# ENEMY
## of the
# GOOD

ALSO BY MATTHEW PALMER

*The Wolf of Sarajevo*

*Secrets of State*

*The American Mission*

G. P. PUTNAM'S SONS

NEW YORK

# ENEMY
## of the
# GOOD

══════════

# MATTHEW PALMER

G. P. PUTNAM'S SONS
*Publishers Since 1838*
An imprint of Penguin Random House LLC
375 Hudson Street
New York, New York 10014

Library of Congress Cataloging-in-Publication Data

Names: Palmer, Matthew, 1966– author.
Title: Enemy of the good / Matthew Palmer.
Description: New York : G.P. Putnam's Sons, [2017]
Identifiers: LCCN 2016041738 (print) | LCCN 2016051716 (ebook) |
ISBN 9780399175022 (hardcover) | ISBN 9780698196018 (EBook)
Subjects: LCSH: Undercover operations—Fiction. | International
relations—Fiction. | Political fiction. | BISAC: FICTION / Thrillers. |
FICTION / Espionage. | GSAFD: Suspense fiction.
Classification: LCC PS3616.A3435 E54 2017 (print) | LCC PS3616.A3435 (ebook)
| DDC 813/.6—dc23
LC record available at https://lccn.loc.gov/2016041738

Printed in the United States of America
1   3   5   7   9   10   8   6   4   2

*Book design by Gretchen Achilles*

This is a work of fiction. Names, characters, places, and incidents either are the product of the author's
imagination or are used fictitiously, and any resemblance to actual persons, living or dead, businesses, companies,
events, or locales is entirely coincidental. The views expressed here are those of the characters and do not
necessarily represent those of the author, the Department of State, or the United States government.

*For Bekica*
*Always*

# ENEMY
## of the
# GOOD

T he basement was cool and damp and smelled of mildew and sour
milk. There were only about twenty of them, hardly an army.
The group included a few graybeards, but most were young, one
or two of the boys barely old enough to shave. Zamira's heart ached
for the youngsters. She was almost fifty and if the secret police put a
bullet through her skull tomorrow it would have been a rich and full
life. The younger ones were risking so much more, even if they did not
yet have the perspective needed to understand that, to recognize their
own mortality.

The agents of the State Committee for National Security—the
GKNB—were both ruthless and efficient. And they were getting
closer. There were only a few places left in Bishkek where the steering
group could meet. Temir, the owner of the restaurant, was a sympathizer, and despite the dangers he let them use the basement. There
was something about meeting literally underground that was deeply

satisfying. It was something primal from hunter-gatherer days, she suspected, the association of the cave with safety and security. But this was their third time in the same place in as many months. And the meeting had already gone on too long.

They called themselves Azattyk, the Kyrgyz word for "freedom," and their ultimate goal was nothing less than the overthrow of the corrupt and despotic regime of Nurlan Eraliev. The one-time Soviet apparatchik had given himself the title President for Life. Some in the movement hoped that Eraliev would read the writing on the wall and flee to Moscow or Beijing to live out his final days in exile. Others in Azattyk were perfectly willing to accept Eraliev's title at face value. As far as they were concerned, he was welcome to reach the end of his reign at the end of a rope, just as long as that day came soon. No one doubted, however, that they would succeed. No one but Zamira.

Zamira cast an appraising glance around the room. These were her comrades, her brothers and sisters in the struggle for a democratic Kyrgyzstan. But for most of them it was a game. Even now, after almost six months of planning, organizing, and skulking in the shadows, they had no idea what they were up against. What the thugs and enforcers of the GKNB would do to them if they were caught. They would learn, and hopefully not before it was too late.

A young man with pale skin, a neatly trimmed beard, and an old army jacket stood up, signaling for attention. His name was Fyodor. He was an ethnic Russian and the informal leader of their radical wing, Azattyk's equivalent of the Young Turks. Hot tempered and impatient, soaked in testosterone, and stupid.

"Enough of this shit!" Fyodor said loudly. He drained his glass and slammed it upside down on the table. The Uzbeks and the Russians, Fyodor among them, were drinking *arrak*, a kind of local vodka. Zamira was Kyrgyz and most of her ethnic kin with their Asiatic features were drinking *kumys*, fermented mare's milk. Zamira didn't much like the taste, but there were those in the movement who still considered her foreign. She had lived most of her life in London, the daughter of dissidents who had fled Bishkek in the 1970s under suspicion—accurate, as it would so happen—of being Kyrgyz nationalists before nationalism in Central Asia was fashionable. Moreover, her sister, Cholpon, was married to an American diplomat. Azattyk's lefty student leaders had no more time for the CIA than they did for the GKNB. So Zamira drank *kumys* more to establish her ethnic bona fides than to appreciate the salty, buttery flavor.

"Enough of this shit," Fyodor repeated. "It is time to stop hiding in the shadows. We are ready to meet our enemy face-to-face on the streets of the city. It is time to stop organizing and start acting."

There was a murmur of assent from the assembled. Fyodor's was a popular sentiment. Azattyk was an underground movement that, so far, had done little more than spray paint furtive pro-democracy and anti-regime graffiti on buildings and bridges. The entire membership numbered no more than several hundred and they had so little money that the steering group had not even bothered to appoint a treasurer.

They were far from formidable, but the regime seemed to be afraid of them, or at least afraid of what they represented. And some of Azattyk's less experienced members, which was to say almost all of them, had begun to believe their own PR.

"It is too soon. The security services would break us like a dry twig." The voice of reason belonged to one of Zamira's contemporaries, a chemical engineer named Chorobek Rustamov, who worked at the state-run fertilizer plant. Rustamov was smart and pragmatic, but he was blunt to a fault, and the younger members of the movement considered him hopelessly bourgeois, which for them was often a synonym for cowardly.

"Chorobek is right," Zamira said, not giving Fyodor a chance to respond. "This is exactly what Eraliev hopes we will do: show ourselves before we are ready. We must build our strength before we come out of hiding. There will be only one chance at this. Fail and we will all be spending the rest of our short, miserable lives in Prison Number One." This was where Eraliev kept his political opponents and those the regime considered enemies of the state.

Fyodor was not rolling over, however. He was clearly ready to fight his corner.

He would not get his chance.

There was a loud crack from upstairs. A gunshot. The room froze into silence. This was a rough part of town. On a typical Saturday night, gunfire would not have been especially noteworthy. But tonight, the restaurant was closed and empty. There was supposed to be no one upstairs except Temir. And Temir, Zamira suspected, was now dead. Reflexively, they all looked up as though they would be able to see through the concrete ceiling.

A series of dull thuds followed, moving across the floor above. Footsteps. Heavy and unconcerned with stealth. That could only mean one thing. There were many of them, enough that it did not matter especially if those below knew they were coming.

The twenty or so conspirators in the basement reached that same conclusion at almost the same moment, their thought processes supercharged by adrenaline, nicotine, and fear. The basement had a back door, a narrow set of crumbling cement stairs that opened up onto the alley behind the restaurant. The would-be revolutionaries dashed for the exit, tripping one another in their haste to reach the illusionary safety of Bishkek's backstreets. All thoughts of comradeship were forgotten in the mad rush for the night air and the cloak of darkness. Zamira saw Mukhamed, a gigantic twenty-year-old ethnic

Kyrgyz prone to bragging about his cat-and-mouse games with the secret police, shove a diminutive Russian girl named Ludmila to the ground, driven by an instinct for self-preservation inscribed in his DNA by millions of years of natural selection.

People were animals, Zamira thought. Herd animals mostly, but with a select few predators. People were both sheep and wolves. And civilization was a thin veneer that concealed nature red in tooth and claw. It was easier to slip the bonds of social norms than most people could imagine, and there was perhaps no society on earth that was more than two missed meals away from anarchy.

Zamira did not join the others in fighting for the stairs. The security services were professional and their agents were anything but dumb. The alley would be a trap.

Instead, she went the other way. There was a small storeroom in the basement where Temir kept supplies for his restaurant, Café Manas. A few weeks earlier, Zamira had stopped by the café for a drink. Temir, a friend of long-standing, had hurt his back and he had asked her to help him bring some potatoes and parsnips up from the basement. In the corner of the storeroom there was a small pile of burlap bags. Under the bags was a trapdoor that concealed a storage bin for root vegetables. Down here, the fall harvest would keep more or less fresh through the long winter until spring. It was March and the bin would be almost empty. There should be enough room for one.

Zamira slipped as quickly and quietly as she could into the storage bin, doing her best to slide the burlap bags back into place as she closed the trapdoor. The potatoes she was lying on were soft and mushy and stank of rot. She hoped that there were no rats in the bin, not because she was afraid but because their scuttling might betray her hiding place.

The thumping of boots on the stairs told her that the police had found the door to the basement. There was a scream, followed by a wet smack that sounded to Zamira like a truncheon hitting flesh. The noise was muffled somewhat by the burlap bags that covered the cramped root cellar.

She concentrated on her breathing, in through the nose and out through the mouth. Slow and regular and, most important, quiet. There was a story she had read once by an American writer about a murderer who thought he could hear the heart of his victim beating under the floorboards of his house. Her own jackhammering heartbeat felt loud enough to be a telltale, and she willed it to slow. It obeyed reluctantly.

There was a creak as the door to the storeroom opened, followed by footsteps.

"Get the lights," she heard a male voice say with the casual authority of someone used to giving orders. Zamira recognized the voice and a pulse of fear ran like acid through her veins. The language was Russian, but the accent was heavy and plodding, as though the liquid Russian phrases had congealed into something thick and greasy. It was Georgian, the accent of gangsters and Stalin. And there was only one man this could be. His name was Anton Chalibashvili. But Kyrgyzstan's democrats and members of Bishkek's intelligentsia had another name for him. Torquemada. The Inquisitor.

There was a room in the sub-basement of Prison Number One where the Georgian, a former KGB major who learned his trade at Moscow's infamous Lubyanka prison, practiced his dark arts in the service of the Eraliev regime. It was called the Pit.

The Inquisitor's job was to secure confessions by whatever means necessary. Everyone confessed in the end.

Zamira shuddered as her mind conjured up medieval fantasies of the Pit and its elaborate methods of torture. And as awful as the visions were, Zamira suspected that her imagination had fallen short of the realities.

A small part of the outline of the trapdoor lit up and Zamira knew that there was no more than a single layer of burlap covering that corner of her hiding place.

"Are you sure you saw her come in here?" the Inquisitor asked.

"I'm sure. There is nowhere else down here where she could be."

Zamira recognized that voice as well. It belonged to a student named Aibek who had joined the group only a few months earlier. Aibek had demonstrated considerable promise as a future leader in the movement. He was smart, articulate, and passionate. He was also, it would seem, a traitor. It was the age-old problem of cabals, conspiracies, and underground movements. Who could you trust? Ultimately, yourself alone, and sometimes not even that.

Temir, she remembered, kept a tool in the storage bin, a steel poker with a fork at the end that could be used to help scoop out the beets, potatoes, and carrots. In the dark, with her enemies standing over her body, Zamira felt frantically around the sides of the bin until her fingers closed around the wooden handle of the tool. With her other hand, she tested the tips of the tines at the business end. They were sharp and the metal was strong. They would find her here, but she would drive the tool into Aibek's reptilian brain before they put her down.

There was a scraping sound as someone—likely Aibek—dragged the burlap sacks off the trapdoor.

"Look what we have here," she heard the traitor say.

"Open it."

The light was bright, and the silhouette of Aibek's head loomed over Zamira in sharp relief. She thrust the long fork up with all of her strength and had the satisfaction of feeling one of the tines pierce an eyeball as though it were a boiled egg. Warm, wet drops sprayed onto her hand and arm. Blood and ocular fluid.

Aibek screamed.

"My eye! Goddamn bitch blinded me."

The traitor pulled his head back and Zamira's second thrust hit nothing but air.

She crouched on the mash of rotten vegetables on the floor of the bin and raised her modest weapon to eye level. If she could take the Inquisitor in the throat or the groin, she could make a run for the stairs.

Aibek rolled helplessly on the floor, both hands pressed up against his left eye. He was whimpering like a dog and Zamira enjoyed a brief moment of satisfaction.

It was a fleeting sensation.

Chalibashvili would not be as careless as Aibek had been. He was not a young man; Zamira would have guessed that he was in his late fifties. But he carried himself with a military bearing and he exuded both confidence and competence. He was tall and broad and his gray hair was cut close to his scalp. He wore a dark suit under a knee-length leather coat that was open at the front. There was a black truncheon in one hand and Zamira could see the butt of a pistol in a holster on his hip.

Chalibashvili just watched as Zamira crawled out of the pit, his lips in an amused smirk.

It was as easy for him to take the weapon from her as it would have been to take a toy from an ill-behaved child.

The handcuffs he used to bind her hands behind her back were heavy and cold.

Chalibashvili led her up the stairs and out the front door, leaving his mole in their group writhing on the basement floor in pain and humiliation, his utility to the security services used up.

There was a black truck parked in front of the restaurant and Zamira's colleagues were being loaded in the back.

Zamira looked up at the night sky. It was late and there were few lights to hide the stars. Her breath formed wispy clouds of vapor in the cold air.

"Yes." Standing behind her, the Georgian whispered in her ear. "Look up. Drink in the sky. It will be a long, long time until next you see the stars."

# TWELVE YEARS
# LATER

═══════

1

HAVANA
MARCH 1, 2016


The four people gathered in the Tank were judge and jury. The executioner already had his orders.

"It's a death sentence," Kate Hollister said, embarrassed by the note of pleading that she could not quite keep out of her voice. As happened so often she was the only woman in the room, and women, she knew, had to be careful about tone. Match the men for toughness and risk being branded a bitch. Speak elliptically and you were weak. Speak plainly and you were a shrew. Kate wanted desperately to hit just the right note. Get it wrong, and her friends were dead.

"I'm sorry, Kate. But Mike's right. We can't take action on what we know without risking the source."

Charlie DelBarco was in over his head, Kate thought. He was a perfectly competent management officer with no meaningful policy experience who had found himself elevated to the position of chargé d'affaires of the American embassy in Havana when the deputy chief of mission had been medevaced ten days ago with appendicitis. The DCM was actually the top dog in the mission. The position of ambassador was vacant because one of Florida's two Republican senators had put an indefinite hold on the nominee's confirmation. The United States and Cuba had restored diplomatic relations after an estrangement lasting more than half a century, but not everyone had gotten the memo.

Temporarily at least, it was DelBarco's embassy, and what happened next was up to him.

The Tank, a secure room in the basement of the embassy, about the size and shape of a shipping container, was the only place in the country where the American staff could hold sensitive conversations. The Cuban services were aggressive and technically competent. The air inside the Tank was pressurized and oppressive. The air conditioners were cranked up high enough to give Kate goose pimples.

In addition to Kate and Charlie, the group in the Tank included the embassy's regional security officer and Kate's boss in the political section, Barry Kriegler. One of the RSO's contacts in the Cuban police had let slip that there would be a raid on a meeting of pro-democracy dissidents at an abandoned cigar factory on the outskirts of Havana that same evening. As ties with America improved, the Cuban government had grown more paranoid about the aspirations of its own citizens. Tonight the police were targeting three of the leading lights in the Cuban democracy movement, including Reuben Morales, who had become popular enough to represent a threat to the regime.

Kate was the embassy's human rights officer. It was her job to network with Cuba's political dissidents, to report on government abuses, and to do what she could to advance the goal of democratic reforms in what was still very much an authoritarian state. Morales was an important contact—and a friend.

"What good is the source if we can't do anything with the information?" Kate said carefully. "Isn't that the point of intelligence? Morales isn't just another activist; he's a symbol of hope. If the authorities lock him up, they'd be taking a chance that he'd become like Nelson Mandela on Robben Island. They won't do that. They'll just kill him and dump his body in the sea."

"And what about my guy?" the RSO asked. "What about the risk to him if the Cubans go looking for who blew the op and they find my guy sitting there when they turn over the rock?"

"This is a big operation," Kate explained for what felt to her like the tenth time. "There are bound to be a lot of people in a position to tip off the dissidents. If we move fast enough, there's no reason the government needs to know it came from the Americans."

"They would assume it was us. When we sneeze, the G2 says bless you. The Cuban services know more about me than my wife does." The G2 was the Dirección General de Inteligencia, the widely reviled and universally feared foreign intelligence arm of the Cuban state.

"I could get Morales a message through cutouts," Kate insisted. "The dissidents know how to get information to one another under the radar of the G2 and without tripping any alarms. They do it all the time."

"It's too risky," DelBarco said. "I can't authorize it without instructions from Washington. We've asked for guidance. We need to be patient."

"It'll take a week for D.C. to make up its mind," Kate protested. "We have four hours."

Kate looked over at Barry Kriegler. He was a good boss. Smart, experienced, and supportive. Although Kate was only a first-tour officer, he had given her considerable responsibility and backed her up when she had pressed the front office and Washington for more open support of Cuba's embattled democrats. Now Kriegler could only shrug.

"You're tilting at windmills, Kate. I know Reuben's important. But we have to play the long game on this island, and that means protecting sources and methods at all cost."

"Five decades isn't long enough for you?" Kate asked, incredulous. "We're on the cusp of real change in Cuba. Finally. And Morales could be the catalyst. But only if he's alive and free."

"If they miss him tonight, they'll just pick him up next week," the station chief said. "Or the week after that. It's an island. There's nowhere to go."

"He could go underground," Kate said. "There's a system in place to move dissidents house to house. They could keep him safe. If it came to it, they could smuggle him out to Dominica or even Miami. We just need to warn him."

"I'm sorry," DelBarco said again. "The answer is the same. No."

Wordlessly, Kate stood up and left. She needed two hands to operate the lever that locked the door to the Tank tight.

Kriegler followed her.

He put a hand on her shoulder and forced her to slow down.

"Kate . . ."

"Yes."

"Don't do anything stupid."

"Don't worry about me, Barry."


There was no ambiguity in her instructions. There was no way, however, that Kate was going to allow her superiors to feed Morales to the sharks. She understood what she was risking. Kate was only on her first tour as a foreign service officer, but she had grown up in and around embassies as a diplomatic brat and she had absorbed many of the State Department's rules and norms by osmosis. What she was about to do was the very definition of insubordination. As an untenured officer, she could be dismissed from the service for cause easily. But there was such a thing as right and wrong. And while it was not always easy to tell the difference between the two, when it was clear, there was no excuse for inaction. She would take the risk.

Despite what Kate had argued in the Tank, getting a message to her dissident friends proved harder than she had anticipated. None of her contacts had cell phones or regular e-mail access, and even if they had, all telephone and electronic communications were monitored obsessively by the security services. Kate knocked on a few doors and tried a couple of the cafés the dissident and activist community would frequent, but she was not able to find anyone in a position to help.

The sky turned from blue to purple and then indigo as twilight fell on Havana. Kate checked the time obsessively, but she knew that a meeting of Cuban dissidents was not run like a meeting of South Korean engineers. The start time for the meeting was notional and there was no official agenda and no chairman. It would start when there were enough people there to begin, and it would last for as long as they had something to say. The debate would be freewheeling and passionately intense. It was Cuba. And Kate had grown to love it. There was no way to know just how much time she had to work with, but she knew that it was not much. Likely not enough.

Finally, at a secondhand bookstore run out of the back of a private house in a residential part of town, she found Paco, a middle-aged man who wrote terrible poetry and cultivated a bohemian air that he used to hit on Scandinavian tourists half his age. Kate thought he was a little skeevy and really only a fringe player on the dissident scene, but he was the best she could find. In hushed tones, she asked Paco to get a message to Morales that the meeting later that evening would be the target of a police raid. In typically florid language, Paco swore a blood oath that he would get the message to Morales. Kate's level of confidence in the third-rate poet was low.

Night had fallen and Havana was a city that only really stirred itself from its tropical torpor after dark. The scattered sodium-vapor lamps cast an ugly yellow-orange glow over Centro Habana. It was still too early for the streets to be crowded, and Kate found herself standing alone in front of a crumbling Batista-era villa now boarded up and abandoned. She checked her watch again. It was almost eight p.m., the time that had been set, in principle, for Morales's meeting.

She made up her mind.

"Okay, here we go," Kate said out loud to no one in particular.

It took her twenty minutes to get to her apartment. Three minutes after that, she was rocketing through the backstreets of Havana headed for the municipality of Boyeros in the direction of the airport. Kate's car, a twelve-year-old BMW 5 series, handled smoothly at high speeds, and in the socialist paradise of Cuba there was little traffic to contend with.

She made it to the old cigar factory in less than fifteen minutes. This part of Boyeros was industrial, or rather post-industrial, as most of the factories and workshops that lined the backstreets had closed their doors decades earlier. The Castillo-Barzaga factory had ceased rolling cigars sometime in the 1970s, but there was still a hint of tobacco smell in the air from where the juices had worked their way deep into the building's timbers.

Kate parked in the shadows and walked up to the front door. From inside, she could hear the buzz of conversation in machine-gun

Spanish. Kate let herself in. As soon as she opened the door, the conversation stopped.

There were, perhaps, two dozen people in the room. Kate recognized about half of them. The room was large and lit only by three naked lightbulbs hanging from the rafters.

"Katie? How did you know we would be here?" Reuben Morales's voice was deep and raspy.

"I'm not supposed to know," Kate replied in fluent Spanish. "But I do. Which means . . ."

"Others know it as well," Morales finished her sentence. "G2?"

"Regular police, I think."

"Just as bad. Are they on their way?"

Kate nodded.

*"Gracias, señorita."* Morales stood. He was dressed in jeans and a white shirt open at the collar. It was hot in the poorly ventilated factory and there was a thin film of sweat on his chest. Morales was no longer young, but his hair was still dark and curly and his mustache was so distinctive it had become a symbol of resistance to the Castro regime. A basic rite of passage for aspiring activists was to draw a Morales mustache on posters of Cuba's unelected leadership. He was an attractive man, Kate thought. Magnetic. The future of the island. But only if he could stay out of prison. Stay alive.

"You have to get out of here, Reuben," she said.

A beam of light shining through the window briefly pierced the gloom in the factory and swept across the far wall like a searchlight.

Morales looked quickly out the window. "It's too late, Katie. They're here."

Kate moved to stand beside Reuben and saw a small convoy of cars turning onto the road that led toward the factory.

"Come with me. I can get you out of here."

"No, Katie. I appreciate what you've done. And I know that it was not without risk to you. But I will not leave my friends."

An idea born of desperation clawed its way to the front of Kate's consciousness. She tried to push it back, but she could not. It made sense to her. It could also get her killed.

She swallowed hard. There was no time to think it through, no time to weigh the pros and cons.

"Get the others out the back. I'll buy you as much time as I can."

"What are you going to do?"

"Something stupid."

Kate ran for her car. Within seconds the heavy BMW sedan was screaming down the road toward the line of Cuban police cars.

The car in front flashed its lights, but there was no siren. The police would not want to alert those they had come to arrest. Kate ignored the lights and the instinct hardwired in her brain to turn away from danger, to turn the car. The distance between them closed with frightening speed.

As the cars barreled toward each other. At the last possible moment, Kate flinched and the BMW struck the Cuban police car in the left front quarter panel. Kate's car spun wildly and the air bag deployed, blocking her view and keeping her from flying through the windshield. Her head cracked painfully against the side window, starring the glass as the force of the spin flung her into the door. Her vision grayed at the edges and she wanted to vomit.

Within seconds of the car coming to a stop, the door was ripped open and powerful hands were dragging her onto the ground. Blood ran down her face from a gash at her temple

Kate lay flat on her belly and she felt the cold muzzle of a pistol pressed up against the back of her skull.

"*Quien coño eres tu?*" Who the fuck are you?

Kate looked Charlie DelBarco right in the eyes, refusing to avert her gaze, to submit to his authority.

"Do you have any idea what you've done?" DelBarco's voice was calm and even, but the vein throbbing in his neck made it clear what an effort it was for him to keep from yelling. They were in his office in the embassy. Only an hour earlier, Kate had been cooling her heels in a Cuban jail. Barry Kriegler had come to get her out, something he had told her had been a heavy lift with the Cuban authorities.

"I had a car accident, Charlie." She touched the bandage on her head like it was a Saint Christopher's medallion.

"Bullshit. I had to call the justice minister himself to get you out of jail. I should have left you there to rot for a week or two, diplomatic immunity be damned."

"What did you tell them?" Kate asked.

"That it was a car accident."

"Well then, that's what it was. It's policy now."

The chargé waved his hands dismissively.

"It doesn't really matter. You won't be my problem for long." DelBarco picked up a legal-sized piece of paper from his desk and thrust it angrily in front of Kate's face. "We got a dip note this morning from the Cubans. They've declared you *persona non grata*. You have thirty-six hours to leave Cuba forever."

The news stung. Kate had known it was a possibility, but to hear it put in such stark terms was painful. She had come to love this island with its warm people and vibrant culture. The loss would hurt. But Kriegler had told her when he escorted her from prison that no one knew where Morales was. The police had not found him and he had gone into hiding. It would cost Kate, cost her a great deal. But it was worth it. She had no regrets.

"The only problem," DelBarco continued, "is that we can't punish you for insubordination in the way you deserve to be punished. Being PNG'd actually protects you. We can't let the Cubans feel they got the upper hand by damaging one of our own. So we won't sanction you, just to spite them."

"Thanks, Charlie. I appreciate the compassion."

DelBarco ignored the sarcasm.

"But it looks like you aren't completely insulated from the consequences of your actions."

"How so?" Kate asked nervously.

DelBarco picked up another document from his desk. This one a regular letter-sized paper.

"A transfer cable with your name on it, Kate. Say good-bye to mojitos and salsa music. I hope you packed a parka."

"Where are they sending me?"

"The icky-stans. You're going to Bishkek. I can't even remember which one of those central Asian backwaters that's the capital of."

"Kyrgyzstan," Kate answered flatly.

"Whatever. Seems they asked for you specifically. I'm not sure if that means someone's looking out for you or if they have it in for you."

"Me neither," Kate agreed. "But I know who it is."

# 2

## THE KYRGYZ REPUBLIC

From thirty-five thousand feet, it looked as though they were flying over a storm-tossed sea. Except that the waves were frozen in place and the whitecaps were really ice and snow. The mountains of Kyrgyzstan's foreboding Ala-Too range stretched to the horizon, and Kate amused herself by mentally flipping the landscape back and forth from rock to ocean like a Buddhist monk meditating at one of the ancient Zen gardens in Kyoto.

This made it easier to ignore her seatmate, a rotund Russian businessman with sweat circles at his armpits who had been popping hard-boiled eggs from a plastic bag like peanuts for much of the long flight and washing them down with liter bottles of vodka. They were still an hour or more from Bishkek, at the tail end of a two-day odyssey that had so far taken Kate from Havana to Toronto, Reykjavik, London, and Dubai. This final leg of the trip was on Egypt Air, known in State

Department circles as Inshallah Airways for the cavalier manner in which the pilots and grounds crew seemed to slough off onto Allah all responsibility for passenger safety and on-time arrival. This was far from the most direct route possible, but the Fly America Act and the regulations governing contract carriers were anything but flexible, and the department's travel office, Kate was firmly convinced, was staffed entirely by sadistic trolls.

The stark, cold beauty of Central Asia was a far cry from Cuba's lush greenery and turquoise water, but for Kate it was a homecoming of sorts. Bishkek was where she had gone to high school. Where she had experienced the joys and heartache of her first serious boyfriend. Where she had gotten drunk for the first time and smoked her first cigarette. Where she had discovered a love for Russian literature and the magical, romantic poetry of Pushkin and Lermontov.

It was where she had buried her parents.

The government had asked Kate, then just a few months into her sophomore year at Georgetown, where to send the bodies. She had not known how to answer. Her father had been in the Foreign Service and had somehow managed to avoid being posted to Washington. Assignments in D.C. were career enhancing, but her father had no interest in the bureaucratic knife fighting that was the essence of the Washington policy process. He turned down every offer that came his way to work at "Main State," the department's sprawling, run-down headquarters building in Foggy Bottom, even with the understanding that without Washington experience he was unlikely ever to make it to the higher ranks. In consequence, before freshman orientation at Georgetown, Kate had never lived in the United States. She had never spent more than three weeks at a stretch in America visiting grandparents in Ohio.

Her mother had no ties to America, not even a passport. Her citizenships were Kyrgyz and British. Her father, meanwhile, had no real connection to the United Kingdom beyond a short stint at the London School of Economics, where the two had met. They had lived together in Moscow, St. Petersburg, Tbilisi, and Kiev. But it was Bishkek where they had spent the most time as a family. They had been happy there, for the most part.

So Kate had made the decision to bury them in Bishkek's Ala-Archa cemetery. The embassy had helped make the arrangements.

She had not been back to Kyrgyzstan since the funeral, a rainy November day with a wind that blew in off the steppes and cut through her black cloth coat like a knife made of ice. Officially, it had been a single car accident on a slick mountain road. But Kate never believed that. It was murder. President for Life Nurlan Eraliev had murdered her parents.

There was no evidence of this crime. That meant nothing. An absence of evidence was not evidence of absence. For Kate, it wasn't a question of evidence. It was an article of faith.

Kate thumbed through her dog-eared copy of Ivan Turgenev's *Fathers and Sons*, but she was too tired and distracted to concentrate. Outside, she could see villages scattered in the foothills, the first sign that Bishkek was close.

The plane began its descent and Kate realized that she had been holding her breath. She was on edge.

The terminal at Bishkek's Manas International Airport was just like she remembered: drab, dirty, and vaguely Soviet in both design and execution. At immigration, she followed a sign that said CD, which stood for *corps diplomatique*, a vestige of another time when the language of international diplomacy had been French, the literal lingua franca. Now, thank god, it was English. In another fifty years maybe it would be Chinese. It was all about power, both absolute and relative.

The immigration officer on duty stared suspiciously at Kate, comparing her face to that on the passport picture with open skepticism. It was a bit of a stretch to conclude that the Eraliev regime would order a low-level functionary to harass her just for sport as she was coming into the country. But it was not entirely out of the question. There was little enough love lost between Kate's family and the Kyrgyz government.

Kate collected her luggage at baggage claim, somewhat amazed that her bags had managed to keep pace with the ridiculous itinerary. Maybe her bags flew direct. It would be just like the State Department to book her luggage on a different—and better—route. The bags probably flew first class as well, or at least business class, waiting in the lounge with a mai tai on the layovers. Kate stretched her back to work out some of the kinks from forty-three hours in seat 36C and its equivalents. She was exhausted, dehydrated, and jet-lagged, the intercontinental trifecta. Kate knew from experience that no matter how tired she was, she would be up at three a.m., unable to sleep, slave to her own circadian rhythms.

It was easy to spot the embassy representative waiting for her on the other side of customs. She was blond, a shade that looked natural rather than dyed. Her outfit—a pink polo shirt and pressed flat-front khakis—looked straight out of the J.Crew catalog. And she was wearing sensible heels rather than the stilettos favored by the locals.

But what really marked her as American was her guileless smile. She looked genuinely happy to be at Manas airport on a Sunday afternoon waiting for the latest new arrival. It was the kind of smile that could not be faked. And there were few Kyrgyz or Russians who would even think to make the attempt.

The final clue, completely unnecessary, was the small cardboard sign she carried that said KATARINA.

The embassy greeter scanned the steady stream of passengers emerging from customs. She looked right past Kate, who triggered none of the "American" signals that made it so easy to spot fellow countrymen across a crowded room almost anywhere in the world. Kate could have been just another well-heeled local returning from a shopping expedition to Dubai or London. She was tall and slim, pretty in her own way but not striking. Her hair was dark and straight and there was something vaguely ethnic about her features that was distinct from the American midwestern norm. It was her mannerisms, however, that helped her blend in. Bishkek was perhaps the closest thing Kate had to home and she walked and dressed and talked like she belonged.

Kate was an American diplomat and she loved her country, but it was a somewhat abstract love, more admiration than passion. It was the kind of love that you might have for a relative whose company you enjoyed on the infrequent occasions of family gatherings. Her feelings for Kyrgyzstan were more complicated, colored by the kind of intimate familiarity she did not have with the United States.

Kate walked up to the bubbly blonde, who continued to look right through her.

"Hi, I'm Kate."

Blondie looked startled, seemingly surprised at Kate's ability to speak such excellent English. Her smile slipped for just a moment, but she caught herself and it reappeared quickly, a cloud passing briefly over the sun.

"Oh, I'm sorry," she said. "I thought . . ."

"It's okay," Kate replied. She tried to smile back at Blondie with the same kind of high-voltage intensity but knew that she was not quite American enough to pull it off.

"Welcome to Bishkek."

"Thanks. I'm sorry to drag you out on a Sunday afternoon."

"Don't worry about it. It's my pleasure. Not much going on here on the weekend. I'm Gabby, by the way, Gabby Rider. I'm the ECON officer and your cubicle mate. I'm also your sponsor."

New arrivals at embassies around the world were assigned sponsors who would show them around town, introduce them to the embassy community, and stock their refrigerators so they would not get mugged on their first night in town looking for a convenience store. Sponsors were assigned by the community liaison officer, or CLO—a position typically filled by an embassy spouse, usually female and always unnaturally chirpy. The CLO was responsible for embassy morale, and the position was predicated on the belief that the psychological impact of intestinal parasites, car jackings, and intrusive surveillance by the intelligence services could be papered over with Halloween parties, children's play groups, and adult pub crawls. In assigning sponsors, CLOs typically tried to pair like with like. That Gabby was not wearing a ring suggested that she was "the other single woman" in the small embassy fishbowl, and the CLO had decided that they would be friends. It was social engineering on the most micro level and Kate found it irritating.

She promised herself that she would not take it out on poor Gabby, who was just doing her job.

"It's nice to meet you."

"Likewise. Looks like you had a rough trip." Gabby touched her temple in the same place where Kate's bandage was visible. Underneath were three stitches.

"I had an accident on my last day in Havana."

"Then how about I drive into town. The traffic here can be a bit nuts. The car's out front, and I thought we'd just go straight to your apartment. You must be beat."

Kate's smile this time was genuine as she contemplated first a shower and then a nap.

"I'd like that, thanks. I'm looking forward to a little downtime."

"You won't get much, I'm afraid. The ambassador has asked you to dinner tonight at the residence. Just the two of you."

Kate shook her head resignedly.

"Yeah. I thought that might happen."

"Are you two . . . ?"

"Yes." Kate's answer was just a little too quick and curt to be polite.

"Sorry. I didn't mean to pry. It's just . . ."

"Don't worry about it. I'm hoping no one treats me different. I'm here to work."

"Of course."

Kate was expecting the typical embassy airport pickup vehicle, an armored SUV suitable for urban warfare. But Gabby had brought her own car, a cherry red Mustang GT convertible with a white racing stripe.

"Sweet ride."

"Only one in the country," Gabby said proudly. "Straight up American muscle. An ambassador for the United States in its own right."

"V-8?"

"Accept no substitute."

Gabby shot up several notches in Kate's estimation. Maybe it was shallow to like someone because of her taste in cars, but so be it. Gabby gained another notch when Kate saw that she had opted for the six-speed manual transmission.

"You do any racing?"

"As a kid. Karting mostly. Both of my brothers were real gearheads. The older one tried his luck at racing for a while, but could never make a real go of it. He runs a Ford dealership outside of Indianapolis."

"So you got a good deal."

"The very best."

Kate's bags just fit in the Mustang's undersized trunk. In an embassy Suburban, the drive into town from Manas airport took almost an hour. They made it in less than half that time, as Gabby pushed the sporty Mustang down the two-line "highway" with reckless abandon.

It was all familiar to Kate. Change was slow to come in this part of the world. Donkeys grazed in the fields on either side of the road. Small farm stands lined the route, piled high with fresh melons and tomatoes, cabbages, beets, and apples. In the middle distance, the awesome Ala-Too mountain range dominated the landscape.

Traffic was light on a Sunday afternoon, which was all to the good as Gabby passed overloaded trucks and underpowered Russian Ladas like they were standing still.

Farmland gave way to an industrial belt around the city and then to residential neighborhoods closer to the center. Kate's building was on a relatively modern, or at least post-Soviet, apartment block no more than half a mile from the embassy.

"You've got a good building," Gabby said. "There are a couple of government muckety-mucks who live here, some of Eraliev's cronies. So the power never goes out. Me, I'm not so lucky. Blackouts once a week minimum."

The apartment was pleasant enough, with two bedrooms, a small balcony, and a kitchen with Italian appliances.

"Anything you need?" Gabby asked after she had helped Kate get settled.

"I'm good for now."

"Great. Dinner at the residence is at seven-thirty. Do you need me to pick you up? I don't mind."

"No. That's okay. I know my way around."

A shower and a catnap made her feel almost human. There was an iron in the embassy "welcome kit," which included linens and kitchenware to see her through the two or three months it would take for her household effects to make the trip from Havana. Kate ironed out the wrinkles in a black knee-length dress. She used minimal makeup, just lip gloss and enough foundation to hide the darks circles under her eyes. The pearl necklace that she chose as her one piece of jewelry used to belong to her mother.

Kate took a look in the mirror, running a brush quickly over a last undisciplined strand of hair. Not bad, she decided, as long as she was grading on the jet-lag curve.

There was a taxi stand a block and a half from the apartment. She had noticed it from the passenger seat of Gabby's Mustang. It was already dark, but street crime in Bishkek was not a serious problem. There were too many police and the punishments were sufficiently severe to ensure that neither petty larceny nor armed robbery was seen as an attractive profession.

There was crime in Kyrgyzstan, of course, but it was organized and high-level. At times, it was also somewhat misleadingly called politics.

It was only a ten-minute ride to the ambassador's residence. Kate did not have any local currency, which was called som from the Kyr-gyz word for "pure," but the driver was only too happy to accept five dollars. The residence was a Georgian mansion in an upscale neigh-boorhood set back from the road behind a high fence and wrought-iron gates. The grounds were spectacular, with mature trees, a tennis court, and a swimming pool. The pool was formally considered an "emergency water containment facility" on the theory that the resi-dence was the alternate safe haven for embassy personnel in the event of an insurrection or natural disaster and the huddled masses would need something to drink. The bean counters at State drew the line at luxury, but did not mind paying for security.

Kate knew the residence well. She had attended scores of diplo-matic parties and embassy functions there over the years. The house itself was a graceful building with a wide stone portico and an enor-mous American flag that hung limply in the windless night air from a pole affixed to the butter yellow façade.

The guard at the front gate recognized her.

"Miss Kate. It's been a long time."

"Nine years, Mehmut. It's nice to see you."

They spoke Kyrgyz together, a language in which Kate was almost as comfortable as she was with English. Although written with the Cyrillic script, Kyrgyz was closer to Turkish than to Russian. Lan-guage was intimately bound up with identity, and Kate's mother had made certain from the cradle that she would grow up fluent in Kyr-gyz as well as Russian.

"You look all grown up," Mehmut said. It was the kind of thing he would not have said to an American officer if they were speak-ing English. The Kyrgyz language broke down the barriers of formality and rank, however, and all that was left was a sense of family.

"Not yet," Kate assured him. "But I'm working on it, I promise."

Mehmut touched a button inside the guardhouse and the gate slid open on oiled hinges.

"The ambassador is waiting for you."

"I'm sure he is."

# 3

The gravel on the driveway crunched agreeably under her boots as she walked up to the stone stairs at the front of the house. The grounds were lit and Kate could see the clearing where the admin staff would set up the volleyball court for the embassy's Fourth of July parties and the flagstone patio that was used for more formal outdoor gatherings. There was the oak tree that her father liked to stand under during receptions, out of the sun, with a gin and tonic in his hand, holding court with a rotating cast of friends, colleagues, and contacts. His loss had left a hole in her life that she knew she could never fill.

The portico with its thick marble balustrade led around to the side of the house. The door opened as she approached. Meryem, the house manager, was there to take her coat, but only after giving Kate a kiss on the cheek.

"It's so lovely to have you back with us," she said. "And I am so sorry about your parents. They were wonderful people."

"Yes, they were. Thank you for thinking of them."

"Always."

Meryem showed Kate into the sitting room, with its familiar over-stuffed furniture.

"The ambassador will be here shortly," she said. "Can I get you a drink while you wait?"

"A glass of wine would be nice, thanks."

Kate sipped the wine and flipped through a coffee-table book of photographs of Kyrgyzstan. It was a beautiful country, and Kate was unreasonably proud that she had been to most of the places featured in the book. There were still a few things she had not seen. Nothing a few months in the country wouldn't allow her to fix, however.

"Good god, you look absolutely lovely."

The ambassador of the United States of America strode into the room like Caesar stepping onto the floor of the Roman Senate. Confident and in command.

He was a big man with silver-white hair streaked with a few traces of black. His tortoiseshell glasses made him look scholarly, like an art history professor or a documentary filmmaker. His blue suit was freshly pressed, and the gray-and-red-striped tie he wore announced to those in a position to know that the ambassador was a graduate of the National War College. Her father had had one just like it, and there was enough of a family resemblance between the two brothers to make her wistful.

Kate smiled. She was happy to see him. Her uncle had reasons for bringing her here, she knew, reasons that had nothing to do with family ties. He was ambitious and subtle, and he never did anything without a reason. He had moved awfully fast to snatch her out of Havana, as though he had been waiting for the opportunity. But Kate knew that he would not simply tell her what it was. She would have to earn it.

She rose from the couch and let the ambassador fold her into a massive bear hug. He kissed her cheek in a manner that was both affectionate and possessive.

"How's my favorite niece?"

"Uncle Harry, did my father have any other children I should know about? If not, I believe I am your only niece, which makes that kind of a low bar."

"You always did set the bar high, Kate. Just one of the many things I admire about you."

Horace "Harry" Hollister was a charming man. He was like her father in that way as well, and it was a quality he both cultivated and appreciated in others.

"What happened to your head?"

Kate was wearing her hair loose and she had tried to style it to hide the bandage, but it was still hard to miss.

"It's nothing. You should see the other guy."

"We Hollisters give as good as we get," her uncle agreed.

Kate patted him on the arm affectionately.

"Thank you for having me to dinner."

"I'm sorry to impose on you on your first night in country, and I'm equally sorry that I couldn't make it to the airport to pick you up. I had to spend the afternoon at the interior minister's hunting lodge. Frightfully boring man. That's the way he hunts, I think. He tells stories to the animals until they shoot themselves to make it stop. I came dangerously close to mounting my head on the wall of his trophy room today. God, the things I do for my country."

"I'm glad you dodged that bullet," Kate said with a laugh. "I hate eating alone."

"And I will feed you well, I promise. But you're going to have to play for me first."

"Now?"

"Absolutely. I'm serving an excellent wine with dinner, and if we wait you'll be too blotto to play and I'll be in no position to appreciate your skills. Come. It's been too long."

Meryem appeared at the ambassador's elbow with a tumbler of scotch and ice balanced on a small silver tray. He took it, nodding his appreciation.

The living room was dominated by a jet black Steinway grand piano. It was an older model, but it looked to have been beautifully maintained.

"Is that beast in tune?" Kate asked.

"It should be. Although it's been a while since the ivories have been tickled by someone of your talent."

Kate sat at the bench and considered what to play. Music had been one of the few constants of her peripatetic youth. She had started playing at five, and at every post she had auditioned successfully for the state-run music academy that was a staple institution across Eastern Europe and the former Soviet space. Kate had been good, at her best better than good, entering and scoring well at international competitions. At one point, she had considered a career in music, but she had chosen a different path and was now more a recreational player than the serious concert musician she had been. Even so, thousands of hours of practice had helped her build a sizable repertoire. And she could still play.

After a moment's thought, she launched into the opening bars of Schubert's Sonata in A Major. Schubert was Kate's favorite composer, and this was one of the first competition pieces she had mastered as a girl. Playing it elicited strong memories of Madame Raisa in St. Petersburg, who would rap her knuckles sharply with a ruler if her tempo ever faltered. It also reminded her of her father, who had loved to sit in his leather chair by the fire sipping cognac and listening to Kate practice. Schubert had been his favorite as well.

When she had finished, Kate transitioned seamlessly to *Estar Enamorado* by the Cuban great Adolfo Guzmán. She glanced at the ambassador, who raised a quizzical eyebrow. This was not the typical music of a pianist trained in the Russian classical tradition. Kate had fallen in love with Cuban music in Havana. It was free and spontaneous, the opposite of what Cuban society had become but also a promise of hope for what it could be again. Culture was stronger than any political system, no matter how repressive.

The last notes of *Estar Enamorado* fluttered lightly from her fingers and she thought about Reuben. Had he made it off the island? Was he sipping rum on the beach in Dominica? Or hiding in a dark basement in Las Tunas waiting for the agents of the G2 to find him?

At the final flourish, her uncle drained the last dram of scotch in his glass as though toasting her performance.

"I see that you've fallen under the spell of the Caribbean communists. Does diplomatic security know about this?"

"It comes from spending all my time there with the anti-regime activists. Many of them were artists of some sort. Painters. Writers. Musicians. Artists make the best dissidents."

"Passion?" her uncle asked.

"Yes. But there's something else about them. They speak a language those with power don't fully understand. It's made up of symbols and allusions and shared cultural touchstones. Authoritarians are literal thinkers, almost entirely concrete. They don't understand art, and they often don't know enough to be afraid of it. It's like the sculptor in Shelley's 'Ozymandias' mocking the Pharaoh by carving his face on a megalomaniacal statue with wrinkled lips and a sneer of cold command. Ozy just knows that the statue is big and imposing. He doesn't have the sense or sensibility to know that he's being ridiculed and that the sculptor's mockery will outlast his empire by three thousand years. The autocrats can't confront the artists on their terms, and in the end art wins. It has to."

"That's pretty profound, Kate. But I am also reminded of a little girl I knew who used to bring home stray kittens and baby birds with broken wings. The patron saint of the forlorn and abandoned."

"What can I say? I'm a hopeless romantic."

"And a hungry one, I hope. I have a new chef. Belgian-trained. And I asked him to make your favorite. Uzgen *paloo*."

"And he agreed?"

"Under protest. Said it was peasant food. I'm sure he's finding some way to fancy it up. Deconstruct it, as they say. Maybe add sea foam or acacia berries or something or other that's all the rage in Brooklyn. Whatever. To the table with us."

Kate giggled. It was good to be with family. The Hollister clan was accomplished but not especially fecund. She did not have many close relatives on her father's side. And her mother's side of the family tree had had nearly all of its leaves stripped, first by the Soviets and then by the Eraliev regime.

The dining room was enormous, much of it taken up by a table large enough to seat at least twenty-four guests. Kate was pleased to see that the staff had set their plates at one corner of the table, so they would not have to talk across acres of walnut. Even so, certain formalities had to be observed and there was a hand-engraved name card at Kate's place setting and a menu card propped up on the table.

*Warm Salad of Seared Scallops, Haricots Verts,*
*and Bell Peppers in Walnut Vinaigrette*

*Uzgen Paloo "Nouveau"*

*Caramel Pear Terrine*

The wines listed at the bottom of the menu were a pinot noir from Sonoma and a sauvignon blanc from the Rogue River Valley in Oregon. Kate recognized the vineyards. These wines were almost a hundred dollars a bottle. It was not the typical embassy function swill.

"You're bringing out the good stuff, Uncle. I'm flattered."

"Nothing's too good for my brother's little girl."

"It's nice to be with family. Speaking of which, how's Beverly?"

"She's well, thank you. You'll see her soon enough. She's in the States visiting the boys. But she'll be back in a few weeks."

Harry and Beverly had twin boys about six years older than Kate. One was an ophthalmologist in New Jersey and the other was a successful commodities trader in Chicago. Like Kate, they had grown up mostly abroad, but neither had been bitten by the foreign affairs bug. She knew little enough of them beyond the exchange of Christmas cards and carefully curated Facebook posts. They had grown up on different continents and they were not close.

A waiter that Kate did not know poured the sauvignon blanc.

Meryem appeared with the first course. It was delicious. The scallops were lightly seared and tender and the peppers sautéed just enough to bring out the flavor while still leaving them crispy.

They talked about family, but there were so few relatives to get caught up on that the conversation veered quickly to shop talk. Kate told her uncle, somewhat sheepishly, about disobeying direct instructions in Havana and warning Morales and the other dissidents about the raid.

"You did the right thing," Harry said. "Although, had you done the opposite, I could have said the same. It's easy enough to argue both sides."

This, Kate thought, was the classic answer of the diplomat. Nothing was certain. Everything was open to debate, interpretation, and compromise. It could be maddening.

"I suppose so. But there didn't seem to be anything else I could do. And the Cuban government couldn't wait to get me out of there. Thanks for giving me a soft place to land."

"There are times when you gotta do what you believe needs to be done."

"Thanks, Uncle."

"But Kate . . ."

"Yeah."

"You ever do that to me and you're on the first plane out of here. Family or not. This is my mission and you're under my orders. Do we still have a consulate in Greenland? 'Cause that's where you'll be, eating fried whale blubber and stamping visas for Inuit pipe welders."

"Understood."

As if to make up for the threat, he poured Kate a glass of the pinot noir.

"Time to switch to red."

As her uncle had promised, the wine was excellent.

"I'm happy to have you here, Kate. You're going to be an important part of this team. And I believe you can do great things here."

"And I'm glad to be back here. Back home."

"Kyrgyzstan has changed since your salad days. There are some things that you really need to know."

Meryem removed the empty plates from the first course and set dishes of Uzgen *paloo* in front of Kate and the ambassador. *Paloo* was the unofficial national dish of Kyrgyzstan, rice mixed with mutton and shredded carrots that had been fried in a large cast-iron cauldron called a *qazan*. Traditionally, it was garnished with whole fried cloves of garlic and hot red peppers. The rice came from Kyrgyzstan's Uzgen region and was brownish red with a slightly nutty flavor. As the ambassador had predicted, the chef had tried mightily to make the humble *paloo* sufficiently sophisticated for the diplomatic table. The rice was formed into a tall cylinder and topped by a three-dimensional lattice made of garlic cloves and hot peppers that looked like the steel frame of a skyscraper.

"See what I mean?" Harry said. "There was no way that Michel was going to do the *paloo* straight up."

"I think it's cute. Thanks for asking him to do this."

Kate took a bite. It was perhaps the best *paloo* she had ever tried, rich and earthy and spicy. But even in the hands of a world-class chef it was never going to be more than the Kyrgyz version of comfort food. It was as if Le Cirque were serving meat loaf or mac and cheese.

The ambassador was less interested in the *paloo* than his exposition on the latest developments in Kyrgyz politics. Dinners with the Hollisters were always like that. Given the choice between talking and eating, talking always won. It was a wonder the Hollisters were not all as thin as sticks.

"When you were here before, our stated goal was regime change. It was the Bush years and that was all the rage. Axis of Evil. No negotiating with terrorists. No compromise. No prisoners . . . well, maybe one or two so we would have somebody to waterboard. It seems a little silly to talk about those days as naïve, but that's what they were. The neocons were ascendant and our plan, such as it was, was to bomb and bully the Muslim world into embracing democracy and the free market and—god willing—start voting Republican. The world as they saw it was Manichaean. Everything in black and white. But the lines in the real world are never quite so crisp and de-fined. It's all shades of gray bleeding into each other.

"Americans have been conditioned to think that victory looks like the surrender ceremony on the deck of the battleship *Missouri*. Un-conditional and absolute. Total domination. A clean win with sharp corners and no room for uncertainty or ambiguity. But that's a fan-tasy, at least in this century. If you insist on absolute purity, you risk coming away with nothing. Diplomacy is the art of the possible. And you should never allow the best to be the enemy of the good. That's the world that you and I inhabit."

"The purists certainly had their comeuppance in Iraq," Kate observed. "Things didn't quite work out the way the neocons had envisioned."

"Indeed not. They promised we would be greeted with flowers as liberators, and at the time I suspect they very much believed that that was true. So now the pendulum has swung back the other way and we are prepared to accept a little bit less purity in exchange for a little bit more security."

"And does that include Eraliev?"

"Up to a point."

"He killed your brother."

The expression on his face betrayed a sense of grief and loss. It was fleeting, but that only made it more powerful, and Kate felt guilty for making the point so bluntly. Her uncle was in a difficult position, caught between duty to country and obligation to family.

"It's possible," he admitted after a moment's thought. "And I understand why you're so committed to that theory. There's no larger meaning in a tragic accident. But there's no hard evidence of government involvement. And even if the rumors were true, it wouldn't really matter. This isn't about me or you. It's about the United States. Regime change is not our policy here. Not for now, at least."

Kate wished that she could be so dispassionate about the man she believed responsible for her parents' death. But she knew that she would never develop that sense of professional distance. It was all too close and too personal.

"But isn't it in the interest of the United States to get rid of Eraliev? To help build a democratic Kyrgyzstan?"

"Without a doubt. But if we aren't prepared to invade and occupy this place to make it so, then we are going to have to learn to work with this government, at least for a while, and support change slowly over time. And until that day, there are certain things that we are going to want from this government, no matter how unattractive it is."

"So what do we want from Eraliev?"

"Birlik."

"The one-horse town down near the border with Tajikistan?"

"One horse, yes. And one Soviet air base, albeit one that needs to be rebuilt from the ground up at considerable expense. But still and all, one that offers unprecedented opportunities to project air power across central Asia. And we are negotiating with the Eraliev government on a ninety-nine-year lease for that base. This will help us amortize the costs."

"Why do we need the base?"

"In a word: China. The Great Game in Central Asia is back on, only with the U.S. and China dueling on the Field of Mars rather than the UK and Russia."

For much of the nineteenth century, the British and Russian empires had rubbed up against each other in Central Asia with the kind of tectonic force that produced the Himalayas. The British were afraid that the tsar's troops would subdue the Central Asian Khanates of Khiva, Bukhara, and Kokand and use Afghanistan as a staging area for an invasion of India, the jewel in the crown of the empire. The Great Game, the struggle for influence and dominance, was played on the battlefield, but it was also played by spymasters and diplomats, journalists, and businessmen. It was the kind of full-spectrum conflict at which successful empires excel, and which can ultimately drain even the most powerful of them dry.

"It's hard to see how one little air base is going to determine the future of big power relationships. We had an air base here until two years ago out at Manas airport. That hardly seems to have been a game changer in the region."

"That was a transit base," her uncle replied. "It was all oriented toward supplying the troops in Afghanistan. That fight was always destined to be a sideshow. The base at Birlik would be the real thing, a platform for power projection across Central Asia and western China with advanced fighters, bombers, and AWACS aircraft. It would force China to shift significant forces inland, away from the Taiwan Strait and the South China Sea, to counter our position in the interior. The Birlik base would actually be bolstering our position in the Pacific, and that's the biggest prize of this century."

"I understand that," Kate said. And she did. It was Great Power Diplomacy 101. "So, are you running the negotiations with Eraliev?"

"I'm just the local muscle," the ambassador demurred. "I work the issues from here, but the overall lead is Winston Crandle."

"The Fossil?"

"The same. Still nostalgic for Mutually Assured Destruction."

Ambassador Winston Crandle was the deputy secretary of defense, a one-time FSO who had transitioned to Democratic Party politics and reinvented himself as the leader of the party's "realist wing" of foreign policy strategists. He did not lack for experience. Crandle had joined the Foreign Service in the early days of the Johnson administration and had been a staff aid to Dean Rusk. Later he had hitched his wagon to a rising star named Henry Kissinger. He had been ambassador three times, most recently to NATO, and although he was well into his seventies, his nickname, the Fossil, was more a comment on his worldview than his advanced age. He was a hardened Cold Warrior—one of the fire-breathers who secretly hoped that China's ascension to the rank of peer competitor of the United States would return a kind of moral clarity to American foreign policy and push the self-defeating "war on terror" to the margins of global affairs where it belonged.

"And he comes here?"

"Regularly. I'll make you his control officer for the next visit, but you'll have to behave yourself."

"I'll be good, I promise. But I have to tell you that I'm not sold on this."

"How so?"

"The base deal would come at a price, a steep price. And I'm afraid that we're falling victim, again, to short-termism. We have a clear vision for what we want this country to become: stable, free, prosperous, democratic, and allied to the West. But we want something from Eraliev right now and we're prepared to mortgage that future in exchange for immediate gratification. It's not a recipe for long-term success in this region."

"I wouldn't use that frame," the ambassador suggested. "What we struggle with, not only here in Kyrgyzstan but everywhere in the world, is what I call values complexity."

"A new term for me, I'll admit."

"My own coinage. The United States of America is an empire. Our interests span the globe and our appetites are all but limitless. Every problem is our problem and we want many, many things. Sometimes our interests are complementary. We want country X to buy American goods, so we hope it's rich enough to afford our airplanes and iPads. As it so happens, country X is also an American ally and a functioning democracy, so we want it politically stable. Prosperity supports both goals. Everyone wins.

"But sometimes our interests are contradictory. We support human rights and religious freedom, but not if it means Saudi Arabia won't sell us oil or make nice to Israel. So we tend to downplay the whole freedom thing when we're kissing al-Saud's . . . ring. We oppose human trafficking and forced labor, but we like cheap sneakers. Democracy is great. But what do we do when the public votes in leaders we find objectionable, genocidal scumbags, for example, or fanatical jihadists? Life is complicated. In any given situation there are hundreds of factors and dozens of values that we need to balance against each other. The process of finding that balance is what we call policy making. It's what you and I do for a living on behalf of the American people, and it is an honor and a privilege to shoulder that responsibility."

"And what about right and wrong? Doesn't that matter?"

"Of course it does. But right about what? And wrong about what? No set of circumstances outside the lab has only one set of variables."

"So Eraliev gets a pass on what he did to our family and what he's doing now to Kyrgyzstan? If he gives us the air base, all is forgiven?"

"It's a little more nuanced than that. It always is. Values complexity again. We can walk and chew gum at the same time, and we can work with what we have even while we work for change. Look, Kate, Eraliev is a loathsome toad. My job isn't to like him; it's to get him to make decisions that are consistent with our interests. Today, that means getting to 'yes' on the base deal. But we can also be laying the groundwork for a tomorrow that doesn't include him. In the long run, a democratic government in Kyrgyzstan aligned with the West will support a broader set of U.S. interests, making it possible for us to do more not only here but in the wider region. You're absolutely right about that."

"So what are you doing to make that tomorrow a reality?"

"Have you heard of a group called Boldu? They actually spell their name with an exclamation point. Boldu!" The ambassador raised both his voice and his glass as though it were a toast. A few drops of expensive red wine spilled onto the tablecloth. He seemed not to notice and Kate realized that he had consumed most of the bottle.

"Boldu? It's the Kyrgyz word for 'enough.' Is it a new political party?"

"It's more a movement. A democracy movement. It's underground for the time being and incredibly secretive."

"I would imagine so, after Kyrgyzstan's last experience with a democracy movement." Kate's tone was bitter and her uncle understood.

"I've made inquiries about Zamira, Kate. I've tried to find out if she's alive, but I haven't learned anything. I'm sorry."

"Mom never gave up hope that her sister was alive somewhere in the black prisons. She was sure of it."

"And you?"

"I'll never stop looking. Tell me about Boldu!" Kate imitated her uncle's exaggerated delivery of the exclamation point.

"There's not much to tell. We don't know much. A few months ago, anti-Eraliev graffiti started to appear around town. Some of it quite clever. The signature was either a collective Boldu or someone using the nom de guerre Seitek."

"As in the grandson?"

"None other."

The *Epic of Manas*, a monumental poem meant to be sung and recited by master singers rather than read, was the heart and soul of Kyrgyz culture. It was the Kyrgyz version of the Torah, *The Aeneid*, *The Tale of Genji*, and the collected works of Shakespeare all rolled up into one package. The Kyrgyz maintained that the epic poem, nearly twenty times longer than *The Iliad* and *The Odyssey* together, was a thousand years old. Modern scholars disputed that figure but would never have dared to challenge it in a bar in Bishkek, many of which were named after Manas or other figures in the epic.

Manas was the father of the Kyrgyz people, who had united the tribes and led them to victory against their enemies. The second book of the Manas epic was devoted to the adventures of his son, Semetei. Seitek was the grandson.

"It's interesting that he chose Seitek rather than Semetei," Kate observed.

"How so?"

"Both Manas and Semetei battled the Kyrgyz' outside enemies. The Oirats, the Uighurs, and the Afghans. Seitek's enemies were in the palace, ersatz allies and those who had betrayed his grandfather's legacy. The name alone tells a story. One the Kyrgyz people would understand."

"We don't know very much about the man who calls himself Seitek. And he has a good reason for using an alias. Eraliev would like nothing better than to mount his head on a pike at the city gates. Boldu operates in absolute secrecy with a cell-like structure, which makes it hard to penetrate."

"Have you met with them?"

"No. They won't meet with us. We're not even sure how to get in touch with them. It looks like they don't trust us and paranoia has served them well so far. But there are things that we can do to help them. Money. Training. Media attention. Resources. We want a viable opposition here. We support what Boldu is trying to do. But we need to find some way to make contact with them so we can prove our bona fides. That, Kate, is where you come in."

"Me?"

"Yes."

"How? You have a whole team of political officers with many more years of experience than I have. I don't really see how I can do something they can't."

"I'd like to pause to admire that moment of genuine modesty. You don't hear that often in our line of work. The faux variety certainly, but you, my niece, are entirely sincere and entirely wrong."

"What can I do?"

"We don't have a good line into Boldu, but we do have some decent intel on some of the likely members."

"And?"

The ambassador reached down beside his chair and Kate saw that there was a briefcase sitting there, the kind that opened from the top. Her uncle had put it there earlier, she understood, for just this moment. It was a bit of diplomatic theater.

He set a plain red folder on the table next to her.

"You went to high school with them, Kate."

The first document was an analytic product from the Defense Intelligence Agency with the subject line "Boldu: An Emerging Challenge to the Eraliev Regime in Kyrgyzstan?" Kate read it through quickly. It was a typical intelligence community piece, heavily caveated with weasel words such as "seems like," "could possibly," and "assess with medium confidence." Even the punctuation was weasly. The question mark in the title was the equivalent of the intelligence community throwing its hands up in the air and saying "your guess is as good as mine." It might as well have been a shrug emoji. Analysts were always wary of expressing opinions too forcefully lest they be called on to account for their failure to predict the future with absolute fidelity.

This particular product was a leadership analysis, outlining what little the DIA knew about the makeup of Boldu. The putative leader, Seitek, was little more than a name. There were no photographs. His family name was unknown. That did not dissuade one of the psychiatrists on the DIA payroll from offering a sidebar assessment of his personality. Seitek was described as a paranoid narcissist with control issues and an uneasy relationship with his father. Evidently the last Freudian shrink still in business had taken a government job.

The analysts had some more information to work with in describing the makeup of the leadership at the next level, the closest advisors to the elusive Seitek. A number of them, the report noted, were graduates of the International School of Bishkek. The members of the inner circle seemed to rely on personal ties and long-standing loyalties to reduce the risk that Boldu would suffer the same fate as Azattyk, betrayed from within.

The report identified half a dozen suspected members of the Boldu leadership, using the caveats and hedges that Kate found so irritating.

Next to three of the names were yearbook photos from their senior year at the International School of Bishkek. ISB included not only the children of diplomats and international businessmen but also the sons and daughters of Kyrgyzstan's elite and a few exceptionally bright Kyrgyz kids on scholarship. The language of education was English, but more than half the student body held Kyrgyz passports.

Two of the ISB students had graduated in Kate's year. One— Valentina Aitmatova—had been a friend. She had known the other— Hamid Ismailov—as well, but they had not been close. He had run with the jocks while Kate had spent most of her time with the art nerds and the math geeks. Ismailov had been good enough to make it onto the Kyrgyz wrestling team for the Beijing Olympics, although not good enough to win a single match once he got there. Valentina's parents were intellectuals. Her Kyrgyz father had taught psychology at the university and her Russian mother was a lawyer. Val herself had always been politically conscious and it was not surprising to Kate that she would be involved with Boldu. Hamid, however, was the son of a wealthy businessman with close ties to the Eraliev government. Kate would not have expected the incurious jock she remembered from high school to grow up a political dissident. But people can change.

There was a second product in the folder, an outline of Boldu's activities over the last six months. Much of it was simple anti-regime graffiti, but the group was growing increasingly audacious in its political stunts. An eight-by-ten glossy photo showed two remotely operated drones carrying a banner over the city denouncing a new law requiring all print media to secure a government license to operate, meaning every newspaper and magazine would have to parrot the regime's line. The banner read in both Kyrgyz and English: WE DON'T NEED NO STINKING LICENSE. And was signed with a stylized red upraised fist and the word "Boldu!"

"Now that's what I'm talking about," Kate said. "I don't think there'll be many people in the government who've seen either *The Treasure of the Sierra Madre* or *Blazing Saddles*. What's with the fist?"

"It's their trademark," the ambassador explained. "They don't want our help, but they certainly seem to want us to know they're there. That's why they use almost as much English as Kyrgyz or Russian."

"How are they doing?"

"They're still small and they know that if they stick their heads up out of the hole the government will cut them off at the neck, but our sense is that they're growing, picking up supporters and momentum. They've struck a raw nerve in Kyrgyz society. And the regime is afraid of them, disproportionately so."

"And what's my role in this?"

"I want you to make contact with these people. Find out more about them and convince them that they have more to gain than to lose from working with us."

"You really think they'll let me in? You've just described them as pretty paranoid, and not without reason."

"You're all ISB alums. I want you to get inside the group and make contact with the leader, Seitek. Find out who he is, what motivates him, and persuade him that we can help. You're practically a local, Kate. They'll trust you."

"I wouldn't bet the farm on that, Uncle Harry."

"No. Not the farm. I'm betting the whole damn country."

# 4

Ruslan's uniform was ill-fitting. It was also ugly. It was supposed to be a waiter's uniform, but it was more like something you might see on a bellhop in a down-market hotel in Eastern Europe than at a bistro in Paris. The white jacket was loose at the shoulders and the black pants were baggy. The rightful owner no doubt sported a prominent belly. Only one of the professional hazards, Ruslan suspected, of a life spent serving rich food to the powerful people of Bishkek and their wealthy friends.

The Hall of the People was something of a misnomer. The grand ballroom—the size of a high school gymnasium with a vaulted ceiling and baroque columns encrusted with gold leaf—was the exclusive playground of the elite. If the people had the temerity to insist on equal access to their hall, they would have been shot. "People's" was one of the adjectives that dictatorial regimes routinely twisted into a kind of Orwellian doublespeak. Control of language was the purest form of power, and in Ruslan's experience, a People's Democratic Republic was like the Holy Roman Empire—nothing of what it purported to be.

The ballroom had been decorated by someone with more money than taste. The walls were hung with mirrors in ornate gilt frames. The ceiling was painted with elaborate scenes taken from *Manas*. Several of the panels featured Seitek, Ruslan's necessary alias in his role as the leader of Boldu. In the central panel, the figure of Manas himself, the father of all Kyrgyz, bore a striking resemblance to President Eraliev. Ruslan knew the artist. In one epic drunken night some years ago, the painter had explained that he had taken the job because he needed the money, but he had exacted a measure of revenge. "I painted Eraliev with no dick," he had explained.

Ruslan looked around the room. The rich and beautiful people of Bishkek were taking their seats at the round tables scattered across the parquet floor. The head table was rectangular and reserved for Eraliev's inner circle. Ruslan saw the finance minister and his fat wife take their assigned seats at a round table in the political equivalent of Siberia. It was a public sign of disfavor, adding substance to the rumors that his star was falling. Meanwhile, the relatively junior minister of transportation was seated at the head table. Ruslan knew he was one to watch; maybe he would be the next finance minister. At a minimum, his seat at this dinner would guarantee that the envelopes of bribes that were the just due of any senior government official would double in size.

Alana, a sultry blonde with dark roots and fake boobs, sashayed to her seat a suitably respectable distance from the head table. It was well known around Bishkek that the pop singer with one name and the president were lovers, but that was no reason to rub Mrs. Eraliev's nose in it. Her table included a number of the "controversial businessmen" who had made their fortunes by being apparatchiks at the right time and benefiting from the Wild West privatizations that followed the collapse of the Soviet Union. There was also a media magnate who pandered slavishly to the regime and both the Chinese and Russian ambassadors.

The other tables were similarly eclectic. But as far as Ruslan was concerned, they had one important thing in common. They were all pigs snuffling at the trough. A point that would be made soon enough in a clear and unvarnished fashion.

Ruslan and the other servers moved from table to table pouring wine for the guests who were there to celebrate the twentieth anniversary of Eraliev's uninterrupted reign. The tables were set with silver and crystal and the official state china bearing the Kyrgyz emblem, a blue circle showing the Ala-Too mountains supported by the wings of a hawk. To facilitate smooth service, the first course—a salad with walnuts and beetroot—was already set out. Once the wine had been served, Eraliev would call for a toast and the eating could begin in earnest. Ruslan had seen the menu. The plan was for six courses of increasingly rich and heavy dishes.

Ruslan and his compatriots had a plan that would spare the guests from the excess calories and the excessive speech making. One by one, he made eye contact with the three other "waiters" who were part of his team. They nodded carefully. All was ready.

Ruslan walked purposefully over to the far wall, where a heavy maroon tapestry hung from the ceiling to the floor. A security guard stood in front of the curtain. He was wearing a suit rather than a uniform, but the spiral cord running from his right ear to his collar was unmistakable, as was the bulge of a concealed pistol under the left breast of his suit jacket. This was an unexpected wrinkle and a potentially serious complication.

Another waiter, an actual employee of the palace, walked by with an empty tray and Ruslan set the wine bottle he was carrying onto it.

"Take this back to the kitchen, please. It's corked."

The harried waiter nodded and rushed off to do as he was told. Ruslan spoke with such authority that it did not occur to the server to question his right to issue orders. He was young, but he was a leader. Men twice his age were perfectly comfortable following his commands.

Ruslan approached the bored-looking guard, leaning in conspiratorially.

"I have a message for you from the president."

"Really?" The guard made no effort to hide his disbelief. "Does he need me to look after Alana for him? I'd like to see if the carpet matches the drapes." He reached behind and tugged on the maroon tapestry.

"No. The president told me to ask you to go to the front gate and wait for a package from a Russian general. You are to bring this package to him immediately. You must give it to him directly and to no one else."

The guard's skepticism wavered.

"Why would he send a waiter to tell me this?"

"Do you think I'm really a waiter?" Ruslan replied. "Look closely. The uniform doesn't even fit. But I was assigned to close protection as a last-minute stand-in. It was the best the Office could do."

The reference to the Office caught the guard's attention. It was how those on the inside referred to the GKNB.

"Why me?"

"Why the fuck not you?" Ruslan insisted. "Listen, I didn't ask for you to do this. The president did. Do you want to go over there and ask him why you should be the one to wait at the gate in the dark and the cold? The night shift at Number One will be delighted. Things have been slow recently."

Here again, the sense of confidence—of command—in Ruslan's voice was more persuasive than any badge of rank. The guard pulled his shoulders back and might have saluted if Ruslan had not signaled him to discretion with a brief cutting motion.

"I'm undercover," Ruslan reminded him.

The guard left, walking with pride of purpose. The president himself had entrusted him with a secret mission.

Poor bastard, Ruslan thought.

"Nice job, Seitek." One of the other faux waiters, a slim, dark-haired woman named Bermet, had joined Ruslan in front of the heavy curtain, all according to the plan, which was back on schedule. The servers' uniforms in the Great Hall included white gloves, which was fortuitous. They did not wish to leave fingerprints.

Ruslan slipped behind the curtain and felt along the wall until he found what he was looking for, a large metal wheel. There was a hatch built into the wall that was secured like the door on a submarine. Behind the hatch was a bomb shelter stocked with enough emergency rations to last the president and his family through a nuclear winter. The seals on the doorframe were rubber. The designers wanted to make certain that the room would be airtight in the event of a gas attack. It also ensured that the room was soundproof. Ruslan knew this because one of Boldu's members had worked on the design team.

Boldu was growing and finding allies among the reluctant servants of the regime. The momentum in favor of the movement was building. Ruslan could feel it. And tonight he would make sure that Eraliev could feel it too.

He opened the door just a crack. There were no lights, but Ruslan could hear something moving in the darkness at the bottom of the stairs to the underground room. Something big. He whistled, a low note that rose quickly in tone. The villagers in Ruslan's home province used this. It was a signal that had been imprinted on the creatures below through experience and repetition. It meant only one thing. Dinner.

"Now," he whispered, and Bermet pulled the tapestry sharply to one side as Ruslan opened the door wide. An unpleasant, barnyard smell wafted up from the shelter along with the sounds of snorting and large bodies jockeying for space. There was a pounding on the stairs and four tons of hungry hog poured out of the cellar and onto the slick floor of the ballroom. There were a dozen Chinese Jinhua pigs, the smallest of which tipped the scales at three hundred kilograms. Ruslan and a team from Boldu had snuck the pigs into the cellar three days earlier, walking them like dogs on a leash from the back of a truck and across a tarp they had laid over the ballroom floor. The pigs had gone seventy-two hours without food, a new and unpleasant experience for them.

The hogs ran wild through the ballroom, slipping on the freshly polished parquet and knocking tables over in their eagerness to get at the food. Waiters had already begun to deliver the next course and they were carrying trays piled high with rice and mutton and grilled vegetables. The pigs pressed eagerly up against the waiters until the trays crashed noisily to the floor, spilling the food in front of them like so much slop.

A few of the women screamed. A guard pulled a pistol and shot one of the pigs, wounding it rather than killing it and only adding to the chaos as the panicked animal scrambled among the guests squealing in pain and leaving a trail of blood. Someone with more sense shouted at the armed guards to hold their fire.

"You'll kill someone, you idiot. Someone who matters."

The other members of the team had their assignments as well. Ruslan watched approvingly from across the room as the Boldu activists produced a stencil and spray paint from under one of the round tables and quickly spray painted a red fist onto the wall. The emblem of the movement. There should be no mistaking the message. Boldu had declared this a party for pigs.

Two of the giant hogs stuck their forelegs up on the head table in an effort to get at the food. The table collapsed as the legs buckled and the plates and silver slid across the floor. The crystal stemware shattered. Eraliev himself tried to rise from his seat, but one of the hogs bumped into him from behind and the president fell unceremoniously onto his ample rear.

It was perfect television, and Ruslan knew that two other Boldu operatives were filming the madness on their smartphones. The video would be uploaded to websites all over the world within hours. This was the Achilles' heel of authoritarian regimes. They were vulnerable to ridicule.

The videos that his team was making would be the only ones available. Computer hackers loyal to Seitek and Boldu had disabled the security cameras. It would not do for Ruslan or the others to be captured on film. They were not yet ready for open war with the regime. That day would come.

Ruslan stood watch as the members of the Boldu strike force drifted away from the madness in the ballroom, stripping off their waiters' uniforms to reveal plain dark clothing underneath and disappearing through the side exits into the garden and then out onto the streets of Bishkek. They were all wearing light disguises: wigs, cheek pads, and makeup. It was almost certainly an excess of caution. No one ever really looked at waiters. They were faceless servants of power.

"Why don't you get moving, Bermet?" Ruslan said. "I'll follow." He would be the last to leave.

"I'm staying with you."

Ruslan started to argue but Bermet shook her head to shut him up. She was not only Ruslan's comrade in the movement, she was his occasional lover and not above exploiting that position.

When Ruslan was satisfied that the others on the team were safe, he and Bermet started toward the nearest exit. They had waited just a beat too long. He pulled up when he saw a small knot of guards standing by the door. The guard he had dispatched to meet the imaginary Russian general was gesturing in their direction. He drew his pistol and tried to take aim at Ruslan. The crowd blocked his line of fire.

"This way!" Ruslan grabbed Bermet by the arm and pulled her in the direction of a hallway that led away from the exits toward the central core of the palace complex.

"That's away from the street," Bermet protested.

"It's the only way out that's not blocked."

The hallway was dimly lit and wove a crooked trail through the palace past office suites and ceremonial rooms that Ruslan assessed as dead ends. They had enough of a head start that they could not see their pursuers, but they could hear them. And Eraliev's guards only needed to get within pistol range. Embarrassing the president was a capital offense.

The corridor took a sharp ninety-degree turn and there was a steel door on the far wall with a push-bar exit. It was unlocked and opened up onto the garden. Bermet held the door open.

"Let's go," she said.

Ruslan stepped through into the shadows of the Presidential Gardens. From here, Boldu had plotted the escape routes. If they could lose their pursuers, there was a chance they could make it out.

The door clicked shut behind him and Ruslan heard the sound of a bolt being thrown shut.

He pounded on the door.

"Bermet," he hissed. "What are you doing? Open the door."

"They're too close." Her voice was muffled by the wall between them, but he could hear her well enough through a vent at the top of the doorframe. "I will lead them away. You are the only one we cannot lose."

"Goddamn it, Bermet . . ."

"Good-bye, Seitek." He heard the sounds of her running down the corridor and then the heavier sounds of the guards. The door shook as one of them pushed on the arm only to find it locked.

"They went left," he heard one of the guards shout.

"After them, you bastards."

Ruslan's eyes stung with tears as he thought about the magnitude of the sacrifice Bermet was making. Sweet, beautiful Bermet. He knew that she loved him. That he did not love her only compounded his feelings of guilt. He wanted to scream his frustration to the night sky. But if they caught him, then Bermet's sacrifice would be for nothing. On this side of the garden, there was a gate that a Boldu sympathizer on the palace guard force had arranged to leave propped open. Ruslan kept low as he moved through the shadows.

There would be an accounting for Bermet, he promised. The ledgers would be balanced.

If the government wanted a fight, then Seitek would give them one. It was time for Boldu to step out into the light.

# 5

Kate did not expect that it would be easy to do what her uncle had asked of her. Even so, it turned out to be much harder than she had thought.

The first few days after the dinner at the residence were the typical whirl of activity that always attended a PCS—a permanent change of station. The State Department, like all government agencies, was awash in acronyms, often to the point that the original meaning of the abbreviation had been lost in the mists of time. Sometimes the acronym did not even save any letters, and Kate knew that her first order of business would be to acquire a POV. No one seemed to find it odd that this government shorthand for personally owned vehicle was both cumbersome and required exactly as many letters as "car."

As had been her father's practice, she looked first at what was available from the German embassy. As much as she hated to traffic in national clichés, the Germans were appropriately obsessive about their automobiles. Kate knew she would find one that had been garaged and carefully maintained with all the records saved in color-coded folders. The German embassy was a dry hole, but Kate got lucky with the Swiss. The Germans' Germans. A third secretary was selling a four-year-old Volkswagen Touareg with only fifty thousand kilometers on the odometer. He was sorry to see it go, the junior Swiss diplomat explained, but he was being transferred to India and the steering wheel was on the wrong side.

The transition at the embassy was not nearly as smooth. The Department of State moved thousands of people around the world every year, many to strange and exotic locales. For all that practice, one would think the bureaucracy would be better at it. But as Kate's father had once said after getting caught up in a particularly infuriating tangle of red tape, every time you moved it was as though the department were doing it for the first time. You mean you're bringing your family with you to post? You have a dog? The school year starts in September? It all seemed like a new experience for the personnel techs and admin specialists who must have, Kate knew, dealt with these same routine concerns a thousand times.

Neither of Kate's government e-mail accounts had been successfully passed from Havana to Bishkek, meaning that it would be at least a week before she would get on either the secure SIPRNet system or the unclassified intranet. Her orders listed a dependent child that she did not have and the embassy management team seemed disinclined to take her word for it. And—as the capstone insult—the shipping coordinator informed Kate apologetically that her shipment of household effects would take six months to make their way from the island of Cuba to landlocked Kyrgyzstan.

In the meantime, she could continue to use the embassy welcome kit with its assortment of plastic plates and cutlery and polyester sheets. It was a fairly average level of chaos for a transfer, and Kate resolved to go shopping as soon as possible. It was because of mix-ups like this that the typical Foreign Service family traveled the world with three mismatched pasta pots.

Kate's boss in the political section seemed like a pleasant enough man, if not exactly a ball of fire. Chester Grimes was somewhere north of fifty with a middle-aged paunch, unfashionable steel-rimmed glasses, and a rumpled safari suit. His skin had an unhealthy, almost waxy sheen. He was also getting a little long in the tooth for the job he had. With almost twenty-five years in the service, Chet should have been running one of the big political sections in a place like Nairobi or Moscow or Jakarta, or making his bones as a deputy chief of mission. The combined political-economic section in Bishkek was small, a total of four officers. In addition to Kate and Chet there was Lyle Koslowski, a "junior officer" on his first tour who was just a month shy of his forty-seventh birthday. He had finished his twenty years in the army as a lieutenant colonel and joined the Foreign Service as a second career. Gabby was the lone ECON officer in the section

Chet had the only office. The rest of them were in cubicles with waist-high walls. Government had come late to the open-office concept and was making the change at just the point where the private sector was having second thoughts. Kate shared a cubicle wall with Gabby. A framed photo of her Mustang was perched next to Gabby's computer monitor.

On her first day in the section, Grimes had sat her down for the talk she knew was coming.

"Is this going to be awkward?" he asked. "You being the ambassador's niece."

Grimes ran his fingers nervously through his comb-over as he talked.

"Not on my part. Ethics gave it the green light. I don't expect to be treated any differently than anyone else in the section. I don't want to be treated differently."

"And I want a full head of hair," Chet replied sardonically. "I don't think either of us is going to get our wish."

"I suppose not," Kate acknowledged.

He had been gracious about it, and Kate understood why Grimes might find her threatening. She would have to be careful, especially at first, not to do anything that would look like a challenge to his authority.

"The biggest thing our section is involved with," Grimes said, "is the base negotiations. The defense attaché, Colonel Ball, has the lead on the issue for the embassy, at least when he isn't running around in the mountains with his Kyrgyz Special Forces friends. But we play an important supporting role. Keeping tabs on the shifting political currents and advocating with various key players. I've taken personal charge of this issue with Lyle backing me up. Your responsibilities, Kate, are primarily democracy issues, human rights, and the opposition parties . . . such as they are. It's not the sexiest portfolio in the section, I'll admit, but it's a good training ground for new officers. I know you millennials all feel you should be measuring the drapes in the ambassador's office, but there's something to be said for a bit of seasoning."

"Of course."

Even as she was settling into her new job and learning the unique rhythms of a new embassy, Kate was working to track down Valentina. Her first stop was the CIA station and its chief, Larry Crespo. The station was located on the basement level behind a massive metal door. Kate hit the buzzer to the right of the door and waited. She stood there for almost four minutes, feeling increasingly foolish until a severe-looking woman with her gray hair pulled back into a librarian's bun opened the door and ushered her in wordlessly. Behind the door was an airlock-like arrangement with an elevator-sized holding area and a second steel door on the far wall. Kate's nameless escort stared straight ahead avoiding both eye contact and small talk. Her demeanor and Kate's long wait at the front door offered an unambiguous message. You may be the ambassador's niece, but down here you're unimportant. The CIA and the State Department were bound at the hip and yet barely tolerated each other.

On the far side of the door was a nondescript open-plan office space and one additional reminder of Kate's low-caste status. On the back wall, next to a line of cheap government-issue clocks showing the time in Washington, Bishkek, and Moscow, a red light lit up, a warning, Kate knew, that there was an outsider in the suite and the staff should watch what they say.

As station chief, Crespo had the only private office in the suite. In Kate's experience, CIA operations officers came in two distinct flavors. There were the former military types—usually army or Marine Corps, occasionally navy and only rarely air force—their knuckles dusty from dragging them on the ground as they learned to walk upright. The other flavor was the back-slapping used-car salesman with an Ivy League pedigree and a passionate interest in tennis. Crespo was of the first sort.

He was short, no more than five foot five, and Kate regretted her decision that morning to wear the pumps with the four-inch heels. Shaking hands with Crespo, she felt like a giraffe.

The station chief's windowless office was ultra-modern, uncomfortable, and Spartan in the extreme. The walls were completely bare, with none of the standard awards and plaques and pictures with "Washington famous" people that made up the I-love-me display that was seemingly de rigueur for senior government bureaucrats. The desktop was clean. The metal in-tray was empty. There were no family pictures anywhere in the office. The only decoration of any kind was a pen set on the desk embossed with the Marine Corps globe and anchor.

And Crespo looked like he still woke up early for PT. He was trim and fit with a regulation-short haircut, and as he shook her hand he looked at Kate with ice blue eyes and the kind of focused intensity she associated with psychotics.

"Thanks for seeing me," Kate said.

"You have ten minutes," Crespo replied. "Don't waste them."

Crespo was thinking to unbalance her, get her on the back foot. Kate resolved not to give ground. He sat in the one chair and gestured for Kate to take the low-slung couch.

"You know why I'm here?" she asked.

"The ambassador's wild sheep chase for Seitek and Boldu."

"Why do you call it that?"

"Because I'm not persuaded that Seitek is a real person. There are some sharp analysts at Langley who think he's just a symbol. It could even be a collective name for a group of people, some kind of politburo. Me, I'm not convinced that Boldu is more than a handful of college kids playing pranks."

"What about last night? That couldn't have been easy to carry off. And their video of chaos at the state dinner had to be deeply embarrassing to the palace."

"Embarrassing for sure," Crespo offered. "But damaging? I don't see that. The government blocks access to YouTube and Facebook. Only foreigners will see that video. Boldu is playing with fire and they run huge risks for minimal returns. Eventually, and I mean soon, they'll take one risk too many and the government will bury them. It won't be the first time. You of all people should know that."

It was an unkind thing to say, a sharp-edged reminder of what Eraliev had done to her family. And it was deliberate, an attempt to establish dominance in the conversation, to blunt Kate's focus. She ignored the jibe.

"The ambassador doesn't see it that way."

"No," Crespo acknowledged. "That's why you're here. And why your ten minutes are with me. I wouldn't ordinarily meet with a junior officer from the political section, even if she is the ambassador's daughter."

"Niece."

"Whatever."

"Let's cut to the chase, shall we, even if it is for wild sheep or geese. The ambassador showed me a number of finished intelligence products about Boldu, including one indicating that a woman named Valentina Aitmatova is potentially in a leadership position in the organization. I'd like your help making contact with her."

Crespo was quiet for a moment as he considered his response.

"No," he said flatly.

"No?" Kate was somewhat incredulous. She was used to the CIA being unhelpful, but they usually did a better job of pretending otherwise. "Why not?"

"Because it's not a priority for my organization. I know about the reports the ambassador shared with you. They're DIA products and I wouldn't use them to wrap fish."

There was little enough love lost between the CIA and the Defense Intelligence Agency, and Crespo did not so much as try to hide his contempt.

"What's wrong with them?"

"The raw intel that informed those products is hearsay. Two people talking about the activities of a third person. It's worthless except as collateral. There's no direct evidence that Aitmatova has any involvement with Boldu—much less a leadership role—or that Boldu even has anything that you and I would recognize as a leadership structure."

"Can I take a look at the raw product?" Kate asked carefully.

"No. I don't think you're cleared for it. Or at least you shouldn't be."

"What do you mean by that?"

Crespo said nothing. He simply stared at her with his arctic eyes. He didn't need to say anything.

Kate understood.

"It's because of my mother, isn't it?"

"Intelligence information about Kyrgyzstan doesn't belong in the hands of a Kyrgyz national."

"I don't have Kyrgyz nationality."

"No. But you could, couldn't you? Your mother was Kyrgyz. Your aunt was a democracy activist disappeared by the government. You spent a good part of your formative years here and you speak the language like a native. I'd say there's good reason to wonder about ultimate loyalties."

Kate felt herself burn and she struggled to tamp down the anger.

"That's one way to look at it," she said in a carefully measured tone. "Another would be that I know this country well, that I understand it, and I can leverage that understanding to advance the interests of the United States."

The CIA was charged with gathering and analyzing foreign government information, but it could be deeply suspicious of the foreign connections that made that possible. The agency's institutional culture valued loyalty above all else, particularly on the operational side of the house. The State Department, in contrast, fetishized expertise and too often valued gut feelings over hard analytics. Both could be blind spots.

"Let me ask you something," Crespo said. "Who did you love more, your mother or your father?"

"What kind of question is that?"

"A simple one. There are only two options. Pick one."

"I can't."

"Of course you can't. Most people can't. Those who can typically had pretty shitty childhoods. So what will you do when your parents are fighting? When the United States and Kyrgyzstan want very different things?"

"I'll do my job. Do my duty."

"I'm sure you will. But how would you define your duty? Don't you worry that you'll be inclined to shade your understanding of U.S. interests in the direction of Kyrgyz interests?"

"I'm fortunate then that they align. I work on democracy, and a democratic Kyrgyzstan is good for the Kyrgyz people and good for the United States. Everyone wins."

"For now maybe. But that could change in a heartbeat. Our strategic interests lie in getting agreement for a long-term lease on the Birlik air base. That's about containing a rising China and beating back a challenge from a resurgent Russia. That's grown-up geopolitics. Democracy promotion. Human rights. NGOs. Rainbows and unicorns. That's social work. It's the policy of luxury, and right now, Ms. Hollister, we cannot afford luxuries. We need to pay the mortgage on our superpower status. National security is not a good fit for people with delicate sensibilities."

"That's short-term thinking," Kate protested weakly. "Longer term we need allies and partners in this region, not vassals and client states."

Crespo snorted derisively.

"You're young. It's okay to believe that when you're young. But you're also awfully close to this particular problem set. Too close for my comfort. And I don't give a rat's ass if you go running to your uncle."

Kate shook her head. She had no intention of complaining to the ambassador.

"*Siz echteke tushungon joksuz.*"

It was a common enough Kyrgyz expression that in a few short words managed to combine "you don't understand me" with "you have no idea what's going on" and "you're something of an idiot."

Crespo just looked at her, blinking. Maybe he spoke some Russian, not that the CIA would give him much chance to practice it by speaking to actual Russians, but it didn't seem like he had a word of Kyrgyz.

"Don't get confused about who you are," he said finally. "Who you work for."

"I don't see how knowing this country and having empathy for the people here can be a bad thing."

Crespo leaned forward in his chair until his face was no more than eight inches from Kate's. She could see the muscles in his jaw clenched tight and there was a twitch at the corner of one eye.

"Because sometimes, sweetie, you have to take your favorite dog out behind the barn and shoot it."

# 6

Kate was shaken by her conversation with Crespo. She had expected some friction in her new post because of her last name and the assumption that she owed her position to nepotism. She had not anticipated suspicion and hostility from her colleagues because of her mother, because of her ties to this country.

Crespo's accusations stung because they were not entirely without foundation. Kate was self-aware enough to know that her identity was somewhat ambiguous, her sense of American-ness occasionally tenuous. But she was a professional, damn it, and Crespo was trying to strip her of that. Kate resolved not to let him succeed.

Nor would she run to her uncle and complain about Crespo's bullying. Once she started down that road, she would never be anything but the ambassador's niece. She would fight her own battles.

So if the CIA wouldn't help, Kate would just have to find Valentina on her own.

She started, naturally, online. There was no trace of Val on social media, no Facebook page or Instagram account or Twitter handle. There were not many people in Kate's age cohort who had not left a thick trail behind them as they blundered clumsily through cyberspace. That Valentina had managed to do so seemed to indicate a deliberate effort not to be found.

Kate's next shot in the dark was the alumni office at the International School of Bishkek. The school was located on the outskirts of town where land was cheap. A high brick wall topped with rusty barbed wire surrounded the campus. The gate was guarded and entry was controlled by a metal arm mounted on a fulcrum. The security overkill was an outgrowth of a special fund established by the State Department's Bureau of Diplomatic Security to harden soft targets overseas that were in some way linked to the United States. International schools around the world were big beneficiaries of the program, and competed aggressively for security dollars for the oldest of bureaucratic reasons. Because they could. Thanks to the largesse of diplomatic security, ISB had acquired a state-of-the-art sprinkler system, biometric ID badges and card readers, and a roving patrol that was expensively trained in surveillance detection.

None of this was strictly necessary. The terrorist threat in Kyrgyzstan was low. But Kate understood the logic. Al-Qaeda had a penchant for attacking the United States where it was strong—downtown Manhattan, fortress embassies in Africa, even a warship making a port call in Yemen—but its affiliates and franchisees were somewhat less discriminating. They were perfectly content to target the United States where it was weak. American facilities around the world were engaged in a security arms race. The competition was with themselves. And the loser was dead.

American diplomatic license plates were something of a golden ticket at ISB. The guard lifted the gate without even bothering to check Kate's ID. The school had changed little in ten years. Three two-story concrete and glass buildings were clustered around an open green space that served as a sports field, parade ground, picnic spot, and dance floor, depending on the season and the occasion. Walnut trees lined the far end of the field along with a few wizened apple trees that produced small, sour fruit that the boys used to throw at one another as they showed off for the girls.

Kate parked in the gravel lot and was somewhat surprised to find a soft, gauzy feeling of nostalgia creeping up on her as she walked across the field to the main building. Kate was only twenty-nine. Too young, she thought, to be sentimental about her youth. But her four years here at ISB had been good ones, and were the last in which she had anything that most people would recognize as a family.

Just on the other side of the main doors, Mrs. Larson was sitting behind the reception desk, as she had every morning when Kate was a student. She was an Australian national married to a Kyrgyz, who had arrived in Bishkek at about the same time Kyrgyzstan had become a country. For more than twenty years, she had been a fixture at the school, serving as registrar, guidance counselor, head librarian, substitute teacher, and informal life mentor to generations of ISB grads. Kate was aware that she must have a first name, but none of the students had known what it was. She was simply Mrs. Larson, and she had not changed. She was wearing the same type of pastel sweater set that she had worn back then. Her gray shoulder-length hair was held in place with a black hair band, and a pair of glasses with rectangular lenses and a tortoiseshell frame was perched at the end of her nose.

Mrs. Larson smiled broadly when she saw Kate and walked around the desk to give her a hug.

"Look at you," she said. "Our little Katie, the American diplomat. And so lovely as well."

Kate blushed.

"It's nice to be back, Mrs. Larson."

"Your father would have been so proud of you, dear. And I'm so sorry about what happened to your parents. Such a terrible tragedy."

"Thank you." There was a small lump in her throat. Kate knew that this was a conversation she would have many times over in the next few months. But that did nothing to make it easier. Being back in Bishkek made it feel as though her parents' deaths were only a few weeks in the past.

It was after-school hours, so Mrs. Larson invited Kate back into the office for tea, which she drank in the Australian way with milk and sugar rather than in the local fashion with honey or strawberry jam.

"You mentioned on the phone that you needed my help with something," Mrs. Larson said after a few minutes of catching up on the events of the last decade. "How can I be of service to you?"

"I'm hoping to reconnect with some old friends while I'm back in town. I've lost touch with most of my old classmates, I'm embarrassed to say. I'm hoping that you can help me track some people down."

"I'll do what I can. Any place you'd like to start?"

Kate could not help but look away for a brief moment, as though she had been caught in a lie.

"I'd like to see if I can get ahold of Valentina Aitmatova."

"Two peas in a pod, you were," Mrs. Larson agreed. "But I was thinking that you might want to begin with that boy. What was his name? Oh my, I'm getting old."

Kate knew that there was no chance Mrs. Larson had forgotten the name of her high school boyfriend. The Aussie was both famous and infamous for her encyclopedic memory of everything that had happened at ISB and everyone who had walked through the doors of the school since its founding.

"He's long gone, alas. Last I heard he left for Moscow and then Berlin and then I lost track of him."

"You were such a sweet couple. As a high school guidance counselor you see a great deal of young love. Most of it is of the puppy variety. But you two were something else. There was something quite . . . mature about the two of you. It was unusual."

Kate knew she was right. Their affair had been relatively brief, the final eight months of their senior year and the summer before Kate left for college. But it had also been intense, and the first time they had made love was a memory that still burned bright and hot. It had been the first time for both of them, and Kate kept it close to her heart along with other memories of him that she had strung together like the beads on a rosary. Kate had had other lovers since, of course, including one at Georgetown that had been serious, at least for a while. Nothing, however, had quite measured up to that first flush of young love. Kate had no desire to discuss this with Mrs. Larson.

"He was special," Kate agreed. "But a girl can't live in the past."

"No, of course not," and for a moment Mrs. Larson had a faraway look in her eyes as though she were remembering her own youth and an early love that had offered, at the time, so much hope and promise.

"But about Valentina . . ."

"Oh, yes. I'm afraid that we've lost touch with her. Alumni outreach has always been one of our weak spots here at ISB. I can give you the last address that we had for her parents, but there's no guarantee that it's still good. I heard that her mother died, poor thing, and her father was a drinker. I remember some stories from PTA meetings that would curl your toes. Valentina had a lot on her plate, what with her brother and all. I don't know what happened to him. Kyrgyzstan isn't especially well equipped for that sort of thing."

"No, it's not," Kate agreed. Val's brother was maybe five years younger than they were and he had been born with cerebral palsy. It was relatively mild, Kate remembered, but even mild CP was severely debilitating, especially in a developing country like Kyrgyzstan. Val had not spoken of her brother often, but Kate knew that she had been devoted to him.

"Maybe there's something I can do to help. I'll take the old address if that's all you've got."

Mrs. Larson went into the back room and returned a few minutes later with the address written in neat block letters on school stationery.

"Good luck, dear."


Kate's luck was not good.

Valentina's old apartment had changed owners at least twice. In an awkward exchange conducted over the apartment's aging intercom, a tetchy old man speaking in Russian had denied ever hearing the name Aitmatova. When Kate asked him the name of the person from whom he had bought the apartment, he hung up. Kate understood. Soviet-era abuses had so clouded the issue of property rights that even the most benign requests for information could come across to the nervous current occupants as a potential threat of litigation.

A café across the street from the apartment building offered Kate an opportunity to drown her sorrows in cappuccino and contemplate her next move.

How did you find someone in Bishkek who didn't want to be found? For that matter, was Valentina even in Bishkek? What if Crespo was right, and the evidence that she was a key player in Boldu was a red herring? Either a misreading of the intelligence or deliberate misinformation. Boldu's version of *maskirovka*. In that case, Valentina could be anywhere. She could be in London or New York or Timbuktu. Asking the Kyrgyz government for help was out of the question. Kate's objective was not only to find Valentina but to win her trust and gain access to Boldu, to find out who the mysterious Seitek was, to learn whether—in fact—he existed at all.

Kate was convinced, however, that Valentina was in Bishkek. The conversation with Mrs. Larson had jogged her memory about the brother. If the parents were out of the picture and unable to care for him, it was impossible for her to imagine that Valentina would abandon her brother to the mercy of the state.

Kate stiffened abruptly and almost spilled her cappuccino. Of course. The brother was the key. There were only a few institutions in the entire country that would be equipped to provide the kind of care he would need. Assuming, of course, that he was still alive. And Kate felt guilty for even thinking about measuring the value of a young man's life in terms of how it furthered her mission. There was a part of her chosen profession, however, that required using people as instruments. A bias toward transactional relationships was one of the more unattractive aspects of diplomatic practice.

Val would want to visit him on a regular basis. If she could find out which facility her brother was in, Kate would know the place

Valentina would be, if not necessarily the time. It was the best idea she had. The only idea she had.

Kate left without finishing her coffee, and twenty minutes later she was back in her cubicle. The embassy nurse gave her the contact number for a local neurologist who the medical unit had vetted for referrals. The doctor, in turn, gave Kate the names of every institution in Bishkek, public and private, capable of managing a patient with cerebral palsy. It was a short list, four public hospitals and two private clinics. Kate felt like she was minutes away from success.

Forty-five minutes later she was back at square one.

None of the hospitals or clinics had a record of a patient named Aitmatov.

With a sudden insight, Kate realized her mistake.

"Oh my god, I'm such an idiot."

"I promise not to tell anyone," Gabby said from the next cubicle.

"Thank you."

"Your secret dies with me."

"Take your time."

Kate had been asking the wrong question. She had been looking for someone with the family name Aitmatov. But if Valentina was trying to hide, she would not want to use that name. She would have registered her brother under a different family name. It was doubtful, however, that she would have wanted to change his first name. Cerebral palsy was often associated with intellectual disabilities, and it would have been confusing to her brother to force that change on him.

She dialed Mrs. Larson's number at the school.

"Hello."

"Mrs. Larson, it's Kate. I need a quick favor."

"Anything, dear."

"Valentina's brother. Do you remember his first name?"

"Of course. It was Zhyrgal, dear. Zhyrgal Aitmatov."

"Thank you, Mrs. Larson."

Half an hour later, Kate had the answer she was after. One of the private clinics had a resident patient named Zhyrgal Dobrynin. The clinic had no set visiting hours, but the nurse who ran the unit said Kate was welcome to visit anytime.

The next morning at nine o'clock, Kate pulled up in front of the NeoMed Clinic and parked her Touareg in the shade of an enormous walnut tree. The clinic was a converted stone villa in a residential part of Bishkek. From the outside it seemed pleasant enough, albeit in need of a little upkeep. Kate walked in through the glass doors carrying a shiny red gift bag she had picked up in the embassy commissary.

The nurse at the front desk was petite, brunette, and pretty, with features that could have been either Slavic or Kyrgyz, a product of the great Central Asian melting pot of cultures. The reception area was not fancy, but it was clean and there was a faint odor of antiseptic. This was a private clinic and Kate knew that it was considerably nicer than the state-run hospitals. Bishkek central hospital was a grimy, gray, cinder-block monolith where underpaid doctors and nurses treated patients like marks, shaking the families down for petty bribes for everything from appointment times to prescriptions.

"Welcome to NeoMed," the nurse said pleasantly. She spoke in Kyrgyz. "How can I help you?"

The concept of customer service was just one more indicator that this was a private clinic.

"I'm here to see Zhyrgal Dobrynin," Kate said.

"Are you a relative?"

"Friend of the family."

"Can you please sign the log?"

The nurse pulled a bulky three-ring notebook off a shelf behind her and flipped through it quickly until she found the page she was looking for. She set it down in front of Kate.

Each resident evidently had an individual page in the log book. At the top of the page was the patient's name—Zhyrgal Dobrynin—and a room number. Beneath that was a list of visitors with arrival and departure times. There were almost twenty visitor entries on Zhyrgal's page, but all from the same person, a woman named Natasa Semirova. She visited Zhyrgal every Thursday in the early afternoon between two and three o'clock, as regular and dutiful as only family could be.

Zhyrgal's room was on the second floor. Kate knocked softly on the door.

"Come in." The voice was high-pitched and the words were slurred.

Zhyrgal was sitting in a padded wheelchair at the window looking out over the courtyard and gardens. His body was twisted and his limbs bent at unnatural angles. His face looked as though it had been crumpled in an accident, and a thin strand of saliva dangled from a corner of his mouth. His black hair was greasy. But there was a spark of intelligence and curiosity in his eyes that was unmistakable and instantly appealing.

"Hello, Zhyrgal."

"Who are you?" The question was open and natural and not colored by suspicion. Kate could see that he had to strain to speak clearly.

"My name is Katarina. I'm a friend of your sister's."

Zhyrgal's face tightened in what looked at first like a grimace. It took Kate a moment to realize that it was, in fact, a smile.

"A friend of Natasa," he said, almost as though he were reminding himself of his sister's name.

"Yes," Kate agreed. "Natasa."

She looked quickly around the room. The walls were a cheery yellow, but the paint was chipped and sun-faded in places. A hospital bed with a frame made from chunky aluminum tubing stood against one wall. There was a poster tacked over the bed featuring FC Dordoi, one of the big Bishkek football clubs. Football loyalty in Kyrgyzstan was a family affair and Val's family had been Dordoi supporters.

Kate held up the bag she carried.

"I brought you a present."

"I like presents," Zhyrgal said.

"Who doesn't?"

She pulled a white baseball cap with FC Dordoi's blue-and-yellow soccer ball logo out of the bag.

Zhyrgal beamed.

"Would you like to try it on?"

"Yes, please."

Kate put the cap on Zhyrgal's head, adjusting it so that the bill would not block his view of the garden.

"You look great in it," she said.

"I know."

Zhyrgal's laugh was more like a bark. His enthusiasm was evident and infectious.

"Do you mind if I visit with you a while?" Kate asked.

"I don't know. I had plans." He laughed again. Louder.

They talked for twenty minutes about football and the weather and the food in the clinic. It took a little practice to follow his slurred speech, but Kate realized quickly that the mind trapped inside his

83

broken body was strong. She could not bring herself to ask directly about Valentina, to confront the fact that she was using Zhyrgal. Lying to him, in essence.

"Will I see you again?" Zhyrgal asked when Kate rose to leave.

"Most definitely."

"When?" he demanded.

"On Thursday, Zhyrgal. I'll be back on Thursday."

# 7

Three days later, Kate was back at the NeoMed clinic. It had been a frustrating seventy-two hours. Kate had had little luck finding any other leads on Boldu and even less in getting cooperation from the CIA. Even her own boss in the political section seemed largely uninterested in Kate's efforts to establish contact with Ruslan and the democrats. Nor had Kate seen much of her uncle since their dinner at the residence. He had been wrapped up in the base negotiations. The few times she had bumped into him in the embassy, he had been encouraging but vague and distracted, and Kate was left to wonder how much importance he really placed on the issue of Boldu. But why then had he pulled strings to get her transferred from Havana to Bishkek? Maybe it wasn't because he really cared about a fringe democracy movement in a small country most Americans had never heard of. Maybe he was just looking out for his brother's little girl. The poor little orphan. Kate hated that idea. She did not want to be condescended to. Under the best of circumstances, it would be hard enough in her field for people to see past her family name.

So it was with an edge of nervous tension that Kate approached the clinic. If Valentina did not show or if Natasa Semirova turned out to be someone else entirely, she would be back at the beginning.

At least she no longer felt like the bride of Frankenstein. The embassy doctor had cut her stitches out yesterday, and a little concealer and foundation helped make the angry red laceration at her temple much less noticeable. She would have a scar, but it was one that she would bear with pride.

The nurse at the reception desk seemed surprised to see her again so soon. Kate was disappointed to note that Semirova had not yet arrived. It meant little, however. She had timed her arrival at the clinic to coincide with the front end of the window in which Semirova had signed in on Zhyrgal's page in the visitor book. There was no reason to be nervous, at least not yet. But Kate's palms were damp and she wiped them surreptitiously on the cool metal desktop.

She made her way up to Zhyrgal's room. He was happy to see Kate and he seemed to appreciate the bag with fruit, nuts, and chocolate that she had brought to share.

She peeled an orange for him. Watching him struggle to eat the fruit without making too much of a mess tugged at her heart. Kate had been struck in their earlier conversation by Zhyrgal's positive attitude, his sense of humor, and his generous spirit. It was painful to see that potential trapped in a broken vessel. They talked about football and music. Zhyrgal was a big fan of Michael Jackson.

Half an hour later, Zhyrgal's sister arrived. She stood in the open doorway, leaning against the frame with a look on her face that seemed to combine amusement, irritation, and uncertainty. It was an eloquent expression.

"Hello, Kate," she said in English.

"Hello, Val," Kate replied in the same language.

"It's been a long time."

"You look good. "

This was a lie. Valentina Aitmatova was not an attractive woman. She was tall, almost six feet, and anorexically thin. Her face was so long that one of the boys at school had suggested cruelly that she had modeled for one of the giant heads on Easter Island. Val had laughed it off, but Kate had found ways to make the boy's life miserable until he had apologized.

Many people grow out of their awkward teenage bodies. A few lucky ones transform into swans. Valentina was not one of them. Her features all seemed one size too big for her face. Her nose was both prominent and slightly off center. And her ears seemed set on her head at slightly different heights. But Val carried herself with confidence and style. She was wearing tight black jeans tucked into square-toed boots and a bright yellow silk blouse open at the throat. Her only makeup was a hot pink lip gloss.

Val walked over to her brother and kissed him softly on the cheek. She pulled a book out of her purse and set it on the table next to his wheelchair. It was a coffee-table book about football teams in England's Premier League.

"Brother," she said switching to Kyrgyz. "Kate and I need to talk. I'll be back soon to see you. I promise."

"Okay. Don't be too long."

Val turned to Kate and gave her an appraising look.

"Coffee?" she asked.

"That would be lovely."

Val led Kate to a coffee shop across the street from the NeoMed clinic. It looked like a student hangout with an eclectic mix of mismatched tables and chairs and trendy young people serving espressos and cappuccinos to other trendy young people.

"How have you been, Val?" Kate asked in Kyrgyz after a short woman in a shorter skirt had brought them their coffees and a small plate of biscotti that smelled like ginger and nutmeg. Bishkek had certainly become a more worldly city in the years Kate had been away. It was a little like seeing a beloved niece or nephew after some time apart and realizing with a shock that someone still fixed in your mind as a small child was now all grown up.

Val offered her a wisp of a smile.

"It's complicated." She spooned some sugar into her coffee. "What were you doing in Zhyrgal's room?" Val asked, and there was an edge to her voice that Kate understood reflected a mix of anger and fear.

"I'm sorry about that. I didn't have any other way of getting in touch with you."

"I suppose not."

"I wouldn't have done it, if it wasn't important."

"How did you find me?"

"I went to see Mrs. Larson. She reminded me about Zhyrgal. The rest wasn't difficult."

Valentina pursed her lips, her concern evident.

"If you did it, then others can too."

"Only if they know to look for you."

"Which begs the question, why are you looking for me? Did I forget to sign your yearbook?"

"I'm back with the embassy, Val. Only now I'm a diplomat rather than a dependent."

"Your father would have liked that." Valentina covered Kate's hand with her own. She had been at the funeral.

"I heard about your mother from Mrs. Larson. I'm sorry."

Val withdrew her hand.

"She was sick. It's better for her."

"How's your father?"

"Not well."

"It must be hard on Zhyrgal."

"Yes. Why did you want to find me so badly? Especially after it must have become obvious that I did not want to be found."

This was the kind of conversation Kate had had scores of times in Havana with skittish Cuban dissidents. She knew how to navigate this sort of exchange, with its subtext of suspicion and its abrupt shift in subject matter, even with a woman she considered a friend.

"I'd like to talk to you about the reasons you've tried to stay off the grid, at least inasmuch as that's possible to do."

"As an old friend or as an American diplomat?"

"Both. Either. Neither. Does it matter?"

Val was thoughtful.

"I don't know yet," she acknowledged.

Kate took this as an opening.

"We can help you, Val. I can help you. We know about Boldu and your role in it, you and some of the others from ISB who are close to Seitek. Some of our analyst types don't think there is such a person, that he's a symbol rather than a man. Others disagree. I happen to be among those who thinks Seitek is real."

For a brief moment, Kate thought Val was going to laugh as though at a private joke.

"Why would you think that I'm involved with this group to begin with?"

"Some others have spoken about you," Kate said, and regretted her choice of words almost as soon as they were out of her mouth.

"Spies," Val said bitterly, shaking her head. "You remember that in the stories Seitek struggled primarily against the internal enemies of the Kyrgyz tribes. The betrayers and the turncoats."

"It's nothing like that," Kate hastened to reassure her old classmate. "The information is from something else."

"From phone calls then. The NSA."

Kate didn't answer. She didn't have to.

"What do you want from me?" Valentina asked.

"I'd like you to vouch for me. I'd like to meet Seitek."

There was that smile again, as enigmatic and knowing as anything Mona Lisa had managed.

"Even assuming for a moment, for the sake of argument, that I could do this thing, why would I? You were a friend, Kate. I like you. But high school was a long time ago. I don't really know you."

"No," Kate admitted. "I suppose not. But you know my family. Where they stand. What my mother tried to do for democracy in this country. What her sister sacrificed. What the Eraliev clique did to my family and why. How could I be anything but loyal to what they fought for? What they, in fact, died for."

Val's eyes were moist and soft.

"I loved your mother. She had so much to give and they took it all, the bastards."

"And I want them to pay," Kate said. "I want an accounting."

"I understand that. And I would never doubt your sincerity. But you aren't here as Katarina Hollister, daughter of Kyrgyzstan. You're here as a representative of the global hyper-power, the world's policeman. And your track record in this part of the world is not especially inspiring."

Kate knew what Valentina was talking about. The United States paid lip service to the importance of democracy and human rights in

Central Asia but turned a blind eye to the Uzbek president stealing an election, the entrenched elite rigging the vote in oil-rich Kazakhstan, or the ruling party in Tajikistan crushing the opposition and locking it out of the assembly.

There was always a good reason: overland access for military equipment to supply front-line troops in Afghanistan or a crackdown on Islamic extremists that the United States did not want to endorse but did want to succeed. It was Uncle Harry's value complexity in action.

Just a little further afield, Washington was ready to broker a power-sharing deal with the Taliban and continued to engage in the summary execution by drone strike of suspected militants in Pakistan's largely ungoverned tribal belt. It was easy to see how Valentina could harbor doubts about America's ultimate reliability as a partner in the long struggle for democratic change.

"It's a complicated part of the world," Kate said with hesitation.

"Not for those of us who live here." Valentina's response was passionate, bordering on angry. "Freedom. Dignity. These are the only things that matter. And they are not especially complex ideas."

"Val, you can't do this alone. I've seen it up close. I've lost family to it. We can help you. I can help you. I did it in Cuba." Kate made the argument with force and conviction, but the still fresh memories of losing the fight with the chargé d'affaires and the RSO in the embassy's Tank weighed on her. When it all hit the fan, could she really count on her own government with its infuriating inclination to hesitate, vacillate, and hedge its bets? Unconsciously, she ran a finger along the now largely healed laceration at her temple.

"What are you offering?" Val asked.

"First and foremost is validation. If the United States and other governments start highlighting Boldu as a legitimate expression of democratic ideals rather than anarchists or just a bunch of disaffected kids, it would strengthen your hand. You'd get attention to the cause, converts, allies. You'd raise the costs for the regime of simply quashing you under the boot of the GKNB and the Special Police. There would be more positive media attention, not only in the West but here at home as well. We could train your supporters in grassroots organization, poll watching, and public relations. The nuts-and-bolts stuff of a democracy movement. And, if you need it and want it . . . but only if you need it and want it . . . we could help you with money."

Val sipped her coffee and seemed to be thinking over carefully what Kate had said.

"Do you remember Dr. Geisler?" she asked finally.

"How could I forget? Eleventh-grade honors literature. It was a requirement for the IB diploma." Both Kate and Valentina had been part of the international baccalaureate program at ISB, an intense standardized curriculum that made it easier for globe-hopping third-culture kids to move from school to school.

"Remember how he was always force-feeding us Goethe?"

"It was better than the philosophy class we took with him senior year. All that Nietzsche and Kant with his accent so strong it was like listening to it in the original German."

"I suspect you also remember when he had us read *Faust*."

"It's not like that, Val."

"Isn't it? The good doctor bartered earthly success in exchange for his soul. I'm sure it seemed like a good idea at the time."

"So does that cast me in the role of Mephistopheles?"

"You tell me."

"If I remember right, Faust made it to heaven in the end. Thanks to the grace of the eternal feminine. That sounds more like you and me."

"Goethe didn't have the courage of his own convictions. And he was kind of a sap. If he were alive today, he'd be writing romantic comedies for some cable channel. But it's an old tale, and most versions end with Mephistopheles carrying Faust's soul to hell."

"It doesn't have to be that way. I'm not asking you to sell your soul or sign some contract reeking of sulfur and written in blood. I just want to meet with Seitek and offer my help. Our help. He doesn't have to take it. I just want him to hear me out."

Valentina finished her coffee. She turned the cup upside down on its saucer as though she were a village woman about to read Kate's fortune in the pattern of the grinds at the bottom of the cup. But she had been drinking a latte rather than a Turkish coffee and the old ways of the village did not mesh well with the modern world.

Valentina reached into her purse and pulled out a violet five-hundred-som note. She held it up so that Kate could see the face on the front before setting it down on the table to cover the cost of the coffees.

The five-hundred-som bill featured an image of Sayakbay Kara-laev, a renowned Manaschi, one of the reciters of the *Epic of Manas*. It was a good omen.

Valentina stood up.

"Don't look for me," she said. "I'll come to you."

# 8

I want to get her out of there."

Ruslan was emphatic, and his tone brooked no argument. He got one anyway. Such was leadership in a democracy.

"Bermet's in Number One. She might as well be on the moon. All you'd accomplish is to get her rescuers killed."

Daniar Nogoev was a good man, loyal to the cause and absolutely fearless, at least when it came to his own personal safety. Nogoev was a Red Army veteran, an infantry officer who had fought the mujahideen in the harsh, unforgiving mountains of Afghanistan. He was in his sixties, reliant on bifocals, and what was left of his hair was steel gray, but he still carried himself like a soldier. His courage was beyond question. When the subject at hand was a risk to the movement, however, Nogoev could sometimes be, in Ruslan's opinion, overly cautious.

Meetings of the council were always dangerous. This was the inner circle, the only people in Boldu who knew that Ruslan was Seitek. One security slip and the GKNB could decapitate the entire movement. They were all of them sensitive to what had happened to Azattyk. None were eager to repeat that mistake. A bottle of vodka shared among them helped to take the edge off the tension.

They were meeting in an apartment, one of hundreds in a nondescript block of concrete high-rises. The eight members of the Boldu Council sat in a rough circle in the living room on mismatched chairs. The shades were drawn. Tchaikovsky's Symphony no. 5 played on the radio to help mask their conversation from any listening devices. A single floor lamp in the corner of the room cast dark shadows. Conspirators' shadows. The apartment belonged to Nogoev's sister. Family ties were the closest proxy they had to a thorough background check. Even so, this was the one and only time they would meet here.

"What do we know?" Ruslan asked. "Askar, what have you learned?"

"It's not good," Askar Murzaev replied, choosing his words carefully, clearly concerned that an inaccurate word or an undisciplined phrase could push the Boldu leader into a rash decision that would cost lives they could not afford to lose. Murzaev measured all his words, spending them reluctantly as though each were a gold coin in a miser's purse. He was short and slight with features that were so Asian he could have passed for Chinese. His stock-in-trade was information. Murzaev had spent nearly fifteen years in the military intelligence directorate. He had been purged after exposing a major case of military contracting fraud that led back to Eraliev's brother-in-law. In truth, Murzaev had been lucky to escape with his head still fixed to his shoulders. Few who crossed the Eraliev family could make the same claim.

He kept his cards close to his chest, a habit that Ruslan both understood and respected, but one that could be infuriating if you were playing as partners.

"Tell me," Ruslan demanded.

"We have some supporters on the prison staff, not guards unfortunately. Just clerical. So there are some gaps. What we know is that Bermet spent the last six days in solitary confinement. There will be a show trial in three days' time. It shouldn't last more than a day or two. Then, I'm afraid, she is likely to be sent to the Pit for interrogation."

Ruslan shook his head.

"I won't allow that."

"She won't last long," Murzaev said. "Two days. Maybe three. She'll tell Torquemada everything she knows. Please tell me that she doesn't know your name."

That was the risk. As awful as Ruslan felt about Bermet's sacrificing herself to keep him from getting caught, Murzaev and the others on the council had to think first about what she knew. What she could be compelled to divulge. Boldu was extremely security conscious, bordering on paranoid. The group used a cell structure to minimize the number of activists that any one prisoner or turncoat could betray. As far as the Kyrgyz system was concerned, Ruslan Usenov was living a comfortable life somewhere in Europe. If they knew his real identity, the security services could and would threaten his family. Ruslan had no close relatives in the capital. His father was dead and his mother was safely in exile, but he had grandparents and cousins and aunts and uncles, all of whom would be targets for revenge. He kept a low profile as Boldu gathered its strength, but Ruslan believed that the time to strike was approaching rapidly.

"Not so far as I know," Ruslan answered Murzaev with more confidence than he felt. "She knows me only as Seitek."

"Even during pillow talk?" Predictably, Valentina was the only one with the courage or the lack of tact to ask what Ruslan knew they were all thinking. She was a leader, and the de facto spokesperson for the younger members of the council, the former Olympic wrestler Hamid Ismailov and the Tatar twins Albina and Yana Garayev, who were also graduates of the international school.

"Bermet was using your stage name in bed?" Val continued.

Ruslan held up his hands in a gesture of surrender.

"Yes. She asked about my real name, of course. It's only natural. But I thought it would be dangerous for her to know."

"And for you," Valentina added with a hint of steel. Ruslan knew that she had never approved of his casual affair with Bermet, considering it a vulnerability. It was easier and easier to see her point.

"That too."

Ruslan knew he had a reputation as something of a womanizer. He did not enjoy the reputation, but he did seek out female company. And he knew he was attractive to women. He was tall for a Kyrgyz and slim with a thick shock of black hair and eyes as dark as onyx. He had an easy smile and a charisma that drew women in in the unconscious way a planet might capture a moon. None of the relationships was serious. It had been a long time since Ruslan had been serious about a woman, about anything but his mission and his responsibilities as a leader of idealists and amateur revolutionaries.

"I just don't want you making decisions on behalf of all of us because you and Bermet were making the beast with two backs."

"*Romeo and Juliet*?" Ruslan asked.

"*Othello*. But half credit for Shakespeare."

Valentina could always be counted on for a good literary allusion. She had once jokingly suggested to Ruslan that she'd like to be minister of culture in his government when Eraliev had been deposed.

Ruslan had replied quite seriously that he needed Valentina as minister of foreign affairs. Typically, her riposte had been a quote from the American revolutionary John Adams: I study politics and war so that my children might study mathematics and commerce and their children might study music and poetry.

Valentina was an intellectual and an artist. Ruslan respected that, but he was not a thinker. He was a doer.

"Don't worry. I'm not some lovesick puppy," Ruslan replied. He knew, however, that this was personal, not because he and Bermet enjoyed the occasional dalliance, but because of the way she had thrown herself bodily to the wolves to save him from their pursuers. If he could rescue her, he would. Even at great cost.

He said none of this to Valentina. She would not have understood.

"What are our options, Askar?"

The Boldu security chief shook his head.

"None that jumps off the page. Her cell in Prison Number One is entirely secure. According to our source, once the trial is over, Bermet will be sent directly back to the prison and transferred to the Pit."

"Can we break her out of her cell?" Ismailov asked. He was hunched forward on the edge of his chair, a lit cigarette dangling from the corner of his mouth. He had an athlete's predilection for action. "Can our agent get us inside?"

"No," Murzaev was matter-of-fact about it. There was little room for sentiment in his profession. "Another prison, maybe. Number One is too carefully guarded."

"What about the Scythians?" Ruslan asked.

Boldu was a political movement, but the council did not expect the Eraliev regime to pack up its tents and slink off into the night. The ruling clique would fight to hold on to power, and Boldu would have to be ready to respond in kind or risk being slaughtered like spring lambs.

Nogoev was an experienced soldier. He and Ismailov had hand-picked a group of Boldu supporters—young and fit men and a few women—and trained them as the armed wing of the movement. Murzaev had been able to get them a small cache of military-grade weaponry from his contacts in the Kyrgyz army. The country's sparsely settled countryside offered countless places where they could train without fear of being observed by government spies. When the time came to challenge the Eraliev government openly, the movement would not be defenseless. Nogoev had given his small strike team the name Scythians, a nomadic horse-riding culture that had dominated the steppes of central Asia some three thousand years ago and cast a shadow that stretched as far as the Nile before being eclipsed by Alexander and his Macedons.

"I can get us inside the prison," Nogoev said. "But I doubt very much that I can get us back out. The Scythians are getting better. But they're not Spetsnaz. Not by a long shot."

"What about the courtroom? It should be less well guarded than the prison. Can we raid the trial?"

"It's possible," Nogoev said. "But it'd be bloody. There would be civilian casualties. Maybe significant casualties. In my opinion, it's not worth the risks and the costs."

Ruslan bit back the impulse to tell Nogoev that in his opinion nothing was ever worth the risk.

"So where does that leave us?" he asked instead, trying to make the question sound conciliatory. If he was going to find a way to save Bermet, he was going to need Nogoev's enthusiastic cooperation.

He was not there yet.

"Mourning a falling comrade. This is a war, Ruslan. There will be losses. Grievous losses."

"I need a better answer than that."

"If they were going to transfer Bermet to one of the labor camps, and we knew which one and when, we could potentially ambush the convoy. The Scythians would be up to that, I think."

"Any indication that Eraliev may be planning to do that? Send Bermet off to one of the labor camps."

"No. At least not before she's been summoned to Torquemada's house of pleasure. And there won't be much left of her after that, I'm afraid."

Ruslan knew what Nogoev was doing. Baiting him. Hoping that he would get angry with his military advisor rather than choose a course of reckless desperation because of anger at either Eraliev or himself. He knew that Nogoev was not unaffected by thoughts of what awaited Bermet in prison. He had liked her. Ruslan squeezed his right hand into a fist and tamped down the anger that Nogoev had succeeded in fanning.

"So we need to get Bermet transferred to a labor camp now," Valentina said. "Before the trial."

"Only the president can do that," Murzaev said dismissively. "Somehow I don't see him accommodating us."

"How would it work?" Valentina asked. "If Bermet was going to be transferred to one of the camps, how would the order come down? Who would it be from and what would it look like?"

Ruslan had the sense that Valentina was not merely grasping at straws. That she had something in mind. That the questions were purposeful.

"Bermet's been classified as a Tier I political prisoner. Any order to transfer a Tier I within the prison system has to come directly from the president's office."

"How?" Valentina pressed. "Does the president make a phone call? Send a letter?"

"The transfer order is on a form. I've seen it done for military prisoners."

"Could our person on the inside get a copy of this form?"

"I suppose that wouldn't be too difficult," Murzaev said as though he were making some grand concession. "The form itself should be readily available on the computer system at the interior ministry. But it's only valid if it's stamped with the presidential seal. Without the seal, it's useless. And the seal we don't have access to."

"Who is the keeper of the seal? Surely not the president himself. That sounds too much like work."

"Eraliev's personal secretary keeps the seal. It's almost certainly somewhere in his office."

"In a safe?"

"I don't know. It's possible. But I doubt it. The secretary would need to use it regularly, and the office suite is so heavily guarded that the whole thing might as well be inside a safe."

"Well, that's the answer then. We get a blank form, fill in the order to have Bermet transferred to one of the labor camps, maybe Kosh-Dobo. It's isolated enough. And we borrow the presidential seal for a brief moment to make it all official. Then the Scythians would have a relatively soft target. And it seems like they could use a little field experience."

Murzaev pulled a red pack of Altai cigarettes and a lighter from his jacket pocket and lit one. The cheap local tobacco had a foul smell. "You glossed over the tricky bit. We just waltz into Eraliev's office and ask to borrow a cup of sugar and the presidential seal? Maybe the guards will be laughing too hard to kill us. There's always hope."

"That's one of the things I've always admired about you, Askar. Your sunny optimism."

"Optimism is for the inexperienced."

"What if I said that I had a way of getting access to the seal and getting a stamp on the form, making it all nice and legal."

"I'd say you were a liar."

"Askar. That's not especially helpful," Ruslan admonished him. "Tell us what you have in mind, Val."

She told them.

Ruslan shook his head and whistled his astonishment.

He could not quite decide if the gods had just smiled on him or were laughing at him.

# 9

The symbolism was simple but powerful. A group of thirty or so women ranging in age from eleven or twelve to perhaps eighty stood in a loose semicircle on the wide plaza of cracked concrete tiles. They were all dressed entirely in black, although some more stylishly than others. Each woman held a single white candle that flickered fitfully in the twilit gloom. The sky was an iron gray and the dark clouds threatened rain. The air was cool, almost chilly.

The women stood there stoically without jackets or umbrellas. Their silence was eloquent. Their pain spread out before them as an almost physical thing.

These were the Women in Black. And in addition to the somber hues of the clothes they wore they all had one thing in common. Someone they loved—a father, a daughter, a husband, a sister, a son—was rotting away in a cell somewhere inside the enormous, sprawling prison that seemed to mock them with its impassivity.

A small crowd had gathered behind the protestors, watching the women as they kept their silent vigil. Kate stood with them but off to one side, removed and distant from the emotional currents of the moment as a good diplomat should be.

She hated it.

Kate wanted to be standing there in the half circle of demonstrators, right alongside her sisters, dressed in black and protesting the system that ground so many young lives down to powder. Kate was one of them. In her heart, she was wearing black and honoring her mother's sister. She did not believe Zamira was dead. She could not believe it. She would not allow it.

But diplomats accredited to a government did not go out in the streets and protest that government. Not and keep their jobs. And if Kate was PNG'ed from a second post within the span of a few weeks, the State Department might reassess where it considered the blame to lie.

Diplomats do not march. They do not throw stones or storm the prison gates. They observe and report. So Kate stood to the side, absorbing the scene so that she might later record it faithfully in a stiff, bloodless cable for Washington.

"We do this every Friday." The woman by Kate's side, Patime Akhun, was one of the group's organizers. Ordinarily, Patime would have been out in front leading the protest, but she had invited Kate to come tonight as an international observer and a representative of the powerful American embassy. And a good host did not abandon her guest.

Patime was an ethnic Uyghur woman who looked to be in her sixties but who Kate suspected was at least ten years younger than that. She wore thick glasses in black plastic frames and her gray hair was cut close to the scalp as though she were a cancer patient who had recently finished a round of chemotherapy. Her black dress hung on her shapelessly. The body underneath seemed an almost perfect cylinder with no breasts or hips to break the line.

Her son was a poet who had blended the Russian and Uyghur traditions, publishing long, literate sonnets that had been well received in a small rarefied circle of cognoscenti. He had also been active in Azattyk. Twelve years ago, he had gone into Prison Number One and never emerged. Patime had accepted that her only child was dead. But she could never forget. And she would never forgive.

"Your parents used to join us here on occasion," Patime continued. They spoke in Russian. "When I heard that their daughter was back at the embassy, I jumped at the chance to get you here. Your uncle always seemed . . . less interested . . . in what we are doing."

There was a note of bitterness in her voice, the inevitable result, Kate suspected, of a decade spent protesting in front of an inanimate object that could not react in any way to the entreaties of even the most passionate demonstrator.

"Are these guys always here to keep you from tearing down the walls with your fingernails?" Kate asked.

A line of Special Police stood between the Women in Black and the prison gates. They were stone-faced and unsmiling, as hard and implacable as the prison itself. Their black tactical gear, a dominatrix-themed mix of Kevlar and leather, seemed to have been chosen in an ironic tribute to the protestors. They wore helmets with tinted plastic faceplates that, for the moment at least, were pushed up and locked in the "open" position. The rectangular clear plastic riot shields were held at their sides rather than interlocked like a legion of Roman foot soldiers. Their slick black batons were holstered at the hip.

"There's usually a police presence," Patime said. "But I've never seen this many before. And it's not typically the Special Police. Look at us. We're hardly the most physically imposing group."

"Are you worried at all about this? That video of the pigs running wild through the Hall of the People seems to have put the government on edge."

"We've been doing this for years," Patime said reassuringly. "I don't see them deciding all of a sudden that we're a real danger. Change will come, but it will come slowly."

Kate was not so sure about that. Change had a way of sneaking up unnoticed and often uninvited and then announcing itself with a bang and a crash of cymbals.

As though they had been listening in on her thoughts, the Special Police—with the precision of well-drilled soldiers—lowered their faceplates.

Kate's guard went up.

"That can't be good," she muttered.

"I don't understand," Patime said, seeming to speak more to herself than to Kate. "We haven't done anything threatening."

"Patime, you are something threatening."

The half circle of female protestors stood their ground, but they shrunk together, closing ranks with the defensive instincts of a herd. The onlookers similarly refused to back down. Without anyone seeming to lead, the group of some fifty ordinary citizens took a step forward in a show of solidarity with the demonstrators. To Kate, there was nothing special or noteworthy about them. It was the same cross section of people she might have seen waiting for a bus, a mix of young and old, prosperous looking and working class. Most wore Western clothes, but a few of the older men were dressed in traditional Kyrgyz embroidered jackets with the tall felt hats called *kalpak*s.

Kate pulled her phone out of her purse and unlocked it. She

activated the camera function and took a few quick pictures of the face-off between the demonstrators and the police. The moment felt as though it were poised on the edge of a precipice—balanced just on the tipping point, such that the lightest breeze could knock it back onto solid ground or send it over the brink into free fall, spiraling out of control.

"Ready!"

With their tinted faceplates pulled down, Kate could not tell which of the riot police gave the command. But the black-clad paramilitaries raised their shields, and the sound of batons being drawn from their leather holsters was a reptilian hiss.

Kate took a picture.

"Advance!"

The police stepped forward three paces until they were face-to-face with the demonstrators. The no-man's land between the two lines was no more than half a meter. One of the Women in Black who looked like she might have been about college age began to sing. Her voice was light and brittle but clear. Kate recognized the song, a Kyrgyz folk ballad of longing and lost love. She knew the words. They all knew the words and one by one the demonstrators and bystanders added their voices to the chorus and the singing became an act of pure defiance, a gauntlet dropped at the feet of the RoboCop-like police. Kate joined them, linking arms with Patime and abandoning any pretense of diplomatic neutrality.

As the last notes of the song died away, a single stone thrown from somewhere in the back of the crowd struck one of the Special Police on the helmet. The policeman reacted instinctively, pushing forward with his shield and knocking two of the Women in Black, including a young girl, to the pavement.

The fragile truce dissolved in an instant with riot police swinging their truncheons and the crowd of onlookers grabbing their arms and clawing at their shields.

Kate snapped photographs.

One of the Women in Black ran past Kate, blood streaming down her face from where a riot trooper's baton had left a gash on her scalp deep enough to expose the white of her skull. A man with a dark coat and the build of a wrestler got ahold of one policeman's shield and dragged him to the ground.

But it was an unequal fight. And it did not take long for the Special Police to establish control, scattering the demonstrators and handcuffing the die-hards who continued to resist. Patime had waded into the melee and was one of those lying facedown, her hands tied behind her back with neon yellow flex cuffs.

One officer, a large man with broad shoulders and legs like tree trunks, approached Kate. He lifted his faceplate and stretched out his hand.

"Give me your phone," he said in Russian. "No pictures."

"I am an American diplomat and this phone is U.S. government property. It is covered by the Vienna Convention. It's inviolate. So am I for that matter."

The cop blinked hard. The uncertainty was plain on his face, but so was the skepticism. Kate realized her mistake. Her Russian was perfect and if it was at all accented the accent was Kyrgyz. He did not believe Kate was an American because there was nothing "foreign" about her.

"You do not want incident international." Kate tried to make her Russian sound American and she deliberately screwed up the grammar, but it was too late to correct the first impression. The riot trooper stepped in close and grabbed her wrist. He took Kate's phone, a brand-new Samsung Galaxy, and smashed it on the concrete. He seemed to think for a moment about shoving Kate to her knees and strapping her wrists together with flex cuffs but instead chose discretion as the better part of valor, on this point at least.

Kate bent to one knee and gathered the broken pieces of her phone. Maybe something could be recovered from the memory. She watched as the Special Police bundled the Women in Black and their supporters—the broken fragments of the demonstration—into the back of a windowless van.

Here and there, the cement tiles of the plaza were slick with blood.

To the extent that Kate had anticipated that others in the embassy would share her outrage at the heavy-handed treatment of the Women in Black, she was disappointed. As required, immediately after getting back to the office, she had filed a report with the regional security officer that focused primarily on her own confrontation with the police and the destruction of embassy property. Within the hour, she had been called to the ambassador's office.

Her uncle was solicitous and obviously concerned about her safety, but there had been an undercurrent of annoyance as well, as though it were somehow Kate's fault that the police and the demonstrators had come to blows. "I'm doing everything I can for you, Kate," he had said to her, "but if there's a rerun of Havana here in Bishkek I won't be able to protect you." Although it was unlikely that he had meant it that way, it sounded to Kate almost like a threat.

Kate had written up the incident in a cable for Washington. Her narrative laid the blame for the violence squarely at the feet of the Special Police, who had needlessly escalated the confrontation with a group of nonviolent demonstrators. She had described the ensuing violence in graphic detail and added a comment paragraph at the end that described the actions of the security services—including the Special Police—as reflecting a growing nervousness on the part of the Eraliev government about pressures for democratic change building just beneath the surface of Kyrgyz society. When the pressure grew to be too much for the security services to contain, Kate's report had warned, there would be a volcanic explosion to rival Krakatoa.

That had been the first draft.

Kate was required to clear her cables with a number of other sections in the embassy, including the regional security office and the defense attaché, as well as the deputy chief of mission. What had come back from that exercise in sausage making was a bland, deracinated report so weighed down by caveats and false equivalences as to be almost entirely without value. This cable, Kate knew, would sink without a trace into the ocean of information lapping at the shores of the Washington policy process. It might as well never have been written.

Kate stayed late that night, updating the matrix of actions and events that she would use in drafting the annual human rights report in the spring. If she could not get an accurate accounting into the system through a same-day cable, she could bundle it together with other data points in the congressionally mandated report and use that to help shape the overall narrative. Her father had taught her that no decision in Washington was ever final, and patience was the indispensable virtue.

By nine o'clock, she had just about wrapped everything up when she heard the door to the political suite click open. A moment later, Lieutenant Colonel William Ball, USAF, turned the corner and made a beeline for Kate's cubicle.

"Kate, do you have a minute?" The defense attaché was wearing his service dress uniform, a light blue short-sleeved shirt with an open collar and dark blue slacks. The salad bar of decorations over the left shirt pocket included a bronze star with a small *v* for valor.

"Sure thing, Brass."

Even talking to civilians, military pilots preferred to go by their call signs, no matter how obscure or embarrassing in origin. Over the last few years, however, the air force higher-ups had cracked down on some of the more risqué or scatological call signs. Kate knew two pilots—Jason "Skid" Marks and Gordon "Maker" Moan—who had been forced to pick new radio monikers. But Carl "Notso" Bright could keep his and evidently "Brass" Ball had made the cut as well. That one, Kate suspected, had been right on the bubble.

As a lieutenant colonel, Brass would have to be somewhere in his late thirties, but he looked considerably younger. The only feature that threatened to betray his age were the lines at the corners of his eyes that seemed to speak of long hours spent squinting into the sun. The eyes themselves were a dark brown the color of chocolate, but there was nothing soft or warm about them. His hair was a little long for military standards, more "fighter pilot regulation" than regular air force. He was fit and handsome, albeit in a way that Kate found somewhat bland and conventional. The most interesting thing about his face was a thin white scar along the length of his jawline that hinted at some long-ago act of violence.

Kate had spoken to Brass a couple of times since she had started at the embassy. He was the lead on the air base negotiations and her uncle seemed to think highly of him. Kate was not so sure.

When she had asked, Brass had told her that he flew the F-15C and the F-22. He was a pure air-superiority specialist, the absolute apex of the air force's informal hierarchy. And he carried himself with a concomitant arrogance that Kate found off-putting.

Brass took a seat in the one guest chair that would fit in Kate's cube. He sat with his back straight and his shoulders set as though he were delivering testimony at a court martial.

"I wanted to talk to you about your cable from earlier today, the comment paragraph in particular." Although Brass had a sizable team under him in the attaché's office, he had edited Kate's report himself with a red felt-tip pen.

"The one you slashed to pieces and fed to the fish?" Kate asked. She tried to smile as she said it to make it seem like a joke, but it was hard to do. It had been a long and difficult day.

"That's the one," Brass said, and there was no humor in his response. "I'm concerned about the way you tried to link the human rights situation in this country to the base negotiations. They need to be kept completely separate. The negotiations are going well. We have a very good chance of closing this deal in the next couple of weeks and transforming our strategic posture in Central Asia. But a message like yours—in the wrong hands—risks stirring up the goody-two-shoes contingent back in D.C. and adding a new set of requirements to the negotiations. If that happens, if some democracy or human rights conditionality gets attached to these talks by the Hill or the poodle-hugging parts of the State Department, this process is going to crash and burn."

This was an old argument, one that people who cared about human security had been waging, and largely losing, against the hard security types for years. The pendulum swung back and forth, but at the moment the hard security "realists"—a name they chose for themselves—had more or less succeeded in marginalizing the human security advocates as "social workers" and their policies as unaffordable luxuries in a dangerous world. Kate believed strongly that this view was myopic and one-dimensional. She was not going to win this fight, she knew, but she would give it her best shot.

"I hear you, Brass. And I understand where you're coming from. But we can't be too short-term in our thinking. I promise you that Eraliev and his cronies are thinking ten years down the line. They see change coming and they want to hold that day off for as long as possible. I see it coming as well, and I want to make sure that we're on the right side when it comes, not because I believe in unicorns and fairies but because it's in the long-term interests of the United States. It doesn't do us any good if we win the air base and lose the country. We can't have one policy for the base negotiations and another policy for everything else. It's all tied together and our job is to find the balancing point."

This was pretty close to the values complexity speech Kate had gotten from her uncle, albeit with a bit of a twist intended to benefit her position. It was a perfectly reasonable argument, which made Brass's reaction all the more surprising.

A shadow passed across the attaché's face like a dark cloud. For a moment, Kate thought that he was going to lose his composure, but with a visible effort of will the fighter jock wrestled back into submission whatever demon had temporarily broken free of its restraints.

"You're young," he said flatly. "And naïve. I understand that. I even respect it up to a point, but your inexperience is dangerous and I won't allow it to endanger our prospects for success. And don't think for a minute that your uncle will be able to protect you because he won't. He can't. He's not the one in charge of this. He's really just a bag boy for Winston Crandle, and I don't give a damn if you tell him I said that.

"Stay in your lane, Kate, or you're going to get run over. This isn't a kid's game. This is big-boy stuff."

Kate decided right then that her first impression of the fighter pilot had been correct. She did not like Brass Ball.

"What exactly are you threatening here?" she asked.

"I'm not threatening you," Brass replied, and the angry demon look reappeared for a brief moment before once again being subdued. "I'm just pointing to a big steaming turd pile and warning you not to step in it. Be smart, Kate. Don't undercut the single most important thing we have going in this country."

Kate knew that it would seem hopelessly naïve to point to a nascent underground democracy movement as being more important than the base negotiations, even if she believed that over time this would turn out to be the case. And she did not want to damage her relationship with the defense attaché in her first few weeks in the country. It was time to sound the retreat.

"Thanks, Brass. I'll keep that in mind next time."


About an hour later, Kate was walking back to her apartment from where she had parked her car on the street. As she was nearing the front door of her building, a kid who looked to be maybe ten years old approached her. He was small and dark and dressed in a dirty white T-shirt and jeans. It was cold, but he was wearing flip-flops, probably the only footwear he had.

"Chiclet?" he asked, stepping into the weak circle of light cast by the streetlamp.

"Sorry," Kate said in Kyrgyz. "I don't have any gum."

"Well, I have something for you, Ms. Kate."

Kate's internal threat radar started screaming. It was late and they were the only two people on the dimly lit street. She looked around quickly, expecting to see the kid's grown-up accomplices emerging from the shadows with murder in their eyes. But there was nothing. No one else.

"How do you know me?" Kate asked.

The young boy stepped in close to her and Kate reflexively shifted her purse to the far side and pulled it close against her body.

"I have a message for you," the boy said, ignoring her question altogether. Although he was a child, he seemed to be the one in control of the situation and Kate felt vaguely embarrassed by that.

"From who?"

"Your friend from school."

Val.

"Yes?" Kate was now eager to hear what he had to say, her earlier fear gone.

"She said to meet her in the place you used to go to smoke cigarettes."

"I remember. When?"

"Midnight."

And the boy stepped back out of the light from the streetlamp and disappeared into the darkness.

# 10

During the day, Kara-Su Park was lively. Families with young children picnicked in the grass. Older kids enjoyed the dangerous pleasures of a few antiquated and rusted-out carnival rides. Young lovers strolled hand-in-hand through the well-kept gardens.

Nighttime was a different story. A few streetlamps formed an archipelago of weak, sickly light in an ocean of dark. Kate avoided the lights, navigating around them as though they were hazardous shoals. If there was something threatening hiding in the dark, she would rather not make herself easy to find. The dark was safer. Even so, she walked with her hand in her purse and her fingers wrapped lightly around a small canister of pepper spray.

The route she chose led past the bumper cars and Ferris wheel in the small amusement park that was open every day despite looking like it had been abandoned years earlier. The path took a hard turn to the right and dipped down toward a pond, passing under a stone bridge that would not have looked out of place stretched across the Seine. Kate and Val and a group of friends from ISB would sometimes gather here in the evenings, away from the eyes of prying adults, to smoke and drink and flirt and carve their initials into the soft limestone using crumpled bottle caps as chisels.

Under the bridge, it was ink dark. Kate could not see her hand in front of her face. The air was damp.

"Hello?" she said in Kyrgyz, feeling both nervous and foolish. Her greeting echoed off the walls. "Is anyone here?"

There was no response. Kate resisted the urge to call out Val's name.

Just as she was about to abandon hope and turn back, a match flared brightly only a few feet away. Kate almost jumped out of her skin. She closed her eyes against the sudden light and green dots danced on the inside of her eyelids. When she blinked her eyes open, the match light had been replaced by the warm orange glow of a lit cigarette. Val's long, angular face was barely visible in the light it cast.

"Smoke?" she asked.

"Thanks."

Kate did not smoke often, typically when she was drunk or nervous. And she was nervous. She took the cigarette Val offered from a pack of Marlboros along with a thick kitchen match that she struck on the tunnel wall just like they had done as high school students a decade earlier.

"So you still remember the place," Val observed.

"It's hard to forget."

"Yes, it is," and there was a depth of pathos in the response. It was hard to forget many things. Harder still to forgive.

"Do you have a cell phone?" Val asked.

"In my purse."

"Take the battery out, please."

Kate did as Val asked, somewhat sheepish that she had not thought of this herself. It was a reasonable precaution. Cell phones were transmitters with built-in microphones. Even the most cut-rate spy agency had the software necessary to turn them on remotely and use them to record conversations. It was even easier to do this with a compliant state-run telecom monopoly.

"I'm glad you reached out to me," Kate said. She took a deep drag on the cigarette and felt the nicotine rush into her blood, speeding up her heart and focusing her thoughts.

"You may not be when you hear what I have to say."

"Really? Is there some kind of problem?"

"For us. And maybe for you. We'll see."

"Us?"

"Boldu."

In the dark, Kate smiled. She had her foot in the door.

"Thank you for trusting me," she said.

"Well. We have our reasons."

Kate leaned against the limestone wall of the tunnel. The rocks were cool to her touch. Her eyes had adjusted to the dark and she could see in the dim glow from the burning cigarettes graffiti on the tunnel walls that looked like cave paintings. She ran one finger lightly over a spot where someone had carved a set of initials into the stone. Evidently K.R. loved M.T. In stone, at least, it would be that way for many years.

Val lit a second cigarette off the end of her first and crushed the butt against the wall. Kate did the same. She could not remember the last time she had chain-smoked in this way. College maybe.

The cigarette smoke floated between Kate and Val like a fog.

"I'd like to meet the others. I'd like to meet Seitek."

"Hold on, girl. There are some things we need to talk about first."

"Tell me."

"You saw the video of the pigs crashing Eraliev's party."

"Of course."

"We lost someone there, a woman named Bermet who was picked up by the police."

"Where is she now?"

"Prison Number One."

"Oh."

"Yeah. As in oh, shit. We need to get her out of there before her case goes to trial and she gets sent to the Pit."

"Torquemada?" Kate asked apprehensively. "He's still there?" Kate's father had told her about Eraliev's chief inquisitor, and her mother had had nightmares of her sister being subject to the mysterious Georgian's less than tender ministrations.

"He's a vampire. He'll never die."

"Does this woman know something in particular that needs to be protected?" Like Seitek's real name?

"No. That's not it."

"Then what is it? I don't mean to sound callous here, but you're not playing Parcheesi. Revolution is a dangerous game. There will be losses. What's so special about this one?"

Val was quiet.

"You need to be straight with me if you want my help." Kate kept her voice even and level. These conversations were like fishing. Too much tension would snap the line.

"Bermet and Seitek were close," Val admitted. "Maybe too close."

"She's his girlfriend?"

Val snorted.

"I wouldn't use that word. Bermet might, but she'd be the only one. Still, he seems to feel an outsized sense of duty to her, both be-cause he was . . . ploughing her field . . . and because she was arrested saving him from capture. So unless we can find a way to get her out, there's a real chance of Seitek doing something foolish. And he's the one man we truly can't afford to lose. Without him, Boldu is finished before it begins."

"So what does this have to do with me? You think the American embassy can get Bermet out of prison? We don't have a great track record there." Kate was thinking of her aunt and the countless hours her parents had invested in trying to find her.

"No," Val replied. "Believe me, if we thought there was a political angle, we'd take it. This isn't about the American embassy, Kate. This is about you."

"Me?"

"We can't get into the prison. It's too hard a target. We need to get the prison authorities to move Bermet out, preferably to one of the labor camps in the countryside. But Bermet's a Tier I political pris-oner. Which means that the only way to do that is to get the transfer form stamped with the official presidential seal."

Kate had a sinking feeling in her stomach. It did not take a clair-voyant to see where this conversation was headed.

"I don't suppose that's a terribly easy thing to do," she said.

"No. It's not."

"Where's the seal kept?"

"In Eraliev's office. His secretary keeps it. Probably somewhere close at hand. His desk, perhaps."

"Perhaps?"

"It's the best we can do."

"And what do you want from me?"

"Isn't it obvious? We want you to take this form," and Val pulled an envelope from her shoulder bag and held it out to Kate, who took it. "And get it stamped with the presidential seal to make it nice and official."

Kate opened the envelope, but it was too dark to read what was inside.

"How the hell am I supposed to do that?" she asked, making no effort to disguise her skepticism.

"You're a smart girl. You'll figure something out."

"Why me?"

"Because none of us can get into Eraliev's office."

"And you think that he and I meet for coffee every Wednesday?"

"He meets with your uncle often enough. And there's also your diplomatic immunity to be considered. Any of us who tried and failed would be sent to the Pit. They wouldn't do that to an American diplomat. You'd just be sent home."

"I am home, Val."

"Back to Washington then."

Kate thought about her parents' car lying in a crumpled wreck at the bottom of a ravine.

"You really think that's the worst thing this government would do to a diplomat?"

Val understood what Kate meant.

"I'm sorry. I didn't mean . . ."

"It's okay."

The two were silent for a moment. Kate wanted a drink to go with her cigarette.

"And if I don't do this?" Kate asked. "If I can't do this?"

"Then this is as close to Boldu and Seitek as you're ever going to get, Kate. I'm sorry. But you understand."

"And if I do succeed? What then?"

"Then we'll see what happens next."

"Bring me the broomstick of the Wicked Witch of the West," Kate said bitterly.

Val chuckled softly. She had been educated in international schools since she was five. She understood the reference.

"I know you have the brains," Val said. "Now what we want to know is if you have the courage to go with them. And a heart."

# 11

Dorothy had made it look easy. Three loyal friends and a bucket of water, and that was all she wrote for the Wicked Witch and her flying monkeys. Kate had no illusions about what she was up against, but she did know where to begin. Like Dorothy, she would have to get inside the witch's fortress. The intrepid Kansan had been protected by some magical electric field emanating from the ruby slippers. If she was caught, Kate would have to hope that her diplomatic immunity could serve the same purpose.

She tried not the think about the witch's plan for overcoming the force field.

The ambassador had a meeting with Eraliev in two days' time to take stock of progress in the base negotiations. It was a complex process, covering not only the terms of the lease but the all-important status of forces agreement establishing the protections and privileges that would be afforded American military personnel deployed in Kyrgyzstan, everything from their tax status to their legal rights in the event they were charged with a crime. SOFAs were, sadly, essential to any base agreement. Gather a large enough group of twenty-something males and the likelihood of one or more committing a violent crime was depressingly close to one hundred percent.

Brass typically accompanied the ambassador to meetings with the president, representing the interests of the Defense Department and handling the purely military aspects of the negotiations. He was also, Kate suspected, acting as a spy for Winston Crandle. Kate's boss, Chester, covered the political angles. The best way to get into Eraliev's office, Kate reasoned, was as part of the ambassador's team. And if that meant she had to play the family card, then so be it.

Kate asked Rosemary, her uncle's longtime office management specialist, for ten minutes of his time. She got it. No questions asked. No other junior officer would have that kind of access to the ambassador. As always, when her nose was rubbed into it in this way, Kate was a little chagrined by the extent of the privileges afforded by her family connections in the Foreign Service. But as Frederick the Great reportedly said of Austrian empress Maria Theresa when it came time for the big powers of the day to divvy up Poland among themselves: She wept, but she took. Kate may not have earned it on the merits, but she got the time.

There were several people waiting in the outer office when Kate was buzzed into the executive suite. The suite, which in every embassy is known as the Front Office, was home to both the ambassador and the deputy chief of mission. Harry's DCM was a twenty-year veteran of the consular service who focused more on embassy administration than on policy.

The Front Office in Embassy Bishkek was expensively decorated. One wall of the suite was covered in marble the color of dirty snow.

Lithographs by Andy Warhol and Willem de Kooning hung on the walls courtesy of Art in Embassies, a State Department program that arranged the long-term loan of museum-quality pieces to American missions around the world. It was ironic that this program intended to project American soft power overseas was used to decorate the executive suite, which was located in the embassy's controlled-access area and out of bounds for foreign guests.

The ambassador stepped out of his office looking the part of the proconsul. Her father's suits, Kate remembered, had always looked like he had just picked them up from the floor, wrinkled and shiny at the elbows. His brother's clothes looked like they were fresh from a bespoke tailor on Savile Row. The tie was Italian. The perfectly polished alligator-skin loafers were Brooks Brothers. Men could be extraordinarily vain about their bald spots and never seemed to appreciate that women were more likely to be impressed by their footwear than their comb-over. Uncle Harry had it down; and somehow he made it look natural rather than affected. More power to him.

Kate knew she was trading on his affection for her. And to her relief, her uncle did not hug her or pat her head and tell her how much she had grown. Not in front of the colleagues waiting their turn for an audience.

"It's good to see you, Kate," her uncle said instead. "I'm sorry I've been so busy the last few weeks. Come on in."

"Thanks for making some time for me, Ambassador." Kate was always careful to use his title when there were other people around. Never "Harry" or, god forbid, "uncle." It would be like calling the pope "Stinky" because that was the nickname you knew him by in elementary school.

The ambassador's private office was surprisingly small, consistent with the global design for new embassy compounds. The furniture was nice enough but standard government issue. It simply would not do for a visiting congressional delegation, or CODEL, to launch a long and expensive fact-finding investigation into why the American ambassador in the Central African Republic had a walnut desk and an executive-model leather chair. It would be far from the nuttiest thing the Congress had ever done.

They sat facing each other on a pair of cream-colored sofas. The ambassador poured Kate a cup of black tea from a plain silver samovar.

"How are things going?" he asked broadly. "You settling in okay?"

"I am. It's a little weird to be back here, but in a good way."

"How's Grimes treating you?"

"The way he would any second tour officer, I suppose."

"Good. That's what I told him to do. I don't want you coming out of this job thinking that you're already a superstar. You will be. I have a lot of confidence in you. But you can learn a thing or two from someone who's been around the block a few times."

"Chet's certainly done that," Kate said mischievously.

"He is a little old for the job. And maybe not a ball of fire. But he's a good man. You'll see."

After that exchange, Kate was a little chagrined about what she had come to ask. But there was no turning back. Kate took a sip of the tea. It was bitter and tannic from steeping too long in the samovar.

"So how's the hunt for Boldu going?" the ambassador asked. "Any leads?"

"As a matter of fact . . ."

"Really?"

Kate was a little hurt that her uncle seemed surprised at this news.

"Yes. I was able to get in touch with Valentina. It took a little work, but she was ultimately prepared to admit that she was with Boldu. Somewhere in the leadership, I think."

"What about Seitek? Have you met him yet?"

"No. I'm going to need to earn the privilege of an audience, I'm afraid."

"How?"

"By showing them that I can be useful. Val was my friend in high school, but that only goes so far. The leadership of Boldu has good reason to be paranoid."

The ambassador leaned back on the sofa and sipped his bitter tea. Her father had liked his the same way. Maybe there was a gene for it that skipped a generation.

"This is what you wanted to see me about, isn't it? Whatever it is you need to do to prove your bona fides. All right. I'm all ears."

Uncle Harry was impressively perceptive. He was maybe not the kind of serious intellectual that her father had been, but Kate's dad had frequently praised his older brother's emotional intelligence. Harry Hollister could read a room, he said, the way regular people read the newspaper. It was easy and automatic, and he was as skilled in one-on-one exchanges as he was in the more macro diplomacy.

"I need to show Val and the others that I matter. That I have access. That I can do things for them."

Kate was loyal to her uncle, of course, but she had had absolutely no intention of sketching out just what Boldu had asked her to do. It was insane. Potentially high reward, but very, very high risk. If Kate put her plan forward as a serious suggestion, the only sensible response would be to get her on the next plane back to D.C., ideally under sedation. She understood that omitting all this from her narrative could be seen as bad faith. The end would have to justify the means.

"Do you need some walking-around money?" the ambassador asked. "I'm sure Crespo would be able to help out with that if that was the price of admission to the inner circle."

"No. I think that would be the very worst thing we could do." Kate tried not to make it sound like she was teaching her uncle how to suck eggs, but she had seen the CIA muscle in on too many developing relationships and then squash them with their bull-in-a-china-shop lack of finesse.

"It would scare them off," she added. "Make it seem as though we were trying to buy them. We'll need to be patient."

"So what do they want?"

"They want to know that I'm worth their time. That I have influence."

"They must know that you have pretty easy access to me."

"That comes from blood ties, but I need to show them that I'm more than your niece, that I'm on the inside of the policy circle as well as the family circle."

"How do we do that?"

"You're seeing the president tomorrow."

"Yes."

"Take me with you."

Harry shook his head.

"Presidential protocol is pretty tight on numbers. Principals plus two. That's me and Brass and Chet. It might be possible to ask for another seat, but not in twenty-four hours. This place doesn't move that fast. You know that, Kate, better than anyone."

"I don't mean as the third wheel," Kate said. "I mean instead of Chester."

Her uncle smiled like the Cheshire cat.

"You understand what you're asking?"

"Of course."

"And it's safe to assume that you haven't mentioned this to Chet?"

"Of course."

"He not going to like it."

"Of course not."

There was a long pause as the ambassador digested his niece's proposition, one of which Machiavelli himself would have been proud.

"This will help you get close to Boldu?"

"No guarantees. But, yes. I think so."

"That's more important than poor Chet's ego."

"Agreed."

"This would have to be my idea, you understand. Not yours."

"That's why I'm here."

"Will you be able to handle the fallout with Grimes? He'll still be your supervisor. And no matter how I frame this, he's going to see this as favoritism."

"I don't doubt it."

"Okay then. I'll set it up."

The look on the ambassador's face was almost that of parental pride. It made Kate feel both warm and sad.

Diplomatic messaging is a subtle game. Players keep score according to an arcane set of rules rooted in long tradition but often with a modern twist. In the court of Louis XIV, rank and status dictated a complex set of privileges. Whether a particular nobleman could sit in the presence of the king and on how many cushions. How many horses he could use to pull his carriage. How many attendants he was entitled to.

Kate was a part of the ambassador's small delegation headed to meet the president. That said something. But it was Brass who rode with the ambassador in the limousine while Kate was relegated to the follow car, a dull gray Ford Taurus. That said something too.

The supercharged engine on the ambassador's aging up-armored Cadillac was so loud that the embassy staff had nicknamed the limousine Humbaba after the fire-breathing monster in the Sumerian *Epic of Gilgamesh*. Humbaba was also, the embassy's cultural attaché insisted, the onomatopoeic sound the Cadillac would make on a cold morning as the engine struggled to turn over. It was the kind of joke that only college professors and overeducated diplomats would find funny.

The small motorcade—Humbaba, Kate's Taurus, and the police follow car with the ambassador's security detail—drove past Ala-Too Square, which many considered the heart of Bishkek, before turning onto a narrow cobblestone side street that led to a covered stone portico and the bronze doors to the Presidential Palace. The honor guard soldiers stood on either side of the doors, one tall and broad and Slavic looking, and the second shorter, stocky, and Kyrgyz. Their sky blue jackets were heavy with gold braid and they carried their Kalashnikovs at port arms with bayonets fixed to the barrel. They were both handsome, but neither would make eye contact with Kate as she hurried up the stairs past them. They stood ramrod straight staring out at some unseen threat to the safety and security of the head of state.

Presidential protocol was there to meet them at the front door.

"Good afternoon, Ambassador." The protocol officer was, as they so often were in the former Soviet space, pretty and blond. She gave Kate's uncle a smile that could have melted the Tian Shan glacier. She was almost six feet tall, but Kate guessed that a good three inches of that could be attributed to heels that would not have been out of place on a stage with a brass pole. Her white suit was cut just a little too tight, leaving her breasts straining against the fabric. The ambassador seemed oblivious to this, but the defense attaché stared unabashedly at her chest.

"Good afternoon, Svetlana," the ambassador said, returning the greeting.

"Hello, William," Svetlana said to Brass, and the smile she offered him was more come hither than the one she had given the ambassador. "And you must be Katarina, daughter of Kyrgyzstan. The president is especially looking forward to meeting you."

Her smile had somehow gone cold—her beauty now that of the stark northern mountains rather than the soft plains.

Kate shook Svetlana's hand and looked her hard in the eyes, refusing to be intimidated. Inside, however, Kate was on edge. Her stomach twisted in on itself as she tried not to think about what she had come to do. If she thought too much about it, she would not be able to go through with it.

The lithesome Svetlana led them up a grand set of marble stairs covered in threadbare Soviet-era carpet. Brass walked right behind her, looking lecherously at the protocol assistant's shapely ass. Men were idiots.

The president's office was on the second floor. The formal meeting room was oval-shaped with massive oil paintings on the walls. Dark colors in heavy gilt frames. Mostly landscapes and portraits. The kind of art that might convey with the purchase of a castle in Transylvania.

The flags of Kyrgyzstan and the United States stood next to each other on polished wood poles capped by brass hawks. A semicircle of chairs was set up in front of the flags. It was one of the odd diplomatic arrangements that had the principals in the meeting sitting almost side by side and having to twist their bodies to look at one another. Their advisors sat in a row of armchairs to either side that curved away from the principals like wings. While somewhat impractical, this setup had one compelling advantage. It looked good on television.

"The president will be out shortly," Svetlana said, and with a final flip of her hair and a last flirty look for Brass, she took her leave though a set of French doors that led to the presidential office suite.

Kate stared eagerly through the open doorway. She could see the secretary's desk on the other side of the threshold. It was piled with papers. A young, slender man with a neatly trimmed beard sat behind the desk typing. He wore a white dress shirt open at the collar. No tie. Kate reasoned that he must be the president's personal secretary.

The printer along the back wall hummed briefly and disgorged a document. The secretary picked it up and carried it back to the desk. After a moment rummaging through the drawers, he pulled out a metal stamp with a long black handle and used it to fix a raised seal to the document. Kate had used something similar in her consular training when she had learned how to notarize documents for Americans overseas.

This nondescript hunk of metal was Kate's sole reason for being there and she had to force herself not to stare. She was afraid that her interest in the seal was obvious to everyone. The young secretary returned the machine to its drawer, but Kate could not tell which one it was. If she could not find some way to get time alone in the president's outer office, it was all moot in any event. The seal was no more than fifteen feet away, but it may as well have been on the bottom of the ocean.

Kate was so intent on tracking the seal that she almost jumped out of her skin when Eraliev stepped out of his office and into her field of vision.

# 12

For all the outsized influence that the president of Kyrgyzstan had had on her life, this was the first time Kate had seen Eraliev up close and in the flesh. He was a massive figure, with the body of a sumo wrestler and the arms of a butcher. His hands were thick and covered in dark hair. The president's features were flat and expressionless, his porcine eyes set so far apart that they seemed to be looking in separate directions. One of the jokes that periodically made the rounds among members of Bishkek's political class was that Eraliev needed three hundred and sixty degrees of vision to keep the knives out of his back.

The president was sixty-four, but he looked younger. His hair was crow black and as shiny as his shoes. The wags had it that he used the same product to color them both.

Eraliev smiled when he saw Kate, a toothy grin like that of a hungry shark. He walked over to her with light, mincing steps that belied his bulk and offered his hand. Kate took it and tried not to shudder as his greasy palm wrapped around her fingers.

"Ms. Hollister," he said in Kyrgyz. "It's a pleasure to meet you. Your deep roots in this country are well known. And you're so much more attractive than your uncle's regular cast of advisors."

"Thank you, Mr. President," Kate said calmly, even as she suppressed a fantasy of stabbing her pen into the vein she could see pulsating at his temple. "It's a pleasure to be back in the land of my mother's birth . . . and death."

"Your mother, yes. What happened to your parents was a terrible tragedy. You have my condolences. Our mountain roads can be so treacherous."

"Treachery is so often fatal," Kate replied, her expression studiously neutral. She was grateful that neither the ambassador nor Brass spoke Kyrgyz.

Eraliev looked uncertain for a moment, which was itself sufficient compensation for Kate's decidedly undiplomatic response.

Switching to Russian, the president greeted the other members of the delegation and exchanged a few whispered words with the ambassador. Eraliev's "plus two" introduced themselves to Kate. Aziz Isherbaev was the president's national security advisor, and the second man was a relatively junior official from the defense ministry who, like Kate, would be expected to take notes and keep quiet.

They took their seats in the lumpy armchairs, and the lovely Svetlana led a group of scruffy photographers into the room to take pictures of the president and the American ambassador chatting amiably about nothing in particular, their words drowned out by the clicking shutters and the hum of the motor drives. After less than a minute, Svetlana ushered them out so the real work could begin.

"Have you given any consideration to my latest proposal, Ambassador?" Eraliev asked. "I think it represents a fair compromise."

Kate's uncle had briefed her on this earlier. Eraliev wanted to use the base as a source of political patronage. He wanted the government—meaning Eraliev and his Kyrgyz National Party—to pick the companies that would provide services to the base under fixed-cost contracts, with the costs to be fixed by . . . Eraliev.

Even the U.S. military, infamous for procuring eight-hundred-dollar hammers, had its limits. Both Crandle and the ambassador saw these proposals as a black hole sucking tens of millions of U.S. taxpayer dollars into another dimension.

"We're making progress on this point, Mr. President," the ambassador lied smoothly in excellent Russian. "We understand the value of ensuring seamless linkages between the government and the operations of the base. But the numbers need some work."

Kate took notes. It would be her job to write the reporting cable back to Washington.

Eraliev and Harry went back and forth on the issue for the better part of half an hour. Brass occasionally chimed in on the more technical parts of the discussion, always careful to express "the views of the secretary of defense" rather than his own. Brass's Russian was heavily accented and his grammar was spotty, but he followed the discussion easily enough and had little trouble making himself understood.

Kate had trouble concentrating. A small part of her brain directed her hand to jot down notes on the back-and-forth over trash pickup and cafeteria services. But she kept looking across the room at the French doors that led to the president's outer office. The doors were closed and the glass was frosted, but in her mind's eye Kate could see the oversize birch-wood desk with the presidential seal tucked away safely in one of the drawers.

In her jacket pocket, Kate had the prison transfer form folded up neatly in an envelope. She needed thirty seconds alone with the seal, and she had no idea how she was going to get that. As her uncle and the president sparred over the base agreement and Kate mechanically wrote down what they said, most of her brainpower was concentrated on solving this puzzle. Even without any flying monkeys to worry about, it was not an easy problem. Each of the elaborate scenarios she spun out in her head ended with her being shot or lying flat on the ground with one of the handsome honor guard soldiers pointing his rifle at her head.

After mentally rejecting a dozen different plans, a germ of an idea took root. It was simple and that was its strength, but it was still high risk with a number of branching variables she could not hope to control. Kate would have to play it by ear. In music at least, the part of her that was classically trained rebelled at that idea. But the part of her that was a student of Cuban jazz was ready and eager.

Kate realized that she had missed the last couple of exchanges between the ambassador and Eraliev. She could only hope that it had not been anything important.

Why was she doing this? Kate asked herself. Why was she so invested in the success of a secretive organization that three weeks ago she had never heard of? The risks she took and the sacrifices she made in Cuba were something else. She did it for her friends, for people she knew and cared about. She did it for Reuben. She did it for love. So why? Was it for love of her mother's country?

Kate looked to her left at Kyrgyzstan's obese head of state with his sallow skin and bulging bullfrog-like neck, and she understood. Hate. She hated this man and she would gladly see him dead. He had murdered her parents. As a motive, hate may have been less pure than love. But it was just as honest.

Eraliev would not die in bed, not unless one of his many mistresses stabbed him in his tiny heart. Eventually, he would reap what he had sown. But Kate was impatient. If there was something she could do to hurry the day of his demise, she would do it and damn the risk.

At the forty-minute mark, the two principles wrapped up the conversation with a ritualized exchange of pleasantries. Kate had only been half listening. The report she would write would be something of an exercise in creative writing. That was the least of her worries.

As she stood up, Kate used her foot to push her shoulder bag under the chair and out of sight.

Eraliev shook hands with the ambassador and Brass and turned to Kate. She wondered if he could see the hate in her eyes. Did he know? Would he care if he did?

The president took her hand in both of his and leaned in close as though he were going to kiss her. She could smell garlic on his breath and it made her stomach turn.

"I will be watching you," he whispered to her. It was disturbingly intimate. Like a lover's promise.

Svetlana the protocol assistant emerged from the office suite and led the small American delegation back down the grand stairway.

Halfway to the car, Kate stopped.

"I'm sorry, Ambassador. I forgot my purse," she said. "Don't wait for me. I'll meet you back at the embassy."

Brass looked at her condescendingly as though to say a man would never forget his purse. Bite me, Kate thought.

"After that last set of negotiations, you may want to cancel your credit cards," her uncle joked. "The president may be putting a new air defense system on your Amex as we speak."

Svetlana laughed lightly and touched the ambassador's arm flirtatiously.

"Is it okay if I pop back upstairs to get my bag?" Kate asked Svetlana in Russian. She was afraid that she was talking too fast. Her breathing, meanwhile, was too shallow and the muscles in her back were like tightly coiled springs.

"Of course."

"Don't wait for me, please, Ambassador," Kate said to her uncle as she concentrated on keeping her agitation from showing on her face.

"No worries, Kate. See you back at the office."

Svetlana led her now diminished delegation back to the motorcade and Kate started up the stairs fighting back the urge to take them two at a time. She scooped up her purse from where she had left it and knocked confidently on the door to the outer office. Moments later the president's secretary opened it, looking annoyed.

"Yes?" he asked curtly.

"Sorry to bother you. But the ambassador asked me to get the president a copy of my notes for the meeting as a record of the negotiations. Could I ask for your help with that?" Kate did her best to smile warmly, but it felt unnatural and she was afraid that it would come across more as nervous than friendly.

"The president asked for this?"

"I'm afraid I don't know. It's possible. I only know that I was asked to share the notes and I'm under a little time pressure. Could you help me?"

The damsel-in-distress routine was not a role Kate had much experience with. But the secretary did not seem to be much of a theater critic either.

"Let me have them, please," he said.

Kate handed over her notebook.

"Wait here. I'll be right back."

The secretary disappeared down the hall and Kate was alone in the president's outer office. Eraliev himself was just on the other side of the door. Kate did not know how long she had. It should take at least a few minutes for the secretary to make copies of the ten pages or so of notes on her steno pad. But Svetlana could return to the office at any moment. And it was equally possible that Eraliev could open the door to his office with no notice and catch Kate with her hand in the proverbial cookie jar. There was no time to waste.

Kate searched the desk methodically, going through each of the drawers, her frustration mounting as each one came up empty. Where the hell was it?

A part of her listened for the click-clack of Svetlana's high heels on the thin carpet in the halls or the softer sounds of the secretary's loafers.

It took no more than a few minutes, but it felt like an hour. The seal was wedged into the back of the right middle drawer. Kate's fingers closed eagerly around the cold metal handle. She pulled the form out of her jacket pocket. It was already filled in and the president's distinctive signature had been expertly forged. She slipped the paper under the seal and pushed the handle down, leaving a raised mark over half the signature. Now it was an official state document and the instructions on it would be obeyed by the regime's functionaries without question.

She put the seal back where she had found it and closed the drawer. No sooner had Kate stepped across the threshold into the formal meeting room than the secretary returned with Xerox copies of her notes.

"Thank you," Kate said. "Please give them to the president with the ambassador's compliments."

"Of course."

Kate's legs felt rubbery and she almost tripped walking down the stairs. Svetlana was at the front door, doubtless waiting for the next set of guests.

"I'm glad you found it," she said, gesturing at Kate's bag.

"So am I," Kate said.

Now all she needed to do was deliver the broomstick to the Great and Powerful Oz.

# 13

Ruslan had always believed that the mountains were the soul of his country. The plains were the source of wealth and the cities were the centers of power, but the Kyrgyz were a mountain people and it was only in the hill country or on the back of a horse that their hearts were truly at rest.

It was a nice thought, but at the moment, even up here in the mountains, there was nothing restful about Ruslan's heart. A potent cocktail of anxiety and responsibility had it beating with an urgency he could feel in the tips of his fingers. His grip on the wood stock of the rifle he carried was tight enough to whiten his knuckles. Nogoev, the old soldier, noticed his unease.

"The waiting is the most difficult part," he said reassuringly. "The foot soldiers deal with it as they will. But you are a leader. Talk to your people. They expect that of you. They deserve that from you."

Nogoev was right, Ruslan realized with some chagrin. He should not be thinking of himself or even Bermet at this moment but of them. He briefly surveyed his army. There were sixteen of them, including Nogoev and himself. Ismailov the wrestler was the only other council member. The rest were Nogoev's Scythians. Ten men and three women, although they were considerably closer to boys and girls. They were brave enough and they were all good riders, but in purely military terms they were—at best—half trained. They would need their leaders to keep them alive.

Ruslan slung the rifle over his shoulder and joined a small circle of Scythians who stood deep in conversation.

"Are your horses rested and ready?" he asked.

A small, dark woman named Nazgul was holding the reins of a horse with similar characteristics. She stroked the nose of the tough-looking mountain pony.

"He's ready, Seitek," she said. "We all are."

The others nodded their agreement. This was their first test and they were eager to prove themselves. Their desire was never in doubt. Nazgul had lost both a father and brother to the Eraliev regime's never-ending war against its opponents, real and imagined. Most of the Scythians had suffered a personal loss at the hands of the state. They were ready to risk everything. But Ruslan had no idea how they would respond at the moment of truth. Or how he himself would respond, for that matter. Of all of them, Nogoev was the only one who had ever fired a weapon in anger. Ruslan understood, however, that it was important to pretend to a confidence and a certainty he did not possess. This was not merely the price of leadership; it was a form of leadership.

"You all know what's at stake today," Ruslan said, trying to speak with gravity but without sounding pompous. It was a surprisingly difficult balance to strike. "This is tantamount to a declaration of war, and generations from now a free Kyrgyz people will look back on this day and remember that this was when we struck the first blow for their liberty."

Ruslan paused to gather his thoughts for a suitable peroration, but before he could launch into it, the sound of a single motorcycle engine reached their ears. The Scythians rode horses, mostly one at a time, but Nogoev had mounted a few scouts on 125-horsepower motorbikes. They had been posted as pickets looking out for the convoy that would be carrying Bermet to the labor camp near Kosh-Dobo. That sound meant that the scouts had made contact.

The radio on Ruslan's belt squawked as the scout reached the crest of the hill that had been blocking the signal.

"This is Rice Rocket Two, do you read me?"

Ruslan pulled the radio from its holster.

"Go ahead, Rice Rocket Two," he said. "This is Control."

"The convoy is ten minutes out, Control. I will continue tracking."

"Okay, Rice Rocket. But keep your distance. Don't let them see you."

"Roger, Control."

"Ten minutes," Ruslan shouted at the Scythians stretched in a loose line in the shadow of a ridge that would shield them from view as the convoy approached on the road that ran along the floor of the valley. The Scythians would have to make certain that the convoy had taken the bait before closing the trap shut.

The young warriors mounted their horses and tried to pretend that they did not care about what would happen next. Ruslan loved them for it. And he knew that he would gladly die for them.

"It's a terrible feeling, isn't it?"

He turned to see Nogoev standing behind him holding the reins of two horses. He handed one set to Ruslan.

"Battle?" Ruslan asked.

"Command," Nogoev answered. "It's easy to surrender your own life. It'll be much harder to see these children lose theirs. There will be casualties in this war, Seitek. There always are. Good boys and girls will die. You must be ready for that."

Ruslan grunted his understanding and mounted his horse, a beautiful black mare he called Akkula, after Manas's own horse.

He again pulled the radio from his belt. The Scythians had chosen this position carefully and they had a plan.

"Bo Peep, this is Control."

"I read you, Control."

"Execute."

"Roger."

Ruslan wrapped a long gray scarf around his head and face until only his eyes were visible. Nogoev and the Scythians did the same. They looked like a Berber raiding party in the North African desert.

"This would be easier," Nogoev said, "if we did it my way."

"There'll be no unnecessary killing," Ruslan admonished him. "These are our countrymen, even the servants of Eraliev. And they have sisters and cousins and children and friends who would have cause to hate us if we simply slaughtered our enemies like so many sheep. We will use the force we must, and no more."

Nogoev snorted his disagreement, but he did not press the point. For Ruslan, his aversion to excessive violence was, in part, a matter of principle. But it was more than that. It was a strategic choice. It would do no good to win the battle and lose the war. As experienced as the Red Army veteran was, Nogoev was also limited, like a man with a hammer who saw every problem as a nail.

But as averse as Ruslan was to killing his enemies, he was even more reluctant to see his own people die. The paramilitaries escorting Bermet to the labor camp could not be given the opportunity to bring their heavy weapons into play against the Scythian cavalry. The riders would be murdered before they got within fifty meters of the truck carrying Bermet.

Ruslan and Nogoev rode to near the top of the ridge and dismounted. Ruslan handed the reins to the Scythian commander and walked the last few meters to the peak. He lay down in the tall grass. From here he had a clear view of the valley road and the convoy of prison vehicles that was throwing up dust. A pair of compact but powerful binoculars brought the scene into sharp focus. The lead vehicle was a blue-and-white police car with its lights flashing. Behind that was a gunmetal-gray prison transport truck, heavy and armored with a steel grille welded to the front and a big winch that could reel the truck from the mudflats that formed on the back roads after heavy rains. The third car was a black Toyota Land Cruiser. This was the most dangerous vehicle. There would be Special Police inside with long guns, machine pistols, and ballistic vests.

"All this for one girl?" Ruslan had asked Murzaev incredulously when the intelligence chief had explained what they were likely to encounter.

"She's not a girl," Murzaev had replied. "She's a Tier I political prisoner. This is a standard package."

The valley was narrow and the dirt road paralleled a small stream with steep banks. Ruslan watched through the binoculars as the prison convoy rounded the last turn and was forced to a stop by a sizable flock of sheep meandering in the middle of the road. The incompetent shepherd was wearing traditional Kyrgyz clothes, including a wool cloak that concealed a squat Russian Bizon-2 submachine gun.

The next few minutes would mark the difference between success and failure. Victory and death.

Ruslan wanted desperately to mount Akkula and charge down the slope firing his rifle into the sky. But he had to make certain the Special Police in the Land Cruiser would not mow down the Scythians as they rode across the open ground.

The police car in the front honked at the sheep, who bleated but gave no indication that they acknowledged the authority and supremacy of the state and its designated representatives. The cop in the passenger seat leaned out the window and seemed to be shouting something at the shepherd. Ruslan could not hear him, but it did not look like an exchange of pleasantries.

With all the attention focused at the front of the convoy, only Ruslan saw the two figures emerge from their hiding place in the waist-high grass behind the convoy. One was carrying a long metal pipe. They moved swiftly to the Land Cruiser at the tail end of the column. The larger of the two, Ismailov, swung the pipe into the SUV's rear window, shattering it. The other figure, one of the women on the team, tossed two small objects into the SUV through the jagged hole in the glass.

Even before the explosion, Ruslan was on his feet signaling to the Scythians and running for Akkula. The Scythian cavalry leapt forward over the crest of the hill as the flash-bang grenade exploded. Inside the confined space of the Land Cruiser cabin, the effects would be magnified. The Special Police would have their eardrums blown out. Blood would be leaking from their noses and their ears. They would be blind and disoriented. To add to the confusion, the second grenade filled the SUV with a thick, acrid smoke that would— *inshallah*—shield the Scythians from view.

Ruslan charged down the slope, letting Akkula pick her own line.

He saw the shepherd spray the hood of the marked blue-and-white police car with his submachine gun and then point it at the cops in the front seat, his message unmistakable.

The Scythians had their assignments. One team of six circled the Land Cruiser. They dismounted quickly and pulled the stunned Special Police out of the car, stripping them of their weapons and radios and forcing them to lie flat on the road. Three of the horsemen joined the shepherd in dissuading the two regular policemen in the lead vehicle from martyring themselves in an unjust cause.

The rest, together with Ruslan, assaulted the hulking prisoner transfer truck. Ruslan approached the driver's-side door, his rifle now slung over his shoulder. The door was locked and the window was made of reinforced glass that was bullet resistant if not necessarily bulletproof. The driver was young and fit looking with the chest and shoulders of a serious weight lifter. And an attitude. He looked at Ruslan and shook his head. Then he held up his fist in what was known locally as the "fig sign," with his thumb tucked between the index and middle fingers. It was a gesture of refusal and defiance. And it was not especially polite.

Reaching into his saddle bag, Ruslan pulled out a greasy orange block of Semtex plastic explosive and slapped it firmly onto the glass right by the driver's head. The detonator was already lodged in the center of the lump of putty. Ruslan held up the trigger and looked at the driver, tilting his head and shrugging his shoulders as though to say "your call."

The prison driver raised both his hands in surrender. Ruslan gestured at the door and the driver opened it. Without getting off his horse, Ruslan grabbed the man by the shoulder of his uniform and dragged him to the ground.

"Keys," Ruslan said. The driver looked Slavic, so Ruslan spoke to him in Russian.

The bodybuilder turned prison driver pulled a set of keys off his belt and held them up awkwardly.

Ruslan took them.

"Which one opens the back?"

"The big silver one."

"Tie him up," Ruslan instructed one of the Scythians. "And watch him closely."

The locking mechanism turned easily enough and Ruslan tugged the rear door open eagerly. Inside, four people in drab prison uniforms sat facing one another wearing handcuffs and shackles. All of them were men. Bermet wasn't there.

Nothing is easy.

"Where is she?" Ruslan demanded of the driver.

"Who?"

"Bermet. The woman you were supposed to be transporting to Kosh-Dobo."

"Believe me that you wouldn't want a woman back there with those boys. They must have put her on the helicopter."

"Helicopter?"

"The commander at Kosh-Dobo is rotating back to Bishkek. Guys that senior get to fly. I heard that they were going to use the helicopter for one of the Tier I's. That must be your girl. Now can I sit up, please?"

The driver started to pull himself up off the dusty ground into a sitting position. Ruslan put a boot between his shoulder blades and pushed him back onto his belly.

"Not until we're finished here," he explained. "What's your name?"

"Bogdan."

"Okay, Bogdan. Can you contact the helicopter?"

"Yes. In an emergency."

Ruslan pulled a pistol from his belt and kneeled in front of the driver, pointing it at his forehead."

"Do you think this might qualify?"

"Y-y-yes."

"Good. You may sit up."

Bogdan did so.

Ruslan gestured at the Scythian to cut the plastic flex cuffs holding his hands behind his back.

"Now show me how to reach the helo."

It was not difficult. Ruslan listened with a part of his brain while Bogdan explained how to use the radio. The bulk of his gray matter, however, was busy sorting through options, trying to formulate a plan. What he came up with seemed entirely crazy. It would have to do.

Ruslan gathered a small circle of Scythians that included Nogoev and Ismailov and explained his plan. Nogoev laughed.

"You would have been right at home in Afghanistan, Seitek. All the best officers were slightly mad."

Ismailov gave the Scythians their assignments, while Ruslan tried to raise the helicopter on the radio in the truck cab. Bogdan was sitting next to him in the passenger seat.

"Do you know the pilot?" Ruslan asked.

"Yes. But not well."

"What's his name?"

The driver was silent.

"You do not want to be a hero today. If you won't be honest with me, Bogdan, I'm afraid we're going to have to ride off and leave those boys in the back of the truck in charge. They don't look like especially nice people, do they?"

Bogdan shook his head

"What's the pilot's name?"

"Umid." It was an Uzbek name.

"You're quite sure about that?"

Bogdan nodded miserably.

"Excellent. I think we're going to be friends, you and I. What's the radio call sign for the helicopter?"

"Eagle Flight."

"And yours?"

"Stallion."

Ruslan had to bite back a laugh.

"If you're lying to me, Bogdan, you'll need to change that to Gelding. Do you understand?"

"You're the one they call Seitek, aren't you? From Boldu."

"I have the privilege."

"You can't beat them. They will kill you in the end."

"They'll have to find me first."

As Bogdan had instructed, Ruslan set the radio to channel three.

"Eagle Flight, this is Stallion. Do you read me?" Ruslan dropped his voice to match Bogdan's deeper tones, but he was relying on the tinny sounds of radio communications and the ambient noise of the helicopter to mask the difference.

There was a burst of static.

"I read you, Stallion. How's the drive? Dusty?"

"Umid, we have a problem." Ruslan let a note of urgency creep into his voice and used the pilot's name both to establish his bona fides and to send the subtle message that some emergency had made him grow sloppy in his radio discipline.

"What's the issue, Stallion?"

"There was an attack on the convoy. RPGs and machine guns. We beat them back and killed a few, but we have casualties. One critical. We need an air evacuation."

"I can relay the message to base, Stallion. And they can send up another flight."

"That'll take too long. Sascha's got a sucking chest wound. He'll die before they can get here. We need you." Ruslan was acutely aware that he was making things up as he went along, things like the name of the wounded guard. The more he said, the greater the risk that he would say something that would give the game away. But he had to keep talking and not allow the pilot time to think.

"I have a prisoner on board, Stallion," the pilot protested.

"Does she have someplace to be? That bitch will be in Kosh-Dobo for the next twenty years. She can be a little late."

There was silence on the other end as Umid considered the options.

"Sascha reports directly to the Georgian," Ruslan said in what was either a flash of inspiration or a desperate grasping at straws. But no one, he reasoned, wanted to get on Chalibashvili's bad side. "The bastard will be very unhappy if he dies."

The pause lengthened and Ruslan tried to think of another angle. He was coming up empty.

"Roger, Stallion. State your position."

Ruslan had no real religious leanings, but he offered up a short prayer to Allah and read off the GLONASS coordinates from the screen mounted on the dashboard.

"I'm ten minutes out," the pilot said. "Keep him alive."

"Thank you, Eagle Flight."

Ruslan opened the door to the cab and shouted to the Scythians that they had eight minutes to get ready. Then he turned to his prisoner.

"Bogdan."

"Yes."

"I'm going to need your clothes."


Minutes later, a single helicopter, a Russian MI-8 transport, flew in low and hard, following the bend in the river. Seven of the Scythians were dressed in police uniforms, their original owners stuffed standing room only into the back of the truck.

"Sorry about this," Ruslan had said as he shut the door. "But I need the weight."

The emergency gear in the truck included a backboard and Ismailov was lying on it, his chest soaked in sheep's blood. Another half dozen Scythians, Ruslan among them, lay scattered on the ground "dead." From the air, he hoped, it would look like a scene of panic and chaos. As long as the pilot did not look too closely or start wondering where all the horses had come from.

Two of the Scythians waved frantically at the helicopter, pointing at a flat patch of ground that made for a suitable landing spot. The only obstacle, a dead raider in a gray head scarf, was easy enough to avoid.

The pilot settled the helicopter down skillfully and the rotors kicked up a wave of dust and small stones that forced Ruslan to shut his eyes. Otherwise, he did not move. Choking would spoil the illusion of being dead.

The rotors slowed perceptibly and the cloud of dirt settled on Ruslan's upturned face. He opened his eyes a crack, but he did not dare turn his head. The MI-8 was no more than ten meters away settled hard on its landing gear with the rotors turning slowly enough that he could make out the individual blades. Deprived of centrifugal force, the blades were starting to bend to the will of gravity.

The pilot and copilot were visible in the front seats. Ruslan strained to get a glimpse of Bermet, but the MI-8's windows were too small and the plastic too rough and pitted.

Four Scythians hustled to the helicopter carrying Ismailov on the backboard. The side door of the MI-8 swung open and a short, squat man in a green jumpsuit beckoned them forward. Ruslan started to crawl toward the helicopter, dragging the cable from the winch at the front of the truck. When he was still five meters from the helicopter, the rotors quickly began spinning and the helicopter started fighting against the pull of the earth. The pilots must have realized that something was wrong. Abandoning any pretense of being dead, Ruslan rose to a crouch and scuttled the last few meters to the belly of the helicopter. He pushed the cable through the frame of the landing strut and wrapped it around the base of the wheel three times before securing it with a chunky carabiner just as the MI-8 gathered sufficient torque for liftoff.

The stocky crewman in the doorway pulled a pistol from a shoulder holster and started shooting. But it would have taken both great skill and phenomenal luck to hit a moving target from a lurching helicopter. His shots went wide.

Ruslan ran back to the truck, hoping that whoever had welded the winch in place had been a master craftsman. He also had to hope that the truck designers had not stinted on the armor plate. The MI-8 could lift a sizable load.

As he settled into the driver's seat, the helicopter reached the end of its tether and the entire front end of the truck lifted up almost a meter into the air before settling back to the ground with a crash of metal. The MI-8 lost altitude but recovered quickly, and the cable was pulled taut as a guitar string.

The winch controls were simple. Ruslan tried to reel in the helicopter. The MI-8 was a strong machine, however, and the winch did not have enough power. The motor whined as it strained and Ruslan was afraid that the cable would snap at any moment. The truck was running and he put it in gear, driving forward toward the helicopter. The cable went slack briefly and Ruslan used the winch controls to haul in five meters or so of its length before it tightened up.

After that, it was like catching a big fish. Ruslan drove backward with the MI-8 fighting him for every centimeter. Then he reversed direction and wound in another few meters of slack. If the helicopter had been armed, it would not have been possible. But the crew did not seem to be carrying anything more powerful than the pistol that had already demonstrated its impotence.

When the MI-8 was no more than eight meters off the ground, Ruslan pushed it toward a stand of trees. The message was clear. The pilot settled the aircraft down with a petulant thud and the Scythians quickly surrounded it.

Bermet was the only passenger and she ran to Ruslan, throwing her arms around his neck and burying her face in his chest.

"I knew you would come for me," she said.

"Of course I did," Ruslan replied, stroking her hair. "No one gets left behind."

# 14

If Kate had thought that Boldu was going to send her an engraved invitation for a private meeting with the mysterious Seitek or otherwise roll out the red carpet, she was doomed to disappointment. She had heard nothing from Val since their prearranged meeting under the stone bridge in Kara-Su Park to deliver the transfer order with the presidential seal. Val had been visibly impressed.

"You know, I really didn't think you were going to be able to do this," she had said.

"Gee. Thanks, Val. Your confidence is inspiring."

Valentina had stuck out her tongue.

"Does this earn me an audience with Oz himself?"

"We'll be in touch."

But they had not. And Kate was frustrated.

Screw this. She wasn't the type to sit breathlessly by the phone waiting for some boy to call. She was an American diplomat and she would engage the powers of that position to figure out what the hell was going on.

The transfer form had included a date. Bermet, the Tier I political prisoner and Seitek's sometime girlfriend, should have been moved from the central prison to the labor camp at Kosh-Dobo three days ago. Boldu had been planning to intercept the convoy and free Bermet. So had that happened? Had Boldu succeeded? Or was Seitek himself now confined to a prison cell somewhere in the dungeons of Number One? From what little Kate knew of him, the Boldu leader did not sound like someone who would put minions at the point of maximum danger while he "led from behind." Maybe he was dead, lying in some shallow grave in the mountains after a failed rescue attempt.

There had been nothing in the Kyrgyz press about an attack on a prison convoy. But there wouldn't be. The press was hardly free. The newspapers published whatever the Eraliev family told them to publish. Television was even worse. So what did the United States government know about what had happened? More to the point, what information did it possess that it did not yet know about? The intelligence community spent some sixty billion dollars a year on collecting and analyzing information from around the world. And that did not even count the classified budget for military intelligence operations and some of the more exotic space-based collection systems.

The various collectors gathered up significantly more data than the analysts could process. Orders of magnitude more. Often, a particularly interesting or important data point or piece of information would float unrecognized on an ocean of information until it was too late to be of utility. After 9/11, the intelligence community was sharply criticized for failing to connect the dots and provide law enforcement with the leads that might have disrupted the plot. But what was poorly understood by the public and the pundits was that those particular dots were only really meaningful in retrospect. On the tenth of September, those particular dots had not formed an especially alarming pattern. There were, in fact, so many dots that you could draw from them whatever picture you might like.

Somewhere inside the system, Kate suspected, was some information about what had happened three days earlier somewhere on the road from Bishkek to Kosh-Dobo. All that she needed to do was to find that one particular needle in a haystack-sized pile of needles.

There was no getting around it. She would need Crespo's help. The CIA station chief had largely ignored her since their first unpleasant conversation. It might have been possible to avoid talking to him if Kate had been willing to go directly to the ambassador, but that would require dancing around the question of how she knew enough to go looking for a particular event. She certainly had no intention of telling either her uncle or Crespo about "borrowing" the president's personal seal. And she did not want to lie to her uncle. Lying to the CIA was something else. That was only fair. The boys from Langley were professional liars. They lied for practice. Even, at times, when it was easier and more efficient to tell the truth.

Rather than try to set up a meeting through his scheduler, which would likely have taken days, Kate walked up to the imposing metal airlock in the basement and hit the buzzer. It was a good five minutes before the angry librarian opened the door.

"Can I help you?" she asked with a level of enthusiasm that implied she would have been happier to find a group of Jehovah's Witnesses or vacuum cleaner salesmen buzzing at the station's door.

"I'm here to see Larry."

"Do you have an appointment?"

"He'll want to see me."

"Really?"

"It's important."

"Wait here."

Kate spent another ten minutes standing in front of the door tamping down her growing impatience. Finally, the door opened again with a pneumatic hiss, and Crespo's sour assistant ushered her in.

The CIA station chief was sitting behind his cheap particle-board desk poring over a stack of paper reports. His jacket was draped over the back of his chair, but his tie was pulled up snug to his stiff collar. There was nothing relaxed about Larry Crespo.

"Sit down, Kate," he said without looking up.

Kate sat on Crespo's uncomfortable couch.

"Thanks for seeing me."

"You're persistent," Crespo said, still giving more attention to the papers on his desktop than to Kate. "I've gotta give you that."

"Thank you. I suppose."

"What can I do for you?"

"I need your help."

"I don't chase geese."

"No need. I caught the goose."

Crespo looked up at her for the first time. He put down his pen.

"What do you mean?"

"I made contact with Boldu."

Crespo smirked.

"Or someone pretending to be Boldu," he suggested.

"I don't think so."

"Have you met Seitek?"

"Not yet. But I'm close."

"Sure. You keep telling yourself that."

Kate ignored the jibe.

"Well, here's something you may be interested in. Boldu conducted its first direct attack on Eraliev's security forces three days ago." Kate tried to project absolute confidence in this statement with none of the caveats or qualifiers that too often led type A–plus men like Crespo to dismiss the opinions of women as tepid or—worse still—uninteresting.

"You have my attention."

"How generous of you."

"But not for long," Crespo warned.

"Valentina Aitmatova is, in fact, in a leadership position in Boldu. I believe she may be in Seitek's inner circle. But I need more time to confirm that. A woman named Bermet, who is reportedly quite close to Seitek, was arrested at the palace when Boldu turned the pigs loose on Eraliev and his cronies. Seitek wanted to get her out. They arranged somehow for Bermet to be transferred to a labor camp in the Kosh-Dobo region, and they made plans to hit the convoy and free her."

"Hit the convoy with what?" Crespo asked.

"I don't know," Kate admitted.

"Why did Aitmatova tell you this? What did she want in return?" It was a shrewd question, but one Kate had anticipated.

"Val wanted us to know they did it. If the government tried to pin the blame on ISIS, or the Taliban, or some Russian criminal gang, Boldu wanted to be on record announcing the operation in advance."

"And you didn't think to report the conversation at the time?" Crespo asked skeptically.

"To what end? There was no evidence beyond this one claim, and we weren't going to do anything about it in any event. We didn't have a dog in the fight."

"So what happened?"

"I don't know. There hasn't been anything in the press about an attack on a prison convoy."

"And you haven't heard anything from Aitmatova?"

"Not a thing," Kate said with just a hint of apprehension. Crespo, of course, was trained to pick up on exactly these kinds of clues.

"And you're afraid that she's dead," the station chief said without any trace of sympathy. "That Seitek's dead. That they failed to free this girl, Bermet, and instead the government succeeded in decapitating Boldu in a single strike."

"Something like that," Kate acknowledged.

"And what do you want me to do about that? Ask the local services if they've misplaced any prison convoys?"

"No. Nothing active. I'd just like you to ask Langley to review the database for any information about an incident on the road somewhere between here and Kosh-Dobo over the last three days. I'd like to know what we already have in the system that we haven't looked at yet."

Crespo was quiet as he considered the issue. The muscles in his jaw quivered as he clenched and unclenched his teeth. A nervous habit, Kate supposed. She had never met a man who burned with such nervous energy as the chief of Bishkek station.

"All right," he said finally. "I'll ask. No promises."

"Thanks, Larry." Kate tried to smile, wishing that she was better at it.

The next afternoon, Kate was sitting in her cubicle trying to finish a draft of the annual labor relations report when the phone rang.

"Hello."

"Mr. Crespo would like to see you." It was the angry librarian. Kate still did not know her name and she had never seen her anywhere other than in the world of the subterranean.

"When?" Kate asked.

"Right now, of course." She sounded somewhat surprised that the answer to that question was anything other than self-evident.

This time the door opened almost as soon as Kate buzzed.

"This way, please."

Wow. Please. Kate was definitely moving on up.

Crespo was sitting at his desk, wearing the same blue suit, white shirt, and striped tie that he had been wearing the day before. He probably had a closet full of the same cheap suits and the same shirts from Macy's or Nordstrom's—extra starch.

Crespo's desktop was clean with the exception of three documents spread out in front of him like cards on a blackjack table. Kate sat in the chair directly across from him and Crespo pushed the documents to her side of the desk. They were already oriented for Kate to read.

"That's all there is," he said.

"What are they?"

"Two pieces of imagery from NGA. One NSA intercept." The National Geo-Spatial Intelligence Agency was a little-known member of America's sprawling and expensive intelligence community. Among other things, NGA was responsible for taking pictures from space. The National Security Agency's particular area of expertise was signals intelligence, or SIGINT, principally listening in on other people's phone calls.

"No HUMINT?" Kate asked using the standard intelligence community abbreviation for human intelligence.

"Too early. And we didn't know to ask."

"So what's the upshot?

Crespo pointed to the picture on the left, a single sheet with a black-and-white image of what Kate could see was a road cutting through improbably steep mountains. The satellites could, of course, take color photos, but the analysts preferred to work in black and white, which offered greater contrast. There were vehicles on the road. Without special training in imagery analysis, however, it was hard to tell what they were. White text boxes with arrows pointing to details in the picture served as a helpful guide to end users like Kate who were policy people rather than analysts.

"The first piece of imagery shows the wreckage of a helicopter, a Russian MI-8, being hauled on the back of a flatbed from an area not far from Kosh-Dobo in the direction of Bishkek. This may or may not be related to the rumored attack on the convoy."

"Why do you call it rumored?"

"Because I have no actual evidence. Intelligence is an empirical game. If I can't see it and touch it and fuck it, as far I'm concerned, it doesn't exist."

"So what do you believe?"

Crespo stabbed a finger at the paper in the middle, another black-and-white image.

"That somebodies are dead."

The second piece of imagery looked to Kate to be a high mountain valley with a stream running parallel to a narrow road. A small group of vehicles was parked in a neat line on the side of the road, each one helpfully labeled by some nameless NGA imagery analysts. The important part of the picture, however, was in the lower right corner on the back side of a ridge that overlooked the road. It was a rectangular patch of ground that was a different shade of gray from the rest. A black arrow pointing at the shape led back to a dialog box that said euphemistically "recently disturbed earth."

Kate's stomach turned.

"A mass grave," she said.

Crespo nodded.

"Big enough for twenty to twenty-five people," he said.

"Do you know who?" Kate asked the question, but she did not want to know the answer.

"Read the intercept."

The piece was written in the dense and turgid style typical of NSA products. One of the challenges of interpreting SIGINT was that people who knew each other well enough to say anything interesting typically spoke in shorthand. An individual conversation was usually a snapshot of a larger exchange that was part of a long-term relationship, often stretching back years. Participants rarely needed to return to square one to explain the context to each other. They understood what they were talking about. It was the eavesdropper who was most at risk for misunderstanding.

There was even a classic 1970s Francis Ford Coppola movie called *The Conversation* that revolved around a garbled intercept and the critical difference between "he'd *kill* us if he got the chance" and "he'd kill *us* if he got the chance." SIGINT was far from an exact science.

No matter how you wanted to parse this particular product, however, it was disheartening and disturbing.

Kate read one sentence out loud.

"Chalibashvili told Major (unidentified) to execute the subjects and dispose of the bodies."

"That's the money line," Crespo agreed.

"I have to assume that's the same Chalibashvili who runs the interrogation program at Prison Number One. The one they call Torquemada."

"I don't know another one. He's an unpleasant little creature. But we only know him as Eraliev's current torturer in chief. This is unusually operational for him."

"What did he mean by subjects?"

Crespo shrugged.

"That's everything we know."

"But you think it's Boldu. That Seitek is dead."

"If there even is a Seitek. I'd say the odds are good."

"Shit."

The club was not crowded. But there were enough people there to make Kate feel a little less like she was drinking alone. It was nine o'clock on a Thursday night, and there should have been a bigger crowd. The drinks were cheap and strong and the music was good, a pianist who was playing mostly jazz standards but who Kate could tell had had classical training. She was on her second vodka tonic. Dinner had consisted of olives and peanuts.

It was possible, Kate had to acknowledge, that Val was dead, lying in some shallow grave in the Ala-Too mountains alongside Seitek and all hope for a better future for Kyrgyzstan, just another sad, futile casualty in the long and so far unsuccessful war against the Eraliev family.

She hummed along to "My Funny Valentine," the vodka tonics already starting to do their job, numbing her brain and her soul. She fished the slice of lemon out of the drink and bit into it, relishing the way the sharp, sour taste cut through the alcoholic fog. Together with the olives and peanuts, the lemon would make for a complete meal.

Kate was signaling the bartender for another drink when she felt a hand on her arm. She turned to find a woman who until that instant she was afraid was dead.

"You want to pass on that next drink," Val said.

Kate looked her over quickly for some sign of injury. There was nothing visible. Val was dressed casually in slacks and a silk top. Her eyes were shining.

"How come?" Kate asked

"Seitek wants to see you."

"When?"

"Right now."

# 15

Valentina's car, a nondescript Japanese hatchback that might have been a Mitsubishi or a Nissan in a dark color that might have been blue or black, was parked a block away from the club.

"Where are we going?" Kate asked.

"Off to see the Wizard," Val said.

"I won't ask what road we're going to follow. I won't give you the satisfaction."

In the green glow of the dashboard, Kate could see Val smile.

The yellow brick road evidently looped around through Bishkek's backstreets, because that's the route Val drove. Kate had enough training in counterintelligence and defensive driving to recognize this for what it was. The "cousins across the river" in Langley called it SDR, a surveillance detection route. Val drove with one eye on the road in front of them and one eye on the rearview mirror.

"See anything?" Kate asked.

"Nothing. But I won't see the one that gets me. The GKNB is pretty good at this kind of thing."

"You look like you've had some practice yourself. Was I sick the day they taught this kind of stuff at ISB?"

"We have a guy with some experience that he's been willing to share. If everything goes right, you may meet him tonight."

After half an hour or so of hard turns, switchbacks, and at least one block going the wrong way down a one-way street, Val hit the edge of town and veered left into the dark foothills. About fifteen minutes later, she turned onto a rutted gravel road. A kilometer down the road, she pulled over to the shoulder and killed the lights and the engine. Rolling the window down, she stuck her head out into the cool night air and listened.

"No lights behind us, and I don't hear anything but the wind. I think we're clear."

The road ended after another three kilometers at an old farmhouse. Val parked in front. Kate could see other vehicles parked in the shadows of the house and barn.

Val led Kate up to the front door and then stopped.

"Kate. Before we go in there, I want you to know that I'm sorry I didn't tell you earlier. I couldn't. The risks are too great."

"Tell me what?"

"You'll see."

She opened the door and they stepped inside, and Kate understood what Val was talking about. Goddamn her. This was not fair. Seven people sat in a rough circle on wooden chairs and benches drinking and smoking. Clouds of cigarette smoke floated up into the rafters. A kerosene lantern sat on a table in the middle of the room, casting a warm yellow light.

It was a mixed group. Young and old. Kyrgyz and Slavic. Most looked like educated, urban sophisticates, but there was one older man in traditional Kyrgyz dress.

Kate's eyes were drawn to one man sitting on the far side of the room. The others were all turned to face him. It was clear to Kate that this was Seitek. He had a slim build and dark hair. He was handsome, with eyes that had the intensity of a hawk's. He looked to be about Kate's age, but she knew he was older than she was. By forty-five days. She knew his birthday and his favorite music and the name of his first horse.

He stood up when he saw Kate. He was tall and Kate remembered how she had had to tilt her head back to kiss him.

"Hello, Kate," he said, and the familiar sound of his voice sparked a frisson of excitement in her chest.

"Hello, Ruslan," she said.


Ruslan stepped in close to her and leaned over to kiss her on the cheek. His lips were soft against her skin and Kate flashed back on the first time they had kissed. They had been young and inexperienced, but that first kiss had been neither awkward nor furtive. Standing under the old walnut tree that still dominated the courtyard at ISB, Ruslan had kissed her as tenderly and confidently as if they had been longtime lovers. They had been drinking sweet tea at a bonfire celebrating Nowruz, the Kyrgyz holiday that marks the vernal equinox. His mouth had tasted of honey and wood smoke.

"Thank you for what you did," he said, switching from English to Russian. "It was a lot to ask."

"Yes," Kate agreed. "It was." *I hope she's worth it.* Kate was pleased that she kept that last thought bottled up. Even six months ago, she might have said it out loud. She was growing up. Cuba had changed her.

"What you did was a minor miracle. We owe you and I won't forget."

"Consider it a contribution to the campaign."

"Oh, we do." This voice too was familiar.

"Is that you, Hamid? I didn't recognize you."

The former wrestling champ looked different. He was leaner than he had been in high school, with a new hipster beard and round wire-rimmed glasses. The real change, however, was something beyond the mere physical. Where ten years ago, Hamid had been the proto-typical athlete, all swagger and ambition, he seemed now to be re-served, sadder. And to Kate, at least, his eyes seemed to speak to a depth of character that had been lacking in the younger Hamid with his glossy, untroubled surface. Kate understood instinctively that the regime had taken someone from him too.

"You look the same, Kate. As beautiful and serious as ever. It's good to see you."

Kate knew the Garayev twins slightly, but they had been a few years behind her at ISB. The older man in Kyrgyz dress was Ruslan's uncle from his mother's village in Choktal. Ruslan introduced the others, including the Red Army veteran Nogoev and Boldu's chief of intelligence Murzaev. Kate thought that Nogoev looked a little like Clint Eastwood, square-jawed and flinty-eyed. It was easy to imagine him standing on the back of a tank surveying some sunbaked rill in an Afghan valley and scanning for mujahideen. Murzaev reminded her of Yoda, squat and ugly and wrinkled as a Shar-Pei. He would be easy to underestimate. Kate promised herself that she would not make that mistake.

"These two are the men who make Boldu different from every failed democracy movement that has come before," Ruslan explained. "Murzaev has given us an intelligence network that may be smaller than Eraliev's but is no less skilled. And Nogoev has built an armed wing for the movement that for the first time gives us the ability to hit back. You're here right on the cusp of real change, Kate. We're happy to have you."

Kate saw from the slightly sour expression on Murzaev's face that not everyone in the movement shared this sentiment.

She took a seat in the circle directly across from Ruslan. Val pressed a ceramic mug into her hand. The dark liquid inside had the cloyingly sweet smell of homemade wine.

"So, Seitek," she said, taking a sip of the wine to give herself a moment in which to organize her thoughts. "Congratulations on everything you've accomplished. I was worried that you were dead. And I am pleased to be wrong."

"What made you think I was dead?"

"I knew you were planning to ambush a prison convoy somewhere on the road to Kosh-Dobo. When I didn't hear anything from Val after I passed her the transfer order, I went looking through the intelligence. There's a fresh grave near the highway, big enough for twenty or more. It was reasonable to fear that your raid had not gone well."

To Kate's surprise, Ruslan looked stricken at the news.

"A grave?" he asked. "You're certain?"

"I can't say too much about the specific intelligence," Kate replied. "But it was pretty definitive. We've had an unfortunate amount of practice spotting mass graves from space over the last decades."

"Poor Bogdan."

Kate looked quizzical.

"Who's Bogdan?"

"One of the guards. They're just pawns really. Almost as much victims of the regime as the prisoners they keep under lock and key. I didn't want any of them to die."

"Eraliev could not allow them to live," Murzaev said, his tone matter-of-fact. "It was always a risk. The regime is vulnerable to ridicule, and if the guards had spread the story of how the great Seitek had gotten the better of them, it would have been another blow to the government's credibility. I'm frankly not surprised they did it."

"I didn't want it to happen that way," Ruslan said, and Kate was struck by the depth of sadness in his voice. He was young and the burden he was carrying was heavy.

"It wasn't you," she said. "It was that pit viper, Chalibashvili." Kate knew that she needed to be careful about revealing information that pointed to intelligence sources and methods. But Ruslan's obvious need for succor pulled her right up to that line. The young leader of Boldu shook his head resignedly.

"Someday," he promised. "Someday soon, he's going to be made to answer for his crimes."

"This is another sin to add to the pile already on the scales," Val agreed. "But we also need to look forward. Kate, you asked for this meeting and you earned it. The floor is yours. What do you have to tell us? How do you want to use this time?"

Kate had practiced her speech in her mind. She had even made a few notes. But she had never imagined delivering it to her high school boyfriend.

"We share the same goals," she began. "The United States wants to see a democratic transition in Kyrgyzstan and we see Boldu as an ally in this. We want to work with you, find ways we can help."

For diplomats, the first-person plural was the default pronoun. Just who exactly "we" were was always a little undefined. This was the nature of the profession. Diplomats did not merely tolerate ambiguity, they needed it in the way plants needed water and sunlight. But sitting here in a farmhouse with a group of people risking their lives for a cause they passionately believed in, Kate felt herself questioning which "we" she really belonged to. It was an uncomfortable feeling. Too close to the charge of divided loyalty that Crespo had leveled against her.

"It seems to me that the United States and Eraliev also have certain interests in common." This was Murzaev, and it felt to Kate like the old spy was reading her mind. "Your negotiations on the air base agreement, for example, seem quite . . . advanced."

This was the problem with speaking to this group on behalf of the U.S. government. It was the flip side of the values complexity dilemma that her uncle had addressed so eloquently. The United States was big and multidimensional. The American government wanted many things, and if Kate had come here to speak only as a U.S. government official, she would have to own them all.

"I hear you," Kate said, and it felt good and natural to slip into the singular. "But I'm here to represent my family as much as I'm here on behalf of my government. You know what my parents gave to the cause. I am as committed to freedom for the Kyrgyz people as my mother was. Or her sister. My uncle sees things here as clearly as his brother—my father. He asked me to reach out to you and offer our help, not because it is another item on his to-do list, but because he cares about this country. And as for me . . ." Kate paused and looked at Val, Hamid, and Ruslan in turn. "You know me. You know why I'm here, and just how much I'm willing to risk to help you win."

"How much, Ms. Hollister?" Murzaev asked.

"Everything."

"So what do you propose, Kate?" Val's question was open-ended, a lifeline she could use to haul herself out of the swamp of Murzaev's suspicion. She was grateful for it.

"It depends in part on what you need. We have some experience with this. I have some experience. I can help you with information. I can help you make contact with other pro-democracy groups in the region. I can arrange for material assistance. If you don't want to take American money—and I would understand why not—there are independent organizations that could step in and provide help. You've done amazing things to date, but this is a big lift and you don't need to carry it all yourselves."

The debate this triggered among the members of Boldu's leadership was intense, passionate, and compelling. They did not seem to mind arguing with one another in front of Kate. Two distinct camps emerged. Val and the twins backing an alliance with Kate and the Americans. Murzaev and—to Kate's disappointment—Hamid leading the charge against. Ruslan listened to both sides, but kept his own cards close to his chest. As a leader should, Kate thought.

They smoked foul-smelling Turkish cigarettes and drank the sweet wine and argued. Kate highlighted the way U.S. support had made the difference in the Maidan Revolution in Ukraine, the student movement in Serbia that had brought down Slobodan Milošević, and the long and ultimately successful struggle for democratic change in Burma. Murzaev pointed to Iraq's Anbar Awakening, the failed "Sea of Green" protests over a stolen election in Iran, and the aborted Denim Revolution in Belarus as examples of U.S. support evaporating at the critical moment, leaving the protestors swinging in the wind, at times with a rope around their necks.

"You seem like a nice girl," Murzaev said at one point in a voice lacking all sincerity. "But you are young, and very junior. Even if we decide to trust you, what would prevent your superiors, meaning, let us speak frankly, just about everyone in your government, from changing their minds and selling us to the Eraliev regime for thirty pieces of silver?"

It was a fair point.

"My uncle is hardly junior," Kate protested weakly. "And he feels the same way I do."

"For now," Murzaev noted coldly.

The conversation began to wind down, and Kate glanced at her watch, surprised to find that it was almost two o'clock in the morning. The issue of the future relationship between Kate and Boldu was still very much in doubt.

"We clearly have more work to do," Ruslan said. "This is not a small decision and it is important that we are all of one mind. Kate, we are grateful for the risks you took on our behalf and the risks you may yet run. Stay alert. We will come to you."

Ruslan walked Kate and Val to the door. As he leaned forward to kiss her cheek, Kate felt him press a piece of paper into her hand.

"I've missed you, Kate," he whispered into her ear in English.

Kate slipped the paper unread into her jacket pocket.

"You okay?" Val asked when they had started down the dark road for Bishkek. "That had to have been something of a shock."

"Yeah," Kate admitted. "But not an unpleasant one."

"He still cares about you. You should know that, but you should be careful with it as well."

"Careful?"

"Why do you think we brought you out here for this meeting tonight?"

"Because I delivered that prison transfer order with the presidential seal."

"No. That would likely have earned you a meeting with Nogoev and Murzaev. Hamid and the twins would probably have been there as well. But there is no secret we have more important than the real identity of Seitek. He's the only one of us who can't be replaced."

"So why was he there tonight?"

"Because he insisted on it. He wanted to see you. Murzaev was against it. So was I," she added.

"Et tu, Val? I thought we were friends. It is March, so at least that sentiment is seasonally appropriate."

"Ten years is a long time, Kate. And there's too much at stake to make this a test of friendship."

"Ruslan seems to feel differently."

"Yes. I'm not certain that he ever got over you."

"He seems to have landed on his feet."

"Who? Bermet? In her dreams, perhaps. She's a . . . diversion. And I don't mean that in a bad way. Ruslan is never anything but kind to the women who have shared his bed. But that's all that he's shared. He has given them nothing of his heart. And Bermet's already gone."

"What do you mean?"

"She can't stay here. It's too dangerous for her. She's been smuggled to Germany where she can join up with the group raising money from the diaspora. It's better for her . . . and for him."

Kate was quiet. Her own feelings were confused. She knew that she had never really moved on from Ruslan herself. Seeing him tonight had been like a wrinkle in time. Their first kiss and their last kiss and his lips pressed close against her cheek, all part of a single moment. The decade since she had seen him no more than a fleeting dream.

Kate reached into her pocket and found the note from Ruslan. She ran her fingers over it as though it were written in Braille and she could somehow absorb its message through her skin.

"You have to promise me something, Kate."

"Promise you what?"

"Not to tell anyone Seitek's real name. You owe him that. He wanted to see you for reasons of his own and we couldn't deny him that. But every person who can draw a straight line from Seitek to Ruslan Usenov adds an exponent to the level of risk. Keep this confidence, Kate. Please. Don't tell anyone. Not even your uncle."

Kate was silent. She did not know what she could say to this.

"And there's one more thing," Val said, her tone careful and measured.

"There's more?"

"Yes."

"Does it involve turning lead into gold?"

"Stay away from him."

"Huh?"

"Don't try to see him. Turn him away if he comes to you. And for god's sake, stay out of his bed."

"You're getting a little ahead of things here, Val."

"I'm not so sure about that. But I'm serious. They'll follow you and they'll find him. And when they do . . . they'll kill him."

The rest of the trip into town passed in silence.

Val dropped Kate a block from her car. Bishkek was a safe enough city that Kate was at little risk on the streets, even late at night. This was the upside of life in a police state.

It was growing cold, and Kate's breath formed a few weak clouds, just barely visible in the light from the streetlamps.

As soon as she was in the car, Kate pulled Ruslan's note from her pocket and turned on the Touareg's map light to read by. The handwriting was the same as she remembered it, thin and spidery and urgent. It was in English.

> *Kate. I need to see you. Meet me tomorrow at 6 p.m. at the stables where we used to ride. Bring your boots. R.*

Kate was no longer cold. She felt flushed and, for the first time in a long time, happy.

# 16

Rosemary, It's Kate. I need five minutes."

"Today? Not possible. He's booked wall to wall."

"It's gotta be today. Trust me. He'll want to do this one."

"Five minutes?"

"Scout's honor."

"Washington minutes, not Bishkek minutes."

"How long is five Washington minutes?"

"Three minutes."

"I'll take it."

"Be here at two-thirty and I'll try to fit you in before he has to go meet with the injustice minister."

It was an old joke, but Kate laughed politely as a show of respect. Rosemary's position as the guardian of the ambassador's schedule was one of considerable power. Junior officers, Kate knew, even favored nieces, would do well to remember that.

"I'll be there."

Kate hung up the receiver and looked over at her computer screen where the blinking cursor and the blank page mocked her efforts to write a report on the events of last night.


The Front Office was the usual hum of activity. A disparate group of embassy personnel representing various agencies formed a small scrum in the waiting room, leafing through briefing papers or one of the coffee-table books about the "Beauties of Kyrgyzstan" that government officials liked to give as gifts and that migrated to the Front Office with the predictable regularity of swallows returning to Capistrano. The ambassador was evidently running somewhat behind schedule. Although she had forgotten to bring anything with her to occupy the time, Kate resigned herself to a potentially long wait.

Rosemary, however, motioned her to go into the ambassador's office at precisely two-thirty. Kate offered the scrum of embassy supplicants what she hoped was an abashed smile as she jumped the queue. When dealing with royalty, and at least in their own embassies, ambassadors were royal in all but title, it was sometimes good to be a princess.

"Kate, how are you?"

Her uncle was sitting behind his desk with an intimidating stack of papers and color-coded folders piled up in front of him. The paperless office had been just around the corner for as long as Kate could remember. Somehow, she doubted that they would ever get there. Each week, the bureaucratic machinery of the U.S. government killed more trees than the chestnut blight.

As always, the ambassador was impeccably dressed. Today, the suit was a charcoal gray with subtle white pinstripes. His shirt was monogrammed on the pocket and his cuff links were embossed with the Great Seal of the United States in black and gold.

"You look sharp, Uncle Harry."

"Thank you. I gotta keep up. I'm going over to meet the justice minister in a few minutes, and he dresses like a man who sells underworld mobsters immunity from prosecution at twenty thousand dollars a pop."

"Imagine that."

The ambassador walked around the desk, putting one hand affectionately on Kate's arm and steering her to the sofa. Kate sat and smoothed her skirt. Her uncle took a seat in a cream-colored leather chair set at a ninety-degree angle to the couch.

"I only have a few minutes. Rosemary said it was urgent. What's up?"

"Boldu brought me in last night for a meeting with the senior leadership. I wanted to tell you about it. Val arranged it. The information about Ismailov being part of the leadership team is accurate. And there were a couple of others from ISB. But the real power players are older former Soviet types with backgrounds in the military and intelligence agencies. Serious people. They're still not sold on me, or the United States, but I think I have a shot at bringing them around. The door is at least open."

"What about Seitek?" her uncle asked a little too eagerly. "Was he there as well?"

This was it. The decision point. The thing that had been keeping Kate from writing so much as a single word of her report. Did she tell Washington about Ruslan? Did she tell her uncle? Kate had made the appointment with every intention of telling her uncle everything. But now she hesitated, uncertain about the right thing to do. She would not only be telling her uncle. The information would go into channels. Telling him meant telling a large number of people. She could not say something to the American ambassador and expect it to stay between them. That expectation would have been childishly naïve. Telling her uncle Harry that the great and powerful Seitek was actually her old high school boyfriend Ruslan Usenov meant telling Crespo and Ball and a basement full of intelligence analysts in Washington and the other U.S. embassies in Central Asia. Even if the report went out in one of the "captioned" channels that limited distribution, too many people would ultimately have access to the information. Moreover, the government's recent track record of protecting classified information was somewhat less than inspiring.

Her father would not have hesitated. He was first and foremost a creature of duty. He would already have written the report and brought it with him to this conversation so it could be cleared and out on the wires by close of business. Equally, her mother would have known what to do. She had grown up in the Soviet system and had learned to be deeply distrustful of authority. She had been a firm believer in the old adage that three people can keep a secret as long as two of them are dead.

Kate could almost hear her mother's voice whispering in her ear to be cautious and to always assume the worst. She had learned that lesson from bitter experience.

Was Kate her father's daughter or her mother's? The distinction had never before seemed quite so stark and binary.

She wanted to do her job. Do her duty. Make her uncle—the closest thing she had left to a father—happy and proud. But she was also sensitive to Val's warning about the risks for Ruslan of expanding the circle of people who could connect him directly to Seitek. And then there was Ruslan himself, and the note he had passed to her. Why the cloak-and-dagger? Who was he keeping in the dark? Murzaev? Val?

All of this shot through Kate's mind in an instant, a complicated tangle of thoughts and feelings. Problems with no solution.

The ambassador seemed to notice her hesitation.

"Seitek, Kate. Was he there last night?"

Kate looked her uncle in the eye and for the first time she lied to him.

"No, Ambassador. Not yet. I'm closer. But I need a little more time."

An expression of disappointment, almost irritation, flashed across his face, but so briefly that Kate would have missed it if she had not been attuned to the nuances of Hollister family communication.

"You're doing well," he said. "You've made more progress in two weeks than we've made in the last six months. Keep at it. And keep me looped in."

Kate was experienced enough to know when a meeting was over.

"Thank you, Ambassador."

She walked out of his office deeply ambivalent about the choice she had made and uncertain about the reasoning behind it. To top it off, when she tried to parse her emotions, the only feeling that stood out with clarity was excitement over her upcoming meeting with Ruslan. She did not want to like the feeling, but she did.

"Don't be such a high school girl," she muttered to herself.


"What do you think of the new guy?"

With a subtle movement of her head, Val directed Kate's attention to a boy sitting by himself two tables away. He looked Kyrgyz, with high cheekbones and black hair that reached almost to his collar. He had broad shoulders and a trim build, but there was something about him that made him seem more the artistic type than an athlete. He was certainly good looking. Kate had noticed him earlier that morning in the registrar's office. This must be his first day at the school.

"He's cute," she said, turning back to Val before it become obvious that she was looking. "Do you know his name?"

"Ruslan. He was with me in European history this morning. Seems smart."

"I like smart."

"I know you do."

"Do you think I should go over and introduce myself?"

"He does seem like he could use a friend."

"Couldn't we all?"

Before Kate could muster the courage, however, a group of boys in jeans and dark T-shirts walked up behind Ruslan, pinning him in. A large boy with acne-scarred skin and a substantial belly tapped Ruslan on the shoulder. This was trouble. A hush fell over the cafeteria as the students turned to watch.

"You're in my seat." Maksim Orlov was the son of the minister of defense and the grandson of one of the wealthiest men in Kyrgyzstan. This gave him status that Maksim used along with his bulk to intimidate both students and faculty. Maksim had pulled a group of the older boys into his orbit, using them to enforce a rough hierarchy in the school with Maksim himself at the apex. He did not seem to have any particular objective in mind. He wasn't dealing drugs or running a low-level protection racket. The goal, if there was one, seemed to be dominance for its own sake. It was a microcosm of Kyrgyz society, an irony that was not lost on anyone except Maksim and his enforcers.

Ruslan looked unperturbed.

"I'm sorry," he said in a tone that came across as genuinely sincere.

"It's my first day. I wouldn't want to upset the natural order of things." Maksim had spoken to him in Russian and Ruslan had responded in the same language.

Ruslan tried to push his chair back, but one of Maksim's boys—a star wrestler named Hamid—stopped him.

"That's mine too," Maksim said.

"What is?"

"Wherever you were going to move."

"That's kind of a problem, isn't it?"

"For you."

"You're Maksim, aren't you? I've heard about you."

"It's all true."

Ruslan ignored him. He pushed the table forward to create space in front of him and then stood, turning to face the boy holding the back of his chair.

"But you, Hamid," he said, switching from Russian to Kyrgyz. "You disappoint me. This one," and he nodded dismissively in Maksim's direction, "has nothing of his own to offer, so he trades on the accomplishments of others, his father in particular. Maybe this appeals to some. You, however, have accomplishments of your own. You are a champion wrestler who could one day, perhaps, carry the Kyrgyz flag in the Olympic stadium. And yet here you stand, doing the bidding of a lesser man. Why would a champion follow a second-rate braggart and a bully? Can you explain that?"

It may have been Ruslan's first day at the school, but he had clearly done his homework on whom he would need to know. Hamid looked confused and Maksim appeared flustered. This was not the response they had anticipated to what for Maksim and his crew was a routine effort to reinforce the school's social order.

"You should do what Maksim says," Hamid mumbled.

"Why? Because he's bigger than I am? Is that how you measure a man?"

"No."

"Then is it because his daddy's the defense minister? What are we? Five years old? You should value a man on his achievements and the strength of his character. How does this boy measure up?"

Kate was struck not only by the sophistication and maturity of his argument but by the calm and persuasive way that Ruslan delivered it. It could not have been clearer that he was not intimidated.

"Teach him some manners, Hamid," Maksim commanded.

"Is that your master's voice?" Ruslan asked the wrestler. "Let him do his own dirty work. I doubt he's ever fought his own battles. I wonder if he has courage."

Ruslan turned to Maksim and looked him hard in the eyes. "How 'bout it? Are you anything but a shadow of your father? Show me what you are."

Ruslan leaned forward as though daring Maksim to hit him. The warmth and openness that he had offered Hamid was gone, replaced by steel. Sharp and cold and strong. There was no doubt or uncertainty in him, just a quiet confidence.

"Hamid," Maksim barked.

The wrestler stepped back, leaving space for Maksim and Ruslan to bring their dispute to resolution. The other two students who had been part of Maksim's entourage did the same.

"Looks like just you and me," Ruslan said, softening his voice and—Kate realized—giving Maksim a face-saving way to de-escalate, to back down. "What do you think?"

Maksim looked genuinely scared. And Kate almost felt sorry for him. But too many of her friends had been subject to his bullying for that feeling to last for more than a fleeting moment.

Maksim balled his hands into fists but kept them at his sides. Hesitating. Uncertain. Off balance. He seemed to recognize that no matter what happened next, he had already lost.

Without saying anything, Maksim turned and walked out of the cafeteria. Hamid and the other boys left by a different door. And Kate knew that things at ISB would never be the same. The room began buzzing as students at the other tables began processing what they had just witnessed.

Ruslan sat back at the table and took a bite of his sandwich, seemingly oblivious to the chatter around him.

Val nudged Kate in the ribs with her elbow.

"Well?" she asked.

Kate got up and walked over to Ruslan's table, taking the seat across from him and placing her school books on the chair beside her. His eyes were dark. Darker than brown, she thought. When he looked at her, she felt looked at.

"Hello," she said. "My name's Kate."

"I know."

Ruslan had spent the better part of the last two years playing a dangerous game of hide-and-seek with the GKNB. He had come within a whisker of being picked up maybe half a dozen times. He had been smart, but he had been lucky too. There was no denying that.

Even so, Ruslan could not remember the last time he had been as anxious as he was now. His normal unflappable demeanor had deserted him. His stomach was knotted up and he paced around the room with a nervous energy that would not dissipate.

What if she doesn't show?

"Get a grip," he said out loud.

Ruslan looked again at the watch he had been checking obsessively for almost an hour. It was five minutes after six. She would want to see him, he thought. They had so much to talk about. Could she be angry with him? She's the one who had left. Or at least that was how he had understood it. Maybe she had a different narrative about the end of their relationship. There was nothing quite so Rashomon-like as love. No two people were ever in the same relationship.

Ruslan did not know what he wanted or what he expected. He only knew that he needed to see her. From the moment Val had told him that Kate was back in Bishkek, he had been plotting how to make that happen, while also avoiding the prying eyes of both the GKNB and his own well-meaning handlers. Sending Bermet to Germany had been the right thing to do, the smart operational move. She had not wanted to go. The regime, however, would have turned Bishkek inside out hunting for her. The GKNB would find out soon enough that she was out of the country, but the Kyrgyz services did not have the international reach to get to her in Berlin. Murzaev had pushed hard for it. It was also—he acknowledged—personally convenient. This compounded his guilt over having agreed to her exile.

Ruslan had chosen this place because he hoped Kate would remember it fondly. And because it was private. It was an old stable located in the foothills about a half-hour drive from the city. The Kyrgyz took their horses seriously, and some of the wealthier denizens of Bishkek kept a weekend horse the way rich Russians had dachas. Back in high school, Ruslan and Kate had not had horses of their own, but they knew the couple who ran the stable well enough that they let them ride just about whenever they asked. They would come up here as often as two or three times a week to ride on the mountain trails and gallop madly across the *djailoo*, flat-bottomed valleys where the shepherds would graze their flocks.

There was one particular field by a clear stream where Ruslan would lay a blanket and they would make love with a passionate intensity. Ruslan could remember the last time they had done this, knowing that it was the last time and willing it never to end. Kate, he hoped, carried the same memories.

At fifteen minutes after six, a gray VW Touareg pulled up in front of the wooden house where the caretakers lived. The driver's-side door opened and a pair of boots got out, followed by legs that Ruslan could still remember wrapped around his waist.

Kate was older, of course, a woman now rather than a girl. The changes were subtle. She was slim and tall and graceful, as she had been a decade ago. But where she had been light and carefree, there was now a sadness about her that had not been there before.

She was dressed for riding, in black leather boots, stretch pants, and a thick fleece. Her dark hair was pulled back in a ponytail. She wore no makeup. She had never used much. Ruslan walked toward her, and as he bent to kiss her cheek he noticed that the pattern of small freckles on her cheekbones was just as he remembered it. It had been too dark at the farmhouse last night for him to make out that small detail.

"I was afraid that you weren't going to be able to make it," he said.

"Sorry to be late. I had to finish up something I was working on in the office."

"About us? About Boldu?"

"Yes."

"Did you tell them about me?"

"No."

Ruslan took her hand and squeezed it.

"Thank you, Kate."

"Is that what you wanted to see me about," Kate asked.

"No. Of course not."

"Why were you so secretive about wanting to see me? Who are we hiding from? The GKNB? Or your own people?"

"Both, I'm afraid."

"They don't trust me. Murzaev and Nogoev in particular. But Hamid as well. Maybe even Val."

"We've been underground for a long time. It can make you a little paranoid. All they can see is risk. It's better that they don't know we're here . . . together."

"Do you trust me?"

"With my life." And my heart, he wanted to add.

Kate seemed to take pity on him. She changed the subject.

"How is it that you became a revolutionary, Ruslan? You were never especially political back in school."

"No. I was more into girls."

"So what happened?"

"They took my family from me."

Kate reached out to him and touched his arm in sympathy. Of all people, he knew, she would understand.

"What happened?"

"My father had started a bank in Bishkek. It was doing well. Well enough that some people with ties to the government wanted it for themselves. He wouldn't give it to them. A day later, the tax authorities were there with the Special Police. They arrested my father and charged him with every financial crime you could imagine. He was sent to Prison Number One and he never came out. They told us that he committed suicide, but they wouldn't let us see the body. I brought my mother to live in Germany. She's still there, but she's not the same."

"I'm so sorry. I know you and your dad were close."

"And I'm sorry I wasn't there when you had to bury your parents. I was already off in Germany and I didn't hear about what happened until it was too late. I should have written you, but . . ." He trailed off, the reasons he hadn't reached out to Kate too complex to put easily into words.

"It's all right. I'm just as responsible for leaving things the way we did. Unfinished."

"We have a lot to catch up on."

"There's time," Kate said reassuringly. "Tell me how you got started in all this."

"It started with fund-raising with the diaspora and took off from there," Ruslan explained. "I guess I had something of a talent for it. Boldu was already in place, but it was only able to function abroad. I wanted to bring it back home to Kyrgyzstan, and the only way to do that was underground. Askar was part of the movement and he helped me with that. It wouldn't have been possible without him."

"There's so much I want to know," Kate said.

"And so much I want to tell you, but there's not much daylight left and I promised you a ride."

"Are Myrzakan and Adilet still in charge of this place?" Kate asked. "I should say hello to them first."

"They are getting on in years, but they're still running the stables. And will be, I suspect, for as long as Myrzakan has the strength to muck out the stalls. But they're not here today. It's just you and me."

Had she leaned in toward him as he said that? Or was it his imagination? Ruslan wanted to reach out to Kate, take her in his arms. But he was afraid to do anything that might shatter the moment. Kate too seemed reluctant to cross the last few centimeters of distance between them.

"Let's go for a ride."

Ruslan grinned.

"You're going to like what I have for you."

He took her hand and led Kate to the stable. Inside, the horses were already saddled. A dapple gray stallion with a broad chest and dark eyes and a chestnut-colored mare so sleek and lean that even standing still she looked fast.

"Pick one," Ruslan said.

"I'll take the big boy."

Kate let go of Ruslan's hand and unhooked the reins from the iron ring bolted to the stable wall.

"What's his name?"

"Aravan."

"That's a beautiful name."

"Have you kept in practice?" Ruslan asked. "He's handsome enough but a little headstrong."

"I knew a guy like that once. I think I can handle him."

Ruslan laughed.

"He's all yours."

"We'll see about that."

They walked the horses outside and mounted up. The sky was already starting to turn purple and orange. It would not be a long ride. Ruslan led Kate up the hill on a path that wound gently through a forest of pine trees and holly. Shrikes and swallows flitted through the trees calling to each other, looking for mates. Somewhere in the forest, an owl hooted as he stretched his wings in preparation for a long night hunting mice in the forest and fields.

On the far side of the hill, the landscape opened up into a *djailoo*, rich and green and flat as a racecourse. Kate turned to Ruslan with a mischievous look on her face. She pulled a riding crop out of a holster on the saddle and held it up to him.

"Fancy a race?" she asked.

Ruslan understood what she meant. The crop was not for the horse. Kyz Kuumai was a traditional Kyrgyz game, sometimes translated as kiss-the-girl. A boy and a girl race each other on horseback. The girl gets a running start, and if the boy can catch her before the finish line, he gets a kiss. But if the girl wins, she beats him with a horsewhip.

Ruslan was perhaps a better rider than Kate, but if so by only a fraction, and Kate was mounted on the stronger horse.

"I don't know," he said coyly. "It's been a while since you've ridden. It might not be fair."

"Catch me if you can." Kate turned the stallion's head and took off at a gallop. Ruslan was right behind her, and he heard Kate whoop with joy as she bent over Aravan's neck and pushed him hard.

Ruslan's mare was smaller, but she was young and had a big heart and loved to run. They pulled up on the right flank of Aravan, and Ruslan stroked the neck of his mount and whispered to her in Kyrgyz that she was both strong and brave. Still the mare could not quite find the extra gear she needed to overtake the stallion, until with no more than fifty meters of open grassland left in front of them, Aravan stumbled briefly and the mare shot forward, edging just barely ahead before the riders had to pull up out of the gallop. The horses and riders were equally breathless and their hearts were beating hard and fast.

Ruslan eased his horse alongside the stallion's flanks. Kate turned to him, her lips parted slightly. He could not remember ever wanting anything as much as he wanted to kiss her at that moment. Her lips were soft and warm and her hair smelled of lavender. When Ruslan finally pulled back from the kiss, he ran his hand across the side of

Kate's face, tracing a line with his finger lightly across her freckled cheekbone.

He smiled.

"You lost on purpose, didn't you?"

Kate shrugged.

"Hard to say. But I'm glad it worked out that way."

Their second kiss was even better than the first.

# 17

Kate had never needed an alarm clock. She was an early riser and her body always seemed to know when it was time to get up. The price to be paid for this talent was that there was no sleeping in on weekends. Her body had never learned the difference between Sunday and Monday.

Kate rolled over in bed, glanced at her phone to check the time—twenty minutes after six—and thought about checking her e-mail. Logging on to her State Department account would require inputting three separate passwords. Screw it. She would do it after her run.

It was supposed to be a cool morning, so she chose a hooded sweatshirt with the Georgetown Hoyas bulldog logo and black track pants. Kate boiled water and used a French press to brew a single cup of coffee. She ground the Kona beans fresh. Life was too short to drink bad coffee.

She drank the Hawaiian coffee black and ate half a banana imported from South Africa while skimming the headlines in both *Vecherniy Bishkek* and the *Washington Post* on her iPad. The brassy Cuban timba group Los Van Van played in the background over Pandora. After her run, she planned to do the *New York Times* crossword puzzle. The world grew a little smaller every year. Her father's Foreign Service career had been in an entirely different era, when living behind the iron curtain, even in the sheltered bubble of diplomatic life, had meant giving up many of the daily luxuries Americans took for granted. Globalization had changed all that, and the combination of online shopping and the diplomatic pouch meant that it was possible to live an American middle-class lifestyle in the most far-flung corners of the planet.

It was comfortable, but it did remove an element of adventure from the career. Kate's generation of diplomats was not required to be nearly so intrepid as their predecessors. She could not help but think that something important had been lost in the transition. On the other hand, women and minorities had not been especially welcome in the Foreign Service when her father had joined. So maybe it was just as well that things had changed. Isolation and spotty communications capabilities had only reinforced the Ivy League old-boys club of the earlier era.

Kate laced on her running shoes and headed out the door of her apartment. She tried to run every morning, no matter the weather, and she had mapped out a four-mile loop that took maximum advantage of the available green space. This early on a Sunday, the streets were largely deserted. The air was brisk and Kate set a comfortable pace that she thought would put her at about a seven-minute mile.

As she ran, Kate thought about Ruslan. It had been two days since they had raced each other across the *djailoo* and shared a kiss as emotionally powerful and confusing as any she could remember since . . . well . . . the last time she and Ruslan had kissed.

This was not going to be easy, she realized. Learning that Seitek was Ruslan had been a shock. Learning that Ruslan still cared about her and beginning to plumb the depths of her own feelings for him had compounded the sense of a world upended. Kate's world was already so unstable that the idea of further complicating it by rekindling a romance with Ruslan filled her simultaneously with fear and desire. It was a heady mixture.

Kate had tried to parse her own emotions with as much honesty as she could muster. Her feelings for Ruslan were like the coals in a fire that had been carefully banked. The ashes were cool enough to the touch, but it would take little more than a breath of air to spark a rich orange glow and a heat that Kate feared might consume her.

Could she afford the risk? Could she afford not to take the risk? She had been lonely for too long. Looking for something that she could not quite define. Was this it? She wished that she could talk to her mother about it. Or her aunt. Both had been wise in the ways of the heart. The flash of anger that she felt on thinking again about what the Eraliev government had taken from her was a welcome distraction from the more complicated emotions that Ruslan had stirred up. Anger was the simplest of emotions. It was neat and clean with bright lines and sharp edges. It helped focus the mind. Thinking of Ruslan made her feel unfocused, uncertain, and—she admitted uneasily—hopeful.

Kate's breathing was still smooth and easy at the two-mile mark when she turned into Oak Park. Her route wound through a small urban forest of stately oak and black pine. The sun was up higher now, warming the air and offering a promise of a beautiful spring day.

Kate heard a car engine behind and she drifted over to the side of the road to leave it plenty of room. Glancing over her shoulder, she saw a white van driving a little too fast. She stepped off the asphalt onto the packed earth. Drivers in Bishkek did not have a great deal of experience sharing the road with joggers.

The van pulled up alongside her and the side door opened suddenly. The van screeched to a halt and two men in black *balaclavas* jumped out, grabbing Kate by the arms and tossing her into the vehicle before she had a chance to either scream or run. She landed hard on the metal floor. A third man waiting on the inside clamped one hand over her mouth and pressed the other to the back of her head. He was so strong that Kate gave no thought to the idea of fighting back.

God, she had been a fool.

Diplomatic security had drilled into her from her first day in the service the dangers of being predictable. An older agent named Ray, a large man—muscle gone to fat—who liked to boast that he had once had a tryout with the Cleveland Browns, had taught the Security Overseas seminar.

"Terrorists are after you," he had warned the junior diplomats. "ISIS would like nothing more than to put a picture of your severed head on Instagram. Don't give them the opportunity. Vary your routes and times. Be unpredictable. Let them cut the head off the third secretary from the Russian embassy instead. The bad guys will go after the easy mark. Don't let it be you."

Sorry, Ray.

Kate had let her familiar surroundings lull her into a false sense of security. She ran the same route each morning at about the same time, in violation of the first rule of personal security. And now she would pay for it.

She knew instinctively, however, that this was not ISIS or al-Qaeda or some other Islamic terrorist organization. This was purely local.

Maybe the GKNB had figured out that she had supplied Boldu with the notarized transport form that had enabled the ambush on the prison convoy. Maybe one of Eraliev's spies had followed her to the stable where she had met Ruslan.

If so, it was likely that they were taking her to Prison Number One, where Torquemada was waiting in some dank basement interrogation room. Kate felt a chill. She was an American diplomat. The government could never afford to acknowledge that it had kidnapped her off the street and tortured her. If they started down that road, there could be only one ending. They would kill her.

She felt the pressure on her mouth ease as the big man with hands the size of dinner plates loosened his hold.

"Who are you?" Kate demanded as soon as she was free to speak. "Where are you taking me?" She spoke in Russian.

"All in good time," the man said back to her in the same language. "Now, be quiet." He ripped a length of duct tape off a thick roll and slapped it forcefully over Kate's mouth. Her teeth cut the inside of her lip and she tasted blood. He pulled Kate's arms forward and used the tape to bind her wrists together. From behind her one of the other kidnappers slipped a black cloth bag over her head. He cinched it tightly around her throat with a leather cord and Kate's anger began to give way to fear.

It was okay to be afraid, Kate told herself. But she'd be damned if she would let them see it. She sat cross-legged with her back pressed up against the side of the van and concentrated on her breathing.

No one spoke. Kate sat stock-still, bound and gagged and blind. She could do nothing but wait to learn her fate.

With her heart racing, time was difficult to measure. But it felt to Kate as though at least an hour had passed before they came to a stop. The door swung open with an ugly rumble of metal rollers. Two men lifted Kate bodily from the van and frog-marched her about twenty feet before pushing her down onto a cold metal chair. Someone cut the tape at her wrists with a knife and then taped them again to the arms of chair. Someone—maybe the same person, maybe someone else—taped her ankles to the chair legs. A strap of some kind was wrapped around her chest, sitting just over her breasts. A second strap was wound around her abdomen, passing right over her diaphragm. They were tight but not painfully so and they did not seem to be tied to the chair. Kate was not certain what it was. Experimentally, she tried to move the chair just a bit, only to find that it was bolted to the floor.

A hand at her throat made her freeze for an instant, but it proved to be just one of her captors loosening the knot that held the hood tight.

When the hood was pulled off, Kate blinked hard as her eyes adjusted to the light. She was in a warehouse or a hangar of some kind, with a high ceiling and shelves along the walls piled with boxes and what looked like engine parts.

As gloomy as it was, this was not a prison, and Kate felt a shiver of relief. Her situation was hardly ideal, but it was not yet her deepest fear.

Kate could not see behind her, but she sensed that the men in the *balaclavas* were somewhere in her blind spot. In front of her was a wooden table with a metal box on it. Cords running from the box connected it to the bands strapped around Kate's torso. A man sat at the desk in a short-sleeved dress shirt. If a toad was turned into a man and the process had somehow broken down at the halfway point, this was what he might look like. The man was small. His face was wrinkled and decorated with a forest of moles, warts, and lumps of uncertain origin. The thick glasses he wore had black plastic rims, and they magnified his eyes to the point where he looked almost amphibian.

The hair on his head grew in mangy patches. The follicles on his ears were seemingly more reliable. He was an ugly troll of a man, and Kate sensed that he was someone she should fear.

From behind her she could hear the sound of heels clicking on the cement floor of the warehouse. Even though this was not the central prison, Kate was still certain that the men who had taken her were GKNB. If this was Chalibashvili, maybe he had his reasons for interrogating her outside the formal system. The Kyrgyz authorities were children of the Soviet Union. They kept records.

Kate fought the instinct to crane her neck to see who was behind her. It would look weak. Desperate. She would learn soon enough. The man stopped right behind her and Kate could feel him studying her. Slowly, he moved clockwise around her. When he had reached her shoulder, Kate turned her head and looked up.

It was Askar Murzaev, the Boldu chief of intelligence.

"I suppose I should be surprised by this," she said. "But I'm not especially. Are you in the market for a wife? I wouldn't have pegged you as a traditionalist." Ala Kachuu, or bride stealing, was a custom with deep roots in Kyrgyz history. Depending on the circumstances, it could be either an elaborate form of elopement or a kidnapping followed by rape and forced marriage. As many as a third of Kyrgyz brides were taken against their will.

"You flatter yourself, Ms. Hollister," Murzaev answered. "But I have other surprises for you."

The Boldu intelligence chief was dressed in a dark suit and tie as though for work, which—Kate supposed—this was.

"Are you working for Eraliev?" she asked. "Are you a traitor?" Did you sign Ruslan's death warrant? she wanted to ask.

"We'll see who the worm in the apple really is," Murzaev said flatly. He pointed to the box on the table. "Do you know what that is?"

"Yes."

When he was secretary of state, George Shultz had successfully protected the Foreign Service from the intrusive indignity of regular polygraph testing. But Kate recognized the machine easily enough. And she had heard from her friends in the intelligence community what it was like to go "on the box." It was the kind of thing that would make Mother Teresa come to doubt her own virtue.

"Yuri here may not be much to look at, but I assure you that he's the very best at what he does." The man-toad sitting at the table scowled at Murzaev, an expression that seemed to suit him and perversely made him fractionally less ugly.

At a signal from Murzaev, one of the musclemen who had grabbed her off the street pushed the right sleeve of her sweatshirt up over her elbow and wrapped something that looked like a blood pressure cuff around her forearm. Then he straightened the fingers on Kate's left hand and slipped a metal clip over her index and middle fingers, securing it with medical tape.

"Yuri is going to ask you a few questions to calibrate our little device," Murzaev said. "And then . . ." He paused and stared at Kate with the intensity of a lover. "And then, I'm going to ask you some questions."

The questions from the examiner were mundane: her name, her birthday, her address, her place of employment. Most were phrased as "yes" or "no" questions. To some, she was instructed to answer falsely.

Finally, it was Murzaev's turn.

"How long have you been working for Eraliev?" he asked.

"What?" Kate was in turn flabbergasted, relieved, and angry. "Is that what this is about? You don't trust me? Jesus, we could have had this little chat without the kidnapping bit."

"Please just answer the question. For how long have you worked for Eraliev?"

"When did I stop beating my dog?"

"Answer the question, please."

"I don't work for Eraliev. He murdered my family. I'd sooner work for Stalin."

Murzaev looked over at the examiner, who shook his head.

"Yuri doesn't believe you."

Kate remembered one of her friends in the CIA telling her that the polygraphers would sometimes accuse the test subjects of lying, even when there were no physiological indications, just to shake them up. The box was based on questionable science, but it was an ace interrogation tool.

Kate's father had been scrupulously honest, and he had tried to instill that same damn-the-torpedoes forthrightness in his daughter. Her mother, however, had grown up in the Soviet Union and her relationship with the truth was less dogmatic than that of her husband. It was more practical. Even transactional.

"I thought you said he was the best," Kate said, striving to project both confidence and disdain. "I hope you didn't pay him in advance."

"How much does Eraliev pay you?" he asked.

"I told you—"

"Who is your handler with the GKNB?"

"I don't—"

"Did you tell him Seitek's real name?"

Kate noted that he did not use Ruslan's name, and she resolved to do the same. There were a large number of people in the room and she did not know if they were all privy to that information. They would not learn it from her.

"Did your ambassador instruct you to make contact with Boldu?"

"Yes."

"Why?"

"Because he thought we could help you, and he thought you would talk to me."

"Because of . . . what do you Americans say . . . old school ties?" The last phrase was delivered in English that was heavily accented but intelligible.

"Yes."

"Did you tell anyone Seitek's real name?"

"No."

"Not even your ambassador?"

"No."

Kate saw Murzaev glance over at the man-toad, who made a gesture that she could not interpret.

"I will ask you again, and I want you to answer truthfully this time. Did you tell the American ambassador to Kyrgyzstan—your uncle—Seitek's real name?"

"No."

"Did he ask you if you knew?"

"Yes."

"And you didn't tell him?"

"No."

"Why not?"

"I don't know," she admitted.

"You withheld important information from your ambassador, from your father's brother. You lied to him, even when he asked you a direct question?" Murzaev's skepticism was plain as day in his tone.

"Yes, I did. And when you put it that way, it doesn't sound too good."

"I'd imagine not. And you do understand why this is somewhat difficult to believe?"

"I do."

"Have you seen Seitek since the night on the farm?"

"You should ask him."

"I'm asking you."

"Asking me what?" Kate was stalling for time.

"Have you seen Seitek after the meeting at the farm? When and where?"

Kate vaguely remembered reading somewhere that curling your toes as hard as you could would confuse the polygrapher. She had no idea if that was true, but she curled them just the same.

"No." It was her first lie.

"No, what?"

"No. I haven't seen Seitek since the farm."

Kate was now keeping so many different secrets from different players that it would be difficult to keep them all straight. In spite of that, or maybe because of that, Yuri seemed to accept her answer.

The next question caught her unprepared, as the slick and experienced Murzaev knew it would.

"Do you love him?" he asked

"Huh?"

"It's a simple enough question. Do you love Seitek?"

"It's really none of your business."

"Of course it's my business," Murzaev sneered. "Love is a weakness, a vulnerability. I need to know if you love him and—more to the point—if he believes he loves you, if I am to have a comprehensive picture of the strengths and weaknesses of an organization that quite literally holds my life in its hands. Now I will ask you again and I expect an answer this time. Do you love him? Do you love Seitek?"

"No. I do not love Seitek."

Murzaev seemed to realize his mistake, the loophole he had left for her.

"What about the man who is Seitek?" Murzaev again avoided using Ruslan's name.

"What about him?"

"Do you love him?"

"I don't know," Kate said miserably.

Murzaev looked over at Yuri, who nodded almost imperceptibly.

"Congratulations, Ms. Hollister," Murzaev said. "I believe that's the most honest thing you've said all morning."

"Yes," Kate agreed.

There was more. The questioning went on for hours, with Murzaev repeatedly circling back to the issue of whom she had told about Seitek and how she felt about him.

"I assure you," Kate said when Murzaev had asked for the twelfth time in twelve different ways whether she was in love with the great leader of Boldu, "no one is more frustrated that I am about my inability to answer that question."

Finally, it was over.

Murzaev himself cut her loose and released the straps from her chest and abdomen.

"All right, Ms. Hollister," he said. "I am reasonably satisfied that you are what you say you are, which is not the same as saying that I like it."

"I understand. Paranoia is no doubt a priceless asset in your profession."

"Quite. I am sorry about this."

"Me too."

"You understand why it was necessary?"

"Because if I had failed this little test, you didn't want anyone to know that you were the last person to see me alive, especially not Ruslan." They were standing together alone, and with the others out of earshot, Kate saw no reason to maintain the fiction.

"That is the long and the short of it, yes. I am a hard man; it is true. But this is a hard world."

"I don't really get you," Kate admitted. "I checked out your background. You're the consummate insider, a veritable alphabet's soup of Soviet, Russian, and Kyrgyz security services. This is kind of an unusual résumé for a democrat and a dissident, isn't it? Why are you doing this? Why are you with Boldu?"

Murzaev was quiet. The expression on his face was almost wistful.

"I was born here in Bishkek," he said finally. "My family was Kyrgyz, but my father was a real Soviet man. Above ethnicity. A servant of the party and state. That's what he taught me. Growing up, my best friend was Chorobek Rustamov. We were inseparable, Chorobek and I. We even lived together when we went off to Leningrad for college. I studied politics and Chorobek was a budding chemical engineer. After graduating, I went to Moscow and began a career in intelligence, and Chorobek returned to Bishkek and joined Acron Group, the state-run fertilizer manufacturer. We stayed close. I moved from the KGB to the FSB when the Soviet Union broke up and later joined the GKDO, Kyrgyz military intelligence. I never married or had children of my own. Family is not a good fit for spy craft. But Chorobek's children were like mine. And then the fool had to go and develop a political conscience. He became a democrat and sided with Azattyk against Eraliev. He was arrested, of course, and tortured before they murdered him."

The spymaster's expression hardened as he relived the insults visited on his childhood friend by Eraliev's inquisitors. Kate wondered if Chorobek had known Zamira. He must have. Azattyk had not been that big or that careful about security.

"Azattyk were amateurs," Murzaev said as though reading her mind. "And I promised that the next time the opposition would be ready to match the regime for ruthlessness."

"You're doing an excellent job," Kate said.

Murzaev almost seemed to smile at that.

"Your aunt. Her sacrifice. That's why I agreed to your initial meeting with Seitek. But I had to be certain about you."

"I understand."

They stood in silence, and to her irritation Kate found herself respecting the old spy, even liking him in a certain way.

"I have a little something for you," Murzaev said.

"A nice set of monogrammed thumb screws?"

Murzaev looked confused, then seemed to decide, correctly, that Kate's answer was pure sarcasm and could therefore be ignored.

"It's just a phone." The old spy pulled a cell phone out of his pocket and handed it to Kate. It was an older, clunky candy bar–style phone and seemed to have been designed purely for function. There was no manufacturer's mark on it. It was a plain tool.

"Is this like one of the toys Q would give James Bond at the beginning of the movie? Does it have a laser?"

"It just makes calls, I'm afraid. Actually, it makes one call to one number already programmed in. All you need to do is enter the value of pi to five places and hit the pound key. It will call me. If any other number is entered, the guts of the phone will melt down. It will be quite hot, so try not to burn your fingers. When I answer, you will say, 'His forefathers were all khans.' That means that you are not under duress. You recognize the line?"

"Yes. It's the first line in the Manas epic."

"Good. You will remember it then. This phone is clean. But there is no such thing as risk-free electronic communication. Use it only in an emergency."

"You think this is necessary?"

"I do."

Kate put the phone in her pocket. It was heavy.

"I'll have the boys drop you back at your apartment," Murzaev said.

"Thank you."

Kate felt numb, emotionally drained by what she had been through. Her tracksuit was soaked with sweat, first from the run and then from the tension of the interrogation.

"There's one more thing," Murzaev said.

"Let me guess," Kate answered, thinking of her earlier conversation with Val. "You want me to stay away from the great Seitek."

"No." Murzaev sounded genuinely surprised by that. "Denying you to him would only make you more enticing. He's that way, you see."

"Of course."

"I think it would be better for all concerned, however, if he didn't learn of our little chat today."

"Better for you, you mean."

"Me among others. My methods are somewhat extreme, I grant you, but I am committed to this cause, and if we are going to do it, then we are going to do it the right way. There are some aspects of the right way that should be kept away from idealists like our mutual friend. He is indispensable but not infallible. He has his blind spots. This would be one of them. You understand, of course."

"I understand that you're concerned about protecting your position in Boldu."

"Boldu relies on my ability to do my job. Should Ruslan decide that he no longer requires my services, the cause would suffer a grievous blow. There is no one else in the movement with my background. My training. It would be a shame for the organization to lose this particular set of skills unnecessarily. Revolution, Ms. Hollister, is not for the faint of heart."

Kate knew he was right, but she hated it nonetheless.

"You're asking me to protect you after you kidnapped me and interrogated me for hours under white-hot klieg lots and then casually threatened me with death."

"Lights?" Murzaev looked around the dimly lit warehouse as though searching for something he had misplaced.

"The lights are metaphorical."

"I see."

"Don't patronize me."

"I wouldn't dream of it. But you do understand my point."

"Are you certain that Ruslan would be so quick to cast you out because of our little tête-à-tête here?"

"My profession is based largely on reading people. Their strengths and their shortcomings. Their desires and ambitions and frustrations. Espionage is really a branch of psychology."

"And what does your training tell you, Doctor?"

"That Ruslan's feelings for you are real and deep. Maybe more so than even he knows."

Kate felt herself blush, embarrassed at how much she wanted this statement to be true and wary of being manipulated by a self-confessed master manipulator.

"All right," she agreed. "I'll keep your secret."

Another secret to keep. She was going to have to start writing this all down.

# 18

For the first time since her return to Kyrgyzstan, Kate found herself back at Manas International Airport. This time she was in Gabby's role, waiting patiently for a new arrival. As he had promised, the ambassador had made Kate the control officer for the visit of deputy secretary of defense Winston Crandle.

Managing official visitors was an unavoidable fact of embassy life. In some of the nicer western European embassies it could be a significant burden. Every executive branch visitor and congressional delegation required a control officer, an embassy official who set up the meetings, arranged the transportation, and wrote the reporting cable after the fact. Embassies in major capitals like London or Tokyo or Buenos Aires—or consulates in touristy towns like Florence and Capetown—were so deluged with visitors that they functioned as little more than informal travel agencies.

In a small post like Bishkek, however, official visitors were few and far between. There had not been a congressional delegation in town since the closure of the transit base on the military side of the airport. They were not missed. Congressional delegations, or CODELS in State Department argot, were almost always a source of anxiety and frustration. Many visits involved more shopping and sightseeing than government business. Somehow or other there always seemed to be some important issue requiring congressional attention in Paris in the spring. And away from the stifling confines of Washington and after a few drinks, elected members of Congress could be as rowdy, boorish, and ill behaved as Dartmouth frat brothers at a freshman mixer on Saturday night. After such visits, the control officer was responsible for coordinating the official apologies.

Another of the control officer's duties was "meet and greet," which is why Kate was at the airport waiting for Crandle's military aircraft—or MILAIR—flight to touch down. Kate's diplomatic credentials allowed her out on the tarmac, and she stood in the early morning sunshine with Alisher, the embassy expediter who would take care of the luggage and visa formalities.

Crandle's aircraft, a U.S. Air Force C-20, landed on time. Kate and Alisher waited planeside as the ground crew maneuvered a set of "VIP" stairs covered in a ratty, stained red carpet into position. The door swung open and an airman in a green jumpsuit locked it into place before stepping back to make way for the VIP to exit first. Crandle appeared at the top of the stairs, shading his eyes against the sunlight. And there was something vampiric about the deputy secretary. He was tall and angular and almost entirely bald. The skin on his face was pulled tight as though it were too small for his skull. His aquiline nose was shaped like a hawk's bill and defined his face as, Kate suspected, it had defined his childhood. His dark suit added to the impression that he was one of the undead.

When he reached the bottom of the stairs, Kate offered her hand. Crandle shook it noncommittally, his pale gray eyes seeming to look past her for somebody important. The liver spots on the back of his hand matched those on his skull. He gave off the faint odor of cologne, as though he were trying to mask the stench of cadaverous decay. The Fossil was a suitable enough nickname, Kate decided.

"Mr. Crandle, I'm Kate Hollister, your control officer."

At the mention of her name, Crandle stopped scanning the tarmac and focused his attention on her with a suddenness that Kate found mildly disorienting.

"Hollister? Yes. The niece. I knew your father. He was a talented officer. It was unfortunate that his attachment to the periphery of the Russo-sphere limited his career the way it did. Otherwise, he might have been somebody. You're here alone?"

Crandle's blithe dismissal of her father's thirty-five years of service to the United States stuck in her craw, but Kate understood that the deputy secretary had been trying in his own way to say something complimentary.

"Alisher is here to help with the expediting," she said.

"Alone then. Your uncle had something more pressing it would seem."

There was a subtext to the conversation that Kate could sense but not interpret. Ordinarily, she knew, an ambassador at a mission the size of Embassy Bishkek would go to the airport to meet a visitor at this level, but it was hardly a requirement. The way he had zeroed in on her family name made Kate feel like there was more to that story, however.

"He'll meet you at the residence for breakfast," Kate said. "In the meantime, if Alisher can take your passport, we'll get the formalities sorted out."

"Brian will get it for him," Crandle said dismissively.

A harried-looking twenty-something aide stumbled down the staircase carrying three bags and juggling a cell phone and an iPad as he scanned frantically for a signal. He was overweight with unruly hair and a tan suit that looked like it had been slept in. But he was cute in a Jack Black sort of way. Alisher stepped forward to relieve him of the bags.

"I'll get these over to the hotel," he said. "And I'll deal with immigration if you leave me the passports."

The aide handed him two brick red official passports and mumbled his thanks.

"Let's go," Crandle said impatiently. "We're on taxpayer time."

Kate signaled to the "motorcade," which was only two cars long, to pull up planeside. She and Crandle and the aide, Brian, piled into the Suburban with the deputy secretary in the right rear "seat of honor," the aide behind the driver, and Kate up front. No one needed to be told where to sit. It was all according to diplomatic protocol and as second nature to all of them as breathing.

The follow car was for security, provided as a courtesy by the Special Police. Autocrats were always careful to extend courtesies to the powerful.

Neither Crandle nor his aide turned out to be much for small talk, and Kate knew that they would not want to talk business in a serious way with their Kyrgyz driver listening. The ride into town passed mostly in silence, with young Brian dealing with urgent e-mails and text messages while Crandle sat in his seat unmoving, staring straight ahead as though sleeping with his eyes open.

This is what Nosferatu must have looked like lying in his coffin, Kate thought to herself, and she glanced in the rearview mirror half expecting to see that Crandle had no reflection.

Breakfast at the residence was on the austere side—coffee, orange juice, and croissants—and Kate wondered whether there was a message in that as well. Protocol and subtle signals. The language of diplomacy could sometimes be so elliptical that it was all too easy to misread the message, even when both parties shared a single culture and a long history.

"It's nice to see you, Winston," the ambassador said, although there was nothing in his tone to indicate that this was, in fact, true.

"And you, Harry." Crandle's greeting was equally distant, his handshake as limp and disinterested as the one he had offered Kate at the airport.

Crandle was more effusive in greeting Brass. Kate was not especially surprised to find that the defense attaché had been included in the breakfast, but neither was she especially pleased to see him. Brass had already made clear where his loyalties lay in whatever dispute existed between the two ambassadors.

Breakfast was served at the small table in the sunroom rather than in the formal dining room. Meryem poured the coffee, and they helped themselves to pastries. The ambassador's chef, Kate was happy to learn, was even better at baking than he was at *paloo*. Brian took a cup of coffee and sat by himself at a side table, tapping away nonstop on his phone.

"How are things going with the Fifty-fourth, Colonel?"

"Progressing, Mr. Secretary. We've cycled most of the unit's leadership, including Colonel Shakirov, through advanced training, and we've equipped the brigade up to near-NATO standard."

"Good. Eraliev needs to know he can count on the Fifty-fourth to defend him personally, and he needs to know who made that possible."

"You did, sir."

"Yes. I did."

"What are your priorities for this visit, Winston?" the ambassador asked. "We're seeing Eraliev at ten. What's the message you're bringing from Washington?"

"The Eraliev meeting will be fine. I'll meet him halfway on the base services issue. He can dip his bill, but only up to a point. I'm confident he'll be reasonable, which I am defining here as not embarrassingly greedy, or at least not publicly so. But what I'm really here to do, Harry, is to light something of a fire under your ass about Boldu."

"Do tell," the ambassador said with an icy calm.

"I've been following the reporting. And it looks like you've finally started to make some progress on identifying the leadership. Congratulations. But I'm worried that it's too little, too late. The second tier, really. I hope you appreciate the urgency of this particular task."

The ambassador broke his croissant in half and dropped a spoonful of strawberry jam into the center.

"We'll see," he said, and Kate suspected that biting into the pastry helped him bite back a sharper response. "As you said, we are making progress. The credit really belongs to Kate here. She's the one who made contact with Boldu and has started earning their trust."

Crandle turned to Kate and examined her in what seemed an almost clinical fashion.

"Not enough trust, it would seem. How much progress are you making, Ms. Hollister, in identifying the real name of the mysterious Seitek?"

"Why does it matter so much?" Kate asked. "What his real name is? His profession? His hometown? Whether he even exists? Boldu is real enough and there are people in the movement we know by name who are willing to work with us, people with influence in the organization and a demonstrated commitment to a democratic Kyrgyzstan that I hope we all share. Isn't that enough? We can work with the movement through the people we know, even if we never see a copy of Seitek's birth certificate."

Kate was afraid that she had gone too far, that she had embarrassed her uncle in front of a powerful bureaucrat she had come to dislike deeply in a remarkably short time. But when she glanced over at him, there was no hint of disapproval. Instead, the ambassador winked at her as though they were co-conspirators and offered a discreet thumbs-up that would have been hard for anyone else to spot.

Crandle was not, however, thrown off his game. He smiled a vulpine smile that was entirely lacking in warmth.

"Ms. Hollister, if this was a charitable enterprise, I might agree with you. We toss a few hundred thousand dollars to the group and hope for the best. No great loss if things don't work out. But we would be committing more than money. What we are talking about is a partnership with this organization. We would be investing political capital in the group. Consider it a form of insurance against the collapse of the existing political order in this country. It could be seen as a vote of no confidence in Eraliev. There's even a chance that our open support for Boldu could trigger the kind of safe-haven seeking that can hollow out a tyrant's kingdom in a remarkably short time."

"But why is it personal?" Kate asked. "Why the focus on Seitek himself rather than on what we can do with Boldu as a broader movement?"

"Our outreach to Boldu is essentially a business proposition. For better or worse, Seitek is the CEO of a company with which we have proposed a merger. How can I go to my board—which in this case includes the president of the United States and the secretary of state—

and recommend that merger without ever having met the chief executive? How can I judge him? How can I take the measure of the man, if I don't know who he is? It would be a form of malpractice."

When Kate was young, she had loved Dr. Seuss. She had made her father read the Seuss books until the pages fell off the spine and together they had worn out the DVD of *How the Grinch Stole Christmas*. In that story, Little Cindy Lou Who catches the Grinch, dressed as Santa Claus, stealing the family Christmas tree. He feeds her a line of crap about fixing a broken light at his workshop in the North Pole, gives her a glass of water, and hustles her off to bed.

Kate did not enjoy being treated like Little Cindy Lou Who.

Crandle's heart was as shrunken and leathery as that of the Grinch and she did not believe a thing he said.

"Deputy Secretary Crandle has it exactly right, Kate." Brass managed to convey both condescension toward Kate and fawning admiration toward Crandle in a single eight-word sentence. It was no mean feat, even for a practiced sycophant. "We don't know enough about Boldu to take the risk of backing them, at least not openly. Maybe if we knew more . . ."

Brass had already shared with Kate his private opinion of Boldu. He was using her to position himself, but who was the audience? Crandle or the ambassador?

"We know a hell of a lot more than we did even three weeks ago," Kate said. "My sense is that support for Boldu is broad and growing. The more they do to challenge the regime publicly, the more credibility they earn with a populace that's had about enough. It's a big tent and it would be a mistake to focus exclusively on the name of the ringmaster."

"It is something of a circus," the ambassador agreed, seemingly in an effort to lighten the mood. "We're a superpower," he continued, directing his comments at Crandle. "We can walk and chew gum at the same time, meaning that we can leverage our engagement with the Eraliev government to advance the base negotiations, even as we work to build a relationship of trust with Boldu. That should eventually include a face-to-face meeting with the titular head of the movement. In the meantime, we work with them, help them, but also learn more about them. It's not going to happen overnight, Winston. You'll need to be patient."

"Patience is an overrated virtue," Crandle replied. "It is impatient people who do great things. I want that goddamn name, Harry. And I don't care how you get it. I will not be either 'patient' or complacent. And I don't expect you to be either."

"Fair point. We'll make establishing direct contact with Seitek our top priority. Kate, you have your orders."

"Yes, sir." Kate did not offer anything else, afraid that anything she might say would be a lie.

"You're doing well," her uncle said gently. "Keep it up."

"Yes, sir."

"It's almost ten. We should head over to the palace. Kate, this is all going to be about the military aspects of the negotiation. I'm going to take Brass with us, but I'd like you to take Brian back to the embassy. I'll fill you and Chet in on anything you need to know after the meeting."

"Of course."

Kate did not let anything show on her face, but she was unhappy at being excluded from the meeting. The one positive aspect of control officer responsibilities was the opportunity to get into top-level meetings. Her uncle was taking this away, and while there was no reason to believe it was intended as a punishment, it sure felt like one.

It was well into the twenty-first century, and the delegation heading off to meet with the head of state was still three white men. It was the kind of delegation that was the exclusive norm when Crandle had begun his career in the early days of the war in Vietnam. That was supposed to have changed. But it hadn't really.

*I'll take care of the dishes.* Kate was proud of herself for keeping that retort bottled up. In diplomacy, knowing when to shut up was at least as important as knowing what to say. And ulcers were as much a professional hazard for diplomats as alcoholism.

The men took their leave, and Kate and Brian stayed behind, finishing their coffee and croissants. The windows of the sunroom looked out over the residence's rose garden and Kate admired the view. Brian barely looked up from his phone, intent on managing his e-mail or responding to whatever D.C.-based crisis was demanding his attention.

Kate reflected on what had been a strange conversation. She turned it over in her mind as she sipped her coffee. It was not easy to parse the exchange between her uncle and Crandle. There was a level to it that she was not privy to. Brass, she suspected, knew more of the background than she did.

What Kate did know was that she neither liked nor trusted the deputy secretary of defense. And she had no intent of sharing Ruslan's name with him.

She trusted her uncle. She had to. But who, she wondered, was calling the shots?

# 19

This time, he was sure she would come. Ruslan had sent Kate a message asking her to meet him here. He wanted to show her. It was important that she understand. And it would be easier to explain what he had in mind if Kate could see it for herself. He needed her to understand. He needed her help.

She would see it. She would understand.

He was sure of it.

At least he was sure about something. Everything else about Kate confused him. He knew he had never gotten over her. She seemed still to feel something for him as well. All the rest would have to wait. There was work to do.

It was early evening. There was enough daylight left to see, but it was dark enough that it would be hard for the GKNB to track them from a distance.

Ruslan stood on the corner of Kiev and Panfilov streets a half block from Ala-Too Square, the center of civic life in Bishkek and the site of several mass demonstrations over the years that had attempted to challenge Eraliev's right to rule in perpetuity. All had been crushed. The regime had responded to these threats with overwhelming force.

He saw her the moment she rounded the corner onto Panfilov Street. She walked with confidence and purpose, as much at home on the streets of Bishkek as Ruslan himself. Her jeans were tucked into calf-high boots. It was a warm evening, and the short jacket she wore over a white top was open at the front. She wore her chestnut hair loose, brushed sleek and straight down to her shoulders. Ruslan did not hide the fact that he was staring at her.

God, she was beautiful.

The distance between them was closing rapidly, and when she was only a few meters away, Ruslan suffered a brief moment of panic. How should he greet her? Should he kiss her? Would she want that? Ruslan had now led men and women into battle. He had played bell-the-cat with the security services and taken unconscionable risks as the leader of Boldu. This was worse. He did not want to make a mistake. Say the wrong thing. And he knew instinctively that it would be easy to do.

Better not to speak, he decided.

Without a word, he stepped toward her and leaned forward to kiss her on the lips. Not passionately. But gently, questioningly.

The kiss back was the answer he had been hoping for.

"A nine-year-old told me to meet you here."

"You really shouldn't let kids order you around like that."

"Then maybe you should stop employing child labor."

"I missed you," he said.

"You too." Kate's smile was shy and natural.

"There's something I'd like to show you."

She put her arm in his and stared him hard in the eyes.

"I'll follow you anywhere."

Ruslan felt himself flush and he looked away shyly, as nonplussed by Kate's flirting as he was calm in the searchlights of the GKNB.

"Good to know," he said as casually as he could manage.

Ruslan led Kate toward Ala-Too Square. They walked arm in arm and they fit together naturally, as though no time had passed since they had been together. Kate leaned in against him just slightly.

Ala-Too Square was a broad open plaza of concrete and stone. A bronze statue of Manas on a red marble plinth dominated the square. The modernist Kyrgyz National Historical Museum loomed over the plaza on the far side of Chuy Avenue, which bisected the park. Triumphal arches to the east and west of the square managed to combine the worst aspects of Islamic and Soviet architecture in white marble and fake gold. The square was cold and windswept in the winter and hot and stifling in the summer. In the fall and spring, it was merely ugly.

To the north, the snowcapped peaks of the Ala-Too mountains seemed to rebuke the eponymous square. Nothing mankind could build would ever compare to the power and glory of those mountains.

The Presidential Palace was visible from the square, sheltered behind high walls and strong gates. This was where Kate had somehow managed to get Eraliev's personal seal on the transfer order that had made it possible for Nogoev's Scythians to free Bermet before she vanished forever into the Pit.

"Want to stop by the office and see if you can lift Eraliev's wallet and watch? Maybe steal his car?"

Kate shuddered.

"Don't remind me. Scariest five minutes of my life."

They crossed Kiev Street, and walked to the base of the Manas statue. The father of all Kyrgyz was mounted on a horse with his sword sheathed. Although it looked like it had been there forever, the Manas sculpture was really only a few years old. It had replaced a winged woman on a globe meant to symbolize Kyrgyzstan's independence from the USSR. Fittingly, that sculpture had replaced an enormous statue of Lenin, his arm raised as though hailing a cab on the streets of Moscow. To the left of the statue, there was a large fountain. The water was stagnant and choked with leaves.

"This is what you wanted to show me?" Kate asked. "Ala-Too Square? It's like bringing a Muscovite to the Kremlin."

"If you bring one Russian to Red Square, it's a picnic. If you bring fifty thousand, it's a revolution."

Kate looked at him sharply.

"Haven't we seen that movie already? I didn't like the ending."

"This time would be different," Ruslan promised.

"Revolutionaries always believe that. And then they hang."

"Not this time."

"What makes you so sure?"

"Because this time we're ready to fight."

"To the battlements. Like the French Revolution?"

"Like Maidan."

"That was pretty ugly too," Kate said sadly.

It was true. In 2014, tens of thousands of average Ukrainians had risen up against a Kremlin puppet government under Viktor Yanukovych. Protestors had taken over Maidan, the main square in Kiev, building a tent city surrounded by walls hastily thrown up and guarded by angry young men. They called their movement Euromaidan, and they asked for nothing more than the opportunity to choose for themselves whether to be part of the East or the West.

They wanted a European future that the Russian president, Vladimir Putin, and his cronies were determined to deny them.

Tensions built over weeks and months, finally exploding in a spasm of violence that left several hundred dead, more than a thousand injured, and Yanukovych in exile in Russia. For a few brief weeks, everything seemed possible. But then Russia invaded and annexed Crimea, and the revolutionaries proved to be better at overthrowing governments than running them. Patriotic as they were, they turned out to be almost as corrupt and inept as the quislings they had displaced. As in Orwell's story, the pigs had started walking on two legs.

"We will do better," Ruslan promised.

"Really?"

"We have the chance to learn from their mistakes and choose not to repeat them. We have the discipline and the training to defend the little tent city we will build here on Ala-Too and enough support from the people that the regime will not choose to slaughter us."

"You hope."

"Yes. I hope. And it is hope that drives me to action. But there is a problem."

"Just one?"

Ruslan smiled resignedly.

"More than one," he admitted. "But one in particular."

"One that I can help you with, I presume."

"You always were a quick study, Kate."

"Is that what this is all about? You and me?"

"No," Ruslan protested. "That's not it at all."

"I know. I'm sorry. That wasn't fair."

There was a stone bench by the fountain. They sat holding hands with their backs to the water, looking out over the square.

"It's perfectly fair. I've asked a lot of you. I'm the one who asked you to go into the president's lair and get the seal on the transfer order."

"To rescue your girlfriend."

"My comrade. A woman who risked her life for mine. You and I had something special, Kate. Maybe we still do. God knows, I hope so. But the movement . . . Boldu . . . It has to come first. It's too important."

"Tell me what you need."

"There's a man who I'm afraid could force a confrontation before we are ready. A violent confrontation that we would be likely to lose. Even if we won, it would only be at a terrible price."

"Who is it?"

"His name is Talant Malinin. He is the current head of the Special Police. And a sociopath."

"Hmm. That does sound like a problem."

"The moment when we first take the square will be the moment of maximum vulnerability. Malinin will know it. And he won't hesitate to use the Special Police and their heavy weapons to crush us like bugs."

"How do I fit into this?"

"Malinin has a deputy. An ethnic Kyrgyz named Davron Kayrat uluu. He's young and thoughtful and—we believe—sympathetic to our cause. At least that's what his sister thinks, and she's one of us. It would be better for us if Kayrat uluu was the head of the Special Police rather than Malinin."

That Malinin's deputy appended the suffix "uluu" to his name was itself a signifier. Like "Mac" in Scotland, it meant "son of" and was part of a Kyrgyz tradition more common in the countryside than in the Russified capital.

"You want me to fire him?"

"In a manner of speaking. We want you to start a rumor that

Malinin is planning a palace coup. Eraliev lives in fear of ending his life like Caligula or Pertinax. Murdered by his own Praetorians. If word gets back to him that the Special Police are plotting against the palace, Malinin will be out and Kayrat uluu will be in. He will give us the time we need."

Kate shook her head.

"What makes you think I can do something like that?" she asked incredulously.

"I think you can do anything. Put the word out in your diplomatic circles. You know that the GKNB listens to every word you say on the phone. Call people and talk about it in a coded fashion that would be easy enough for them to understand. Leave them the dots to connect themselves. They'll believe it that way."

The hairs on the back of Ruslan's neck jumped to attention. Something had tripped his subliminal alarm bells. He had learned from experience to take those warnings from his subconscious seriously. The feelings of fear emanating from deep in his lizard brain. The fear of being hunted. Moving cautiously. Carefully. He scanned the square the way that Murzaev had taught him, casually but systematically, looking for something that seemed out of place.

There! By the gates to the Presidential Palace. A man standing by himself with a camera around his neck. Even at fifty meters, Ruslan could see that there was something about the man that did not feel right. In a time when just about everyone carried around a minimum of eight megapixels of photographic resolution in a shirt pocket, this was a bulky SLR with a telephoto lens. Who needs that kind of power? The man was wearing a dark suit and a long black jacket cut like a trench coat. He was taking pictures of the square, zooming in on the Manas statue and the museum. Tourist photos. But he did not look like a tourist.

To the right of Ruslan and Kate, on another park bench, an older Asiatic man wearing a white felt *kalpak* sat reading the newspaper. The light was fading now and Ruslan judged that it was too dark to read comfortably, but the pensioner—whose eyes were almost certainly not what they once were—seemed not to mind as he studied the paper in his hand. A nearby coffee shop with a view of at least a part of the square would have offered ample light, but the man seemed to prefer the bench, where, among other things, he had a clear view of Ruslan and Kate.

"What is it?" Kate asked. "Do you see something?"

"Time to go," Ruslan answered.

"Is someone watching us?"

"Maybe. Or maybe I'm growing paranoid. But paranoids live longer. Follow me."

"Where to?"

"Someplace safe."

Ruslan stood up from the bench with a studied, casual air and offered Kate his hand. He led her toward Erkindik Avenue, a busy street that ran north-south parallel to the square. At Murzaev's insistence, Boldu had acquired a couple of small apartments scattered across the city that could serve as safe houses. They did not use the apartments for regular meetings. They were held in reserve for emergencies. But if he and Kate were being followed, Ruslan reasoned, than this situation was awfully close to clearing that bar. It depended on who was following them.

He risked a quick glance over his shoulder. Cameraman was pointing the telephoto lens right at them.

Damn it. He was almost certainly GKNB. It seemed that they had grown a tail. It would have to be cut off. His hope was that they were following Kate, not him. If this was routine surveillance of an

American diplomat, there might be no more than two or three operatives watching them. If the security service had even an inkling that she was meeting with Seitek—Public Enemy Number One—there would be hundreds of them and he was as good as dead.

Murzaev had taught them all the basic principles of surveillance detection and evasion. Ruslan had not had many opportunities to practice, but now seemed like a pretty good time.

He and Kate turned north on Yusup Abdrahmanov Street. It was growing dark rapidly and the streetlights came on as Bishkek transitioned from afternoon to evening.

"Stop here for a minute," Ruslan said as they walked past a bakery with a window display of French-style cakes and pastries. The lights on the inside made it impossible, however, to get any kind of reflection off the glass, and Ruslan risked a quick look behind them. He caught a glimpse of a figure in a dark jacket stepping out of one of the pools of light cast by the streetlamps and then back into the shadows. It was too brief and too far back for Ruslan to be able to judge with certainty that it was Cameraman.

A family passed Ruslan and Kate, walking in the direction of Ala-Too Square, a multigenerational gaggle out for an evening stroll. None paid them the slightest attention.

Ruslan and Kate continued north, turning right onto Frunze Street. A middle-aged woman stood on the corner looking at a display of clothing in a store window. Judging by the tight skirts and crop tops on the mannequins, the store was targeting a much younger demographic. Maybe she was shopping for a daughter or a niece, but maybe she was not interested in the clothes at all.

Passing a narrow alley, Ruslan pulled Kate by the hand into the sheltering darkness. This was the old part of the city. The alleyway street was cobbled and the stones were slick with the greasy residue from the trash cans lined up along the walls. The air was still and stank of rotten food. A fat rat skittered behind a pile of plastic garbage bags. Ruslan and Kate were pressed up against the wall in the deep shadow cast by a commercial-grade dumpster.

Kate leaned in close and whispered softly in his ear.

"You always did know how to show a girl a good time."

She kissed his cheek. Ruslan squeezed her hand.

"Stay still."

They watched the entrance to the alley and marked the passers-by. A pair of young men talking animatedly about football. A group of women carrying shopping bags. A boy and a girl holding hands. A shopkeeper wearing an apron.

"Let's keep moving," Kate suggested in a whisper.

"A little longer."

An elderly man in a white *kalpak*, walking by himself, passed the alley entrance. He looked into the gloom in their direction, but he did not stop or turn off the main street. It was a different jacket, but Ruslan thought it was the pensioner from the square.

"We need to get off the streets," Ruslan said quietly.

"Where?"

"Not far."

He led Kate down the dark alley. They moved slowly so as not to make noise banging into trash cans. The alley ended at Gogol Street.

Ruslan scanned the street in both directions. He did not see anything that would have indicated GKNB surveillance.

"Let's move. Not too slow. Not too fast."

After twenty minutes of zigging and zagging through the winding streets of the old city, they reached their destination. Ruslan was reasonably certain that they had slipped the surveillance coverage.

"In here," he said.

The apartment building was old and had seen better days. The mailboxes in the entryway were rusted and buckled and the paint was peeling. The boxes were labeled with numbers, but no names. The lock on box number 14 was broken. On the inside lip overhanging the door of the box Ruslan's fingers brushed over a piece of thick tape. Carefully he peeled it off and removed the keys that had been left there.

The first key opened the door to the building. It was dark inside and Ruslan had to search for the switch that illuminated the stairwell. It was three flights up to number 14, which turned out to be a simple one-bedroom apartment with a sitting room and a galley-style kitchen.

Before they turned on the lights, Ruslan made sure that the heavy curtains were drawn tight. Paranoia saves lives.

There was a couch and two tattered armchairs set around a low wooden table. The floors were parquet. They might once have been nice, but they were now so stained and scratched as to be good for little more than firewood. The walls were bare and mottled with the plaster scars of repairs performed with a minimum of skill and enthusiasm. A single bulb dangling from the ceiling was the only source of light.

"Charming," Kate said, and although her tone was jaunty, Ruslan could see that her face was flushed and her breathing was quick and shallow. She was scared. So was he.

"We revolutionaries have to be careful about cash flow. And Murzaev wanted a place that was both safe and low profile. He doesn't care much about the niceties."

"No," Kate answered. "He certainly doesn't." There was something about the tone of her response that caught Ruslan's attention, a negative reaction to the mention of Murzaev. But he sensed that she was in no mood to be interrogated.

"Let's see if the spymaster remembered to stock the fridge."

There were two things in the refrigerator, a jar of Chinese mustard and a bottle of Russian vodka. Ruslan found two glasses in a cupboard and wiped them clean with a hand towel.

"All of life's necessities," he said as he set the bottle and glasses down on the coffee table. He poured a stiff slug of vodka into the glasses and they toasted in the Russian style, looking each other in the eyes as they downed the shot in a single gulp. It was cheap vodka and it burned Ruslan's throat on the way down. Kate coughed and her eyes watered.

"That's awful," she said.

"If it were good, do you think someone would have left it here?"

"Maybe it gets better as you drink it."

"Everything does."

The next thing he knew, Kate was in his arms and he was kissing her mouth and her neck and the hollow of her throat. The years that they had been apart simply evaporated. The sensation of touching her was simultaneously new and familiar. And it was intoxicating. She pressed her body up against his. She bit his earlobe gently and whispered to him with a fierce urgency.

"Put your hands on me."

He did.

They undressed each other as they made their way slowly to the bedroom.

Tomorrow there would be a war to fight. And Ruslan's own desires would be subordinate to the needs of those who looked to him to lead. But tonight belonged to him and Kate. And all they could do was make the night last for as long as possible.

Tomorrow would take care of itself.

# 20

"Kate, he'd like to see you."

Rosemary did not need to explain who "he" was. This was an embassy and he was the American ambassador.

"When?"

"Right now."

"Okay. I'll be there in thirty seconds."

"No. He wants to meet in the Cone."

"What's going on?"

"Better you hear it from him."

Every embassy had a secure room for sensitive conversations. And every embassy had its own unique name for it. In Cuba, it had been the Tank. Other missions called it the Bubble or the Star Chamber or the Bunker. Here in Bishkek, some long-ago officer had christened their room "the Cone," after the Cone of Silence in the old *Get Smart*

TV show. Its name aside, the Cone was almost indistinguishable from the Tank.

Kate was evidently the last to arrive. Arguably the four most powerful and influential people in the embassy had gotten there before her. The ambassador, Crespo, Ball, and the regional security officer, a one-time Chicago narcotics detective named Frank Barrone who saw himself somewhat dramatically as the last line of defense between a helpless embassy community and the rampaging Golden Horde of Batu Khan.

They were seated abreast on one side of the table. Kate's seat was directly across from them. There was no uncertainty about what this was. An interrogation. That her inquisitors were all white middle-aged men in dark suits only made that all the more evident.

She looked to her uncle for some indication of what this was about. But he had a diplomat's self-control and his expression was impossible to read.

Steeling herself for whatever was to come, Kate took the seat opposite the ambassador and folded her hands in front of her on the table.

"Thanks for coming on such short notice," her uncle began.

"I didn't know I had a choice."

"You always have choices to make, Kate. We all do. The challenge is to make the right ones."

There was something sad, Kate thought, underlying that statement, but nothing specific, nothing she could place. It was ineffable.

"We want to talk to you about Boldu," Crespo said unnecessarily. What else could this be about? Kate's progress to date in preparing the embassy's annual labor report?

"Have you been entirely transparent with us about your interactions with the organization's leadership?" Brass picked up from Crespo as smoothly as an Olympic baton pass.

"And have you reported on all your personal contacts with Kyrgyz nationals as required by the FAM?" Barrone added his voice to the chorus of accusation and innuendo, citing the provisions in the *Foreign Affairs Manual* that entitled the State Department to demand visibility into an officer's personal life when stationed abroad.

"What are we talking about here?" Kate asked, genuinely uncertain.

Crespo set a plain buff folder on the table and slid it across. Kate had a reasonably good idea as to what was inside. She looked at it as she might a poisonous snake. Nothing good could come of touching it.

"Have you been following me around, Larry?"

"Should I be?"

Kate opened the folder and inside found what she had been expecting. Pictures of her and Ruslan together. Walking arm in arm in Ala-Too Square. Sitting side by side on the bench by the fountain. Kissing.

It was a profound violation of her personal space.

"Those were your guys," Kate said, looking at the station chief accusingly. "Short hair. Black coat. And the pensioner with the *kalpak*. You set them on me like dogs."

Crespo held up his hands as though warding off a blow. "Not my guys," he insisted. "You'd never make my guys. They're professionals." The look he shot in Barrone's direction was both fleeting and subtle, more an unconscious micro-expression than a considered response. It was enough.

"Your people then, Frank. The surveillance detection team maybe. Why would you do that?"

"Because I asked him to," Brass said, his voice cold and sharp.

"To what end?"

"I had reason to believe that there were things you weren't telling us about your involvement with the leadership of Boldu. That for whatever reason, you knew more than you were willing to say."

"You are aware, Ms. Hollister, of the regulations in the *Foreign Affairs Manual* describing your responsibilities to report any and all close and continuing contact with foreign nationals?"

"I am."

"Would you say this qualifies as close and continuing?" Barrone stabbed a long, crooked finger onto the picture of Ruslan kissing Kate on the mouth.

"Not yet," Kate said defiantly.

Barrone reached into a briefcase sitting on the floor next to his chair and pulled out another photograph. This one was the apartment building where Kate and Ruslan had spent the night together. Apparently, they had not been as successful in shaking their tail as Ruslan had thought.

"Do you want to reconsider that answer?"

"No."

"Are you involved in an intimate relationship with a foreign national? And is there a reason you neglected to report that information to my office?"

The ambassador made a quick cutting gesture with his right hand, silencing the RSO.

"Kate, who's the man in the photograph? Is he Boldu? Is this Seitek?"

If her uncle had asked her when they were alone—as family—she might have told him the truth. She wanted to tell someone, to unburden herself of what she was being asked to carry. But with Brass,

Crespo, and Barrone lined up across from her, worming their way into her private thoughts, there was only one possible answer.

She laughed.

"Is that what you think? That I've fallen under the spell of the Great Seitek and I'm ready to play Bonnie to his Clyde. Helen to his Paris."

"The thought did cross our mind," Crespo said dryly.

"You're the one who told me that there was no Seitek, that he was a composite rather than a man."

"There's always an element of uncertainty in intelligence," Crespo replied. "I like to hedge my bets. Assuming Seitek is a single individual—and I'll grant you that seems increasingly likely—then I want to know who he is. And I want to know if our interests overlap enough that we can be of use to each other. So, the question is, do you know more than you're telling us?"

"I've told you everything I know about Boldu," Kate insisted. "The man in the photograph is an old boyfriend. We have renewed our . . . friendship. And before you ask, Frank, yes, I am familiar with the reporting requirements in the FAM and the definition of close and continuing. If I sleep with him once, it's none of your business. If I sleep with him again, I have to fill out your damn contact reporting form. If it becomes necessary, I assure you that you'll be among the first to know. And I hope that will satisfy your somewhat prurient interest in my social life. Maybe you should get out more. Voyeurism is really something of a disorder."

Barrone's face turned bright red with suppressed anger. Kate knew that what she had just done was stupid, and she would do it again in a heartbeat.

"You're quite sure about that answer?" Crespo asked. "That the man in the photograph is not connected to Boldu?"

"Quite sure, yes."

"That's interesting, because I had our people do a little drill down into that building. Most of the apartments are deeded to families. All simple and normal. But one of them—number fourteen I believe—is registered to a shell company based in Dushanbe that is little more than a post office box. The ownership structure of the company is opaque, all of it drawn up by some clever lawyers. Who does that kind of thing, Kate? In my experience, it's a pretty short list. Mafia bosses, big-time narco-traffickers, and spies occupy the top spots. I read your report about your meeting with the Boldu leadership. Askar Murzaev is a name we know. He would be more than capable of setting up a shell game like this. Seems like quite a coincidence."

Kate was silent.

"Who is the boy, Kate?" the ambassador asked gently. "What's his name?"

Kate would gladly surrender what was left of her career before giving Ruslan's name to the three-headed monster her uncle had brought to the meeting. She did not at all like how easy it was becoming for her to lie, but one falsehood seemed to require two or three more to sustain it. Her father had warned her about that. It would be best, she understood, to stick as close to the truth and to say as little as possible.

"His name is Grigoriy Vetochkin," Kate said. "We dated briefly in high school. He left for Moscow to go to university. I didn't realize he was back in Bishkek. Mutual friends put us back in touch. We had lunch. And I had sex with him." Kate was looking daggers at Barrone. "Three times that night if you're curious, Frank, so maybe I should have filled out your form after all. Sorry about that."

The stricken look on her uncle's face made Kate feel guilty for the way she had twisted the knife, but the RSO had it coming.

"What does the virile Mr. Vetochkin do for a living?" Crespo asked her.

"He has a law practice in Moscow. He's here looking at the possibility of opening up a branch in Bishkek."

Kate wanted to keep her answers short and simple. She was making this all up as she went along and she would have to remember the lies. There really was a Grigoriy Vetochkin. He had been a year ahead of her at ISB. And he had had an unrequited crush on Kate. She remembered that he had gone to Lomonosov University to study law. Elements of the story at least would check out if Crespo decided to investigate. It was the best she could do.

"What kind of law?"

"I don't know. That wasn't really what we were talking about."

There was an awkward silence as her inquisitors looked for a face-saving way to end the second interrogation she had endured in the last three days.

"If you're going to see this guy again, you'll have to come by my office and fill out the proper forms." It sounded terribly lame and Barrone knew it.

"Sure thing, Frank. We all have our job to do."


Kate needed to get a message to Ruslan. Fortunately, before they had said their good-byes in the predawn light two days earlier, Kate had insisted on having her own channel. She did not want to communicate with Ruslan through Val and she did not want to wait for some nine-year-old to show up at her apartment with a handwritten note that asked "u awake?" She was nobody's booty call.

Ruslan did not use a phone or e-mail or anything that left electronic footprints. Murzaev knew what the GKNB was capable of, and he insisted on this precaution. Boldu preferred couriers and dead drops, and the movement had friends and supporters in the most unlikely places. There was a newsstand a block and a half from Kate's apartment that was run by an elderly couple who had lost a son to one of the regime's periodic crackdowns on suspected dissidents. A message given to them would move through Boldu's courier system, a branching capillary-like network that ensured the channels of communication remained unpredictable. Ruslan, similarly, could get messages through the kiosk to Kate.

It was not fast, but it was secure.

Kate stopped by the kiosk on her way home from the embassy. She picked a copy of *Chui Baayni*, a weekly newsmagazine with a pro-Eraliev slant, off the rack and dropped two one-hundred-som notes on the counter. The wife was on duty that evening, a heavyset woman in her early sixties with a perm and eyes set so deep in their sockets it was a wonder she could see. They exchanged a few pleasantries, and Kate watched as the woman extracted the folded blue notecard from underneath the bills, slipping it into the front pocket of her apron with the practiced finesse of a stage magician. On the card, Kate had written only: "Need to see you soonest. important." The blue card—which came out of the political-section supply cabinet—meant that it was from Kate and the lower case *i* in important meant that she was not under duress. There was no way of knowing how long it would take the message to reach Ruslan and how long it would be before he could respond. Ruslan had told her that he thought it would take less than forty-eight hours, but there were too many variables to be confident about that.

Back at her apartment, Kate changed from a suit to a black cocktail dress. She picked out a gold bracelet and a necklace with a ruby solitaire from the modest collection of jewelry she had brought with her from Cuba. After a moment's reflection, she matched her outfit with a pair of Jimmy Choo pumps with three-inch heels. The Swedish ambassador was a tall man and she wanted to equalize their height to compensate for their unequal rank.

Kate checked herself out in the bathroom mirror. The dress was low cut, a little on the risqué side for a diplomatic function, perhaps, but only enough to draw attention rather than criticism. She freshened her makeup. The scar on her temple was now little more than a thin white line, a reminder that she would carry forever of a particular choice, one she did not regret. A little foundation hid it reasonably well.

In her clutch, Kate carried her embassy ID, a hundred dollars in Kyrgyz som, and the engraved invitation to a reception at the Swedish residence. She had met the ambassador a week earlier at a roundtable on press freedom organized by a Kyrgyz human rights group. Anders Larssen had seemed quite taken with her, and the woman who had organized the meeting later warned Kate that the ambassador was a notorious skirt chaser.

The invitation to the Swedish reception had arrived by courier the morning after the roundtable. It was a perfect opportunity to make good on her promise to Ruslan.

The cab dropped her off in front of the residence, an elegant villa in one of Bishkek's most upscale neighborhoods. It was a warm evening and the party spilled out of the house into the gardens where the guests clustered in small groups drinking and smoking and gossiping. Gossip was the fuel of the diplomatic engine. Almost by definition, it was more valuable than news, which belonged to everyone. Gossip was personal and private, and the race to know something first was the way that diplomats kept score.

The crowd was a mix of internationals and Kyrgyz, with the local guest list seeming to favor independent journalists, academics, and activists of various stripes over government officials. It was a fair enough reflection of Swedish foreign policy. There were also a number of attractive young women with long legs and short skirts. Here the connection to Swedish national interests seemed somewhat tenuous.

Ambassador Larssen noticed her almost as soon as she stepped into the foyer, and Kate thought he seemed very much like a leopard springing out of the tall grass onto an impala. An ambush predator. Inside of thirty seconds he was standing just a little too close to her with a glass of prosecco in each hand.

"So very glad you could make it this evening, Ms. Hollister."

Kate took the glass he had extended to her.

"Thank you for having me, Ambassador. You have a lovely home."

"Please call me Anders."

"And I'm Kate."

Kate let him chat her up. Anders Larssen may have been a rogue and a womanizer, but he was charming and witty. And while he was about twenty years too old for her, he was not unattractive. The ambassador had been in Bishkek for more than two years and he was knowledgeable enough about currents and tensions within the Eraliev government to be interesting. Kate let him lead, but she was looking for an opening as well.

"Eraliev certainly seems to fear Boldu and the ever mysterious Seitek," Larssen said about ten minutes into a conversation that was closer to a monologue. "But he has no real reason to. Boldu's greatest victories have been little more than university pranks. The security forces are loyal, and there's no threat to his rule as long as he maintains their backing."

"Are you so certain of their loyalty?" Kate asked. "Is Eraliev?" There was just enough insinuation of inside information to catch Larssen's attention.

"Is that really a question, or do you know something?"

In a heartbeat, the ambassador had transitioned seamlessly from would-be Don Juan to gossipy fishmonger's wife. Just about anywhere in the world, America's diplomatic service had a well-earned and carefully cultivated reputation for being among the first to know vital information. The Scandinavian services, among others, actually trained their junior diplomats to make friends with their American colleagues, who typically had access to host government officials well beyond what they could hope to achieve. Now, Larssen sensed that Kate knew something that would be useful to him, and he wanted to have it. This was how the game worked.

"Well," Kate began carefully. "I understand that there have been questions raised about Talant Malinin's ambitions."

"The chief of the Special Police."

"None other. Malinin has position and influence, but like all of them he's hungry for more. There are rumors of a palace coup, and Malinin reportedly has designs on the top job himself. Eraliev may have more to fear from his own Praetorians than from the democrats."

"And what's the president's likely response to this threat?"

"A purge, I would expect. An *ishembi* night massacre." Kate used the Kyrgyz word for "Saturday." It was a diplomat's joke, layered and complex and requiring both a knowledge of American history and an understanding of the Kyrgyz language. That it was not especially funny was irrelevant. Kate was flattering the ambassador's intelligence. He likely knew that, but he liked it nonetheless.

A few minutes later, the ambassador took his leave. He needed to mingle with the guests. He shook Kate's hand, but his attentions were considerably less focused than they had been when she had walked through the door. The only thing a typical diplomat cared for more than sex and booze was brokering information. And Kate had given him something irresistible.

Over the course of the next hour, Kate found a few more marks with whom to drop hints about Malinin's sharpening the long knives. She was confident that Larssen was doing the same.

Toward the end of the evening, as Kate was out in the garden sipping too-sweet chardonnay from a clunky IKEA wineglass, a somewhat drunken official from the Kyrgyz Ministry of the Interior confided in her that he had heard rumors about the chief of the Special Police being under surveillance for suspicion of disloyalty. Kate listened to him with the open admiration he expected from a young woman as "one in the know." If he thought that this display of insider knowledge was going to result in sexual conquest, however, he was to be disappointed.

Kate had everything she needed. A government official had told her something that was simultaneously salacious and relevant to American national interests. She had an obligation to report it to Washington in a front-channel cable.

Even if the cable was never sent, it would be read by Brass, among others. And what the defense attaché knew, Crandle was certain to learn about as well. And what Crandle knew, Kate had increasingly come to suspect, would eventually make its way to the ear of Eraliev, President for Life of the Kyrgyz Republic.

# 21

The Swedish ambassador made an excellent stalking horse. And the story about the chief of the Special Police falling under suspicion for organizing a palace coup was sufficiently titillating and credible that Kate knew it would spread like kudzu through the diplomatic community. With each retelling it would pick up a new detail or embellishment, often keyed to highlighting the importance or acumen of the individual telling the story. And like a game of Chinese whispers, there was no knowing for certain what would come out on the far end.

It was a good start, but it would not be enough, so the morning after the Swedish party Kate called an old friend of her father's. Marat Jalilov had been a crusading journalist at the dawn of Kyrgyzstan's independence from the USSR. His enthusiasm for the republic was ultimately crushed by the oppressive regime that rose to power, and Marat spent the next quarter century in and out of trouble with the government. He was a gadfly with a serious drinking problem, but he was also recognized around the world as a former prisoner of conscience, and it was cheaper and easier for the authorities to tolerate Marat than to eliminate him.

It was almost eleven, but Marat sounded as if Kate had woken him when he picked up the phone.

"Allo?"

"Marat? It's Kate Hollister from the American embassy, Vergil's daughter." Kate spoke in Kyrgyz. Marat was a nationalist who had preferred to speak Kyrgyz exclusively long before it was the norm in Bishkek's power circles.

It took a moment for Marat's alcohol-soaked synapses to process the information.

"Little Katie? It's been years. I heard that you were back in town. I haven't seen you since—" He stopped awkwardly in mid-sentence.

"The funeral. It's okay, Marat. My father loved you. I'm glad you were there, and you don't need to worry about reminding me of it. I'll never forget."

"He was a great man."

"Thank you. There's a lot we have to catch up on. Can I buy you a cup of coffee this afternoon?" Kate wanted to meet Marat as early in the day as possible to maximize the chance that he would be at least semi-sober.

"I don't see why not. Do you remember that place we used to meet up, your father and I? You came along a few times, if I recall."

"I remember."

"Well, it burned down years ago. You and I will need a new place. There's a decent establishment on Toktogul Street not far from the university called the Augean Stables."

"A café or a bar?" Kate asked suspiciously.

Marat laughed.

"A café. I promise you. Two o'clock?"

"Perfect. See you there."

Marat was twenty minutes late, which was ten minutes early by Central Asian journalist standards. Kate was shocked at how old he looked. It had been nine years since her parents' funeral, but Marat seemed to have aged at least twice that. He was tall and broad but walked with stooped shoulders as though carrying a heavy weight on his back. His shock of white hair had thinned considerably and the flesh around his jawline hung loose and saggy. His eyes were puffy and bloodshot from last night's drinking. The whites were slightly yellowed, and Kate could only imagine the demands Marat had placed on his liver over the years. Journalists in the successor states to the Soviet Union lived hard lives, and Marat's life had been harder than most.

Kate stood to greet him and he enfolded her in a bear hug, kissing her roughly on both cheeks.

"You look beautiful, Katie. So like your mother."

A wave of shame washed over Kate as she thought about how she was about to use and manipulate this man who had loved her father. It was cold and calculating, but it was also in the service of a goal that Marat would have embraced as wholeheartedly as he had just embraced the daughter of his friend.

Here again, it was Uncle Harry's damn values complexity conundrum in operation. Do something wrong to do something right. Choose the lesser evil and hope the ends justify that choice. She understood it. She accepted it. And she was ashamed of herself nonetheless.

"So tell me, how do things look to you?" Kate asked after they ordered coffees. "You always had the best sources in town."

"I did and I do. I may look old, but I haven't slowed down. You've come home at an interesting time, Katie. I know a lot of people are dismissing Boldu as little more than a horsefly on Eraliev's ample rump, but this is the most serious challenge to the regime since Azattyk. And the Boldu leadership seems to have learned something from that experience. Eraliev is afraid of them and he has reason to be. I know some of the people in the movement's leadership . . . or at least I think I do. You might be surprised at the names."

The look he gave Kate was enigmatic but also somehow light-hearted, almost amused. If he knew about Ruslan and the rest of the ISB mafia in Boldu, his sources were indeed more than good.

Kate knew that if she told him something interesting, Marat would use it as trade bait with his sources, and the word would spread on another network that overlapped like a Venn diagram with the diplomatic channels she was working through the Swedish ambassador. It would be an echo chamber. The separate reports seeming to come from independent sources would confirm one another and validate the story. But Kate had to make it interesting.

The waitress brought their coffees and two small bottles of mineral water.

"Is Boldu the only thing Eraliev has to be afraid of?" Kate asked.

"Not at all. The fat prick could have a stroke or a major coronary event any day. God willing."

"What about his own security services?"

"A knife in the back? I haven't heard anything like that."

"I have."

"Who?"

"Malinin."

Marat raised an eyebrow that was so thick it looked like a caterpillar was crawling across his forehead.

"Interesting."

There, Kate thought, was the magic word.

"Ain't it?"

"Tell me more."

Kate did, assuring herself that she had made the only possible choice and hating herself for it at the same time.

After work, Kate stopped at the newsstand. She picked up a copy of *Vecherniy Bishkek* for fifty som. It was the husband on duty tonight. In contrast to his corpulent bride, he was short and slight and the bones in his wrist were clearly visible as he made change, his movements as light and delicate as a bird's.

There was no eye contact, nothing that might give Kate a clue as to whether Ruslan had received her message, whether he had been able to respond.

Back at her apartment, Kate leafed quickly through the paper. Tucked inside the sports section, she found a small scrap of paper with a few words written in Ruslan's spidery scrawl. It was a little more than an address and a time: 164 Serova St. Block 13. Apartment 11. 24:00. As an additional layer of security, Kate and Ruslan had agreed on a simple code. They would subtract two from every number in any message, meaning that Ruslan would meet her at 162 Serova St., Block 11, Apartment 9, at 10 o'clock. It wasn't much, but Ruslan told her that little bits added together could make a big difference.

Kate felt a rush of excitement at the prospect of seeing him. It was a feeling she had not had in so long, she had almost forgotten what it was like. Her face was flush and warm, her pulse elevated, her palms damp. She wanted to rush to the address in Ruslan's note, but it was only seven o'clock.

And she was cautious. Barrone had tracked her to their last meeting. It would be potentially disastrous if he were to do so again. It was even possible that the RSO's surveillance detection team was parked out in front of her apartment right now on the assumption that Kate's response to the grilling she had endured would be to do exactly what she had done before, set up a meeting with the man that the embassy security team suspected might be Seitek.

If she dashed out into the night, lovestruck and heedless, there was a good chance that she would be leading her embassy minders to another Boldu safe house. This time they might have equipment that would allow them to listen in on their conversation, lasers that could read the vibrations off the windowpanes of the apartment, or something even more exotic on loan from Crespo's office.

Kate waited. She did not rush to the window straining against the dark to spot the men who might be out there watching her. She would assume that they were there and act accordingly. Fortunately, Kate had just the thing to help pass the time and focus her thoughts. The living room was dominated by an older but lovingly maintained baby grand piano that she had bought from a local dealer and had had delivered the week before. The Kyrgyz took their music seriously and it had not been difficult to find a quality instrument she could afford. It was a German mark, Bechstein, polished sleek and black. Most of the pianos on the local market were Russian made. Kate steered clear of those. Ironically, the Russians, who produced many of the world's finest pianists, also produced some of the world's worst pianos.

Kate sat and played from memory. Rachmaninoff and Roberto Fonseca. Chopin and Hilario Durán. The disciplined act of playing helped calm her emotions and focus her thoughts. She played for an hour and a half before taking a quick shower and changing into jeans and a soft gray sweater.

It was twenty minutes after nine when Kate left her apartment. She took the stairs down to the basement and used the service door at the back of the building that opened out onto a narrow alley. The alley took her almost a full block from her building before intersecting with Mosovskaya Street, which even this late was busy and well lit. Kate slipped into the crowd and walked another six blocks before grabbing a cab and taking it to within two blocks of the address Ruslan had given her. She had not been able to spot anyone following her. But Kate was aware that she lacked the training and experience to be certain of this.

The apartment building was older and unprepossessing. There were hundreds just like it throughout the city, a monument to Soviet design. The front door clicked open when Kate hit the buzzer for apartment 9. The stairwell was clean and the lights worked.

Ruslan opened the door to the apartment wearing black jeans, a white shirt, and two days of stubble.

There was so much she wanted to tell him, but without so much as a hello she found herself in Ruslan's arms, kissing him hungrily. Greedily. As though they had been apart for years.

Ruslan propped himself up on one arm and used his free hand to trace the gently curved form lying next to him. Kate's skin was warm to the touch, and Ruslan had spent the last couple of hours exploring every square centimeter of it. With some chagrin, he knew that if he were magically granted one wish right now it would not be for a free and democratic Kyrgyzstan. It would be for time to stop. For this moment of clarity and purity to last forever. Was it possible, he wondered, that he was falling in love so fast, or was it that he had never fallen out of love with Kate Hollister? Had he been carrying her with him for more than a decade? And was that the source of the weight that he had felt on his heart? The reason why the women who had been so numerous had meant so little to him?

Kate made a contented sound, like a low purr, as Ruslan stroked her hip and thigh and she pressed her body against his in invitation.

He was tempted, but there would be time for that later.

"Talk first," he said.

She kissed him.

"You sure?"

"Absolutely," he lied. "I am a committed revolutionary. Sacrifice comes with the territory."

Kate laughed and her laugh was familiar, reminding him of easier days when the calculus midterm was his most serious worry. She sat up in bed, letting the sheets fall to her lap. She had a dancer's body, strong and lean.

"You said you needed to see me. I am more than overjoyed to see you, but your note made it sound like something was wrong."

Kate's expression was troubled, almost guilty.

"I know who Cameraman and the Pensioner are, or at least who they work for."

"Who?"

"Us."

"The Americans?"

Kate nodded.

"They work for the embassy security office. They must have followed me to Ala-Too Square."

"Why would they do that?"

"Because both the CIA and the Defense Department think I'm

holding back on them. That I know more about Boldu than I've been willing to say."

"The identity of the Great Seitek?"

"Pretty much. Our defense attaché is an air force pilot who goes by Brass Ball. No, seriously. That's his name. Brass is obsessed with you. And he's much too close to the government for my liking. I don't trust him to keep a secret."

"So what did you tell him about the picture? That I'm just some guy you met in the park and kissed? That wouldn't be the dumbest thing the CIA has ever believed."

"Fair enough. But I told them the truth, or most of it. I said that I was hooking up with my old high school boyfriend . . . Grigoriy Vetochkin."

Now it was Ruslan's turn to laugh.

"Grigor? What ever happened to him?"

"I have no idea. And I'm hoping that they don't care. It was the best I could do on the spot, but my story has holes you could drive a truck through. I don't know if it's going to hold up for long. And if it doesn't—"

"Then they may very well figure out who I am." Ruslan finished her sentence.

Kate looked stricken.

"I'm sorry, Ruslan. This is all my fault. I should have spotted them following me and not come to meet you at Ala-Too."

Ruslan reached out to stroke her hair and rest his fingertips lightly on her shoulder.

"You're a diplomat, Kate, and a musician. Not a spy. You couldn't possibly have known they were tracking you. This was always a risk. And if someone needs to learn who I am, better it be the CIA than the GKNB."

"Are you sure there's a difference?"

"There has to be."

"I'm worried, Ruslan. This focus on Boldu and on you is intense and hard to explain. I don't think they're going to let it go easily."

"So you're worried, eh? Well, we Kyrgyz know how to handle worries."

Ruslan got up and padded to the kitchen, returning a few minutes later with two glasses of vodka. Murzaev had evidently made sure that each safe house was stocked with the essentials.

They clinked glasses and drained them in a single gulp.

"Better?" he asked.

"It's a start."

He put his arm around her and Kate snuggled in close, laying her head on his chest.

"So what do we do?" she asked. "Wait and see?"

"I don't think so."

"Then what?"

"The plan that I told you about for occupying Ala-Too, our own little Maidan revolution?"

"Yes."

"We need to accelerate it. We don't sit and wait to be hunted. We go after them."

"Are you sure about that?" Kate asked, and Ruslan could hear the concern in her voice. He knew she was thinking of what had happened to Azattyk, to her own family.

"Who can be sure about anything?"

"The biggest thing you've tried to date has involved no more than thirty people. To take over Ala-Too Square, to challenge the regime, you're going to need hundreds, thousands maybe. Does Boldu have that many followers?"

"Boldu? No. But I know where I can get them."

"You're going to order them from Amazon? Do you get free shipping with that?"

Ruslan laughed.

"Too slow."

"Where then?"

"The clans."

Kate cocked her head. "From the villages?"

"From the whole countryside."

Kate looked skeptical . . . and beautiful. Ruslan leaned over and kissed her neck lightly.

"You're Kyrgyz, Kate. But you're a city girl. You don't know the countryside. We are still, at heart, a nomadic people. Clan identity is a serious matter. Even the word 'Kyrgyz' means 'we are forty,' as in the forty clans unified by Manas. Eraliev is not just the president. He's the head of the Sarybagysh, who owe their privileged position to the patronage of Joseph Stalin. The other clans are jealous, and the Solto and Buguu and Adygine and Kara-Kyrgyz are looking for a chance to hit the political reset button. The Buguu, for one, were the most powerful clan until the bloody purges of the nineteen thirties. They haven't forgotten."

"This was always your plan, wasn't it? Focus Eraliev on the threat close at hand—students and democracy activists in the city—so he doesn't see the danger from the countryside. That's what you were doing with your pranks and spray paint. It's like the way a stage magician uses misdirection."

"You're pretty smart. Bishkek is the anvil. It's the clans that are the hammer. And we've been working on this for the better part of a year. I think they're ready. Do you know how Cortés, with five hundred men and a dozen horses, managed to conquer the Aztec empire?"

"Guns and steel."

"That didn't hurt. The key thing, however, was local allies, all the other peoples that the Aztecs had kept down and exploited. Cortés gave them a rallying point, but it was the Aztecs' own subjects who brought them down. We can do it here too."

"Can the other clans really challenge the Sarybagysh? They're so much smaller."

"Individually, that's true. But there are dozens of clans and they are organized into three 'wings.' The Sarybagysh dominate one wing. The Adygine lead another. The third wing, the Ichkilik, is the most diverse. Some of the clans in that wing aren't even Kyrgyz. We will need to mobilize both the Adygine and the Ichkilik if we are going to have a chance. Murzaev has close ties to the Ichkilik. My job is the Adygine."

"When will you be ready?"

"Soon. Very soon."

Ruslan's tone was calm and confident, his voice level and even. That was for Kate's benefit. He had no idea whether the clans were really ready, who would answer the call when it came. But there was only one way to find out.

# 22

Kate left the next morning before dawn, sneaking into her apartment building through the back door just in case Barrone's people or the GKNB were watching the front entrance. She was simultaneously exhausted and exhilarated.

At the office, Kate felt dreamy and detached from a combination of sleep deficit and what she realized was an emotional state dangerously close to love. How could that happen so fast? she wondered. It was as though she and Ruslan had hit the pause button when they were eighteen, and it took only the lightest of touches for the music to start playing again.

Her cubicle mate noticed that something was off.

"You okay, Kate?" Gabby asked about halfway through the day, leaning over the low partition that separated their work stations.

"Hmm? Oh yeah, never better."

"You've been sitting there for forty-five minutes without touching the keyboard or picking up a piece of paper, looking at the ceiling. What are you doing, playing chess in your head?"

"I'm thinking, Gabby. I need the practice."

She saw her uncle only once that day, walking down the hall talking animatedly to the embassy management counselor, an African American woman who had taken her Taiwanese husband's name and was now Carol Zhang. Par for the course in the Foreign Service. The ambassador had nodded at Kate absentmindedly as he walked past, paying her no more attention than he would have any of the hundreds of others who worked in his embassy, as if their meeting in the Cone the other day had never happened.

Kate left work early and took advantage of the comfortably crisp weather to walk back to her apartment. She left her car in the embassy lot, planning to get a good run in the next morning and finish up at the embassy. She could shower in the basement gym and change into one of the outfits that she kept in the supply closet.

The walk helped Kate clear her head and focus on what was going to happen next. Ruslan had explained his plan for occupying Ala-Too Square and forcing a Maidan-like standoff with the government. He was confident that the regime was weaker than it seemed. Brittle. Vulnerable. Kate was not so sure.

"What happens if the security services open fire on the protestors?" she asked.

"They won't," Ruslan had promised her.

What Kate knew about Boldu's plans was precisely the kind of thing that the United States government paid her to learn . . . and report. But she had no intention of writing up what Ruslan had told her as a cable or a memo. Crandle and Brass could not be trusted to keep the secret, and if Eraliev knew about the threat he would move quickly to crush it. She thought about telling her uncle, but she was uncertain about what he might do with the information, whom he might tell. Kate was aware that she was picking a side, drifting seemingly inexorably into the Boldu camp and violating her oath as a foreign service officer. Her professional responsibilities were clear, but so was the right thing to do. If it cost Kate her career, that would be a small enough price to pay for freedom for Kyrgyzstan and, if she was being honest, revenge on Eraliev.

Kate stopped at the newsstand on the way home, not really expecting that Ruslan would have left her a message quite so soon after their tryst, but not entirely unhopeful. The wife was on duty this evening, and Kate's pulse quickened when she placed her copy of the *Times of Central Asia* near the register—and out of sight—while making change. Sure enough, back at her apartment, Kate found a small square of translucent onionskin paper with a note that told her to be at the corner of Ochakovskaya and Patrice Lumumba at nine-thirty.

Kate should have been overjoyed. But there was one problem. The handwriting was not Ruslan's.


So if the note was not from Ruslan, then who was it from? Was this a trap of some kind? And did that mean that Ruslan was already in the Pit at Prison Number One, surrendering secrets like Boldu's network of newsstand messengers a little bit at a time as the Georgian Torquemada exercised his dark inquisitor's arts?

There was no one to ask for either information or advice. Kate thought fleetingly of using the phone Murzaev had given her. It was sitting like a brick at the bottom of her handbag. She quickly dismissed the idea. That was for genuine life-and-death moments.

The decision she was faced with was largely binary. She could show up at the appointed time and place or not. Kate knew immediately that she would be there.

The hours until nine-thirty crawled by as her anxieties expanded to fill the void in her knowledge. She tried to play but could not feel the music. The Mozart concerto she attempted sounded flat and dull. "Paseo Iluminado" by Cuban jazz great Gonzalo Rubalcaba was, to her expert ear, cacophonous and atonal.

She took a shower and changed, more to pass the time than because she needed to.

At the appointed hour, she was standing as instructed on the corner of Ochakovskaya and Patrice Lumumba. Waiting. Unsure of whom she was meeting or why. It was hard for Kate to know how to dress for the occasion. She wore black jeans and a short jacket. The boots she had chosen had low heels in case she needed to run and steel caps in the toes in case she needed to defend herself. The can of pepper spray in her purse was wholly inadequate for any actually dangerous situation. But it was better than nothing, she reasoned.

The neighborhood was more commercial than residential. After business hours, there were few people on the streets and traffic was light. An older Chinese model caterpillar bus roared past, belching a noxious cloud of diesel fumes.

At 9:35, a metallic silver late-model BMW pulled up to the curb. The passenger side door opened. Shaking her head slightly at the risk she was taking, Kate got in the car.

"Hello, Kate."

Hamid Ismailov was behind the wheel, wearing a black leather jacket. He did not look happy to see her.

The BMW pulled smoothly away from the curb.

"What's going on, Hamid? What happened?"

Kate felt an icy stab of fear for Ruslan.

"Not yet. Not here."

Hamid offered nothing more. Kate knew he did not trust her, and she had to admit that she did not entirely trust him.

After about fifteen minutes on mostly backstreets, Hamid pulled into an underground parking garage. This part of Bishkek was all but deserted at night. The garage itself was dark and empty. Kate's fear for Ruslan's safety expanded to include herself. Revolutionaries were notoriously fratricidal. And although he was less bulky than he had been in high school, Hamid was still far stronger than she was.

Hamid parked on the lowest level of the garage, deep in the shadows. There were no other cars visible.

"What are we doing here?" Kate asked. "Is it about Ruslan? Is he in trouble?"

"Albina is dead."

So Ruslan was safe, and Kate felt a brief and dislocating happiness at the terrible news about Albina. She hated herself for it.

"How?" she asked.

"The Special Police raided their apartment this morning. Albina didn't want to be taken alive. She knows too much. The twins kept a pair of pistols in their bedroom. We have a friend in the Ministry of Interior who told us that she got into a gun battle with the police. Wounded two of them. Albina made sure that the police had no choice but to shoot her."

"What about Yana? Is she okay?"

"She was out shopping. We have her in hiding. But she'll never really be okay."

"I'm so sorry."

"Are you?" Hamid's voice was cold.

"What do you mean?"

"I mean that there has been a pretty significant breakdown in security. This happens not long after you are invited to a meeting of the council. And you'd have to be stone stupid not to wonder whether these two things are related."

Hamid shifted in his seat in Kate's direction. There was a bulge visible under his jacket. He was armed. Through the driver's-side window, on the other side of the garage, Kate thought she saw something moving in the shadows. Hamid may have brought Scythians with him to this conversation.

"What is it that you're accusing me of?"

"Nothing yet. But I want to know who you told what. The Special Police got Albina's name from someone. Was it you?"

"No."

"Who did you tell?"

"I wrote a report. The whole point of this was for us to be able to help Boldu. But to do that, we needed to know more about the group, including the leadership. But the report was classified and distribution was strictly limited."

"How limited? Who knew about Albina?"

"I don't know," Kate had to admit.

"Your uncle?"

"Yes. Of course."

"Others in the embassy?"

"Yes."

"The CIA?"

"Yes," she said miserably.

"Who else do they know about?"

"Valentina. That's how I got in touch with you in the first instance. The embassy gave me her name."

"Who else?"

"You," she admitted.

"You told them about me?" There was an edge in his voice that might have been anger . . . or fear. The two were so closely bound together that it could be hard to tell them apart. Like twins. Like Albina and Yana.

"No. They told me about you. But my report confirms what they knew. I also told them about the twins and about Murzaev and Nogoev."

"What about Ruslan? Did you give him up as well?"

Kate felt like she had been slapped.

"No. I told them I didn't know Seitek's real name."

"Why not?"

"Because Val asked me not to, and because . . ." Kate struggled for a way to express her internal conflict.

"Because you didn't trust your own people." Hamid's analysis was too simple, too one dimensional. But it was not wrong.

"That's the long and the short of it, I suppose."

"You killed Albina. You might as well have pulled the trigger yourself."

Kate fought back tears.

"We don't know that," she protested. "There's no reason to believe that it was my reporting that exposed the twins. The Special Police have all kinds of sources."

"Occam's razor, Kate. The simplest answer is the right one."

Kate suspected that he was right. And she thought she knew who was responsible.

"I'm sorry, Hamid. I really am."

"Stay away from us. Stay away from Ruslan. And get out of my car."

Kate stood alone in the darkened parking garage long after Hamid had driven away, thinking about her next move.

The next morning, Kate went to Brass's office with murder in her heart. The defense attaché suite was just down the hall from the political section in the embassy's controlled-access area. In acronym-dependent government speak, the DATT's office was next to POL in the CAA.

The OPSCO, or operations coordinator, opened the door. Chief petty officer Archie Rose ran the day to day of the DATT office. Rose was black and somewhere in his thirties. He had been a sand sailor in Iraq when a roadside bomb cost him the hearing in his right ear and almost ended his career. The navy moved him to intelligence, where Rose had demonstrated a diplomat's knack for discretion and a flair for managing complex programs. Kate liked him and respected him. It was a shame that a man like this had to work for a man like Brass.

"Good morning, Kate. How can I help you?" Rose's smile was warm and genuine. He turned his head slightly in conversation, favoring his good ear.

"I need to see Brass," Kate said. She could feel the anger coiled in her stomach like a snake, but she worked to keep it out of her voice. Her smile, she feared, looked much less natural than the chief's.

"I'm sorry, he's in a meeting."

"He's going to have to reschedule."

Kate brushed past Rose and stepped into the suite. She was being rude to a man whose good opinion she valued, but her anger over

Albina's death and her fear for Ruslan's safety was driving her. There was no time for the niceties of coordinating calendars.

Brass Ball's capacious office would easily have accommodated six or seven of Kate's cubicles. The defense attaché was evidently a collector of military memorabilia, and the office walls were hung with swords, old medals, and battle-scarred flags alongside the more typical framed citations, unit souvenirs, and grip-and-grin photos of Brass with senior military leaders, their shoulders heavy with stars.

The attaché was sitting in one of the brown leather chairs set up in a corner of the office as a place to receive visitors. The CIA station chief was sitting across from him. Thick stacks of classified material were spread out on the coffee table. Crespo was wearing one of the twenty or so identical dark blue suits Kate suspected he had hanging in his closet. Brass was wearing a starched sky blue short-sleeved shirt with a tie and a look of smug self-satisfaction that Kate wanted desperately to shatter.

"Hello, Kate. We were just talking about you."

That could not possibly be a good thing.

"Why'd you do it, Brass? For the air base? For promotion? Do you want a star that bad? Maybe Eraliev is paying you. Or Svetlana is screwing you."

"What are you talking about?"

"Someone's been leaking my reporting on Boldu to the security services. I think it was you. And the Special Police killed a friend of mine this morning because of it. Her name was Albina, and she was twenty-seven years old. Goddamn you to hell."

Crespo watched the angry exchange without saying a word, his head swiveling slightly as Kate and Brass went at it, as though he were watching a tennis match.

"I think you're a little confused about the nature of this profession," Brass said with patently false concern. "And I'm frankly a little offended that you would accuse me of leaking. That kind of thing does happen from time to time, I'm sure. But I'm certainly more disciplined than that. Now, if what you're talking about is intelligence sharing through normal, established channels, that's something entirely different. That's something that our country does all the time as a matter of policy. I would hardly call it leaking."

"So you did turn over my reporting to Eraliev's people. You let them use my information to kill my friend."

"Your reporting? Your information? Your friend? Kate, this isn't about you. That's the fundamental truth that you have been unable to grasp. I understand why you're a little unmoored by what happened to . . . Albina, was it? . . . but I'm not going to share with you what we have passed to the relevant Kyrgyz authorities as part of routine intelligence cooperation. Frankly, you're not cleared for it."

"That was State Department reporting and it was classified at the secret level. It doesn't belong to you. You had no right to share it through DOD channels."

"Take it up with Winston Crandle."

"I will. But first, I'm taking it to the ambassador."

"Excellent," Brass said, and his smile was cold. "We have certain issues that we need to discuss. Together." The defense attaché gestured in Crespo's direction, including him in the conversation for the first time.

"Such as?"

Instead of answering, Brass reached over to the phone on the side table and hit first the speaker button and then a number on speed dial.

Rosemary picked up on the second ring.

"Yes, Colonel?"

"Is he ready for us?"

"Yes. He's expecting you now. Frank is already here."

"Good. We'll be right down."

Brass hung up and looked at Kate. His smile was gone. His eyes squinted almost shut as though he were marking a distant target from the cockpit of his F-22.

"Such as why you are sleeping with Seitek, whose real name it would seem is Ruslan Usenov. And why you lied when you were asked about it. I think I'm going to enjoy hearing your explanation."

And Kate knew that she was now in a great deal of trouble.

"I have to say, Kate, that I'm concerned about what I'm hearing from Frank and Colonel Ball. But I want to hear your side before I make any decisions."

Her uncle looked stern and serious, and almost exactly like her father the night when she was in high school and had snuck out of the house, gotten drunk with her girlfriends, and gotten caught.

"Thank you, Ambassador. But I don't know what you're hearing."

"Frank, why don't you tell Kate what you told me."

The RSO looked at Kate the way he might have looked at a suspected meth dealer back in his days as a beat cop in Chicago. With contempt. He pulled a slim reporter's notebook out of his jacket pocket.

"Ms. Hollister told us that the man we observed her with at Ala-Too Square was Grigoriy Vetochkin, who was, according to her account, an old boyfriend from the International School of Bishkek. I

took the pictures from Ala-Too Square to ISB, where the registrar"—
he glanced briefly at his notebook— "Jane Larson identified the man
in the photos as Ruslan Usenov, who she indicated had been roman-
tically involved with Ms. Hollister. Additionally, Ms. Larson reported
that while there was, in fact, a student at ISB named Grigoriy Vetochkin, he was in the class a year ahead of Ms. Hollister and the two of
them were never, so far as she knew, intimate."

Kate's face flushed with embarrassment as the four men processed
these decade-old details of her love life. She should have thought to
call Mrs. Larson—Jane, she now knew—and ask her to back up the
story she had told. It was too late for that now.

"Kate, what's your side?"

Possible answers to that question cascaded through Kate's mind.
The truth was not one of them. She was loyal to her country, her
family, and her employer, but the circumstances were complicated.
Right and wrong were increasingly murky, free-floating concepts.
Kate had come to understand at a bone-deep level what her uncle had
meant when he spoke of values complexity. She was torn, and the
sensation was almost a physical pain.

Ultimately, Kate was willing to sacrifice what little was left of her
government career to protect Ruslan and defend what he stood for.
The fight for freedom was why she had gone into government in the
first place. She was determined to buy Ruslan as much time as she
could. She had done the same for Reuben in Havana. She would do
no less for the man and the country she loved.

Kate looked her uncle squarely in the eyes. It took considerable
willpower not to look away.

"It's true. The man in the photos is Ruslan, not Grigor. I lied to
you about that. And I apologize. Ruslan is married, unhappily if that

matters, but married nonetheless. I didn't want to make trouble either for him or for me, and when Frank ambushed me with those photos, I panicked and I lied. This wasn't about Boldu. It was about protecting my privacy."

"You have a top secret security clearance," Barrone protested. "You have no right to privacy."

The ambassador cut him off.

"So are you telling me that Usenov is not part of Boldu? That he isn't Seitek?"

"Yes, I am," Kate lied, and a little part of her soul died, sacrificed on the altar of values complexity. "I don't know why you all jumped to the conclusion that he was. I would have expected more intellectual discipline from the CIA"—she turned and looked at Brass—"if not necessarily from the DIA."

Brass shrugged.

"We had our reasons."

"Such as?"

"It fit the profile."

"Seitek's?"

"Yours."

Kate was stunned.

"Mine?"

"We don't know who Seitek is, but that doesn't mean we don't know anything. According to the fragments of intel we have, he's young, charismatic, and reportedly has a weakness for attractive women."

"You don't mean . . ." Kate was at a loss for words.

"If you gained access to the Boldu inner circle, there was at least a reasonable chance that Seitek would seek to establish a relationship with you. Whether you were open to that or not, it would at least let us learn who he was."

"And you approved of this, Uncle Harry?" Kate's tone was sharp and accusatory. "Pimping out your niece? That's pretty low."

The ambassador held up his hands in a calming gesture that only made Kate angrier.

"It wasn't like that at all. I was hoping that you'd be able to make contact with the Boldu leadership, which you did. Anything beyond that was entirely in your control. No one asked you to do anything other than your job. You did good work. But you also lied to me. And I told you when you first arrived that I would not tolerate divided loyalties. I have tremendous respect for you, Kate, but I'm not certain I can trust you."

"So what are you going to do?"

"I'm going to think about it."

The signal was unambiguous. The meeting was over. And Kate was in limbo.

As they stood to leave, Crespo's jacket got caught on Kate's handbag, knocking it onto the floor and spilling the contents onto the carpet, including the phone that Murzaev had given her.

Crespo knelt on the floor with Kate and helped her repack her bag. Kate moved quickly to retrieve the phone before the station chief had a chance to ask about it. She was not supposed to bring any electronics into the controlled-access area. Ball and Barrone were out in the hall, and the ambassador was on the other side of the room already digging through the stack of papers on his desk.

Crespo leaned in close and whispered in Kate's ear.

"They're going to kill him."

He stood and left without saying another word.

Kate left the Front Office suite staggering under the load of what had been an ugly, emotionally charged exchange. She needed air. And she needed to reach Ruslan. Quickly.

Twenty minutes later, half a dozen blocks from the embassy, Kate pulled Murzaev's phone from her bag and punched in the code 314159. Pi to five places.

Murzaev answered.

*"Da?"*

"His forefathers were all khans."

"I've been expecting your call."

# 23

The mountains loomed over the plains as they loomed over the Kyrgyz soul. Dark and forbidding. Eight hundred years ago, Genghis Khan's armies had ridden across these plains in the shadows of these unconquerable mountains.

Ruslan tilted his head back and looked up into a perfect blue bowl of sky, unblemished by even a wisp of cloud. Behind him, the Ala-Too mountains were a dull steel gray. In front of him, the flat plains were all muted browns and tans with only the occasional flash of green where a few farmers scratched a hard living from the thin soil. The Kyrgyz were not farmers, Ruslan thought. They were herders, and raiders, and warriors. The settled life of the village had been forced on them. But their nomadic hearts rebelled at that role.

He had been driving for almost seven hours, more a testament to the rugged roads than the distance. The Russian jeep he was driving was reasonably reliable and it handled well in the mountains, but it was also cramped and uncomfortable. Ruslan had stopped at a bend in the road to both stretch his legs and drink in the beauty of the valley.

The landscape was stark and severe and the Ala-Too would make any man feel small. But Ruslan also felt at home here. He had been born in Kara-Say, a village that clung to the side of these harsh mountains like a barnacle on a whale. He had spent his summers here with his father's extended family, learning to ride as a Kyrgyz should, fearlessly, to shoot, to hunt, and to help a ewe deliver a lamb in a breech birth. Under the watchful eyes of his grandfather, he had competed in the annual horse festival in which young men from across the province challenged one another in traditional games including wrestling on horseback, grabbing bags of silver coins from the ground at a gallop, and the wild and dangerous game of *ulak-tartysh*, a kind of polo with few rules that used a headless goat carcass as a ball.

For Ruslan, Kara-Say was salty meals of mutton and *paloo*, the comaraderie of the wolf hunt, and ice-cold swims in the Naryn River, fed by melting snow from the mountain peaks. He could see the Naryn off in the distance, stretched out across the valley floor like a turquoise green ribbon. The river ran hard and fast in the spring, but for all its vitality the waters of the Naryn would never reach the sea. And by fall, the river would be a mere trickle. It was a good thing to remember, Ruslan thought to himself. Strength fades. Nothing lasts forever. For more than twenty years, the Eraliev regime has seemed invincible. Ruslan hoped that this was about to change.

Back behind the wheel, he steered the tough little jeep down the rutted road that led through the center of Kara-Say and then on to the Chinese border. It had been a few years since Ruslan had been back here, but the town was largely as he had remembered it. The village was far from beautiful, mostly one- or two-story concrete buildings that bore the unmistakable look of Soviet pragmatism, all right angles and rough materials. A kind of brutalist utopia. The Kyrgyz preferred the yurt, rounded and soft-sided. A product of the family rather than the state. Many of the buildings in this village had been painted in pastel colors, pale peach or light blue, the architectural equivalent of lipstick on a pig.

It might not have been picturesque, but Kara-Say was vibrant and alive. The outdoor markets were well stocked with fruits and vegetables, rice, meat, and housewares. Many of the buildings had ground-floor stores with hand-painted signs advertising a variety of goods and services. There was a hair salon and a teahouse and an outdoor restaurant serving roasted lamb and fermented mare's milk.

There was something missing, however. Men. Or at least young men. There were boys and old men in felt *kalpaks* and the padded coat with a high collar called a *chapan*. But there were very few men of working age on the streets of Kara-Say. Nearly all, Ruslan knew, had left for Bishkek or Moscow or Kazakhstan, where they worked low-skill jobs in construction or dirty and dangerous jobs in the oil fields. Remittances from men working abroad were the lifeblood of the Kyrgyz economy. For an extended family, money from even one "guest worker" could be the difference between security and hunger.

Traffic in the village was light, mostly carts pulled by horses or small tractors with a few Russian or Chinese cars mixed in. Ruslan parked in front of an unassuming single-story building made of whitewashed concrete. The shutters were dark wood carved with elaborate scenes of horsemanship and falconry, the two great preoccupations of the building's principal resident. This was the home of Kara-Say's most prominent citizen, Tashtanbek Essenkul uluu. The village was something of a backwater, but Tashtanbek was regarded as the de facto leader of the Adygine, and Ruslan would need his support if his plan for the occupation of Ala-Too Square was going to have any chance of success.

In theory, Ruslan was expected. He had sent a message ahead that should have beaten him to Kara-Say by half a day at least. He would know soon enough.

The door was made of local walnut and the brass knocker was shaped like a horse head. The woman who opened was dressed in traditional Kyrgyz fashion in a maroon skirt embroidered in gold thread and trimmed with fox fur. Her hair—which Ruslan knew was long and streaked with gray—was hidden under an *elechek*, a tall linen headdress that identified her as a married woman. If it were not for her chunky tortoiseshell glasses, she might have been straight out of the time of the khans.

Naz was one of Tashtanbek's innumerable nieces. She had run the clan leader's household for as long as Ruslan could remember.

She kissed Ruslan gently on the cheek.

"He's waiting for you."

And Ruslan knew that his message had preceded him to Kara-Say.

"Thank you, Naz."

The shutters were closed. It was dark inside the house, dark as a yurt. In the center of the main room, a fire burned in a stone pit. The smell of wood smoke was strong but not unpleasant. The walls were hung with *shyrdak*, felt carpets dyed with geometric patterns in bold colors. On the far wall, behind the raised wooden platform where the men sat, a stunning embroidered tapestry called a *tush kyiz* marked the seat of honor. *Shyrdak* were relatively commonplace. Tourists would buy them in the bazaars as souvenirs. *Tush kyiz* were works of art and deeply personal statements about family ties and the connection with the land. They would typically hang over the marriage bed, but Tashtanbek's beloved wife had passed away more than twenty years ago, and the ornate *tush kyiz* that she had brought to the marriage as part of her dowry had been repurposed as a marker of Tashtanbek's status.

The clan leader sat cross-legged on the platform under the *tush kyiz*, sipping tea out of a ceramic bowl. Like Naz, Tashtanbek wore traditional clothing. His *jelek*, a kind of belted coat, was made of brown velvet, and his *kalpak* was tall and four paneled with a pronounced brim that would shield him from the sun and rain when he rode. He was not a tall man, but even at more than seventy years of age his back was straight and his shoulders broad. Tashtanbek's name meant "strong as stone," and it was an appropriate moniker for a man whose impassive face seemed to have been carved from a block of granite.

Ruslan could not recall ever seeing him smile.

"*Kosh kelingiz*, Ruslan," Tashtanbek said, welcoming him. "*Assalom aleykum*."

"*Aleykum assalom*, Grandfather."

Ruslan's father, Taalay, was Tashtanbek's son, the youngest of four. The Soviet education system, as voracious in its own way as the state-run sports programs, had reached out even as far as Kara-Say, and it had identified Taalay early on as an exceptionally gifted student of mathematics. Reluctantly, Tashtanbek had allowed his youngest son to move to Bishkek for high school and to Moscow for university. Taalay had married outside the clan and taken a Russified name. Tashtanbek had insisted, however, that his grandson stay connected to the village and the Adygine. Ruslan was about to test the strength of those bonds.

He sat next to his grandfather on a small carpet and accepted a bowl of green tea from Naz.

"It's been too long since you have been back to Kara-Say," his grandfather said with a hint of admonition in his gravelly voice.

"You're right, Grandfather. And I apologize. Things have been a little crazy at work."

Tashtanbek was one of the few outside the inner circles of Boldu who knew Seitek's identity. For a brief moment, Ruslan thought that the corners of his grandfather's mouth might have twitched up into the slightest of smiles. But it was probably just a trick of the firelight.

"We will talk about your work later," Tashtanbek said. "Family first."

For the next hour, the clan leader spoke at length and in detail about the whereabouts and well-being of Ruslan's entire extended family. Ruslan contributed what he could, but since Boldu had begun to challenge Eraliev, Ruslan had been careful to keep his distance from family. He was dangerous to be around.

At first, Ruslan was restless, wanting to dive straight into the business of revolution he had come to discuss with his grandfather. But he knew that there was no rushing a Kyrgyz village elder. The social conventions were sacrosanct. There would be talk and food before business could be done. So he did his best to relax. And he found that it was both pleasant and refreshingly normal to talk about the day-to-day doings of friends and relatives.

While Ruslan and his grandfather talked over tea, Naz was directing preparations for the mandatory feast. Tables set up in the garden were soon groaning with food. Guests, all of them men, began to arrive and joined Tashtanbek and Ruslan around the fire, drinking bowls of green tea and *kumys*. Many were related to Ruslan in some way.

When Naz signaled that all was ready, they made their way to the tables. The walled garden was spacious and green. It was twilight, and a string of lights hung between two walnut trees gave the dinner the feeling of a festival.

The meal itself, as was the norm in Kyrgyzstan, was protein intensive. A small team of village women served the men from heaving platters of mutton, beef, and horsemeat. Naz was famous for her *beshbarmak*, mutton boiled in broth and served over noodles with coriander and parsley. *Beshbarmak* meant "five fingers" and it was to be eaten with the right hand.

The head of the sheep who had given his life for the *beshbarmak* sat on a plate next to Ruslan. As the guest of honor, it was his responsibility to carve off the cheeks and other choice pieces and distribute them equally among the other diners. There were horsemeat sausages and *shashlik*, skewers of grilled beef served with hunks of raw onion. The *paloo* was made with mutton and smelled of garlic and chilies.

Heavy ceramic plates of dumplings were passed around the table by the guests—*samsa* made of mutton and fat and steamed *manty* filled with ground beef and onions. There were wooden platters piled high with flatbread, and big bowls of *lagman*, thick noodles in a fiery vinegar sauce, sat in the middle of the table.

The men drank *kumys* and vodka and *bozo*, a yeasty and mildly alcoholic brew made from wheat.

The conversation was boisterous and loud and entirely apolitical. The men teased one another about the state of their fields, the quality of their flocks, and their chances in the games at the next horse festival. It was all in good fun, but there was an undercurrent of melancholy to the evening as well. The men gathered in Tashtanbek's garden were mostly older. Their sons and grandsons were working abroad. There were a few younger men, but many of them were sick or injured in some way. One twenty-year-old—Ruslan's first cousin—had lost his left arm at the elbow after an accident in the oil fields of Kazakhstan. An uncle had returned from the coal mines in Belarus with wasting lung disease. He sat at the far end of the table looking gaunt and hollow, picking disinterestedly at his food and coughing into the sleeve of his jacket.

Some hours later, when the guests had eaten their fill and then some, Tashtanbek stood and commanded attention.

"Thank you all for coming this evening to welcome my grandson home. It is my hope that he will soon tire of the city life and return to his people here in Kara-Say with a bride that he has taken in the Kyrgyz fashion."

The men gathered around the tables cheered drunkenly.

"Until that day, and to ensure that he does not forget where he came from, I would ask you, Almaz, to sing for us."

Almaz Beshimov, Ruslan knew, was not only the best Manaschi in Kara-Say, he had a national reputation as one of the most skilled and artistic reciters of the Manas epic in the country. He was somewhere in his eighties but still vital, and he took inordinate pride in his bushy white mustache that curled up at the ends.

A chair had been set up between the tables where all the guests would have an unobstructed view. Almaz had come dressed in his Manaschi best, a *jelek* of dark blue velvet, an elaborately embroidered *kalpak*, and a studded belt buckle that looked to be made of at least two kilos of bronze.

His voice was still clear and powerful and he launched straight into the recitation, a rhythmic and repetitive chant that was familiar to all the guests. He began with the traditional opening that all Manaschi used—"it was a long time ago, and now the eyewitnesses have gone"—before launching into his chosen passage.

Within two stanzas, Ruslan recognized the passage Almaz was

singing. The octogenarian Manaschi had chosen a section from the third book of the epic poem, the story of the grandson Seitek. This was the passage in which Seitek, who had been raised in the enemy's camp unaware of his own lineage, learns of his secret origin and chooses to rise up against the foes of his father and grandfather.

This was not a random selection. Ruslan knew that his grandfather has asked Almaz for this passage. He had come to Kara-Say to ask Tashtanbek for a difficult thing, to deliberately place his people in harm's way. They had much to discuss, but it would have to wait. Now was the time to celebrate the noble history of the forty Kyrgyz tribes.

If this was a message to Ruslan from his grandfather, then the omens were good.


It felt like he had been asleep for no more than fifteen minutes when Tashtanbek shook him awake. Ruslan forced his eyes open and glanced at his watch. It was four a.m. He was hungover and it hurt when he moved his head. His grandfather was dressed to ride and his expression was as affectless and impassive as always.

"Get up, boy," he said. "Time to hunt."

Ruslan groaned, but he did as his grandfather instructed. Someone, probably Naz, had left riding gear out for him. Ruslan fumbled in the dark with the buttons and straps. It had been more than a year since he had worn this kind of Kyrgyz clothing. The plain white *kalpak* was a little too small. Ruslan would have preferred an American-style ball cap, but his grandfather would be happy to see him dressed the Kyrgyz way, and he loved the old man.

Tashtanbek was waiting for him outside. He was mounted on a large black horse. The saddle and felt blanket were decorated with embroidery and yak fur. A hooded goshawk perched obediently on a leather glove he wore on his left hand. His right hand held the reins of a second horse, a roan-colored stallion that was a match for Tashtanbek's mount in size and strength. Ruslan mounted his horse and took the reins from his grandfather. It was a cold morning, and the clean mountain air was already clearing his head. He looked forward to the hunt.

"Lead on," he said.

Wordlessly, Tashtanbek took them down the side of the mountain and across a wooden bridge that spanned the Naryn River. In spring, the water was too high to walk the horses over the ford and too fast to swim them across. The bridge was not strong enough to carry vehicles, but it was more than adequate for horses and riders.

The sun was starting to come up and the mountains were silhouetted against the still starry sky, outlined in bands of red, orange, and violet.

A narrow, rocky path led up the hills on the far side of the Naryn. For all their bulk, the horses were remarkably surefooted on the path. After about an hour's ride, they reached a *djailoo*, lush and green from the spring rains.

Tashtanbek removed the leather hood from the goshawk and spoke to the bird. He told the hawk that it was brave and fierce and loyal, that soon it would kill and feast. As he whispered to the bird, he stroked the feathers on its neck. The hawk glared at him with angry yellow eyes, offering the clan leader obedience but not affection.

Hunting with raptors was the apex of manly skill in Kyrgyz culture. It took patience and discipline and many hours of practice. It was, alas, a dying art, but Tashtanbek was one of the last great masters. He had a kestrel and a saker falcon, and as a younger man he had hunted fox and even wolves with a great golden eagle, but this goshawk was his favorite. His name was Janibar, which meant "one who has a soul."

There was a blur of brown against the green of the *djailoo*. A rabbit. Tashtanbek raised his gloved hand and the goshawk took flight, trailing his leather jesses behind him. The raptor flew low across the *djailoo*. The rabbit spotted the hawk and elected to run rather than hide. It was not a good choice.

Janibar dipped his wings and flew in behind the rabbit, catching it by the back of the neck and lifting it effortlessly into the air. The prey twisted violently as the hawk broke its back.

As he had been trained, Janibar returned to Tashtanbek with his prize, surrendering the rabbit to his master while simultaneously shrieking his disapproval at the arrangement. With his belt knife, Tashtanbek carved off some small slices of rabbit flesh and fed them to the hawk by hand before again hooding the bird and whispering in his ear about his greatness as a hunter.

Then, and only then, did Tashtanbek turn to his grandson and speak to him for the first time since ordering him out of his warm bed.

"Tell me what it is you need," he said.

"It's time," Ruslan replied. "If we don't act now, there will not be another chance. The Sarybagysh are mobilizing to do to us what Janibar just did to that rabbit. If we do not move first, Eraliev and the GKNB will hunt us down and snap our necks."

Ruslan did not need to elaborate. He and Tashtanbek had discussed the plan at length, and while his grandfather had reservations, he saw the opportunity to return the Adygine to a position of power and influence. Tashtanbek was not motivated by abstractions like freedom and democracy. But clan loyalty was something settled deep in his bones. Like most traditional leaders, however, he was cautious by nature.

"It is too soon. We need more time."

"There is no more time."

"When do you plan to do this thing?"

"Six days from now."

Tashtanbek was quiet for a moment as he thought about that answer.

"That is not nearly enough time to get the young men back from abroad."

"I know."

"Who then will fight? We are a village of old men, women, and children. All of the villages in the district are the same."

"I know."

"And that does not give you pause?"

"It gives me hope."

Tashtanbek's face actually betrayed an emotion, if confusion could be considered an emotion.

Ruslan explained what he had in mind.

When he had finished, his grandfather laughed.

It was a good omen.

# 24

Patience was one of the many virtues that an education in classical music was supposed to instill. Kate must have been absent that day. For her, the wait was excruciating. She wanted to see Ruslan right now. To warn him. But also to touch him. To hold him close and rail against the machine, the powerful forces colluding to rip her lover away from her and carry him off to some black pit where demons shaped like men flay the skin and flesh from the bones of those unfortunate enough to fall into the insatiable maw of the security apparatus.

Murzaev had told her to wait. To be patient. To check in through the usual channel for further instructions. Even on a clean phone, the spy had been characteristically evasive. But Kate was left with the impression that Murzaev was not entirely certain where Ruslan was at the moment, or when he would be back.

Kate did not want to go back to the office and face her accusers.

At least not right away. Instead, after her brief exchange with Murzaev, she went to Ala-Too Square, not because she expected to find Ruslan there building a palisade to defend the foot soldiers of Boldu, but because she wanted to feel close to him. Wherever he was, and whatever he was doing, she knew he was thinking about this place. Ground zero for his dreams of a free Kyrgyzstan. Maybe he was thinking about her as well. She hoped so.

It was warm, and the sky was blue and streaked with the thin cirrus clouds called mares' tails. Kate did not want to read too much into that as a sign. She was a rationalist, and not a big believer in God, the gods, or Jungian synchronicity. But it cheered her nonetheless.

There was a café on the west side of the square with a view of the comically heroic statue of Manas. Kate sat at one of the outside tables and ordered a double espresso. As she sipped her coffee, Kate looked out on the square and tried to picture it filled with protestors singing, beating drums, and staring down the rifle barrels of the Special Police. Maybe Ruslan was right. Maybe the regime was brittle, its support limited to a relatively small number of the Bishkek-based elite who had grown rich and fat off Eraliev's largesse. Maybe the Kyrgyz people were ready to rise up against their overlords. If they did, Kate vowed to herself that she would stand with them, no matter where her government came down. Crespo, she realized with a flash of insight that was as uncomfortable as it was clarifying, had been right to doubt her.

That evening, she opened a bottle of decent Spanish rioja and drank too much as she played Chopin until her fingers cramped. Her sleep was fitful and troubled by dreams.

The next morning, Kate woke late, hungover and dehydrated. Breakfast was half a liter of orange juice and three Advil. She forced herself to go for a run. The first mile was agony, but as the blood started to flow, her headache receded and her mood improved. It was Saturday and there was nothing she had to do but wait. Once Kate accepted that reality, it was oddly liberating. Since being picked up off the street by Murzaev's snatch-and-grab crew, Kate had started varying her routes and times the way she was supposed to. She picked her way almost at random through the backstreets and green spaces of Bishkek, mulling over what Ruslan and Boldu were planning and what she could do to help. At this point, there were too many variables and it was impossible to know where she might be able to plug into the equation.

At the end of the run, she stopped by the newsstand and bought one of the local papers, resisting the urge to open it up right there and look for a note. The moment she was back in her apartment, however, she flipped quickly through every page and was disappointed to find nothing.

Uncertain about what else to do with her time, Kate drove out to the stables where she had met with Ruslan alone. The caretakers, Myrzakan and Adilet, were home and they welcomed Kate with affectionate hugs and salty bowls of *kumys*. Myrzakan helped her saddle the stallion Aravan, and Kate rode him up to the *djailoo* where she and Ruslan had played their game of kiss-the-girl. Kate smiled when she thought about how she had pulled back on the reins just a little bit at the end of the race, just enough to lose.

Adilet had packed the saddlebag with a liter bottle of water, a goatskin bag of harsh red wine, some flatbread, and cheese and dried meat wrapped in wax paper. Kate stopped by a bend in the stream and ate lunch while Aravan grazed on the sweet spring grass. Frogs croaked in the shallows and a gray heron marched elegantly along the far bank looking for a meal. It was a peaceful scene, but Kate kept replaying in her mind the last, unpleasant exchange in her uncle's office and Crespo's whispered warning.

They're going to kill him.

The implication was clear. A report on the conversation would be shared with Kyrgyz authorities, the GKNB or the Special Police. They would hunt Ruslan down, turning over every rock and stone until they found him. And they would murder him because there was at least a chance that he was Seitek, and Eraliev was so afraid of Boldu that he would happily kill a thousand innocents for a five percent chance that one of them was his nemesis.

Kate was certain that it was Brass who was leaking intel to the Kyrgyz security services, likely at the instruction of Winston Crandle. And it was hard to escape the conclusion that her uncle knew what was happening. Maybe it was part of a quid pro quo in the base negotiations. It would hardly be the first time the U.S. government had sacrificed its long-term interests for a short-term gain.

Kate knew one thing with a clarity that was so intense as to be almost painful. She needed to talk to Ruslan.

Mounting Aravan, she rode back to the stable and helped Myrzakan unsaddle the big stallion and rub him down. Promising to return soon, Kate drove back to town and, tamping down any expectations, stopped at the newsstand for a copy of *Vecherniy Bishkek*.

She did not wait to get back to her apartment. Sitting in the driver's seat, she opened the paper to the back pages. A small blue note card fluttered out onto the floor. Kate's heart beat faster as she picked it up. The message was simple.

*Tomorrow. 45 Oberon St. Apartment 04. 23:00.*

The note did not say so, but Kate felt strongly that Ruslan would be there. Somehow that would make everything okay.

The next day, at precisely nine o'clock, Kate hit the buzzer next to the number 2 in the entryway of a block of ugly concrete apartments painted a dull yellow. It was a transitional neighborhood, part residential and part industrial. Kate had driven a circuitous route, looking to see if she could spot anyone following her. As near as she could tell with her limited training and experience, she was clean.

The door clicked open and Kate walked down a short flight of stairs to a garden-level apartment with a crooked number 2 nailed to the door.

Ruslan opened the door, wearing jeans and a black zippered fleece. He looked tired and worn out, but he was most definitely alive.

Kate reached for him and he took her in his arms, one hand pressed into the small of her back and the other stroking her hair. She pressed her face against his chest, not certain if she wanted to laugh or cry. Then Ruslan took her face in his hands and kissed her, and time stopped.

Kate pulled back from the kiss.

"I'm sorry about Albina," she said.

"Me too."

"Where's Yana?"

"Hamid is looking after her."

"Close the damn door." Kate recognized Murzaev's voice.

Ruslan ushered her into the apartment and locked the door behind them. Like the other Boldu safe house she had seen, this one was sparsely furnished. But there were chairs in the living room and a low table with a silver tray holding a bottle of vodka and three glasses.

The table and chairs sat on top of a large Turkoman-style carpet dyed a deep red.

Murzaev was sitting in one of the threadbare chairs wearing a black suit that looked like it had been slept in. The spymaster himself looked older, almost frail. Kate walked over to him and leaned down to kiss his cheek.

"Thank you," she said.

Murzaev smiled wanly and gestured at one of the chairs. Kate and Ruslan sat opposite each other and Murzaev poured the vodka.

"I don't think I was followed here," Kate said.

"I know you weren't," Murzaev replied.

"How do you know?"

"Because my boys followed you to make certain you were not. They saw nothing. And if there was something to see, they would have. My boys are good."

"I certainly didn't see them following me."

"No," Murzaev agreed.

Kate turned to the man she loved.

"Ruslan, they know about you. The security team in my embassy didn't believe the story about Grigoriy. They went to the school with the photographs and Mrs. Larson identified you. I should have thought of that and asked for her help. I have reason to believe that what the embassy knows, Eraliev knows. The CIA station chief warned me that the government was going to kill you. He whispered it to me, like it was a secret he wasn't supposed to share."

"And you trust him to tell you the truth?" Murzaev asked.

"No. But I can't see why he would lie about that."

"You can never tell with the CIA. They tell so many lies it can be hard even for them to remember what's false and what's true."

"What can we do?"

"They may know my name," Ruslan said. "But that's not the same thing as knowing where to find me. I just need to keep moving."

"And what about your family? Won't they go after them?"

"Eventually. But I'm hoping that in a few days it'll be a moot point. We'll all be together on Ala-Too Square and then they'll have to come and get us."

"And what happens when they do?"

"There's been some positive news on that front, thanks to you."

"Malinin?"

"Yes."

"What happened?"

"He's fallen from favor," Murzaev said sardonically. "Fallen hard. Seems there were credible rumors that he was plotting a coup. His own men arrested him. Kayrat uluu has taken over as head of the Special Police, and we believe he's sympathetic to the cause. You did well, Ms. Hollister."

"What did they do to Malinin?" Kate asked, although she was not certain that she wanted to know the answer.

"They took him to Number One for questioning," Murzaev replied with no more emotion than he would have displayed reporting on the weather.

"Thanks to me," Kate said, her tone hollow and bitter.

"It had to be, Kate," Ruslan said, and it was clear that he understood Kate's ambivalent reaction to the news. "Whatever fate waits for him in prison is only a small sample of the misery he delivered to hundreds. This isn't on you. It was always his fate. You didn't do this. He did this to himself. Malinin was part of a brutal system that eats its own. Ultimately, it eats them all."

"All except for Eraliev and Chalibashvili."

"They're dancing in the dragon's jaws and they know it. There is no graceful retirement for men like Malinin. Only a bullet or the end of a rope."

Kate's feelings were confused. She knew, in principle, what she had been doing when she started spreading rumors about Malinin. But to have it made real in this way, and to know that it had happened because of her, no matter Ruslan's efforts to shield her from responsibility, was extremely discomfiting. She could not help but imagine the now former head of the Special Police strapped to a chair in one of the dank interrogation rooms in the Pit. And Kate knew, like it or not, that she had put him there. Values complexity.

"You told me that you wanted to accelerate your plans for a Maidan-style occupation of Ala-Too Square. I assume that's where you've been for the last few days, talking to the clans."

Ruslan nodded.

"Clan leadership is a little diffuse, but my grandfather is high up in the councils of the Adygine. He's ready . . . I think. But we have to move quickly."

"When?"

"Three days."

"I've been down south talking to the Buguu and the Kara-Kyrgyz and some of the other tribes," Murzaev added. "Most are cautious. But there are some who are angry enough or greedy enough to take this risk."

"Will there be enough? A critical mass? Will the students and trade unions join them?"

Murzaev shrugged.

"We'll see. Val and Hamid have been working those channels."

"I'll be there," Kate said. "I'm ready to hunt monsters. I'll even bring my own pitchfork, but I may need to borrow a torch."

"I've been carrying one for you for more than a decade," Ruslan said, switching from Kyrgyz to English for the idiom and placing a hand over his heart in mock solemnity.

Kate stuck out her tongue.

"Very funny."

"Tell me what your friends in the embassy know," Murzaev said, shifting the conversation back to operational grounds. "What did they say to you? And what do they want from you?"

Kate gave them a detailed readout on her confrontation with Ball and her subsequent meeting with the ambassador and his entire security team. As she spoke, Murzaev stood up and walked over to the window, looking out into the darkened city intently. It seemed to Kate as though something out there was bothering him.

"Tell me again about Crespo's warning to you," he demanded.

"At the end of the meeting, we had a private moment together and he whispered to me that 'they' were going to kill Ruslan."

"But he didn't tell you who?"

"No. I assumed it meant the Kyrgyz security services, either GKNB or the Special Police, but there wasn't time for much of a conversation."

"Why would he do this thing? Why would he warn you?"

"I don't know," Kate admitted. "There's no love lost between the CIA and Defense Intelligence. There may be something going on between Crespo and Ball that I'm not seeing. But he was pretty emphatic."

Murzaev looked at her briefly and then again out the window at whatever had caught his attention.

"Did Crespo give you anything to carry?" he asked. "A pen? Or a watch? Or anything that you might have with you now?"

"No. I don't think . . . Oh my god."

"Yes?"

"To create the opportunity for our little moment alone, he knocked my purse onto the ground and then helped me repack it."

Murzaev stepped away from the window and without asking took Kate's purse and dumped its contents onto the coffee table, feeling around inside to make certain that he had emptied all the pockets.

"Do you recognize all of this?" he asked.

In addition to her wallet, the pile included a pair of lipsticks, a compact, her phone with the battery pack removed, the phone Murzaev had given her similarly disassembled, a hairbrush, a dozen business cards, three pens, sunglasses, a pack of Tic Tacs from the embassy commissary, tissues, a small pair of scissors, several nail files, and various other bits of flotsam and jetsam. One item stood out for its unfamiliarity. A box of matches sporting the name and logo of a local restaurant.

Kate pointed at it.

"I've never eaten there."

Murzaev picked it up and opened it. The matches inside were cut down and glued together. The space where the missing part of the matchsticks had been was taken up by a small black plastic box from which a coiled silver wire extruded.

Kate's stomach sank. Crespo had set her up.

Murzaev set it on the table and used the bottom of the vodka bottle to crush it as though he were killing a tick. The plastic shell cracked open with a loud pop, and Murzaev fished around inside until he had extracted the small watch battery that powered it.

"We need to get out of here."

"Too late," Ruslan said. He had gone over to the window and he gestured toward the street. Murzaev and Kate joined him and looked outside. Two unmarked vans were parked on the far side of Oberon Street. The doors were open and men were getting out. At least four were dressed in paramilitary gear with bulletproof vests and matte black helmets. They carried carbines. They moved in a crouch and seemed to take their instructions from a large man who wore a knee-length leather duster. In the shadows, Kate thought she could see signs of other men moving into position. The Boldu "safe house" was no doubt surrounded.

"What about the roof?" Kate asked.

"No," Murzaev answered. "There's no time. Help me."

He started to move the chairs off the carpet. Kate and Ruslan copied him.

Under the carpet was a hatch. Under that was a shallow storage space carved out of the concrete foundation with a jackhammer. It was about the size and shape of a coffin. Inside Kate could see a radio, a pair of rifles, four pistols, and a few boxes of ammunition.

"We're going to fight?" she asked incredulously.

"Not unless you want to wind up like one of the gangsters in your American movies. This is for hiding."

"There's only room for one," Ruslan said. "Even if we take the guns out."

"That's true."

"Climb in, Kate. Quickly."

"No," Kate and Murzaev answered at the same time.

"I'm not going to argue about this."

"That's correct. You will not argue," the old spy said. "Kate has diplomatic immunity. She is the safest of all of us. And Boldu is nothing without you. If you are captured, it will all be for nothing. Albina. Azattyk. Everything for nothing. Get in the box."

Ruslan looked helplessly at Kate. If he was hoping for an ally, he was disappointed.

"Askar's right," she said. "I'll be fine. I've been down this road before. They won't hurt me. But hurry. There's not much time."

"But—"

"Ruslan, shut up and get in. This is no time for stupid pride or male bullshit."

Reluctantly, he climbed into the narrow box. Working together, Murzaev and Kate spread the carpet over the hatch and returned the furniture to its original position. Kate quickly swept the contents of her purse back into the bag.

"Are there air holes?" Kate thought to ask. "Will he be able to breathe?"

"Perhaps."

"What's going to happen to you?"

Murzaev poured them each a stiff shot of the vodka.

"They're going to arrest me and take me away."

"To Number One?"

"Yes."

"And what then?"

"They will squeeze me until I tell them what they want to know."

"What will you do?"

"Tell them. Eventually. Everybody does. I just need to hold out long enough until what I know doesn't matter. Then I am useless to them."

"Can you do that?"

"Perhaps. I think so. I thought about using one of those pistols on myself, but I would like to live long enough to see how this all works out."

He raised his glass and waited expectantly until Kate raised hers.

"*Za zdorovie,*" Kate said in Russian.

"*Den soolugubuz üchün!*" Murzaev answered in Kyrgyz.

They drank the eye-watering shots.

The front door crashed open with explosive force.

Two men wearing paramilitary gear that made them look like Ninja Turtles scuttled through the doorframe and leveled their weapons at Kate and Murzaev. In the hall, Kate could see a third cop holding the battering ram he had used on the lock.

Looking utterly unperturbed, Murzaev poured another shot of vodka and held it up in the direction of the police.

"Drink?" he asked.

Kate tried to match his calm, but she was torn between an instinct to flee and a sudden desire to claw out the eyes of these men who had sold themselves to the ruling class.

An odd standoff seemed to have developed, with the heavily armed Special Police on one side and Murzaev—armed only with cool detachment—on the other. Kate already felt like a bystander.

Then a tall man with broad shoulders and gray hair cut close to the scalp stepped through the door and into the room. The man in the leather duster.

"Good evening, Askar," he said in Russian. "Good evening, Ms. Hollister. I apologize for dropping by uninvited."

Kate knew who he was even before he spoke and she heard the distinctive accent. She recognized him from the picture in his CIA bio. This was Anton Chalibashvili and his native language was Georgian. Torquemada was making a house call.

"I'm sorry," Kate said. "I don't believe we've met."

"No," Chalibashvili agreed. "But I know your family. Intimately."

Kate threw her glass at his head.

The Georgian shifted his weight almost imperceptibly, and the glass sailed harmlessly past to shatter against the wall.

"Adding assault to the list of charges for which your government will be required to exercise your immunity? How irresponsible."

Kate wrestled her anger back under control. Dealing with this man, she understood, was like handling a poisonous serpent. It was best done carefully.

"We are doing nothing illegal here. I am sharing a bottle and some conversation with a friend."

"Nothing illegal? Really? Are you familiar with the concept of conspiracy? I believe that your government relies on it quite liberally in the application of what it refers to—quaintly it must be admitted—as justice."

Murzaev snorted contemptuously.

"I'm surprised that you know that word, Anton."

Chalibashvili ignored him.

"Now here's the thing," he said. "I do not, frankly, believe that the two of you were here alone. There is another I am looking for. His name is Ruslan Usenov. And I believe that you know where he is right at this moment. Tell me where he is and you two go home, right now, absolutely free."

"Fuck you," Murzaev replied.

The Inquisitor looked at Kate.

"What he said."

Chalibashvili motioned to the men in the hall and pointed a finger around the apartment. The message was unmistakable. Search the place.

Two men started a thorough sweep beginning with the bedrooms.

"Askar, you disappoint me. You were one of us in the old KGB. Your thinking was clear and logical. To find you consorting with such marginal figures is really quite puzzling."

As he spoke, Chalibashvili walked through the room, stepping at one point onto the carpet covering Ruslan's hiding place. It was as though he were walking on his grave. Kate listened for a telltale creak that would reveal the hollow under the rug. And she tried not to stare at his boots.

"As I am disappointed to find you, Anton, who did such unspeakable things in the service of his country, now peddling his medieval skills to the highest bidder. I am no naïf. The things you do so well can be necessary at times, in pursuit of a higher purpose. But absent that purpose, it is simple cruelty. And you are nothing more than a gangland enforcer or a cheap torturer for hire. I have scraped things from the bottom of my shoe that have more to offer the world than you."

For a brief moment, Chalibashvili seemed to betray real human emotion. Anger. Doubt. But he quickly recovered his composure and pulled the icy mask back over his features.

"And you switched sides simply to avenge your boyhood friend. It's cheap sentimentality, Askar. Like a child crying over a lost puppy. The world is a dark and dangerous place. The brave do what is needed to maintain order. No one knows this better than men like us."

"I am nothing like you."

"No. I suppose you are not. Not anymore. And after your time with us in my . . . office . . . you will not even be a man. Not in any meaningful way."

Murzaev blanched. He knew too well what fate awaited him in the Pit, and Kate thought that he might be regretting his earlier decision not to kill himself.

Having re-established his dominance in the conversation, Chalibashvili seemed to decide that it was time to end it.

He took one of the assault rifles from the Special Police standing guard over the room, carrying it with a casual nonchalance. This was a man, Kate sensed, accustomed to handling instruments of pain and death.

"Let me ask you again about the whereabouts of Ruslan Usenov. Tell me where to find him."

"Fuck off."

Chalibashvili pointed the rifle at Murzaev's head.

"Really?" Murzaev said incredulously. "You threaten a man with torture and then with summary execution. That's kind of a step down, don't you think? You want to shoot me, then shoot me. But until then, fuck off."

The Inquisitor swung the muzzle of the rifle until it was sited on Kate, zeroing in on a point in the middle of her forehead.

"Ms. Hollister? Anything you'd care to add to the conversation?"

Kate swallowed hard, reminding herself that this was not the first time she had looked into the barrel of a gun.

"I think Askar pretty much covered it."

Chalibashvili's smile was sly and superior. The muzzle of the rifle dropped to point at the floor next to Kate's chair. He pulled the trigger, sending a five-round burst into the parquet. A few small pieces of wood landed in Kate's lap. Chalibashvili pointed the gun at another part of the floor closer to Murzaev and fired a similar burst. Then he stepped onto the carpet and pointed the muzzle of the rifle almost directly at where Ruslan's head would be.

He looked over at Kate expectantly and there was little doubt that the Georgian knew full well what was under his feet.

"What do you think?" he asked. "Should I do it?"

Kate was silent. She could feel the muscles in her neck and shoulders strain as she fought to keep her expression calm.

She looked over at Murzaev, who offered her only the slightest of nods, as though passing responsibility for the decision back to her.

Chalibashvili's finger tightened on the trigger. But Kate's eyes were drawn to the gracefully curved magazine, where she knew the jacketed slugs were crammed in like bees in a hive. And like bees they would die after a single sting.

Chalibashvili did not look where he aimed. Instead, he looked right at Kate with the intensity of a lunatic, and Kate recognized that there was a part of him that hoped she would refuse him the answer he wanted, that he would have a reason to fire the weapon. To kill. That he took pleasure in it.

"Stop!" she said. And her shoulders relaxed as Chalibashvili straightened and allowed the rifle to drift away from its aiming point.

"Yes."

"He's there, goddamn it. And you know it."

"So I did. But I wanted to hear it from you. I wanted you to be the one to tell me."

He gestured to the armored police to move the furniture and the rugs.

Chalibashvili stood back as they opened the trapdoor.

"A cornered rat can be dangerous," he said to Kate. "I've seen it."

Ruslan got off two shots from a pistol. The first glanced off the riot helmet of one of the cops and shattered a bulb on the chandelier. The second struck the policeman's armored vest and toppled him backward. His partner used a nightstick to knock the pistol from Ruslan's hand and then club him senseless.

"Are you all right?" the cop asked his partner in Russian.

"Yeah, but I'll be better if you hit him again."

His loyal partner complied.

The cops hauled Ruslan to his feet and used a pair of handcuffs to secure his arms behind his back. Then they did the same to Murzaev, who offered no resistance.

They ignored Kate, who was now standing near the wall on the far side of the room. She stepped forward to embrace Ruslan, but a third cop stepped in front of her and pushed her back.

"I'm sorry, Ruslan," she said. She could feel the tears hot on her face. "I love you."

Ruslan was visibly dazed, his eyes glassy from the beating he had received. He did not respond.

"Thank you, Ms. Hollister," Chalibashvili said. "You've been most cooperative. And your contributions are appreciated. But I believe that you've done everything you can in this country. And now, I believe, it is time for you to take your leave of us. I expect you will be getting those instructions in due time. Good evening."

Chalibashvili and the raid team left, taking Ruslan and Murzaev with them. Kate was left behind. Alone in her misery and her guilt.

She drank the rest of the vodka.

# 25

The wife was working the morning shift at the newsstand. It was early. The sky was still the gray of false dawn, and the scent of fresh bread from scores of small bakeries wafted across the city. It had been eight long hours since Ruslan and Murzaev had been arrested.

Kate needed allies, and she knew she would not find them at the embassy. All she could expect from her employers was a transfer order or a notice of termination. Chalibashvili had been pretty clear about what he expected would happen, and it seemed reasonable to believe that he had an insider's knowledge. Kate's time in the country was limited and she would have to make the most of it.

The woman offered no sign that she recognized Kate or that they shared a secret, no nod or smile, nothing that indicated there was anything between them beyond a small-scale commercial exchange. Her shapeless gray sweater and no-nonsense haircut were, at least in part, an effective form of camouflage, what a naturalist might have called protective coloration. What she and her husband were doing was inherently dangerous, and she did not want to do anything to draw unnecessary and unwanted attention. She would not be happy about what was about to happen. Kate walked straight up to the counter, making no pretense of buying a newspaper or magazine.

"I need your help."

The look of panic on the woman's face was unmistakable. Reflexively, she looked up and down the street to see who was watching, who might be listening in. Kate was breaking every rule of good security. She sympathized with her contact's anxiety, but the stakes were extremely high and this was all she could think to do.

"You would like a newspaper?" the woman asked. She fumbled under the counter and slapped a copy of the English-language *Times of Central Asia* onto the polished wood.

"Not today. I want you to get a message to Valentina Aitmatova. It's urgent."

The woman's eyes narrowed.

"Why are you doing this?" she hissed. "You'll get us both killed."

"They have Seitek. They took him last night. I was there. He'll be in Number One by now. I need Valentina. And I can't get to her without your help. I know this is dangerous, but if we don't take a risk now we have nothing."

Kate pulled a small envelope out of her purse and set it on the counter next to the newspaper. It was unmarked.

"Please," she said.

The newsstand owner looked at the envelope as though it were a scorpion.

"Without Seitek," she whispered, "all is lost."

"Yes."

"And if I do this thing, you can save him?"

"Yes," Kate lied.

The woman nodded, more to herself than to Kate. The look of anxiety on her face faded and what took its place was less determination than fatalism. Somewhat tentatively, she put one hand on top of the envelope and pushed the copy of the *Times of Central Asia* toward Kate.

"On the house," she said. "Just this once."

"Thank you."

Once more, Kate could do little but wait. She took the bus to Prison Number One on the eastern edge of the city. The bus offered security through anonymity. Kate dressed local and looked like just another middle-class resident of Bishkek rather than an American diplomat. As a further precaution, she kept her cell phone batteries separate from the phones. It was still safer to carry them with her. The embassy had a spare set of keys to her apartment.

She had not been back to the prison since the pitched battle between the Special Police and the Women in Black. Prison Number One was a complex of buildings set behind a concrete wall, high and thick and topped with coils of razor wire and bits of broken glass. The main gate was closed. It was made of black steel bars oriented vertically. The gate was built on runners that let the guards open it by sliding it to either side on a steel track embedded in the road. A smaller door built into the frame could be opened separately to admit people rather than vehicles. The aluminum guardhouse was manned by two Special Police wearing ballistic vests and watching a football game on a portable television with a rabbit-ears antenna.

A small sign printed on sheet metal was tacked to the wall by the side of the gate. It announced the identity of the building as the property of the Bishkek Prison Authority. It was superfluous. The grim complex was unlikely to be mistaken for anything else.

Kate walked past the gate without slowing down or betraying any sign that she was especially interested in what was behind the walls. But she could not stop thinking about Ruslan, who at this very moment was likely to be in one of the windowless rooms in the basement level. Maybe it was a dark cell with nothing but rats for company. Or maybe they had already moved him to one of the interrogation rooms with bright lights rather than darkness to disorient and terrify.

She circled the prison. There was a gate on the back side that looked identical to the one in front. Through the bars she could see the prison buildings, blocky and ugly. The doors were all steel and the windows were all covered with bars. If there was a weakness, it was not immediately obvious. As she walked past the back gate, one of the guards stared at her and Kate thought he sensed something suspicious about her behavior. But then he made a few grossly exaggerated kissing sounds in Kate's direction, adding an obscene hip thrust to make his point unambiguously clear. He was just an asshole then. Nothing special to worry about.

She thought about reinserting the batteries in her phone and taking a few surreptitious pictures of the prison, but she had to assume that the security services were tracking her phone, and it did not seem worth the risk of revealing her whereabouts. Instead, she worked to commit the small details to memory. Where did the guards stand? How many were there? Where were the cameras?

Kate did not yet know how she was going to get inside the prison. But she knew one thing, and she knew it with absolute certainty. She was not going to leave Ruslan in there to rot. Or to die. Not alone at least.

———

At seven o'clock that evening, Kate walked through the gate into Kara-Su Park and followed the path to the bridge where she had met Valentina a few weeks earlier. It was dusk, and there were not many people in the park, but it was still light enough to see. Kate did not know how long it might take her message to get to Valentina, or whether Val would be able to come at the appointed time, or whether she would be willing to come at all. Would Val and the others blame Kate for what had happened? Hamid had accused her of killing Albina. What would he say now?

Kate was alone under the bridge. The shadows were deeper here and she stood against the wall where no one walking past would see her. The stone walls were damp and rough to her touch. She wondered if the walls of Ruslan's cell were made of the same stone. Maybe they were concrete or cinder block. But she was certain that they were cold. Dusk turned to night quickly and the shadows thickened and merged. Within twenty minutes, it was too dark to read the graffiti on the walls. As the last of the sunlight dissipated, it grew noticeably colder and Kate zipped her thin jacket tight against her throat.

There was no sign of Val. Kate would try again tomorrow night and the night after that and every evening until she was forced to leave the country. She had to believe her message had gotten through. There was no Plan B.

As she turned to leave, she heard a voice behind her.

"Kate?"

She turned and there were two figures silhouetted against the mouth of the tunnel on the far side of the bridge, the sky behind them just barely lighter than the darkness of the underpass.

"Val? Who's with you?"

Kate walked toward them and needed to get within ten feet before she recognized Daniar Nogoev. A feeling of relief washed through her. Val had come. Kate might not know what to do, but at least she was no longer alone.

Val hugged her quickly but fiercely. Nogoev's greeting was distant but not hostile.

"What happened, Kate?" Val asked.

She told them, leaving out no detail and not seeking to hide or even downplay her own role in leading Chalibashvili and the Special Police to the Boldu safe house. By the time she had finished, hot tears of shame had wet her cheeks.

Val took her hand.

"It's not your fault."

"Of course it's her fault," Nogoev said, his tone matter-of-fact. "But that doesn't really matter. Fault finding is a waste of time, of interest only to housewives and Bolsheviks."

"I'm neither of those," Kate said. "But it matters to me. I'm sorry about your friend."

"Murzaev knew the risks. Ruslan was the only one we couldn't spare."

"So what do we do?" Val asked.

They were quiet as they considered the enormity of that question.

"We rescue him," Kate said emphatically when it became evident that neither Val nor Nogoev seemed inclined to offer that answer independently.

"From Number One?" Val asked, incredulous.

"Yes."

"How?"

"The Scythians," Nogoev answered.

"We just assault the prison? Maybe we could ride in on horseback with bows and arrows. I'll ride naked like Lady Godiva."

"I'm not certain that would have the intended effect."

It was dark in the tunnel, but Kate could see Nogoev's sly smile in the tone of his voice.

"So how would you do this in a way that doesn't end up with your idealistic youngsters shuffling off this mortal coil?" Val asked.

"When we were considering the options for getting to Bermet, you'll recall, Seitek asked us if we could get into the prison."

"And you said you could get in but not get out."

"Not without violence. We weren't ready for that at the time."

"And we are now?"

"Now we have no choice. Bermet wasn't worth it, frankly. Ruslan is. Without him, we lose. With him, we are only likely to lose." There was that smile again.

"Do you have somebody on the inside? Someone in the prison who can help us. Someone sympathetic to our cause."

"I think so. Yes."

"A guard or an administrator?"

"Neither."

"Who then?"

"A prisoner."

"Not really the time for jokes, Daniar."

"I'm one hundred percent serious."

"I'm listening."

"Number One is really two prisons. There's a building reserved for Tier I political prisoners that has very tight security. But the majority of the prisoners are simple criminals and there aren't enough guards to control them. The *obshchak* are really the ones in charge."

*"Obshchak?"* Kate asked.

"Prison gangs," Nogoev explained. "Inside, the gangs run the show, and the gang bosses—they're called thieves-in-law—are lords of their little castles. Even in prison, they can get drugs or cash or girls. They have an understanding with the guards that comes awfully close to a power-sharing arrangement."

"These thieves-in-law don't sound like typical Boldu supporters," Kate observed.

"No," Nogoev agreed. "This is more a personal connection."

"You are friends with one of these thieves-in-law?"

"We are more than friends. We are brothers. Vladimir is younger than I am by almost ten years. I promised our mother I would look after him, but I went off to the army and he fell in with the wrong crowd. He's been in and out of prison his whole life."

Kate did not know what to say to that. And evidently neither did Val. Instead, she fished a pack of cigarettes and a lighter out of her coat pocket and passed them around. While they had been talking, it had grown darker in the tunnel and the glow from the cigarettes offered at least a little light.

"So what's the plan?" Val asked, taking a deep drag and tilting her head back to blow a cloud of smoke up toward the ceiling.

"Plan is a pretty big word," Nogoev offered. "What I have is more like a concept."

"What is it?"

Nogoev explained to them what he had in mind.

"You're insane," Val said.

"Quite possibly."

"And your brother, Vladimir, he'll do this for us just because you ask?"

"No. With the *obshchak* there is always an exchange."

"So what's in it for him?"

"A pardon. I'll promise him that once we come to power Boldu will pardon him and every member of his *obshchak*."

"If he helps us get Ruslan out, Vladimir can have the job as warden of Number One as far as I'm concerned."

They smoked in companionable silence, each of them lighting a second cigarette off the butt of the first. Kate assessed that she had become a cabalistic smoker, only indulging when hiding in the dark and plotting against the state. That, she hoped, was unlikely to be habit forming.

"It's not enough," she said after lighting her second cigarette.

"What's not?" Val asked.

"Breaking Ruslan out of jail. It's necessary but not sufficient."

"What do you mean?"

"I mean that Ruslan and Murzaev started things in motion for the clans to take over Ala-Too Square. They told me about it last night. That's supposed to happen on Wednesday, three days from now. Without Ruslan, they'll be leaderless. Either they won't come, they won't stay, or they'll be cut up by the Special Police. We can't let that happen. They need leadership."

"Can we get Ruslan out before then?" Val asked.

Nogoev flicked the ash from his cigarette.

"We'll see. There're a lot of pieces to this. It'll take time if we're going to do it right. And we have to do it right."

"And what happens to Ruslan in the meantime?" Kate asked.

"My brother told me that they throw the prisoners in solitary for the first three or four days. It's supposed to break their spirit, make them obedient."

"Do they do the same to political prisoners?"

In the dim orange glow of the cigarettes, Kate could see Nogoev shrug his ignorance.

"So what do we do about it?" Val asked.

"Someone has to step up and lead the clans. The Adygine and the Buguu and the Kara-Kyrgyz and all the rest. There won't be many young men with them. There wasn't enough time to get them back from overseas. It'll be mostly women and children and graybeards. But the clans need to be told what to do. And assuming that they show up in Ala-Too as promised, someone needs to be there to lead."

"Are you volunteering?" Nogoev asked.

"Not me, Daniar. Val."

Val snorted her disagreement.

"I'm a good writer and bad poet. I help Boldu frame its message. But I'm a consiglieri type. I'm not that inspiring. I don't belong out in front. That's for people like Ruslan. And you."

"You'll have to do it, Val. There's no one else."

"Why not you? You may be an American, but you're as Kyrgyz as any of us."

"I can't do it. I have other plans."

"Really? There's something more pressing on your calendar?"

"Yeah. I'm going with Daniar and the Scythians and I'm breaking Ruslan out of prison."

# 26

The Scythians bantered and laughed as they climbed into the back of the truck. Twenty-four hours earlier, it had been a bread truck with the company logo—an incongruous singing chicken—painted on both sides. The fresh coat of black paint was still tacky to the touch. Bold block capitals in white spelled out Police in both Russian and Kyrgyz. Metal screens had been welded to the windows in the rear and an ugly metal grille fixed to the front bumper.

It looked like a police van, the type that was sometimes called a Black Maria, or a mother's heart, because there was always room for one more. Underneath the odor of paint, the back of the truck still smelled of fresh bread.

Like the truck, the Scythians were dressed in black. And like the truck, they were intent on passing themselves off as police property. They wore riot gear and black helmets with opaque faceplates. Their gear and weapons had been "liberated" from a Special Police warehouse out by the airport where the guard on the four a.m. to noon shift was a Boldu sympathizer, and now a moderately wealthy one.

Kate pulled down on the back of her heavy ballistic vest, which was riding up uncomfortably under her arms and chafing at the neck. The helmet was too large and Kate had to cinch the chinstrap tight to hold it in place. The pistol in the black holster on her hip was bulky and it pressed up uncomfortably against her side. It was also empty. Just for show. Kate had no intention of shooting anyone.

Nogoev was circulating among his soldiers as a good commander should, exchanging a few words with one, clapping another forcefully on the shoulder. The Scythians were young, and Kate could see that they looked to Nogoev as a father figure. They fought for Boldu and for Ruslan and Kyrgyzstan, but first and foremost they fought for him. Julius Caesar had used the bonds of loyalty he had forged with his legionnaires in Gaul to bring a bloody end to the Roman Republic and set himself up as Dictator Perpetuo. President for Life. The Latin equivalent of Eraliev's current title. Power had the gravitational pull of a thousand suns, and Kate could only hope that Nogoev would not ultimately give in to the temptations of Caesar.

He turned to Kate as though she were just another of his soldiers and put his hands on her shoulders. His eyes shone with a heady mix of confidence and eagerness. Kate could see that this was a man soldiers would gladly follow into battle. That men like Murzaev and Nogoev were ready to fight and die for Ruslan was a testament to his own qualities as a leader. Age was irrelevant. By the time he was thirty, Alexander had conquered half of the known world. Boldu's ambitions were considerably more modest.

"Are you sure that your brother knows what to do?" Kate asked for the tenth time.

"I assure you that no one is better than Vladimir at making

trouble. For the *obshchak*, the borders of the prison are porous. The gangs exist half inside the prison system and half outside. Vladimir and I were able to exchange messages almost in real time. He's organized the riots for two o'clock. We'll show up twenty minutes later as part of the riot response. And they'll let us in through the main gate."

"And after that?"

"The political prisoners are kept separate from the general population. Ruslan and Askar will be in Building D. This is Torquemada's lair and it is well defended. My hope is that many of the guards on duty at Building D will be pulled in to help put down the riot elsewhere in the compound."

"But there's no way to know, is there?"

"Life has no guarantees."

"If it comes to it, do we have enough firepower to fight our way in and fight our way out?"

"Let's go find out, shall we?"

Nogoev's confidence was infectious, no less so for Kate's suspicion that it was entirely feigned. Soldiers on the eve of battle, a Marine Corps friend with two tours in Iraq had once told her, wanted nothing more from their commanding officers than reassurance, and lying to them was not only expedient, it was a moral imperative. Up until this moment, Kate had not really understood that position. Now she welcomed Nogoev's blithe dismissal of the dangers ahead of them and cared little about whether his promises were true.

Kate climbed into the back of the Black Maria. Metal benches had been welded hastily to the walls. At first, the young Scythians continued their banter: light, confident, and boastful. But as the truck bounced down the potholed streets toward Prison Number One, they grew quiet and introspective.

After a thirty-minute ride, the truck stopped. The pass-through between the cargo compartment and the cab had been left open. Kate could head Nogoev's exchange with the nervous gate guard.

"What's the situation?" Nogoev demanded.

"I don't know. There's a riot. The *obshchak* have taken some of the guards captive. At least one of the blocks is on fire. It's out of control."

"Casualties?"

"I'm not sure. There have been a few reports over the radio about guards being hurt, but I don't know how many or how bad."

"What about weapons?"

"The prisoners had knives and clubs and at least one pistol. Now they have more, whatever they took from the guards. And if they get into the armory, god help us all."

The guard sounded scared, and Kate had the feeling that he was right on the edge of tossing his weapon and badge into the nearest storm drain and running back to his village.

"Okay. Settle down, son. Open the gates."

"I'm sorry, sir. We're on lockdown. The gates are supposed to stay closed in lockdown."

"Goddamn it. There's a riot in there and I have a truck full of Special Police whose job it is to break up riots. But they can't do that from out here. Now open the fucking gates or I will make sure that you are held personally responsible for the fate of your fellow guards being held as guests of the *obshchak*. And when they put you in prison, I will see to it that you end up serving your time inside this exact same fucking prison. Do you understand?"

Nogoev was so completely convincing in this role that Kate had to remind herself that it was, in fact, all an act.

There was a grinding sound of metal on stone as the massive gate slid open on its tracks. An unpleasant crawling sensation shot up

Kate's spine, the same feeling she got from a knife set to a sharpening steel. A feeling of dread.

The Scythians around her all sat up straighter at the prospect of imminent action. A few rechecked the weapons they had already checked multiple times.

The truck stopped and the rear doors swung open. The Scythians unloaded quickly and spread out in a semicircle between the truck and the prison buildings. Orange flames licked through the windows of one of the buildings and black smoke poured through a hole in the roof. Small bands of prisoners in matching blue uniforms were running across the courtyard brandishing homemade weapons. There were four buildings on the compound, but one stood out. It was made of concrete rather than crumbling brick, and the bars on the windows were polished steel rather than rusty wrought iron. The front door was massive and metal and imposing. This, Kate knew, was Building D, home to Kyrgyzstan's Tier I political prisoners and anyone else deemed a threat to Eraliev and his family.

The door was guarded by two men, but they were as uncertain, anxious, and inexperienced as the gate guards. Nogoev ordered them to open the door and they obeyed unquestioningly. Thirty seconds later they were both lying facedown on the concrete with their wrists and ankles bound tightly with flex cuffs.

Following the plan, the Scythians moved in pairs through the door and began a methodical search of the building. Kate had teamed with Nogoev, who had agreed to allow her to come on the mission but only if she stayed close to him.

There were a few guards and clerical staff in the front room. One guard reached for his gun and was shot by three different Scythians almost simultaneously. The others surrendered without a fight.

Nogoev ordered them into a holding room and set a pair of Scythians to stand guard.

"Come on, Daniar," Kate said. "Basement level. I'm sure that's where Chalibashvili is keeping them."

"Why so sure?"

"Because rats and snakes like the dark."

They found a stairwell and started down with a pair of Scythians following close behind to provide cover. The stairs went down deep. Building D was an iceberg, with most of its horrors lying beneath the surface.

Four stories down, a steel fire door opened up into a dark corridor lined with rough-cut stone. This level had not been excavated. It had been cut out of bedrock. The walls were damp and slightly slimy to the touch. Plain metal doors were set into the walls at irregular intervals. There were no numbers or nameplates on the doors, just a small slide at eye level that could be opened so the jailers could talk to their charges, or spy on them.

Nogoev slid the first one open.

"Ruslan?" he asked. "Are you there?"

The only sound from within was the jabbering of a madman. The next two cells were empty. It quickly became apparent that there were too many cells to search one at a time.

"We need to find the Turnkey."

"What is it?"

"It's a who. The chief jailer. His name is Karimov and he plays Renfield to Chalibashvili's Dracula."

"How do we find him?"

Nogoev sniffed the air.

"It's lunchtime."

Kate copied Nogoev, and underneath the smell of mold she could detect garlic and chili and fried mutton. The ingredients of *paloo*.

"We used this same trick in Afghanistan when the Muj retreated to their caves. The smell of dal still makes me sick."

The odor of *paloo* was clearly coming from the corridor on their right. They followed it to another split where the cooking smells led to the left. Kate could hear it now, the sizzling sound of frying sheep fat. There was a light coming from an open door up ahead, and Nogoev and their Scythian escorts raised their Heckler & Koch machine pistols to the ready position.

They needn't have bothered.

The Turnkey was alone. And he was far from imposing. Karimov stood little more than five feet tall, with a prominent stoop to his shoulders. His arms were thin and bony. His hairline had receded like a spring tide. He looked up as Kate and Nogoev stepped into the room, his head turned slightly to one side, and Kate could see that his left eye was a dead milky white.

The room looked like it was used primarily as an office, with file cabinets, a desk, and a computer. But Karimov had also set up a small kitchen with a hotplate and a cast-iron skillet. The *paloo* looked excellent.

"What do you want, Captain?" Karimov asked, visibly annoyed and addressing Nogoev by the rank patch sewn onto the sleeve of his stolen uniform.

"Two of your prisoners," Nogoev answered calmly as he leveled the machine pistol at Karimov's head.

"You're not the police, are you?"

"No."

"Who are you then?"

"A man with a gun. But if you don't do exactly as I ask, you can just call me Death."

The jailer seemed unfazed by the threat.

"I don't think so," he said. "I've worked down here a long time. Death and I are old friends. He looks nothing like you. I'd ask you to lunch, but I'm afraid there's only enough for one."

As he spoke, the Turnkey moved his head back and forth as he trained his good eye on Nogoev and then Kate. The Scythians were visible by the doorframe, but he ignored them.

Nogoev stepped over to the hotplate and picked up the skillet with a gloved hand. He dumped the *paloo* on the floor and held the hot metal pan up along the side of Karimov's face.

The jailer's equanimity seemed to falter.

"Who are you?" he asked again.

"Where is Ruslan Usenov?"

"You're Boldu?"

"Where is he?"

"I've tripped the alarm. Help is coming."

"Can they get here before I count to three?"

"They're on their way."

"One."

"You don't have time to free him and save yourselves."

"Two."

"The Georgian will find you. You can't hide from him. No one can."

"Three."

As he said this, Nogoev grabbed the back of Karimov's head with his free hand and pressed it against the bottom of the skillet. The jailer screamed and the smell of burnt human skin mixed sickeningly with the mutton-fat smell of the *paloo*.

When Nogoev released him, Kate could see the ugly red burn marks on his face and the bubbly skin where the blisters would soon form. Her stomach turned. As much as she wanted to find Ruslan and free him, this was torture, and ten minutes ago Kate believed firmly that it was never acceptable. As Murzaev had said about her kidnapping, however, it was complicated.

The Turnkey grabbed the side of his face and cursed in a mixture of Russian and Kyrgyz.

"You will die screaming," he promised.

"Where is Ruslan Usenov?" Nogoev repeated. He held up the skillet in front of Karimov's good eye and moved it slowly toward the unburned side of his face.

"Not far," Karimov squeaked.

"Show me."

The jailer led them through the subterranean maze, stopping before one of the doors, no different than any other.

"You're sure this is it?" Nogoev asked. "Because if it's not, I don't see any reason you should keep that one good eye."

"I know where they all are," Karimov replied, and Kate could hear in his voice how much pain he was in.

Kate opened the slide in the door. The room was pitch black.

"Ruslan? Are you there?"

"Katie?"

"Are you all right?"

"Thirsty. How long have I been in here?"

"Two days. Open the damn door." This last she addressed to the jailer.

Karimov fumbled with the keys at his belt before finding the one he was after. With the muzzle of Nogoev's machine pistol pressed up against his neck, he opened the door.

Ruslan stumbled out, blinking in the unaccustomed light. He looked worn and pale and he staggered slightly. Kate undid her chin strap and dropped her helmet to the ground. Then she hugged Ruslan hard and kissed him on the mouth.

When she finally released him, Ruslan grabbed Nogoev in a bear hug.

"Thank you, Daniar. I knew you would come."

"One more, dwarf," Nogoev said to Karimov. "Where's Askar Murzaev?"

"The Georgian took him for questioning," Karimov protested. "I don't know where he is."

Nogoev pushed the muzzle of the machine pistol up against the Turnkey's one good eye.

"Think harder."

Appropriately incentivized, Karimov acknowledged that he may, in fact, have at least a good idea as to Murzaev's whereabouts. He led them upstairs one level. The third sub-basement looked more like an ordinary jail than a castle dungeon, with whitewashed concrete walls and numbered cells.

"I want you to understand," Karimov said when they stopped in front of the door to the room where Murzaev was being kept. "I had nothing to do with the interrogation. Not my department. That's the Georgian. I'm just the innkeeper." His one good eye blinked rapidly and his Adam's apple bobbed up and down nervously.

"Open the goddamn door."

Murzaev was not in good shape. He was lying naked on a thin rubberized mattress on a metal bed. A single lightbulb hanging from the ceiling cast a harsh light. The old spymaster was badly bruised. His face was swollen and there were burn marks on his chest where, Kate suspected, Chalibashvili had hooked electrodes to his flesh.

Nogoev helped his friend to his feet with a surprising gentleness. Murzaev stirred groggily. When he tried to speak, Kate saw that his front teeth were broken. Torquemada had worked him over hard.

"Don't try to talk," Nogoev said. "And don't worry about identifying the man who did this. We know who it was."

As he said this, Nogoev leveled his machine pistol at Karimov's chest. The Turnkey squealed in fear.

"It wasn't me. I'm not involved in the questioning."

"I don't really care." The muscles in Nogoev's right arm tensed and the gun shifted up slightly to point straight at Karimov's forehead.

"Don't do it, Daniar." The tone of command in Ruslan's voice was unmistakable. This was not a suggestion.

Nogoev looked at him, but the gun did not waver.

"Why the fuck not?"

"Because we're better than that. Better than him. He'll get what's coming to him, I promise you. But in a court, representing the will of the people. Not like this."

The muzzle shifted back and forth just a little but did not drop.

"No, Daniar," Kate said. "I still need him."

"We have Ruslan. That's what we came for. We have to go. Now."

"I'm not going to get another chance like this." She turned to the jailer. "Zamira Ishenbaev. Where is she? You know where they all are. You said so yourself."

There was a flicker of recognition on the jailer's face, maybe as he connected Kate with the aunt she so resembled.

Gunfire in the corridor cut short any answer he might have given.

"The Special Police are here," one of the Scythians shouted from the hall. "The real ones."

"We need to get out of here," Nogoev said.

Karimov, evidently still uncertain about Nogoev's ultimate intentions, seized the moment of distraction to break for the door and step out into the hall, running in the direction of his putative rescuers and waving his arms wildly. They shot him before he had covered five feet, and the Turnkey's last few moments of life were spent twitching like a fish in a pool of his own blood. Kate knew that her best chance for finding her aunt alive had died with him.

With the young Scythians providing cover, they hurried down the hall, running away from the gunfire and in the opposite direction of the stairwell. They moved as quickly as they could with the barely conscious Murzaev in tow. At the far end of the corridor, there was another stairwell, but this led up only one level. One of the Scythians took the point while his partner brought up the rear. Ruslan helped Nogoev lift Murzaev bodily up the stairs.

The next floor up was another maze of cells. They ran down the widest corridor, ignoring the poorly lit branches that seemed to lead off into darkness and nightmares. An oversize red button set at eye level was labeled LOCK DOWN. Kate was afraid that button might seal the doors, but there was no time to stop and examine it.

The Special Police were not far behind. Kate could hear the heavy thud of their boots on the stairs. At the end of the corridor was a metal door. The words EMERGENCY EXIT were stenciled on the door in both Russian and Kyrgyz.

The Special Police fired wildly down the corridor. Bullets from their machine pistols ricocheted off the walls. Right behind her, Kate heard a grunt and turned in time to see one of the Scythians fall, clutching his leg where he had been shot. Automatically, she took a few steps back in the direction of their pursuers to help the wounded Scythian. She had a clear view down the corridor, but without a weapon she could only watch as one of the Special Police hit the red LOCK DOWN button on the wall.

The button's function was instantly and horrifyingly clear. A metal grate dropped from the ceiling and closed off the corridor, with Kate and the injured Scythian on one side and her friends on the other. Ruslan shouted in anger and frustration and threw himself at the grate, struggling to lift it so that Kate might escape. It was locked in place. A burst of bullets forced him to let go.

"She has immunity," Kate heard Nogoev say. "But you do not. And there's no time. We have to leave."

Kate ran to the grate and for a moment her fingers touched Ruslan's.

"Go," she said.

"I love you."

"Then go. Now."

Sparks flew from the steel grate as another wild round of bullets slammed into it.

The uninjured Scythian grabbed Ruslan by the shoulders and dragged him toward the exit.

Kate raised her hands in surrender.

# 27

It was pitch dark in the Pit and Kate had lost all sense of time. It might have been hours since the guards had stripped off her stolen Special Police uniform and closed the door to her cell. It might have been days. Probably not days, Kate told herself. She had no food and no water and while she was both hungry and thirsty, she was not desperately so.

She was, however, cold. Underneath her uniform, Kate had been wearing only a thin cotton T-shirt and underwear. The cell was damp and the stone walls and floor seemed to suck the heat out of her body. She had felt around in the dark looking for a mattress or a blanket, but there was nothing. As near as she could tell, the room was entirely empty.

At one point, something insect-like had skittered across her bare leg and Kate jumped up in alarm, cracking the back of her head against the stone wall. There was a lump there now the size of a robin's egg. It ached dully. When she had to pee, she picked a corner and urinated on the floor, adding a vaguely ammonia smell to the odors of mildew and wet stone.

"At least I can't get sick," Kate said out loud to the dark. "I have immunity." She laughed at her own weak joke.

There was no one to rescue her, she knew. The Scythians had shot their one bolt freeing Ruslan, and the embassy would have no way of knowing she was in the dungeon cells of Prison Number One unless the regime decided to tell them. That seemed unlikely.

Her diplomatic status was only worth something if her government knew what was happening. Without that, she was just another prisoner who had fallen into the black hole. Would they torture her? For what? What would they want from her?

Maybe they would do it for sport, out of sheer bloody-mindedness. A further act of revenge and retribution against her family.

Her best hope, she reasoned, was that she was trade bait. The Eraliev government might give her to the Americans in exchange for some concessions in the base negotiations. How valuable was she? Was she worth the contract for cafeteria services? Maybe Ball and Crandle would prefer that she never see the light of day again. What would her uncle think? What side would he be on? That she was even asking the question was painful.

To pass the time, she played piano in her head, moving her stiff fingers across an imaginary keyboard as best she could. She could hear the music clearly in the silence of her cell. This must have been what it was like for Beethoven, she thought. He had composed his masterpiece, the Ninth Symphony, after going completely deaf and he had never heard a single note of it with his own ears. The mental game both helped her pass the time and keep track of it.

Two concertos, three études, a fugue, and a rumba later, the bolt to her cell door slid open with a crack that sounded like a rifle shot. Kate was sitting on the floor with her back up against the wall, and she unconsciously brought her knees up to her chest in anticipation of some form of assault.

A guard stood silhouetted in the doorway. Without entering the cell, he threw something across the room that landed at Kate's feet.

"Get dressed," he said in Uzbek-accented Kyrgyz.

Kate reached for the bundle. It was a blue prison uniform, with separate shirt and pants rather than a jumpsuit. There was also a pair of rubber slippers about two sizes too big for Kate's feet. She dressed under the watchful eye of the Uzbek guard.

Her T-shirt and underwear were uncomfortably sticky and damp, but it was still a sensuous pleasure to be clothed. The guard was tall and broad, with a boxer's broken nose and tattooed flames on the back of his neck that licked at the collar of his uniform. He led Kate down the hall and up what she believed were the same stairs she and Nogoev had used in their descent to the sub-basement. They went up one flight to the floor on which she had been captured.

The room he brought her to would not have been out of place in a metropolitan police station in the United States. It was entirely functional, with a metal table bracketed to the concrete floor and two metal folding chairs. A steel ring welded to the top of the table was presumably for shackles. The walls were tiled and there was a mirror that did not even try to disguise its identity as an observation window.

The guard said nothing. But he pushed Kate into the room and closed the door behind her. It clicked shut and Kate did not have to try it to know that it was locked. In any event, there was nothing to try. There was no handle on the inside.

Kate went to the mirror, imagining strangers in the room behind it watching her straighten her hair and rub the dirt off her cheeks with her shirtsleeve. Screw them.

She sat at the table and tried not to think about how much she would like a drink. A glass of water first. And then something much stronger.

Keeping her here alone was no doubt part of the elaborate mind games the torturers had learned to play. Kate's defense was the discipline of a classical musician. She waited with her hands in her lap, looking straight at the door.

After half an hour, the door opened and Torquemada himself entered the room. He was wearing a dark suit that looked expensive, with Italian loafers and a black Omega watch. His hair was cut bristly short and was the same steel gray color as his eyes. The body under the suit looked strong and healthy. Torture must agree with him.

He sat across from Kate, his hands resting on the tabletop. His nails, she noticed, were carefully manicured.

"Good morning, Ms. Hollister. I hope you had a good night's sleep." He spoke in Russian with that distinctive Georgian accent.

"The bed was a little firm for my taste. But I won't be staying long. I would like to be released immediately to my embassy. I am an accredited diplomat and inviolate under the Vienna Convention."

"How interesting. A diplomat, you say? Is dressing up in a stolen police uniform, murdering foreign government officials, and releasing dangerous enemies of the state from lawful confinement part of your country's normal diplomatic practice?"

"All your questions will be answered in time. You must release me first, and address your questions to my government in writing through a diplomatic note. We will respond appropriately in time."

"Time. Yes, time. That's really the key factor here, isn't it? None of us have as much of it as we would like. I typically like to leave our guests alone with their thoughts for a few days before we begin our discussions, but you see I'm rather pressed for time, so we are beginning a bit on the early side. I hope you don't mind."

"Beginning what?"

"Questions and answers, of course. I ask the questions and you answer them."

"I don't feel like playing."

"It's not a game, Ms. Hollister. And I assure you, we are not playing."

Chalibashvili's expression hardened and Kate thought he might hit her. She refused to flinch. But the blow did not come. Not yet. All he was doing was giving her a quick look at the tempered steel beneath the velvet glove.

"Let us begin. Tell me everything you know about Ruslan Usenov."

"Who?"

This time he hit her.

Not hard. More a slap. A warning. But her cheek stung.

"No games, Ms. Hollister. Maybe you are uncomfortable with open-ended questions. So allow me to be more specific. What is the name of the Boldu spy in the Presidential Palace?"

This time Kate's quizzical look was genuine.

"I have no idea what you're talking about."

"Someone forged the transfer orders for a Boldu prisoner named Bermet Samsaliev. This could only have been done with the assistance of someone in the president's office. I have . . . spoken . . . about this at some length with Ms. Svetlana, the protocol assistant whom I believe you know, and the president's personal secretary. Both deny their involvement, and I believe that they would have told me what they knew. Under the circumstances."

Kate could imagine what the circumstances were, and it made her sick.

"I believe, Ms. Hollister, that you were the conduit for this document, passing it from someone in the president's circle to Boldu. I want to know who it was."

"Then I suggest you submit that request under cover of a diplomatic note to the American embassy. I will personally make certain that it gets the attention it deserves."

He hit her again. Harder this time.

"What is Boldu planning? We know they intend to strike a blow against the government. What is it? Who is involved? What is the timetable?"

The questions came hard and fast. Chalibashvili did not even give Kate time to answer them. She sensed that she was not expected to. This was part of the softening up. He asked about Boldu, its membership, and its plans. He wanted to know where the leadership met. Who was in the inner circle. How they communicated with one another. It was a long list, and it was increasingly clear to Kate how valuable the information she had was to the government. It was not a pleasant feeling to be in possession of something that Eraliev wanted.

After an hour or more of questioning, Chalibashvili stood and indicated that Kate should do the same.

"Come with me. There's something that I think you should see."

She followed him out into the hall. They walked down the corridor together, almost as though they were colleagues rather than jailer and prisoner. Halfway down the hall they walked past an open door. Inside, Kate could see a steel table with leather restraints built into it.

The table was angled backward and there was a plastic jug of water set on the floor next to it. There were shackles on the wall to chain prisoners upright. And Kate caught a quick glimpse of some of the tools of Torquemada's trade hanging neatly on hooks. Electric cables and leather whips. Pliers and sharp metal probes.

The casually open door was not, Kate knew, a coincidence. It was a threat. Chalibashvili was showing her a stick in the way one might taunt a recalcitrant donkey.

Kate counted the turns. Second right. First left. Third left. They stopped in front of a steel door painted institutional green. The number 374 was stenciled on it in white.

"Do you know whose cell this is?" Chalibashvili asked.

She turned to him and the sharp, sarcastic retort she had intended died on her lips. And Kate realized that she did know. Of course she did. Nothing else made sense. The self-satisfied look on the Georgian's face confirmed her instinctive understanding. Chalibashvili was enjoying himself. But it was the twisted, icy pleasure of a sadist.

"Yes," Kate answered. Her mouth was dry.

Chalibashvili opened the slide and stepped to one side. Kate looked through the opening. It was narrow and the view was partly obscured by wire mesh, but she could see a woman sitting on a wooden bench in the cell. She was wearing a standard prison-issue uniform. The woman was thin and her white hair looked to have been cut by herself with dull scissors and without the benefit of a mirror. The skin on her face was flaccid and lifeless.

"Aunt Zamira?" Kate called softly.

The woman did not react. She continued to stare at a spot on the wall in front of her.

"I'm afraid that we keep her drugged," Chalibashvili explained. "For her own good, really. She's tried to escape a number of times, you see. I've personally watched her blind a man with a fork. I must say I admire your family. Strong women."

If she had a fork handy, Kate would have gladly driven it through his eye and into his brain.

She studied the woman in the cell. Her aunt's hair had been black, but it had been more than ten years. She had not been quite so thin, but prison changed people on the outside as well as the inside. This could be her aunt. She had no reason to disbelieve. She looked for something in the cell that would convince her the Georgian was telling the truth.

And she found it.

A small photograph was taped to the wall by the metal cot. It was a picture of Kate and her mother taken almost fifteen years ago. They were standing on top of a mountain with an incredible panorama behind them. The picture was too far away to make out the details, but Kate did not need to see it up close. It was one of her favorite photographs. She had the same one in a small photo album in her apartment.

"Zamira? It's Kate. I found you."

For a brief moment, Kate thought her aunt was about to turn and look at her. But the moment passed and Zamira's gaze remained fixed straight ahead.

"I assure you that she's of sound mind," Chalibashvili said. "The drugs we give her are powerful, but there are no lasting effects. Once she stops taking the cocktail she'll be as good as new in just a couple of days."

Kate looked at him. She knew what was coming next.

"You can see to that, Kate. All you need to do is cooperate. Tell us what you know. And you and your aunt will be free to go. It's as simple as that."

And there it was. The carrot to go along with the stick. Diplomacy was the same. It was based on incentives and disincentives. Evidently it was not dissimilar from torture in this respect.

"Boldu will be crushed in any event," Chalibashvili continued. "You'd just be helping us do it with a minimum of collateral damage. We'd like to avoid the use of excessive force if that's at all possible. But surgical intervention requires a greater degree of knowledge than we have at the moment. I believe that you can help us with this, Kate."

She was "Kate" now. Not Ms. Hollister. It was like some bizarre game of "good inquisitor/bad inquisitor" with Chalibashvili playing both parts.

"Is that it?" Kate asked.

"What do mean?"

"Aren't you going to offer me more? Money? Power? Position?"

"Name your price." Chalibashvili smiled slyly in accepting her implied offer to negotiate.

But there was nothing to negotiate. Selling out Boldu would not only betray both Kate's principles and her friends, it would vitiate her aunt's twelve years of sacrifice in Torquemada's Pit. Everything she worked for. Everything Kate's mother had worked for. There was only one possible response.

"Go fuck yourself, Anton."

# 28

It's been more than twenty-four hours, Askar. And no word from
Kate. I don't like that at all. What have you been able to find out?"

Despite Daniar's assurances that Chalibashvili would be forced
to respect her diplomatic immunity, Ruslan could not shake the mental image of Kate shivering in the chill dark of a dungeon cell, waiting for a rescue that would never come. A full squad of heavily armed
Special Police was now patrolling Prison Number One as a supple-
ment to the regular guard force. Absent the element of surprise, there
was no way that the Scythians could repeat their successful raid.
Moreover, the *obshchak*'s contacts with the outside, which prison authorities had known about and tolerated, had been cut off. Nogoev
had no word about the fate of his brother.

The core members of the Boldu council were meeting at the last of
Murzaev's safe houses, the only one that had not yet—they hoped—
been compromised. It was a small, dingy two-room apartment in a

mostly industrial part of the city. People who lived in this neighborhood worked with their hands, drank as much as they could afford, and kept to themselves. Even so, every meeting was dangerous. The GKNB and the Special Police were combing Bishkek and the surrounding towns looking for Ruslan and Murzaev. One way or another, it looked like everything was going to come to a head in the next few days.

"There's been nothing moving through the newsstand network," Murzaev said, speaking carefully because of the swelling in his jaw and the dental putty a Boldu doctor had used to patch his broken teeth. "I sent one of the boys around to her apartment building. He didn't ring the buzzer, but there were no lights. It's possible that she was released to the embassy, and if she's there we wouldn't know about it."

"Do you know anyone at the embassy?"

"I could find someone if I had to. But it's dangerous. The Americans are playing all sides of the street right now. If we talk to them, it's impossible to know who's going to hear about it. We can't trust them."

"I need to know, Askar. I need to know what's happened to Kate."

"I understand. I want her out as well. She knows more than she should, even if the most important secret she had has been exposed. Let me see what more I can learn through our own people before we go to the Americans. There's too much at stake."

"If Torquemada is holding Kate," Val interjected, "there's really only one way to get her out of there. We need to take down Eraliev, and the faster we can do that, the better our chances for getting to her before . . ."

Valentina could not finish the sentence. She did not have to. They all knew what happened in the interrogation rooms of Prison Number One.

Ruslan nodded his understanding. He wanted to grab a gun and storm the gates of the prison like Ernest Defarge at the Bastille. But he had responsibilities to Boldu and to Kyrgyzstan and to the revolution that he had launched and hoped to lead. What he wanted to do was subordinate to what he had to do. This, he understood, was the price of leadership. He could only pray that Kate would understand it as well.

"Is everything ready for this evening?" Nogoev asked in a transparent attempt to shift the discussion away from something he considered a mere distraction. The Scythian commander was pragmatic to the point of callous. And he had seen so much death in his long career that its prospect—for himself or others—was of little consequence.

"As ready as it can be," Hamid said. "Val and I have given clear instructions to the clan leaders, but the clans are fractious. They certainly aren't used to working together. The plan isn't especially complicated, but it has a lot of moving parts. Things could go wrong."

"They will go wrong," Ruslan said. "That's unavoidable. We just have to be ready for it and adapt to the circumstances. I can promise you one thing. Tashtanbek Essenkul uluu will not panic. Not even if Eraliev calls out the tanks."

"That's good," Hamid replied. "But he's going to have to work with the Ichkilik and the southern clan leaders. Can he do that?"

"For a while. Let's review the plan one more time."

Nogoev spread a large map of Ala-Too Square out on the coffee table. His briefing was thorough and authoritative. It would not have been out of place at a high-level strategy session in the Kremlin.

Even so, Ruslan was struck by what a wild gamble they were taking, with hundreds of lives and the future of the country on the line. Boldu was his creation and his responsibility. And he was about to bet everything on a single throw of the dice.

It was three a.m. The dead time. The night owls had finally returned to their nests and the early birds had yet to stir. The police presence at Ala-Too Square was at its minimum. There would be only a handful of officers on duty guarding the Presidential Palace. It would take time to organize a response by the Special Police. Time that Ruslan intended to put to good use.

He and Nogoev and a small group of Scythians arrived at the square in the back of a Tata Super Ace, an Indian-made one-ton pickup truck. The Scythians unloaded plywood boards from the bed and laid them across the short set of stairs that led up from the street to the plaza. Ruslan drove the truck up the ramp and onto the square, parking it near the statue of Manas, where two raised planters created a path just about the size of the Super Ace. Six Scythians used levers and muscle power to turn the truck over on its side, blocking the path and making the first barrier.

This, Ruslan thought, was a gauntlet being thrown at Eraliev's feet. Only one of them could survive the duel that must ensue.

Two policemen dressed like traffic cops rather than in paramilitary tactical gear came to investigate the noise. They shined flashlights at the truck and called out contradictory commands in a mix of Kyrgyz and Russian. Ruslan stepped forward. He looked like a Kyrgyz warlord of old in an embroidered jacket with loose trousers tucked into riding boots and a massive *kalpak* on his head. It was uncomfortable. Ruslan was a city boy now, and he rarely dressed like this. But it was part of the plan.

"Greetings, brothers," he said. "Welcome to the dawn of a new Kyrgyzstan."

The police pointed their machine pistols at Ruslan.

"Get on your knees," one of them shouted.

"Never again," Ruslan replied.

Something tapped one of the policemen on the shoulder. He turned to find that he was staring into the barrel of an AK-47. They were surrounded by heavily armed Scythians. Deciding in short order that they did not like the odds, the police held up their hands in surrender. The Scythians stripped them of their weapons and tied them up sitting back-to-back at the base of the statue. Now they had bargaining chips.

The other trucks came quickly, arriving from various side streets near the park and driving up the ramp to the square. Each truck had an assigned spot, and the Scythians worked fast to unload building materials from the back before tipping them up on their sides to make an impromptu wall. Even taking full advantage of all the raised brick-and-concrete flower beds, it still took eleven trucks of various shapes and sizes and three beaten-up old Chinese buses to make a rough, defensible wall that circled the Manas statue. They left one panel van upright that could be used as a gate. The van was loaded with concrete blocks and it sat heavy on its wheels. It was a start.

The buses had disgorged more than a hundred villagers, mostly women and pensioners and a few young men too sick or injured to take work overseas. As Val had instructed, most were wearing Kyrgyz traditional dress, the kind they might wear to a wedding or similar ceremony. It certainly was not what they would wear to work in the fields or the mines or the factories, and it hardly seemed the right dress code for a revolution, but Val had been specific, and the clan leaders, at least for now, had obliged.

The last truck to arrive was pulling a trailer. Tashtanbek dismounted from the passenger side resplendent in a *chapan* with an embroidered collar and a *kalpak* edged in gold. The hooded goshawk, Janibar, was perched on the oversize leather glove Tashtanbek wore on his left hand.

One of the older men from Kara-Say opened the door of the trailer and led two massive horses down the ramp. Ruslan recognized the black stallion and the roan that he and Tashtanbek had ridden on their hunt. Both the truck and trailer were soon added to the walls.

Ruslan walked over to greet his grandfather. By the time he made it through the throng of new arrivals who wanted to touch his arm or exchange a few words with the great Seitek, Tashtanbek was already deep in conversation with Valentina. Like Ruslan and the others, she was dressed in traditional Kyrgyz clothes. Ruslan had never seen her like this. It was not a good look for her.

"Grandfather, thank you for coming. And I see you've already met Valentina. Val, you look . . . great . . ." It was unconvincing.

"She's the reason we're dressed like this," Tashtanbek answered. "Are we here to fight, or are you planning a feast and a dance?"

Val laughed lightly.

"There'll be time to eat after the revolution, I promise. But I wanted us dressed like this because of the contrast it will draw between the demonstrators and the government forces. They'll look like storm-troopers or Cossacks assaulting innocent villagers. I want the world to see that. I want it all on film. We're going to fight the battle in the streets, but we're going to win the war on the BBC."

Tashtanbek nodded but said nothing. With his free hand he reached up and patted the barrel of the ancient rifle slung across his back. The weapon was as old as he was, but Ruslan had seen him use it to kill a mountain goat at eight hundred meters, shooting uphill in the wind.

"We need to get ready," he said.

"Don't worry, Grandfather. We are ready."

Ruslan stepped up on one of the concrete planters to give himself a better view. Everywhere, Scythians and villagers were using the bricks and lumber they had unloaded from the trucks to reinforce the defensive walls and fill in the gaps. As they settled in for a siege, Ruslan planned to improve the defenses further, but they had anticipated that the first attack from the Special Police would come within hours.

It came at dawn. Ruslan stood on a makeshift rampart and watched a squad of Special Police in riot gear form up, their curved plastic shields overlapping. The light was still low and their faceplates were up. Through the binoculars, they looked young and nervous. The Scythians to Ruslan's left and right were, in contrast, calm and confident. They were well led and they believed in themselves as well as their cause. It was a powerful combination.

Nogoev hauled himself up onto the platform and surveyed the scene.

"Are you sure about this, Ruslan? My Scythians could cut them down like wheat if you gave the order."

"I'm sure, Daniar. I don't want to kill anyone unless we absolutely have to. Those are our brothers out there. Our goal is to rally the country to our cause. Murdering police, young men with families, is not the image we want to project. We are better than Eraliev and his thugs, and we have to live up to that."

"Politicians," Nogoev scoffed. But Ruslan could hear the affection buried under the complaint. The Scythians would do their duty.

The riot police marched forward in lockstep carrying long truncheons in their right hands. They were acting as police rather than soldiers. They did not yet understand that this was a war. Three Scythians threw Molotov cocktails that fell short by design. The flaming pools of gasoline were intended to disorient the police and break up their line as they advanced.

When they got closer, the villagers started throwing stones and bricks, forcing the police to raise their shields above their heads. The police tried to climb the barricades, but the Scythians and the younger villagers had the high ground and used blunted farm tools to beat them back. A few police got close enough for the Scythians to grab their shields and rip them off their arms. Ruslan watched one riot cop get caught up in the shield straps and hauled bodily over a section of the wall made of wood and loose brick. Within seconds he had been stripped of his equipment, and minutes later he had joined the growing cluster of prisoners at the base of the Manas statue.

Ruslan hefted an ax and joined the Scythians at the wall. The ax was blunted, but he still used the flat back rather than the edge to beat down on the shields and helmets as the riot police tried to clamber over the planters and the makeshift wall of trucks and buses.

It was all over in less than ten minutes. The riot police retreated, leaving three of their number behind as prisoners. They were battered and bruised, but no one had died on either side. Ruslan knew that they had been lucky in that regard. People would die on both sides before the dust had settled. All he could hope for was to keep that number as low as possible.

The Special Police gave the revolutionaries a few hours of respite as they regrouped. The Scythians and the villagers used the time to improve their defenses. One of the buses had been loaded with food and water and the women from one of the southern villages lit a fire and set large pots of mutton stew on the coals. A group of men set up two large felt-covered yurts. It's a regular village, Ruslan thought, and he was the mayor.

Valentina walked up to him with a small video camera. She had taken footage of the attack and would use her MacBook to edit the film and post it on YouTube. She had already set up a Facebook page and a Twitter feed with the handle @Ala-TooRevolution.

"Easier than you thought?" Valentina asked.

"No. They didn't know what to expect. I knew we'd be able to take the first punch. The next round is going to be tougher."

"I need some footage of you for YouTube. Say something inspirational." She laughed and then turned the camera on and held it up in Ruslan's direction. He made a sour face.

"You have to do this, Ruslan. It's your responsibility. You don't belong to yourself anymore. You belong to all of us. Sorry. But that's what you signed up for. And that's just the way it is. You'd better get used to it."

"I know. I'll do it. And I'll do the best I can."

"Seitek, Boldu has planted its flag here in Ala-Too Square. Is there anything that you would like to say to the Kyrgyz people?"

"My fellow countrymen," he began. "We are a proud people. A warrior people. But we have for too long hung our heads and allowed a privileged few to decide for us how we live our lives. Their time is at an end. And our time is beginning. Come join us here in Ala-Too Square. Stand with us, fight alongside us, and send a message to the Eraliev regime that they cannot ignore. They are yesterday. We are today. And you are tomorrow."

Ruslan had not seen the small group of Scythians and villagers who had gathered behind him while he spoke. But when he finished, they cheered loudly and clapped him on the back, the adrenaline of combat still rushing through their veins.

Valentina lowered the camera.

"That was perfect."


A few hours later, the police tried again, harder this time. There were at least a hundred members of the Special Police, and a few of them carried shotguns or rifles instead of truncheons. A six-wheeled armored personnel carrier lined up on the square directly across from the gate. Two cops stepped out in front of the group and began shooting grenades up into the air. They all knew what was coming.

"Gas!" Nogoev shouted. "Masks, now!"

Among the gear they had confiscated from the Special Police warehouse were three boxes of gas masks. There were enough to equip all the Scythians and almost half of the villagers. Those without masks huddled in the yurts for protection. The tear-gas canisters landed in the middle of the Boldu encampment and began spitting out a white mist that hung low to the ground.

Villagers picked up the individual canisters and tossed them back over the wall in the direction of the police. The attackers donned their own masks, and the net effect on the balance of power was close to zero.

The APC started its engine and moved forward toward the gate, clearly intending to ram it open. The Scythians responded with Molotov cocktails, and soon the front end of the APC was covered in flames. The driver pulled back, leaving behind a black slick of melted rubber from the tires.

"They have guns, Ruslan," Nogoev observed. "What are the rules of engagement?"

"If someone points a gun at your men, you can shoot him. Try to not kill him unless you have to."

"Understood."

Nogoev went to pass the word among his troops.

The Special Police moved forward hesitantly. One man raised a shotgun to his shoulder and almost immediately fell to the ground, clutching his leg where a Scythian had shot him. The message had been delivered.

The police did not seem to have much of a plan. Evidently they had hoped to rely on the tear gas to demoralize the demonstrators and the APC to open a hole in the wall. Moreover, the defenses they were attacking were now stronger than they had been, and the defenders, with one victory under their belt, were more confident.

The results of the second attack were almost the same, with one critical difference. Two dead. One on each side. A policeman trying to clamber up the undercarriage of a truck had fired his shotgun, perhaps by accident. It caught one of the Scythians, a nineteen-year-old named Azamat who had hoped one day to be a pilot, under the chin, blowing off his face. Seconds later, the cop was dead, shot more than a dozen times by vengeful Scythians.

Once the police had retreated, Ruslan ran to the fallen fighter. His comrades had already come to his aid, but the boy was dead. One thing that Ruslan had not thought about was a morgue. What should he do with the body?

The ever practical Nogoev stepped in, instructing the Scythians to place the body of their comrade behind the Manas statue and cover it with a blanket. Ruslan wanted to accompany them, but Nogoev put his hand on his shoulder, stopping him.

"No," he explained. "This is for them. Not us."

Tashtanbek joined them. On anyone else, Ruslan would have described his expression as grave. But on his grandfather, it might well have represented overwhelming joy. It was impossible to say.

"There is a man at the gate," he said.

"Is he selling something?" Ruslan asked, knowing full well that the attempt at humor would be wasted on his grandfather.

"No. It's one of the Special Police. He looks like an officer. He is alone."

"A parlay?" Ruslan asked.

"It does seem early," Nogoev agreed.

"Let's go find out."

At Ruslan's direction, the van pulled forward a few feet and a tall man wearing Special Police tactical gear stepped into the encampment.

Ruslan was there to greet him, along with Nogoev, Murzaev, and Tashtanbek. Whoever this cop was, he was walking alone into the lion's den. Ruslan had to respect that.

"My name is Davron Kayrat uluu," he said, offering his hand to each of them in turn.

Ruslan raised an eyebrow.

"The commander of the Special Police."

"I have the honor."

"But only as of late," Nogoev said.

"True."

"How is your predecessor?"

"Dead by his own hand, I'm afraid."

"Pity."

"This is an unlawful gathering," Kayrat uluu said. "I have come to ask you to disperse before there is additional loss of life."

"Your side is the one that escalated to firearms," Ruslan said. "The consequences are on your head."

"If you lay down your weapons, and return to your homes, I can guarantee the safety of your followers," the Special Police colonel continued. "And I have been authorized to make an additional commitment. If you surrender yourself to justice, the government will release your comrade, Katarina Hollister, without charging her."

"You cannot hold her," Ruslan protested, and he could feel the anger building inside him. "She is an American diplomat, with immunity under international law. You must release her immediately and without condition."

"Not my department, I'm afraid. I have no idea who this woman is. I'm just passing on the message."

"If Chalibashvili hurts her, so help me god, I will rip the eyes from his head."

"We could hold him," Nogoev said. "Trade the commander of the Special Police for Kate."

"Do you think Eraliev or Chalibashvili would take that deal?" Ruslan asked.

"No."

"I'm sorry," Kayrat uluu said. "But I do need an answer."

"Go to hell."

"I thought that might be your position. Very well, the offer is good for the next three hours. Think it over."

"In three hours, I will still want you to go to hell, but there is something else that I want right now."

"What is it?"

"I want your agreement not to use guns. If you do, then we will have to. And boys and girls will die who do not need to die. You, Mr. Kayrat uluu, I believe to be a Kyrgyz patriot. Don't spill the blood of Kyrgyzstan's children needlessly."

"Maybe we should each appoint a champion and they can battle it out in front of your walls. Like Hector and Achilles at Troy."

"I don't think that one worked out so well for the defenders," Ruslan replied. "I'd prefer David and Goliath."

The colonel was quiet as he considered his options.

"Malinin would have already dropped a barrel bomb on you from a helicopter."

"Maybe so," Ruslan said. "But I think you're different."

"Oh, really? What makes you think that?"

"You came here alone. I assume that was so we could talk honestly."

"It's always better to be honest, but you never know who reports to whom."

"Of course. So do we have an understanding? No guns?"

"I'll do what I can," Kayrat uluu promised.

"Remember, Colonel. We are going to win. And for the rest of your life you are going to have to answer for the decisions you make in the next few days. Choose wisely. Choose your country over Eraliev. The fat pig calls himself President for Life. Well, his term is almost up."

Once the colonel had left, Ruslan turned to Murzaev.

"Askar, you said you could contact the Americans if you had to. Let them know about Kate."

"Yes. If I had to."

"Do it. Quickly. Before they decide that she's too dangerous to hold on to."

"You don't think they'll let her go?" Nogoev asked.

"I think they'll kill her."

# 29

He was far from gentle, but Chalibashvili, it seemed, could not quite bring himself to cross the line into torturing an American diplomat. Kate had the impression, however, that he was building up his courage. She had no illusions about her ability to withhold information if Torquemada made the decision to employ some of his more extreme interrogation techniques, waterboarding or electric shock. Nor did she harbor illusions about how valuable the information she had really was. The one meaningful secret she had carried was Seitek's real identity, and she had already compromised that. Everything else was details.

Even so, she had no intention of making things easy for Chalibashvili, and she remained stubbornly uncooperative through three rounds of questioning that were at times conciliatory and at others threatening. Prison Number One's torturer in chief could not seem to make up his mind.

Still, the threat of violence was always there and Kate stiffened when she heard the key turn in the lock of her cell door. At least they had left the lights on. As a mark of her ambiguous status, Kate had been moved up from the dungeon level to the third sub-basement, the same level that Zamira was on. She had a toilet and a bed with a mattress and blanket. After the Pit, it was like being put up in the Waldorf.

The oversize Uzbek guard opened the door and gestured for Kate to follow him. Each "session" with Chalibashvili had been in a different room, as though the Georgian was looking for the right conditions that would persuade Kate to cooperate. All the interrogation rooms had been on the third level, however. This time the guard led her to an elevator she had not known existed and took her up to the ground floor.

There did not seem to be any cells on this level. It was mostly office space. A few prison staff were working at their desks, and they pointedly did not look up from whatever they were doing to stare at Kate as she shuffled past them in her prison uniform and rubber slippers.

The guard knocked on a door at the end of the hall, and she heard Chalibashvili's voice tell him in Russian to come in.

The room behind the door was a Spartan but serviceable conference room. There were eight chairs arranged around a wooden table with a speakerphone on the tabletop and a plastic plant in one corner. Chalibashvili sat at the table facing the door. Two men in business suits sat across from him and turned to look at her when the door opened. One was her Uncle Harry. The other was Larry Crespo. Kate felt a wave of relief and gratitude flood through her, and her knees started to shake from the pent-up fear and anxiety of her days in captivity. It was almost over, she thought.

Her uncle stood and hugged her and Kate had to exercise every ounce of self-control she possessed not to cry.

"Are you okay?" he asked. "Did they hurt you?"

"I'm okay. But I'm awfully glad to see you. You too, Larry."

The station chief nodded but said nothing.

Kate was acutely conscious of how awful she must look. It had been days since she had showered. Her hair was greasy. Her face was grimy and her eyes were bloodshot.

Chalibashvili gestured for her to sit and she took the seat next to her uncle.

"You asked for proof of life, Mr. Ambassador. And as you can see, Ms. Hollister is very much alive."

"And I'm not the only one," Kate interjected. "I found Zamira. She's here. Alive."

The ambassador locked eyes with Chalibashvili.

"Is that true? Are you holding Zamira Ishenbaev here in Building D?"

"We have many guests. I don't know them all by name. But I'd be pleased to check our records for you."

"I saw her," Kate insisted. "Torquemada here brought me to her cell and offered me a deal. I respectfully declined."

"I'm afraid Ms. Hollister may be somewhat delusional. It's been known to happen on occasion to people who aren't used to . . . confinement."

"That's bullshit," Kate said icily. "You—"

The ambassador put a hand on her shoulder, a signal she should stop. Kate swallowed the rest of the sentence.

"First things first," he said. "Mr. Chalibashvili, we'll be leaving now, with Kate. Please produce her things." The ambassador's tone was as smooth and unruffled as if he were discussing the weather rather than the detention and possible torture of his niece. "We can continue this discussion at a later date, to include the issue of Ms. Ishenbaev's whereabouts and well-being."

"I'm afraid that won't be possible," the Georgian replied with equal calm.

"Really?"

"Yes. You see, Ms. Hollister has violated her diplomatic status in the most serious fashion. It will take some time for us to complete the investigation. Formal charges are, I'm afraid, likely."

"You cannot charge her for a crime, no matter how serious, unless my government agrees to lift her immunity. And we do not. You are, therefore, acting in direct contravention to your international legal obligations under the Vienna Convention."

"What is it you Americans say? Sue me?"

"Actually we have a variant of that expression in the State Department. Sanction me."

"I'm afraid I don't follow."

"You are holding an official American unlawfully. There are existing authorities that allow us to add your name and that of your country's leadership, including President Eraliev, to a blacklist that will result in freezing any overseas assets within reach of U.S. financial institutions. Your accounts with . . . I'm sorry, can you remind me?" The question was directed at Crespo.

The station chief removed a small notebook from his jacket pocket and flipped through it slowly. It was all theater, Kate knew, but it was effective theater.

"Chase and Citibank in New York. A total of two-point-five million. There are Swiss and Caymans accounts as well. We can't touch those directly, but we can make it impossible for the money to move anywhere in the international financial system."

"Thank you, Larry. Now you could still, I suppose, fly to the

Caymans and take the money out in cash. But we will make that difficult for you with an INTERPOL Red Notice. That would make international travel . . . interesting. Again, there are workarounds. A Kyrgyz government charter flying direct from Bishkek to the Cayman Islands perhaps. Does your government have a plane with that kind of range? Refueling could subject you to arrest and extradition. It's complicated, I know."

Chalibashvili's expression hardened as he listened to the litany of woes that awaited him.

"And there's more," Crespo offered.

"Do tell." The sarcasm dripped from Chalibashvili's response.

Crespo turned and looked at Kate. "How would you describe your time in captivity here, Kate? Would the word 'terrifying' apply?"

"Absolutely," she answered.

"Inflicting terror on an American official. By definition, I think that would make you a terrorist. And it's a simple enough matter for me to add your name to that list."

"That's ridiculous," Chalibashvili protested. "I haven't planted a bomb in a shopping mall. I have merely been questioning a woman who attacked this prison as part of an armed group and freed a prominent prisoner, who was himself wanted on terrorism charges."

"So you understand how flexible those charges are?" Crespo said. "That's good. It's always a pleasure working with professionals. I assure you that once your name is on the list, the burden of proof to get it removed will be on you. That can take time. A lot can happen in that time. You know how we treat people who make it onto that list? It's so much more efficient than courts, don't you think? You'd be safe enough in downtown Bishkek, I suppose. We've grown averse to collateral damage. But every time you take a trip outside the city limits, driving down some back road in an SUV, you'll have to wonder, is today the day? We have a long reach, Mr. Chalibashvili, and a long, long memory."

Chalibashvili was used to issuing these kinds of threats. Not receiving them. His equanimity was broken. His face was flushed and the edge of anger in his voice was unmistakable.

"How dare you come here and threaten me with your drones. I will bring this to the attention of the president and I guarantee that the base negotiations will be negatively affected by your behavior."

"President Eraliev should be careful," the ambassador observed, "not to alienate too many of the friends he has left, especially in light of the most recent developments. The United States has interests in this country. But those interests are many and varied and they must be balanced against one another. You should please tell him I said that. He'll understand."

Kate did. Values complexity. Her uncle was nothing if not consistent.

The rest was details. Forty-five minutes later, Kate was in the back of the ambassador's armored Cadillac wearing her own clothes. She looked over her shoulder as the gates of the prison receded.

"Don't worry," her uncle said, misinterpreting the gesture. "You'll never see the inside of that place again."

*One more time, maybe. I left something important behind.* She kept this unspoken. Her uncle had likely saved her life, she knew, but she still did not know the full extent of the conflicting values he was balancing. How much was the life of his dead brother's sister-in-law worth to him? But that did not mean that she was ready to let it rest.

"She was there, Ambassador. I saw her. It wasn't a hallucination."

"I don't doubt you."

Something in his tone triggered a connection for Kate, something that she had almost seen but overlooked.

"You knew, didn't you? You knew she was there."

"I suspected," her uncle answered. "That's not the same thing. There was some information. Fragmentary. Not reliable. But not easy to dismiss as noise."

"And you did nothing?"

"No, Kate. I did my job."

This was not a fight that she wanted to have in front of Crespo. It was a family matter.

"How did you find me?" she asked, changing the subject. "Chalibashvili made it sound like a state secret."

"One of your friends in Boldu reached out to Larry through a cutout and let him know where you were." Her uncle seemed relieved that the conversation had moved on from Zamira. "It was a risky thing for them to do. And it says something about your standing with them that they would take that risk."

"Did you have the authority to do those things you threatened Chalibashvili with?"

"Of course not. We were freelancing. But it sounded good, didn't it?"

"You had me fooled. More or less. I'm sorry about the base negotiations," she added. "I know that they were important."

"Not as important as you. There will be other negotiations. You are my only niece."

"And what about you, Larry? You're not family. And the tracking device you put in my purse is the reason I wound up in Prison Number One. I thought you'd be just as happy to leave me there."

"You're wrong, Kate," Crespo said from the front seat. He did not turn around. "My tracker was the reason Usenov ended up in prison.

353

You were there because you decided to violate every imaginable principle of diplomatic practice and join an armed assault on a foreign government facility. It frankly boggles the mind."

Kate was duly chagrined. Crespo's assessment of her actions was harsh but not unfair.

"So why did you come for me?"

"As I told you, I like to hedge my bets."

"What do you mean?"

"You'll see soon enough."

"There've been some . . . changes . . . while you've been away," the ambassador said.

"What kind of changes?"

"Your friends in Boldu have taken over Ala-Too Square. It looks like Maidan, with walls and a tent city, thousands of demonstrators, and a standoff with the Special Police. The situation is pretty fragile. It's not clear how things are going to play out."

Kate felt a surge of joy at the news. She did her best to keep the emotion from showing on her face, but she suspected that her uncle at least knew how to read Hollister family expressions too well to be fooled.

"Values complexity, Kate," the ambassador said. "Never marry your position and never conflate your position and your ego. As circumstances change, we need to adapt. It's what diplomats do."

"I knew they were planning something like this. But I didn't realize it would be quite so big."

"It's pretty big, all right," Crespo said. "The stakes are high, and we don't have a lot of visibility into what's going on from the Boldu end of things."

And suddenly it was clear what Crespo meant by hedging his bets.

"You think Boldu might succeed." Kate said. "That the Eraliev government is in danger of collapse, and you want to make sure that you have your bases covered with the next government if that happens."

"That would be my responsibility, yes."

"And I'm a side bet. Is that right?"

"If you want to look at it that way, go ahead," Crespo said. "But help us here, and the ambassador and I can make sure that nothing about your little misadventure in the Kyrgyz prison system gets back to Washington. And what they don't know, they can't punish."

"So what do you want from me?"

"It's simple, really," her uncle said. "We want you to go inside the Boldu compound and tell us what's going on. We want you to serve as a conduit between us and Usenov. And we want to make certain that if, in fact, Boldu's Maidan-style revolution succeeds, the new powers that be look to the United States as a friend and partner and not as a stalking horse for the restoration of the ancien régime."

"You want me to spy on Boldu?"

"No. You should be completely open about what you're doing. We want you to do your job, Kate. To be a diplomat and represent the interests of your country to Usenov and his people. Do you think you can do that?"

"No secrets? No lies?"

"None."

"I can do it. And I can do it damn well."

"I know you can, Kate."

"There's one condition."

The ambassador rolled his eyes in mock exasperation.

"Tell me."

"We have to stop at my apartment first. I smell like a prison and I'm taking a shower before I see Ruslan."

# 30

An hour later, the ambassador's Cadillac pulled up right before a checkpoint about two blocks from Ala-Too Square.

"Here we are," the ambassador said. "This is as close as we can get."

Kate had showered and changed and she had an overnight bag resting on her lap. She had packed light. How do you dress for a revolution? The clothes she had chosen were more appropriate for a hike in the mountains than a diplomatic reception. She was wearing an old, comfortable pair of jeans, boots, and a black T-shirt under a light windbreaker. It had only been a few hours ago that she was a prisoner locked alone in her cell, but it already felt like that was weeks in the past.

"Will I be able to get through?" Kate asked.

"You should. There are lots of police, but they haven't tried to completely close off the square. People have been able to move in and out, and Boldu supporters have been able to bring food in for the hard-core demonstrators."

"Why are the authorities letting them do that?"

"Because the alternative may be worse. They look at what's happening in Ala-Too like it's a tumor and they're afraid of metastasis. Crack down too hard on the demonstrations and they are likely to trigger uprisings elsewhere, maybe in Bishkek, maybe in some other city or even the countryside. I'm sure that Eraliev's people have looked at the precedents as carefully as Boldu has. For every Maidan that brought down a government, there's a counterexample, like the Green Revolution in Iran, in which the protestors failed. When the government wins, it's usually a result of strategic patience. They wait out the protests and avoid any kind of climactic confrontation that would galvanize the wider public. Basically, they try to bore the revolution to death."

"And that works?"

"Sometimes."

"I'll take those odds."

"There's one more thing," her uncle said. "You're going in there as an American diplomat, not as an avenging angel. I know what you want. And whether you believe it or not, I want the same thing. But we're professionals. I can't have pictures of you dressed up in battle gear, carrying a weapon and standing in formation with the Boldu fighters. I don't want videos of you handing out stewed mutton to demonstrators, or playing 'Moonlight Serenade' on a piano that some septuagenarians hauled in on the back of a yak. You are a dispassionate observer and a representative of the United States of America. Do you think you can handle that?"

Kate took a deep breath and exhaled.

"Yes, I can," Kate said, although she had her doubts. "Wish me luck."

Harry leaned over and kissed her on the cheek.

"You be careful, Kate. If things look like they're getting out of hand, you get out of there. Right away. If anything happened to you, my brother's ghost would strangle me in my sleep."

"Thanks, Uncle Harry. I'll be careful. I promise."

The checkpoint was manned by a pair of ridiculously young police officers, regular beat cops, Kate noted, rather than Special Police. She waved her American diplomatic passport in their general direction as though it represented some kind of authorization. This seemed to confuse them enough that they let her through without subjecting her to any kind of inspection.

The Boldu encampment in the center of the square was sprawling and chaotic. The core of the miniature city was a roughly circular walled-off area dominated by the statue of Manas. The walls themselves were a mix of overturned vehicles, lumber, and brick. It was makeshift but formidable looking, and Kate could see Scythians patrolling along platforms and battlements that had been built along the top of the wall. Outside the walls, more demonstrators had gathered, setting up yurts and market stalls selling food and drink, jackets and blankets. The Boldu-led revolution already had its own economy.

Most important, Kate saw at least half a dozen camera crews scattered about the square. The international media had arrived in force. There was a BBC van, a CNN crew, and al-Jazeera, among others.

The gate to the inner keep was a van with metal plates welded to the side. Two Scythians stood guard. One had been with Kate on the prison raid. She clapped Kate on the shoulder in welcome.

"Seitek will be happy to know you're alive," she said.

"Where can I find him?" Kate asked.

"Try one of the yurts."

The camp was a hive of activity. Some of the protestors were working on strengthening the walls. Others were cooking. A small group of older men sat on a carpet playing backgammon and sipping tea. Many of the people she saw were wearing traditional Kyrgyz dress, which was unusual. Kate suspected Val had something to do with that.

She found Ruslan in the larger of the two yurts, bent over a computer with Val and Murzaev looking over his shoulder.

"Excuse me," Kate said. "I'm looking for the leader of the revolution. Have I come to the right place?"

Ruslan looked up and his expression was one of profound relief.

"Katie! Thank god."

He almost knocked over the table in his urgency. He held Kate tightly, as though she otherwise might slip away, and kissed her, heedless of the others in the tent.

"I love you so," he said. "And I thought I might have lost you."

"I'm only free because you let Askar reach out to the CIA. Thank you for taking that risk."

Kate hugged Val and Murzaev in turn.

"I knew you'd come back to us," Val said.

"How are you feeling, Askar?" Kate asked Murzaev. The last time she had seen him he had been drugged up and badly battered. He still had some bruises on his face, but they were already starting to fade.

Murzaev flashed her a smile, showing off his new crowns.

"One hundred percent better. Thank you for coming for me, Kate. I won't ever forget that."

"It looks like you all have made good use of the time I was away," Kate said.

"It's pretty amazing," Ruslan agreed. "Let me show you around."

He gave Kate a tour of the compound and recounted the story of Boldu's takeover of the square.

"Has the army gotten involved yet?" Kate asked.

"Not yet. It's all police so far. But I think Eraliev missed his opportunity to crush us with force. The first few hours were critical, and the Special Police didn't bring enough to the fight. Now, the terms are almost even. And Val keeps them honest by making sure the whole world can follow what's happening here. I don't think he dares call out the tanks. His rule is brittle and he's afraid the whole country would rise up against him."

"And what about you? Why haven't they come after you directly?"

"It's too late for that. I'm out in the open now. People know who I am. We don't need the mystery of Seitek anymore, even though many people still call me that. The movement has outgrown me. And as a symbol, I'd be more dangerous to the regime dead. I'll tell you though, Kate. Things might have gone differently if Malinin had still been the head of the Special Police. We've been able to reach something of an understanding with his replacement, Kayrat uluu, that's helped us keep things from getting too violent. It's good to have you back with us."

"I need to tell you, Ruslan, that I'm here not just because I want to be. I'm here because my uncle asked me to come, to tell him about what's happening here. Do you have any concerns about that?"

"None. I want you to do that. When Eraliev is gone, we are going to need help. And if America is willing to offer that help, we'll be ready to talk."

He leaned over and kissed her.

"Besides, I like Americans."

"So what do we do now?" Kate asked.

"Now, we wait."

There was more to it than that, of course. Every day, Boldu organized a public event of some sort. There were speeches by Ruslan and Valentina and Hamid and others. Ruslan and his grandfather rode together through throngs of demonstrators on their enormous stallions, with the goshawk Janibar perched on Tashtanbek's gloved fist. Dressed in traditional clothes and looking like he might have ridden alongside Ghengis Khan, Tashtanbek and his hawk were a magnet for the foreign media and fast becoming a romantic symbol for the uprising against Eraliev.

A stage was set up outside the walls and Val organized a series of concerts, both Western-style pop music and more traditional Kyrgyz folk groups. They shared the stage with the Manaschi, who recited long passages of the epic story of the Kyrgyz people, paying particular attention to the book of Seitek. Val organized a group of teenagers who took charge of shooting, editing, and uploading the videos that told the story of the uprising. They competed to see which of them could get their material onto one of the major international networks.

There were also logistical challenges, the unglamorous side of any human endeavor—even a revolution. There was trash to be collected, latrines to be emptied, and two hungry horses and hundreds of people to be fed. Hamid took charge of running the camp and he proved to be a skilled administrator.

On her second day in the camp, he pulled Kate aside.

"I'm sorry about what I said to you, about your being responsible for Albina's death. That wasn't fair. I spoke out of anger. You've sacrificed as much for Kyrgyzstan as any of us. I'll try to remember that."

This time Kate let herself cry.

As the days passed, the size of the protests grew. The country seemed to sense that power was shifting, that Eraliev's time may, in fact, have come. A palpable expectation of change settled over the city, and copycat demonstrations occupied the centers of smaller cities and towns across Kyrgyzstan.

Kate was able to come and go from the compound. The police now recognized her and waved her through the checkpoints easily. At the embassy, she met with the ambassador and Crespo and sent thorough reports back to Washington offering an insider's account of what was now being called the Goshawk Revolution.

Through the embassy, Kate was able to follow developments in Bishkek as they appeared in the fun-house mirror that was the Washington policy process. Kyrgyzstan was page one news, and the coverage was driven by the compelling visuals of the compound, the exotically dressed demonstrators, and Ruslan and his grandfather on horseback. The Goshawk Revolution was a subject for big-power competition as well. The Chinese were openly backing Eraliev. The Russians were opposed, in principle, to any color revolutions. The Europeans were supporting Boldu, and the Americans were on the fence, reflexively supportive of democratic change but mindful of the disappointments from the Arab Spring and waiting to see which side would come out on top. The future of the base negotiations was no small part of the American calculus.

On one visit to the embassy, her uncle called her into his office for a private chat.

"Kate, there are things going on behind the scenes that you need to know about."

"Okay. Tell me."

Harry poured out two stiff measures of Maker's Mark over ice and handed one to Kate.

"You're going to want one of these."

"That bad?"

"Your revolution has gotten caught up in D.C. politics. That's not especially surprising, but this is as bitter and nasty as I've seen in a long time."

"My revolution?"

"No exaggeration. You may not realize it, but you're making something of a name for yourself. The secretary himself is reading your reports."

"So what's the source of the friction? Is this State versus Defense?"

"That's part of it. But it's more personal than institutional. That desiccated son of a bitch Crandle has essentially bet his career on the outcome of the base negotiations. He's pushing the National Security Council to greenlight a strategy for bailing out Eraliev and cashing that check for the base agreement."

"How's he doing?"

"Right now, he's losing. But that's not something a man like Crandle does gracefully. And from what I hear, he's starting to cheat."

"Looking at the policy papers of the boy sitting next to him?"

"This is serious, Kate. Word is that he's leaking intelligence to Eraliev, including some of your reporting."

"That's easy enough to fix. I can stop reporting."

"I think you should stop. But there's more."

"Do I want to know?"

"You have to. There's a lot on the line here, and Crandle and his ilk play for keeps. He's been using Colonel Ball as his surrogate. Brass is the one who I believe has been passing intel to the palace. The FBI has opened an investigation. Success would paper over their multitude of sins. Failure would open them up to all kinds of payback, up to and including charges for espionage. That's life without parole, and that makes men like Crandle and Ball desperate and dangerous. Nothing's out of bounds. Crandle's been urging Eraliev to call out the army, but Eraliev's afraid that if he gives the generals an opening they'll stage a coup."

"That's actually one of his smarter ideas," Kate said. "That is a real risk."

"Indeed. But Crandle may have found a back door. Do you remember that Special Forces unit that Crandle and Ball were talking about at breakfast at the residence?"

"The fifty-something."

"That's the one. The Fifty-fourth parachute battalion under the command of a lieutenant colonel named Shakirov. They're the Kyrgyz equivalent of the Rangers. Real soldiers. Ball has been working with the Fifty-fourth for the last two years, and he and Shakirov are close. Crandle has reportedly ordered Brass to persuade Shakirov to use his troops to crush the Goshawk Revolution and kill Usenov even without a direct order from the president."

"And if that triggers the coup?"

"Then Crandle still wins. Shakirov would be high in the coup government and he would be inclined to give Crandle the base deal as payback."

"So is Brass making any progress with Shakirov?"

"I don't know."

"Why not?"

"Because he's disappeared, Kate. And I don't know where he is."

# 31

I t's time."

Ruslan pointed to the north end of the square, where five armored personnel carriers were lined up and pointed straight at the gate of Boldu's compound. The Special Police were a paramilitary force and they used APCs to provide security at major events. Sometimes they mounted water cannons on the roofs to help pacify unruly crowds. But the Special Police APCs were painted dark blue. These were green. The army had come out to play.

"Is that the Fifty-fourth?" Ruslan asked Nogoev, who was standing next to him on the rickety observation platform.

Nogoev looked through his binoculars.

"I can't see the markings of the vehicles. It's too dark. But I'd bet money it's Shakirov. That man has all the subtlety of a sledgehammer. He's planning to ram the gate and he doesn't care if we know it. Overconfidence kills."

"Watch yourself then, Daniar. We don't want to fall into that same trap. We know they're coming, and the plan is solid. But they still outgun us by a lot."

"Then let's do what we can to make sure that this doesn't become a gunfight."

They had had almost two days to prepare. Kate had passed on the warning from the Americans about Shakirov and their own renegade colonel. Nogoev knew Shakirov. He had been one of the young soldiers under his command in Afghanistan, where he had a reputation for being brave but was also impetuous to the point of foolhardy.

"Is everything ready?"

"Everything's in place. I'll make a sweep and check on the disposition of our forces."

"Such as they are," Ruslan said.

"Such as they are," Nogoev agreed.

"Do you think Kayrat uluu will do as he promised?"

"He had better or we're all dead."

The masses of Kyrgyz camped outside the gate made it impossible for the APCs to run straight at the compound. The police worked to open a corridor for the army unit, but it took time, almost an hour, before there was a clear path.

Ruslan took advantage of the time to review the defenses and to steal a few minutes with Kate.

"I think you should get out of the compound before this begins," Ruslan told her. "I don't know what's going to happen here or how violent it's going to get. But people are going to die tonight. And I don't want you to be one of them."

"I'll do what I can not to disappoint you on that score. But I'm not leaving. I'm going to help Val with the video equipment. If Shakirov knows that he's being filmed, it may encourage him to pull his punches, even a little."

"I can't stay with you, Kate. Nogoev can handle the Scythians. But I need to be with the people. This is about them."

"I know. And I wouldn't have it any other way."

Their kiss was tender and sweet and Ruslan hoped that it would not be their last.

The APCs drove forward down the path that the Special Police had cleared for them. Soldiers in green and gray urban camouflage ran alongside the vehicles. Ruslan and Nogoev watched from the observation platform. Nogoev spoke into the radio he used to communicate with his squad leaders.

"They're coming. Hold your fire. Patience."

"How many of them are there?" Ruslan asked.

"The Fifth-fourth is only about two hundred men total. I'd say there's about a hundred here tonight."

The lead APC had a steel ram welded to the nose and it crashed into the side of the van at what looked to Ruslan like at least fifty kilometers an hour. The speed concentrated too much force at the point of impact, and rather than push the gate aside, the ram punched through the wall of the van and got stuck. The APC was a sitting duck.

"Not yet," Nogoev said into the radio. "Wait. Let them in."

The six oversize wheels of the APC spun on the concrete and Ruslan could smell the burning rubber. Gradually, the vehicle got traction and it bulled the overloaded van forward into the compound. A second APC and scores of soldiers on foot followed. A third vehicle maneuvered to get through the gate.

"Execute. Now. Now. Now." Nogoev did not shout the order. It was delivered with an icy calm. But the reaction was almost instantaneous.

The base of the Manas statue exploded. Shards of brick and marble went flying in every direction. The Scythians and the other Boldu supporters knew to take cover, but Ruslan saw at least four soldiers go down as the stone shrapnel whipped through the compound. The statue itself teetered for a moment and then fell forward, with the giant bronze Manas on his horse leading one last charge.

The bomb maker that Murzaev had found had only one hand. This was not especially encouraging, but he insisted that he had lost the hand in the gears of a conveyer belt and not to the explosive charges he handled for a nickel-mining operation in Kazakhstan. His partner in the operation was a civil engineer, and the two had bickered about the size and placement of the charges, with the engineer relying on math and the miner on gut instinct. They had finally reached an agreement, and whatever compromise they had settled on proved now to be just right.

The statue landed on the front end of the third APC, crushing the armor like it was tissue paper and blocking the gate.

Approximately half of the Fifty-fourth were inside the compound and half were still outside the walls. They had succeeded in dividing Shakirov's force. Now to destroy it.

Ruslan looked around quickly to see if he could find Kate. But it was growing dark and the compound was chaos. The Scythians had lit fires to confuse the soldiers' night-vision equipment.

"Squad Three," Nogoev said into the radio. "Your target is the lead APC. Squad Two. Take the second vehicle."

Two Scythians leapt from the walls onto the top of the first APC. One Scythian trained his weapon on the command hatch while the second leaned over the side and tossed stun grenades in through the firing slits.

Other Scythians lobbed Molotov cocktails at the second APC, which was soon covered in flames. The heat and smoke would drive the soldiers out of the vehicle, or they could choose to die in there.

"Do you have this?" Ruslan asked Nogoev.

"I do. Go."

"Don't slaughter them, Daniar. Give them a chance to surrender."

"They'll have a chance," Nogoev promised vaguely. It would have to do.

Ruslan looked outside the walls and saw what he had been both expecting and hoping for. The police were gone. They had melted away and there was no one to control the crowds. Kayrat uluu had made good on his promise. Ruslan felt a wave of relief. The odds had shifted decidedly in their favor.

Ruslan jumped down from the walls and pushed his way through the crowd to the tent where his grandfather was looking after the horses. He mounted his stallion.

"Grandfather. Find Kate for me, please. Look after her."

Tashtanbek nodded.

Ruslan rode through the crowd, urging them forward. A swarm of ordinary Kyrgyz—women from the village, pensioners from Bishkek, university students, laborers—followed him. Without the police lines to hold them back, they swarmed the soldiers and the remaining APCs, crowding around them and pulling their weapons out of their hands.

The soldiers did not know how to respond. This was not covered by their orders. They had come here to shoot armed traitors, not people who reminded them of their grandparents or their mothers and sisters. The APCs were blocked, unable to move. The drivers refused to run over the demonstrators, who were clearly civilians. The Fifty-fourth was now, for all intents and purposes, out of the fight.

From horseback, Ruslan had a commanding view of the square. To the east, he could see the gates of the Presidential Palace. They were unguarded. The Special Police who had been posted at the entrance to the palace were gone, pulled off by Kayrat uluu along with the others. The gates were not only unguarded, they were open. Now was the moment.

Ruslan pulled back on the reins and the stallion reared and whinnied his eagerness to run.

"Come!" he shouted to the crowd. "Follow me! We end this tonight."

He turned his horse's head and galloped for the gates, trusting that the crowd would follow.

They did.

President for Life Nurlan Eraliev picked up the gun. It was a 9 mm, polished silver with an ivory grip. A gift from Robert Mugabe in Zimbabwe. A man to be admired, Eraliev thought. A man who understood power. A man who though twenty years his elder would outlive him.

Looking out the window of his study, Eraliev could see them. The masses swarming through the suddenly unguarded gates of his palace, trampling through the gardens like wild horses. They would be inside soon enough. The opportunity to loot might slow them down. But they would find him eventually. There were fifteen bullets in the gun and a spare magazine in the desk drawer. The math was pretty easy to do, and the conclusion was inescapable.

He would not need all thirty bullets.

He would only need one.

He wondered how it would end for Mugabe. Would he die in bed surrounded by family and those who had pretended most successfully to be his friends? Would a firing squad offer him a quick and painless death after a hurried trial with a preordained outcome? Or would he be torn apart by a mob?

Someday, he hoped, they would understand. That everything he had done he had done for love of country. He was a patriot. The father of the Kyrgyz people. A benevolent ruler who knew what was best for his children. Someday, they would understand.

He put the gun in his mouth. The silver metallic taste of the gun was overwhelmed by the coppery taste of fear. He calmed his mind.

It would be better this way.

Someday, they would understand.

He pulled the trigger.

It was a madness unlike anything Kate had ever experienced. Soldiers ran through the compound individually and in groups with no clear sense of purpose or mission. Kate admired Val's poise as she recorded the chaos on her camcorder. She zoomed in on two young Scythians who had jumped onto the roof of one of the APCs.

"Someday we're going to build a statue to those two boys," she said.

Kate saw three soldiers cut down by fire from the Scythians posted along the top of the makeshift walls. And she saw one Scythian, a boy really, fall to the ground with the back of his head leaking blood and gore. But with the attacking force cut in half, the Scythians had the advantage. Even to Kate's untrained eye, one thing was apparent. Boldu was winning.

Surrounded and cut off, groups of Kyrgyz army soldiers began surrendering.

"Kate, this is almost over here," Val said. "Let's get up on the walls so we can get some—"

Valentina did not get a chance to finish the sentence.

Kate turned to see Val lying crumpled on the ground. Colonel Ball was standing over her body wearing a Kyrgyz army uniform. He was holding his pistol by the barrel, indicating that he had struck Val with the butt rather than shot her. There was a look of madness in his eyes that Kate could not dismiss as a trick of the firelight.

Ball reversed the weapon and pointed it at Kate's chest.

"Goddamn you. You've ruined it. You've ruined everything."

"It's over, Brass. Eraliev is done. There'll be a new government soon. Then you and Crandle can restart your precious base negotiations. Now put that gun away and let me take care of my friend."

"It's too late for that. This isn't about the base talks anymore. This is about survival. Mine, that is. It's time for me to disappear. Someplace warm and sunny."

"How does killing me help you?"

"It doesn't. This isn't business, Kate. It's personal."

Brass raised the pistol, pointing it straight at Kate's head.

Then he screamed and clawed at his face as a large gray-and-white bird raked furrows into his flesh with its sharp talons. Kate saw that the bird had leather jesses tied to its legs. This was Tashtanbek's goshawk.

Brass tried to pull the bird off his face, but the hawk flew off before he could get a grip on its neck. He turned back to Kate, blood oozing from where his left eye had been.

"I'm gonna find that fucking bird after I kill you and break both its wings."

He raised the pistol and Kate knew that gesture would be fatal.

"Don't do it, Ball. He's watching you."

"Who?"

It was the last thing he would ever say.

A hole appeared in the middle of his chest, the sound of the shot arriving half a second later. Brass fell backward and the gun clattered across the concrete.

Kate looked at the lifeless body of the defense attaché and was surprised and abashed to realize that she felt nothing. Certainly not remorse.

It should be plenty warm in hell, Brass.

Kate turned to see Tashtanbek standing on the observation platform, the ancient rifle he carried around with him resting in his arms. A wisp of smoke drifted from the muzzle.

She waved a quick thank-you and rushed to help Val, who was already beginning to stir. With Kate's assistance, she was able to sit up.

"Val, are you okay?"

The response was incoherent and Kate suspected her friend was concussed.

She pulled Val to her feet and walked her to one of the yurts, where a doctor and two nurses had set up an aid station. There were a dozen serious casualties in the tent, but Kate grabbed one of the nurses and begged her to take a look at Val.

"She'll be all right," the nurse said after a quick examination. "She can sit, but don't let her lie down. She might vomit and aspirate."

By the time Kate located a stool, Val was starting to come around.

"I'll be fine," she said, although her words were still a little slurry and her gaze unfocused. "Go. Go find him."

Kate kissed her on the cheek and ran to see if Ruslan was still alive.

Outside the gate she pushed her way through the crowd. The

demonstrators had taken over the Presidential Palace and she saw Ruslan riding his enormous stallion through the gardens, urging the crowd forward. It was like a weight being lifted. He was all right. And the fighting was over.

She wanted to run to Ruslan and join him in his moment of triumph, but there was something else she had to do.

Kate grabbed one of the Scythians by the arm.

"Where's Nogoev?" she asked, raising her voice to be heard over the triumphant shouts of the exultant Boldu supporters.

The Scythian pointed toward the fountain where Kate could see Nogoev standing on top of one of the planters and addressing a group of his soldiers. She pushed through the crowds to reach him.

"Daniar, I need five Scythians and a truck. And I need them now."

Nogoev studied her for a moment and then nodded his assent.

"Ilhom," he said to one of the Scythians. "Take your squad. Steal a truck. Help Ms. Hollister with whatever she needs."

"Yes, sir."

"Where are you going, Kate?" he asked.

"I'm going back to prison."

# 32

The Scythians found her a truck, a Kyrgyz army transport with a canvas cover.

"Please tell me that you didn't kill anyone to get this," Kate said.

"The keys were in it," Ilhom said unconvincingly.

As the Scythians mounted up, Kate spotted Patime Akhun in the crowd with a group of Women in Black who had been some of the first Bishkekers to join the protests.

"Patime," Kate shouted, catching her attention. "Get in the truck."

Patime and four of her dark-clad colleagues walked over to the truck.

"It's good to see you here, Kate," she said. "What's going on?"

"We're going to get your son. Do you want to come along?"

Patime grinned and got on the truck.

The gates of Prison Number One were closed and locked but

unguarded. It seemed as though the Special Police had their instructions for the night. Go home. Kayrat uluu had bet on regime change and it looked like his bet was going to pay off.

The heavy army truck made short work of the gates, crashing through them in a crunch of metal and a shower of broken bricks. There were guards on duty at Building D, but they were not at all interested in martyring themselves for a spent regime. With the largest of the Scythians offering suitable encouragement, two of the guards admitted to having master keys to the cells. Kate gave one of the keys to Ilhom.

"Help Patime find her son," she ordered. "Find the Scythian who was wounded when we freed Ruslan. He may still be in the infirmary. And release all of the other prisoners in this building as well."

"All of the prisoners?" Ilhom asked. "No exceptions?"

"This is Building D. There are no muggers or rapists here. These are all political prisoners and nothing any of these poor bastards did is a crime. Not anymore."

Kate took a second key and ran to find her aunt.

She paused for a moment at the door to Zamira's cell, both to catch her breath and to prepare herself. It had been more than twelve years since Azattyk had been betrayed. Twelve years since her aunt had fallen hard into the black hole of Prison Number One.

What might the years in prison have done to her? The torture she no doubt endured early on and the long stretches of solitary confinement that followed? Kate had spent a day and a half alone in a dark cell of the Pit and it had rattled her more than she cared to admit. What if it had been a week? Or a month? Or a year? How long could she have endured that before going insane?

She worried that her aunt would no longer be the strong, vibrant woman she remembered from her childhood. Healing the damage they had done to her would take time.

The key turned easily in the lock.

"Zamira? Aunt Zamira? It's me. It's Kate."

Her aunt was as Kate had left her, sitting on a stool and staring at the wall. Her blue prison uniform was worn and faded from years of use. Her once jet black hair was white and feathery, as though all the color had been leeched out by the dark.

"Zamira?" Kate said again in the kind of soft voice she might have used to coax a pet or a frightened child out of its hiding place.

She turned to face Kate.

"Oh god."

A thousand different emotions assailed Kate, competing for a grip on her heart until one came to dominate. Grief. She recognized it easily, as she might an old friend. Kate's knees buckled. Even with her vision blurred by tears, there was no denying the awful truth.

This woman was not Zamira.

Kate had been so certain. The disappointment was crushing.

"I'm sorry," the stranger said in Kyrgyz, her voice slow and deliberate as though she were struggling to keep her focus. "Do I know you?"

"No," Kate said sadly. "You don't."

She sat on the bed across from this woman who looked enough like her aunt to fool her from a distance, at an angle, and across twelve years of imagined suffering. But she did not have Zamira's fiery black eyes or the sharp chin she shared with Kate's mother. It had all been a *maskirovka*. A deception.

Kate looked at the wall where the picture of her and her mother had been taped to the wall. The photograph was gone, but a small piece of tape had been left behind.

It would have been easy enough as part of the deception, Kate knew, to break into her apartment to look for something like that photo. A small keepsake, the kind that a prisoner might be allowed to hold on to. Something personal and intimate that would connect Kate to this stranger on an emotional level, make her see what she wanted to see. Torturers were, at the end of the day, really psychologists of a sort. Leaving the photo somewhere where Kate would have to find it on her own and recognize its significance was a master touch. It made it all seem that much more real.

Chalibashvili knew that Kate's mother had never lost faith that her sister was alive. It was easy enough to conclude that that belief had been passed on to Kate. And he had set her up for exactly what she had hoped and expected to find. He was an evil genius. She was a fool.

And Zamira was dead.

"I thought you were somebody else," Kate said.

"I am somebody else. What year is it? Please?"

Kate told her.

"So long," she said. "So long."

Kate could see the faintly narcoleptic look of disengagement in the woman's eyes from whatever drugs had been mixed in with her food.

"Is it over now?" she asked.

"Yes," Kate said. "It's over."

"I'd like to go home then."

"All right. I'll take you there."

# THREE WEEKS
## LATER

# EPILOGUE

They drove for almost three hours. Spring had turned to early summer and the countryside was lush and emerald green. Murzaev insisted on listening to his music, and Kate indulged his penchant for syrupy Russian folk songs as she pushed the Touareg up the narrow twisting roads in the lower Ala-Too mountains.

"Are you sure you know where we're going, Askar?" Kate asked. Murzaev had not once looked at a map or consulted the GPS.

"Quite sure. Yes."

"Thank you for doing this."

"We owe you this and more. Without you, this new Kyrgyzstan might never have been possible. I'm pleased they let you stay."

"Me too. The interim government's naming Val to head the base negotiations didn't hurt. The ambassador saw value in keeping me on, and Washington ultimately agreed."

"So all is forgiven?"

"More or less. My uncle and Crespo kept D.C. in the dark about most of what happened."

"It's better that way for everyone. How are the talks going?"

"We're almost done. A few loose ends to tie up. But we'll have the agreement ready in a week or two at the most."

"And then what?"

"It needs to be approved by the new government, once it's formally installed. After the elections, it shouldn't take more than a couple of days to put together a cabinet. Then the parliament can vote on the agreement up or down and it'll come into effect when Ruslan—or whoever wins the presidency—signs it."

"Or whoever?"

"Okay, Ruslan's going to win with some ridiculous percentage of the vote. But it'd be good if someone credible at least runs against him. Kyrgyzstan needs a democracy, not a monarchy, and that requires a functioning opposition."

"That may take time," Murzaev said with a trace of regret. "We Kyrgyz have gotten too used to a strongman in the palace."

"We have time."

"Once he's elected, President Usenov will have significant representational responsibilities. These would be so much easier with a First Lady, don't you think?"

Kate downshifted into a sharp turn, forcing Murzaev to grab the dashboard to keep from being thrown against the door.

"He's asked me," Kate admitted. "But it's a huge change. I'd have to leave my job, for one thing. The junior officer in the political section probably shouldn't simultaneously be married to the president of the country to which she is accredited. Too many conflicts of interest."

"So take leave. You can always go back."

"Maybe," Kate said, but she was still dubious. She loved Ruslan and she knew that he loved her. But was that enough? Would their passion cool in the absence of danger? Could Kate abandon her American-ness and embrace her Kyrgyz identity wholeheartedly as the wife of the president? Could she accept a role presiding over tea with the wives of visiting dignitaries? Ruslan would never ask this of her, but Kate knew it would be her responsibility. How would she feel? She pushed it all aside. There would be time to wrestle with those questions later.

"Turn here," Murzaev said, pointing to a dirt track just barely wide enough for the Touareg.

Kate drove carefully down the rutted road. A flat tire out here would be a major inconvenience. A broken axle would be a disaster. After two kilometers, Murzaev told her to stop.

They were in a *djailoo*, a high mountain pasture, and flowers bloomed in the high grass of the meadow. A small stream cut across the field and ran through a culvert under the road before flowing down the mountain in a series of cascades.

Kate and Murzaev got out of the car and walked over to the edge of the field. The sky was blue with a few cotton-ball clouds. A hawk circled overhead. A goshawk, Kate wanted to believe, although the bird was flying too high to say for certain. A small red deer that had been nibbling on the grass raised its head to look at Kate, locking eyes with her for a brief moment before bounding up the hill and out of sight.

"Where is it?" Kate asked.

"This is it," Murzaev answered.

"The whole thing?"

"Yes."

"How many?"

"Eighty-seven."

"And you know who they all are?"

"Most of them. The government kept remarkably detailed records of its atrocities. A holdover from the Soviet days. This is it, Kate. This is where your aunt is buried."

It was a beautiful place and it was hard to believe that it was a cover pulled over so much ugliness. The last resting place of almost ninety of the innumerable victims of Eraliev's reign of terror.

"When did she die?" Kate asked.

"Three days after they arrested her. There was a secret trial and the verdict was carried out immediately. This is where they brought the bodies. Almost everyone here was part of the Azattyk movement."

"And the intel reports that my uncle told me about? The ones that indicated she was alive?"

"Your CIA doesn't share its reporting with me," Murzaev said with a small chuckle. "But I'd hazard to guess that it was a crossed wire. Reading too much into ambiguous information. It happens all the time."

Kate stepped off the road and onto the field, moving slowly, conscious that she was walking on hallowed ground. Murzaev walked alongside her.

"So what do we do now?" Kate asked.

"Whatever you say. You give the word and I will get a team up here to exhume the bodies. We will do our best to identify individual remains using DNA testing and dental records. Then we relocate them to the central cemetery. If that's what you want."

Kate looked around at the stunning natural beauty. The Ala-Too mountains loomed above them as though keeping watch on the fallen.

"I think Zamira would be happier here among her comrades," she said.

Murzaev nodded.

"I think they all would want that," he agreed.

"Maybe we could set up a stone of some sort. A monument to Azattyk."

"That would be nice."

Kate looked up at the sky, hoping for another glimpse of the hawk, but it was gone.

"Can I have a minute?"

"Of course." Murzaev touched her arm affectionately and walked back to the car.

She knelt and put her right hand on the ground, feeling the rich, moist earth under her palm.

"We did it, Zamira," she whispered. "You would have been proud. Mom would have been proud."

Kate walked back to the car.

"Are you ready?" Murzaev asked.

"Yes," she said. "Let's go home."